He Pulled the Jaguar in Front of Her

and motioned her to a side street. Thinking there was something wrong with her car, she obeyed.

He leaned in her window and indicated that she should get out.

She did. Her car must be on fire.

"What is it?" she gasped.

Peter pushed her against the side of the Mercedes and crushed her in his arms, kissing her more deeply, more passionately, than anyone ever had.

There was no space in which she could respond. He had her pinned against the car, against himself.

"Come home with me. I need you. You were brilliant tonight. I couldn't admit it. I don't know why."

His hand was on her shoulder, just above her breast. On her breast. The thin layer of silk was too much. His muscular chest was so large. Could she ever put her arms all the way around it?

Jana snatched the keys out of the Mercedes, rolled up the windows and walked straight to the Jaguar. . . .

Dear Reader:

We trust you will enjoy this Richard Gallen romance. We plan to bring you more of the best in both contemporary and historical romantic fiction with four exciting new titles each month.

We'd like your help.

We value your suggestions and opinions. They will help us to publish the kind of romances you want to read. Please send us your comments, or just let us know which Richard Gallen romances you have especially enjoyed. Write to the address below. We're looking forward to hearing from you!

Happy reading!

Judy Sullivan
Richard Gallen Books
8-10 West 36th St.
New York, N.Y. 10018

Harvest of Dreams

JESSICA DARE

PUBLISHED BY RICHARD GALLEN BOOKS
Distributed by POCKET BOOKS

Books by Jessica Dare

Rhapsody
Harvest of Dreams

 A RICHARD GALLEN BOOKS *Original* publication

Distributed by
POCKET BOOKS, a Simon & Schuster division of
GULF & WESTERN CORPORATION
1230 Avenue of the Americas, New York, N.Y. 10020

ISBN: 0-671-43929-4

First Pocket Books printing December, 1981

10 9 8 7 6 5 4 3 2 1

RICHARD GALLEN and colophon are trademarks
of Simon & Schuster and Richard Gallen & Co., Inc.

Printed in the U.S.A.

Harvest of Dreams

Chapter 1

For forty-five minutes, she had waited for *the* Peter Milford, heir to the Milford fortune and acting manager of this peach ranch.

She had fought off a heavy formation of mosquitoes that were swooning in the 105° heat. The navy linen suit with its long-sleeved jacket was suffocating, and her pantyhose felt like long underwear.

But Jana Robbins had no intention of losing her self-control in this hut of an office. If she walked out now on this so-and-so who couldn't keep an appointment on time, no one in the Chicago office of Havermeyer Harvester would understand.

After years of trying to sell the Mariposa Peach Company half a million dollars worth of peach-harvesting equipment, Peter Milford had finally made the decision to buy—over the objections of his father, Joe Milford. And, as she had been briefed, when compared to the thousands of acres of Milford vineyards and orange groves scattered from the Napa Valley to south of Los Angeles, Mariposa was only the seed of Milford Enterprises. Sales could run well over ten million—*if* she handled everything right.

Under ordinary circumstances, a local farm-equipment

dealer would be in charge of a sale like this. But the local dealer hadn't been able to hold a civil conversation with anyone at Mariposa. Jana's predecessor, a man named Carl Schultz, had finally been at the right place at the right time and had talked Peter Milford into the peach-harvesters.

Havermeyer Harvester executives had concluded that selling more equipment to Milford Enterprises would require unorthodox special attention, and Jana had been given the job.

Jana's experience and education had taught her that American farmers were a very conservative group. Havermeyer, by offering a specialist along with the sale of their equipment, made the farmers feel they had not done something so modern as hire a consultant. But to make matters worse at Mariposa, the harvesters Peter Milford had ordered were late in arriving, and he had been screaming at Havermeyer every day over the long-distance wires.

Jana had come to Havermeyer straight from Harvard Business School, where she had taken a master of business administration degree with a specialization in agribusiness. Before Harvard, she had worked at a firm called Engineered Edibles, which she could not remember without a shudder. Four years at the Massachusetts Institute of Technology and a degree in mechanical engineering had led her to that unfortunate job.

When she had been given the Mariposa assignment, she had thought it would be more or less routine. Now, she wasn't so sure. Jana wriggled uncomfortably in the rickety wooden chair and looked out the screen door.

She had formed a dislike of this part of the country immediately, and would have liked nothing better than to walk out on this arrogant Peter Milford before meeting him. During the hour's drive from Fresno on the seemingly endless straight road through the 450-mile-long San Joaquin Valley, Jana had fought with herself to keep from turning around and heading back to the airport.

The searingly hot valley was not so much cradled as abandoned between two mountain ranges. She felt there was something unnatural about the former desert. All these farmers had to do was plant something, water and fertilize it, and the result was tons of fruit per acre, geraniums that reached up to second-story windows, eerie eucalyptus trees that seemed to stalk the streets and highways, pointing their green fingers down while on the ground their brown leaves curled in on themselves like masses of ingrown . . . she couldn't afford to think about it.

In order not to be tempted to deliver it, Jana rehearsed a speech for this Peter Milford who was forcing her to undergo such a torturous wait.

"Mr. Milford. My suitcases were rerouted to San Francisco; the car I reserved was rented earlier this morning to someone else, or so they said, and I was forced to pay exorbitantly for the white Mercedes you see parked outside. The clothes I have on are inappropriate, unbearably hot, and the conditions in this office. . . ."

She could hear heels drilling into the wooden stairs of the light gray painted boards leading to the porch outside.

The squeaky screen door was flung open by a man in cowboy boots, his shirtless chest heaving, his face streaked with tributaries of mud oozing out from under his dirty straw cowboy hat. "You are J. Robbins from Havermeyer Harvester?" he said. His voice rumbled from somewhere inside the vee formed by a long gold chain with a gold medallion the size of a quarter on it.

Before she could do anything but nod, his black eyes had pinned her down in the chair. "What the hell does that company think it's doing to me? I've got a near-riot on my hands, and they send me a lady under the disguise of J. Robbins?"

Jana flattened her navy pumps into the dust of the bare floorboards and stood up ramrod-straight.

"It was my understanding," she said in a low, seething voice, "that you had requested a representative from Havermeyer to help your peach ranch in its transition from manual labor to machines. I was even told that the Mariposa Peach Company was desperate."

"That's true, but only because Havermeyer has made us desperate. My predicament, J. Robbins. . . ."

"Jana."

". . . . is a direct result of Havermeyer's non-delivery of the peach-harvesters I ordered. I've had to hire the last remaining and therefore the most inept crew of migrant workers in the valley. They've already been offered a better deal by the Calimyrna Corporation up the road. If they knew I'd ordered mechanical harvesters to replace them, they'd do everything in the book—from strikes to sabotage—to keep the harvesters out of the orchards. That's because by the time the damned machines are here, nobody will want to hire them."

Peter Milford was overpoweringly close to her. Staring at his medallion to give her a focus, she stepped back.

"The door is this way," he said, "and you might as well leave through it now."

Instead, Jana sat down on the oak relic of a straight-backed chair where she had waited so long for this brute. To steady herself, she leaned her left ankle against the leg of the chair so tightly that a selection of splinters dug into her flesh and loosed a horse race of runs up her calf.

"Mr. Milford. You are Peter Milford, aren't you? I have a job to do here, and I've no intention of leaving."

Throwing his grimy straw hat down on the floor, he crouched in front of her as if she were a child who had refused to go home from a birthday party.

"All my arrangements," he said slowly for the benefit of her stubbornness, "are for a man. Miss Robbins, you cannot remain here. This is no place for you. Do. You. Understand?"

"You don't want me because I'm a woman?"

"That. Is. Right."

"Mr. Milford, I'd like to remind you that there are laws against discrimination. I would not be the first to invoke them, and this does seem to be a case extreme enough to warrant. . . ."

He swayed, stood up, and looked down at her as if she were a wild creature who refused to behave in captivity.

Her blue suit, prim shoes and blonde hair pulled severely back with a businesslike blue ribbon had thrown him. She looked anything but wild. And she didn't give a damn about his prejudices, his blood pressure or, at this moment, his peach ranch.

She was holding herself in control only because this man was in a position to drop the axe on the speed with which she advanced at Havermeyer. She had worked too hard for that to happen. She thought of those expensive school years and that miserable job she had held with Engineered Edibles in Davenport, Iowa after graduation from MIT. That company was dedicated to creating better simulated strawberries, fake figs, polyester-looking plums. She had joined Havermeyer with two degrees behind her and only because she had felt she could advance further and faster with them. She needed to make a lot of money, and she needed it quickly if she was to help her brother, her mother and herself.

Peter Milford interrupted her thoughts about the forces that had brought her to this little shack of an office. "The government, Miss Robbins, interferes with the kind of pesticides I use, the size of the peaches I send to the cannery, what labor I can hire, how much I have to pay the laborers, where I get my water for irrigation. And now you want the government to intercede on behalf of every blonde snippet who trips in from Chicago waving a string of college degrees?

"Just because Mariposa isn't Del Monte or Dole, Hunt's or Libby's, does Havermeyer think it can send me somebody who hasn't got enough sense not to fly off into an ideological fit the minute facts are laid on the table?"

"What makes you think *I'm* in a fit?" Jana was throwing all her energy into looking and sounding cool.

He ignored her question. What *he* was saying interested him more. "You spend all your time shuffling papers, collecting college degrees, commissions and promotions, primping and driving expensive cars. You can't help me."

If only his hands would halt their accompaniment to his anger. Under the grime were hands that tapered like extensions of his ideas rather than blunt working tools. He couldn't speak without them.

"Mariposa has been working with people for forty years. We've had serious labor problems in the last few years, but nothing like we're going to have this summer because of Havermeyer. We're in a position to lose, not only our working relationship with the laborers we've got, but our reputation as well. We're known for having the finest peaches in the San Joaquin Valley, and part of that reputation is based on the fact that neither your damned machines nor anybody else's have ever gotten their claws into our fruit."

"Our machines don't have claws, as you well know, Mr. Milford. If you'll recall, Mariposa purchased machines that shake the peaches into an inverted umbrella, freeing the peach from the five bruises that inevitably result when a human hand with five fingers yanks the peach off the tree. Was this not one of the factors that caused you to purchase our machines in the first place?"

"Unreal."

"Pardon me?" Jana hated it when people used those two

words as a question, and she had just done it! There was no telling what else she might say or do that was out of character.

"Unreal the kind of people who work for corporations. Look, we could have had the best damned workers in the valley. We didn't sign a contract with them this season because we thought we'd have six new harvesters and each harvester replaces forty men.

"Mariposa is costing Milford Enterprises more than ever this season, and that wasn't supposed to happen. We can no longer continue to drain off profits from my dad's wineries, almond and walnut orchards and orange groves. But how would you, goofing off in air-conditioned comfort in your fancy office overlooking Lake Michigan, know that?"

"Mr. Milford, you ought to know that women aren't secure enough in any corporation to 'goof off.' But, having grubbed around in the dirt for weeks and weeks, you aren't, of course, in a position to know that, are you?"

Jana knew from Schultz's report that this was only his second summer working as manager of Mariposa and that, before, he had apparently disdained the land and gone to Washington as a labor lawyer. He was probably furious with himself when he realized that machines that did not need to be housed, fed and pacified, machines that would not complain or need to sign contracts, would be more profitable than migrant workers.

He put on his hat and moved to the door. "Thank you very much for coming. I hope to see you on the cover of *Time* magazine."

"This is unfair," said Jana, refusing to budge. "Schultz's report did not begin to give an indication of the kind of man or situation I would be dealing with here."

"That's because Schultz never took his eyes off the ladies long enough to absorb the information it would take to—to plug the run in your stocking."

As he watched to see what she would do with his observation, Jana willed herself to move neither her flawed leg nor her flushed face.

"What Schultz didn't know was that I had plans for him to drive a peach truck and from there, learn to know the situation at Mariposa and make friends with the pickers. Since in the beginning any Havermeyer representative would be unpopular, I planned to keep his identity secret—for his own safety.

"The person identified with these machines must first be trusted by the workers, or I'll never be able to convince anyone of anything—nor could he. The health of the fruit industry in this valley depends on the machines—as you know. But introducing them is creating a short-term disruption that is threatening my long-term goals: assembling a crew of year-round *loyal* workers and assimilating as many men as possible into jobs either here at Mariposa or in the Milford vineyards.

"I intended for Schultz to become acquainted with the potential troublemakers and then reason with them on the basis of friendship.

"I know it's hard for you to believe, Miss Robbins, but it's possible that you would be in *equally* as much danger if you are identified as a Havermeyer rep. How about reporting *that* equality problem to the government?"

On the verge of laughter but after this serious speech fighting to control it, Jana motioned to a doorless pickup speeding past, the loose valley dust whirling over its load of full wooden peach boxes. Imagining the bald, red-faced, overweight Schultz driving such a truck, she said, "You were planning to turn Schultz loose in one of those mufflerless wonders?"

The heir apparent looked rattled. Jana saw a man silently working out a puzzle—a man whose eyes were questioning her for clues.

At first, she assumed by his silence that she had won their argument. Instead, he opened the screen door and once again motioned her through it.

"It's been nice meeting you. Maybe I'll see you again someday."

"I know, on the cover of. . . . " Why was his breath providing the only moving air in the room? Why did she feel as gummy and dried up as the figs in the drying shed across the road? And why didn't Peter Milford realize how much she wanted—how much she needed—a glass of water?

Jana ran her hand through her hair, and as she did she could feel her silky, straight locks fall around her face. Her eyes dropped to the navy ribbon that had fallen on the floor, and she bent down to retrieve it at the same time as Peter Milford did.

As they groped under the chair, their sticky hands touched and their eyes met, registering a similar surprise that they

were both human. His hands were as out of place as hers on
the dirty floor. She noticed that the grime had not worked its
way up to his expensive Rolex wristwatch. And his straight,
dark brown hair had fallen down in his face in a pointed fringe
that shaded his black eyes, now beaded with a glimmer of
humanity.

The moment ended when the screen door opened and a
man said, "Just what makes you think that Mariposa can
manage right now without replacing Sara?"

A gray-haired man barged into the center of the room
before seeing Jana, hidden as she crouched on the other side
of Peter.

Peter helped Jana to her feet.

"What about her?" Peter asked the man. "Her references
say she can add and subtract, so she can probably operate a
scale in the weigh house. She's a Harvard Business School
student begging me for a summer job."

"Dammit, Milford, you never fail with the ladies, do you?"
He turned to Jana: "Moose is the name," he said, pumping
both her hands. "Moses Sigourney is what I was called before
this ranch turned me into an animal." He glanced toward
Peter with an unfriendly look.

His stubby hair, hands, jaw, and even cheeks, were
sculpted in squares. His eyes darted under a row of stiff
lashes, and blinked nervously as if he wore contact lenses that
scratched.

"Take her away," said Peter, showing signs of amusement
on his face.

Moose put his hand under Jana's elbow, steered her out to
the porch and down the stairs.

Jana glanced back at Peter, who was standing on the top
step. She tossed her hair out of her eyes and said, "Well, Mr.
Milford, this is certainly better than driving a truck."

For the hundred-foot march to the weigh house, Jana's
thoughts were riveted on the man she was leaving behind.
Black eyes, she considered, had an advantage over blue ones.
Peter Milford had almost won this round because of the
penetrating power of his gaze, and for no other reason.

And look what he had caused her to do. She, who had been
meticulously professional in all her dealings with the men she
had met in her work, was marching off to a grimy job sought
after by college students.

How could she have allowed him to put her in this position?

Why hadn't she, a master at thinking of alternative routes, been able to think of even one?

How surprising it had been to touch his hand; how his chest had lured her eyes over its heaving terrain. The man standing back there on the porch had struck her like a too-heavy thunderstorm in the middle of unbearable heat. That must have been it.

Through the oppressive haze inside the weigh house, Jana met the other weighmaster, Cassie Crofts. In a halter top and bikini shorts, she was clowning around swatting raisins on the floor with a flyswatter for the benefit of a laughing fellow— another shirtless specimen—standing in the door.

As soon as her audience saw Moose, he lumbered out the door, jumped into his pickup and clattered down the dusty road to the orchards.

"Glad I'm not going to be doing all the work around here anymore," said Cassie, laying down the flyswatter and lethargically walking toward Jana, whom Moose introduced as a Harvard student.

Never had Jana seen anyone so perfectly brown, so charmingly berry-round. Cassie's face was frame-fuzzed by a short, curly haircut; her wide-open, light green eyes appeared to be vacantly waiting for a man to furnish the brain behind them with the ideas of his choice.

"Cassie here," said Moose, "is interested in the drivers because they all tend to be students or professors from Stanford, Cal, Cal Tech, UCLA, Fresno State or USC—it doesn't matter to her. She's a fortune hunter, and these fellows are making a bundle from Mariposa, which is one reason we're in so much trouble."

"Moose!" protested Cassie.

"Get your fun while you can, little darling, there may not be a Mariposa after this summer—after this month, if you want to know what I really think."

"Moose is sulky because Peter Milford's pushing improvements on the ranch. He never expected him to return for a second summer."

"Have you ever seen us have more trouble than we've had since Milford arrived?"

"He wouldn't have arrived if you and old man Milford had made improvements all along," said Cassie, removing Moose's cap, which had a Mac Truck bulldog on it. His thick gray hair was damp and he looked exhausted.

Swaying now more like a gorilla than his hoofed namesake, Moose retreated to the door.

"Sugar, don't be upset." Cassie followed and planted a kiss on his cheek. "You're still my favorite fella—remember that."

"I leave you to her," he said to Jana in a softer voice. "*You* figure her out."

As soon as Moose was out the door, Cassie began her own interrogation. "You go to Harvard, huh? Well, I skied, swam and partied *my* way through Sonoma State, and now I teach kindergarten in Fresno.

"And why are you dressed like that? We have to wear *some* clothes at Mariposa, but let's not go overboard. What are you hiding under there?"

Either because of Cassie's urging or her ridicule, Jana rolled up her skirt at the waist until it became a mini and slipped on a tube top Cassie offered. When Cassie pointed to her legs and rolled her eyes, Jana peeled off her pantyhose, certain that a thousand eyes were staring at her through the buckling screens that lined the weigh house.

The air felt wonderfully cool on her midriff; her legs tingled at their release from the stockings. Jana felt like a child being allowed to run through the sprinkler in her underwear on the first warm day of summer. She wanted to giggle like a woman who had come completely unraveled.

"Now," said Cassie, "I'll give you your first and only lesson on how to weigh these trucks."

"Only?"

"Honey, if you need more than one, you'll never graduate from a joint like Harvard. Besides, I don't know what good your credentials will do you here. You know how men are threatened by women who throw around their intelligence. As for Peter Milford, he's already got enough degrees for one peach ranch, so you can keep your hands off him. What are you planning to do when you graduate—run a corporation, or marry one?"

"Really, Cassie. . . ."

"You have to fill out these forms in triplicate. You put the morning weight of the truck here, the weight of the full truck here, and then figure the difference. Doesn't that sound hard?"

Jana felt dumb as she listened to Cassie explain the simple procedure to her. The strangeness of practically stripping in public, and being taught this elementary weighing system when she had taken courses in designing trucks for the twenty-first century, was wrecking her concentration.

Here she was looking to the girl with the vapid green eyes for instructions, hoping that the man with the darting black eyes would return (would not return?) and attempting at the same time to sink into the role of college student.

"All you have to do is shuffle the weights, up here, down there, balance. See? I've got to go, there's a truck on my scales. All there is to this job is waiting until the next gorgeous hunk arrives at your window. You can flirt with him until the truck behind honks impatiently."

This peach ranch was operating in the nineteenth century. The only difference was that dilapidated trucks, instead of rickety horses and carts, hauled the peaches. Plus, there was hand-sorting of peaches, a haphazard arrangement with the canneries in the area, a tendency to stick to old varieties of peaches instead of the new ones that did not bruise, not to mention an unhealthy reliance on chemicals to kill pests and poor marketing and advertising practices. Mariposa was still operating as if the peach business were a little farm-to-market problem instead of big business competing with giant companies like Del Monte.

Introducing machines to a backward labor force was not Mariposa's only problem, not by a long shot. And Peter Milford wasn't really committed to complete modernization or he wouldn't have balked at having a woman show up at Mariposa.

Or was he right? Had a woman no business in a situation where over 250 suspicious, angry, frightened migrant workers were fearful of losing their jobs to machines supplied by Havermeyer? Could she help Peter make them understand? Did he want to disassociate himself from the machines and blame it all on Havermeyer? Could she actually help Mariposa assimilate men and women into other positions? Or should she fly home?

She wondered if she had dug in her heels so resolutely, not because of her confidence that she could make a positive impact here, but because one man with a naked chest had disoriented her reputable radar.

Had Peter Milford actually said something about operating Mariposa with full-time, year-round employees? How could that be possible? It was not, she was certain. But it sounded good and might allay fears for a time. That must be Milford's reasoning.

The first driver to appear at her window was Peter himself. His face was even dirtier than it had been before. His chest had also suffered during the hour since she had last seen him. The black spears from his eyes pierced hers. She let them.

"Okay, let's see you work the scales," he said.

"Peter usually weighs in on my side," said Cassie as she brought over the morning weight of his truck.

"I only want to see if you taught her right, hon. I'll visit you next time."

"I didn't know you drove a peach truck," said Jana. "I thought you were running this ranch."

"I do everything," he said.

"But do you have time?"

Jana slid the weights to the balancing notch, passed the figures out to him through the window in the screen. Peter ran his forearm across his chin, leaving a horizontal streak of dirt on it. He glared at Jana through the window. "There are stipulations I have to lay down if you are to remain here." His lips, jaw, even his cheeks, appeared made of variegated marble.

"Where are you staying?" he demanded.

"A place I found on my way out here. The Plum Tree Inn."

She hadn't mumbled since she was five years old—the year her father had deserted the family. In all that time, she had never allowed herself to be as upset, as topsy-turvy, as she was feeling now. But, at least, by mumbling she hadn't allowed herself to appear upset.

"I know where it is," he said. "I'll pick you up there at seven-thirty tonight."

His eyes touched her bare shoulders like cold, black sticks.

"You can dress for dinner," he said. "This won't be a picnic."

Peter peeled out in his truck. She should have known better than to tangle with him. But for the moment, Jana was more angry with Schultz, who had wangled his way to cool southern China on a new tomato-harvesting experiment. And here she was stuck on this less-than-peachy ranch with Peter Milford, who had just stood outside her screened window like a big, threatening insect.

"Sometimes, we don't leave here until eight," she heard Cassie purr. "But don't worry. We're not far enough into the season to work long hours. I'm just telling you so that you'll be prepared. People like me who've been working here every summer for five or six years already know the ropes.

"You were really lucky to have arrived so soon after Sara quit. She found out she was pregnant. The father is the driver of truck number forty-two. He's gone down to L.A. with her. I imagine they'll stay together. They might even get married."

Jana was fascinated by the way Cassie raised her eyebrows and puckered her bottom lip as though she were pouring her words out through the lip of a pitcher.

"You know, Jana, there's quite a lot of commingling between the drivers and the women in the weigh house. It's only natural. We're the only nubile women on the ranch. The ladies out there on the platform have been here since before the flood—or they look like it, anyway."

Cassie, sitting on her high stool in her bikini shorts, should at least have exhibited a slight fold of fat in her stomach. It was, however, perfectly flat. Jana sucked in her own flat, but not so firm stomach and resolved to exercise. If these Californians looked so great, they must be doing something right.

Jana swung her bare feet and was happy with her more comfortable self. Perhaps it was time she had a California experience. Going from Chicago to the east coast had done wonders for her education, but not much for her social life. Jana wiggled her toes. For a brief second, the one alluring connection between her hand and Peter's flashed through her, and she felt a kind of zig-zag shock from head to toe.

This California experience wouldn't last long. The harvesters would arrive no later than the end of the month. When she returned home, Spenser would be returning, too, after a year in Italy working with a professor on an in-depth book about the bronze Ghiberti doors of the Baptistry in Florence.

Would he be encased in the same bronze as the doors? His pale complexion would probably look better. Spenser could talk for hours about the beauty of the human body, the elegance of the naked form. But he didn't really believe it. Jana had been the one to melt him.

Spenser was the liberal arts course she had never had time to take. She had diligently applied herself to discovering the beast in the poet—a practice that she was sure was totally unnecessary with a California man.

Jana stretched her feet to the floor and inhaled. There was

no part of her that felt sharp or determined—or businesslike. She was almost content to be sitting here idly, waiting for the next truck. Perhaps it was a good idea that she had entered this almost-magic valley where *anything* could grow.

"Peter's aunt—they call her Miss Mari around here," said Cassie, "looks good, but she's getting on in years. She lives right over there in that big white house with the wrap-around front porch. You can hardly see anything but the second story because of all the trees and bushes.

"My dad says that in his day she was the most beautiful woman in this valley. Personally, I think she's still stunning in many ways. In my opinion, she's held up well because she channels her sexual vibes into worthy causes."

"What do you mean?"

"Instead of screwing around. . . ."

"I mean what causes?"

Cassie rolled her eyes and gestured to the unpainted brown boards of the ceiling. "She raises money for the Save Yosemite Committee, which she founded. She also takes in stray animals, and even has a project going to undam the wild river that supplies irrigation water for this ranch. My dad says she got her funny ideas in one of those communist countries."

The eccentricities of this family were piling up. Here was one more complication, one more certain reason why Mariposa was in trouble. If only Jana could focus her attention on peaches instead of personalities, she could be out of here in a week.

"They say she had a lover in Paris," continued Cassie. "He was a famous French film maker. God, I'll bet that was one racy couple. There are also rumors that Peter's mother was somehow involved—a *ménage à trois*. I'd love to know the details, wouldn't you?"

No, but Jana found herself looking forward to meeting Miss Mari—as an isolated experience, of course.

"I don't want you to think," said Cassie, "that just because you have a fancy education you're a perfect match for Peter." Jana sensed that part of Cassie's irritation was caused by her own lack of response to Cassie's revelations about Miss Mari.

"Peter's mine," continued Cassie. "It's been that way for years. And this summer, it's truer than ever, and nobody changes that—certainly not a stranger who wanders in without knowing the *lay* of the land—which Peter Milford certainly is."

While Cassie laughed heartily at herself, Jana squirmed. Everything this woman said knocked her a little further off-balance. How could Jana weigh peach trucks when she could hardly weigh the total worth of a word this woman was saying?

A curly blond head stuck its way through Cassie's scale-side window.

"Who's that?" he asked, motioning to Jana.

"New girl in town."

"I'll be right in."

The dingy weigh house was aglow. Over six feet of suntan were crammed into tight white tennis shorts and a light blue shirt with its sleeves ripped out. His brown legs and arms were sinewy with muscles, and silked over with coarse blond hair. And his eyes were the same utterly blue color as her own.

Until this stunning moment, Jana had always preferred dark-eyed, dark-haired men. This one did not smile or hold out his hand to shake hers. Instead, he helped her off the high work stool in front of her slanted desk. As she stood there waiting for what she feared would be the common exchange of acquaintance, he gently touched her hair on the sides, then in the back.

With eyes that already had everything in common on the color scale, their introduction was flowing faster than words. However, she believed he said his name was Andy Goodwin in a voice that was either choked up or naturally husky.

He cupped both her shoulders with his hands. Her bones were melting. She was fourteen years old and wondering how his kiss would taste.

"At first, I thought we'd met before." That was his first complete sentence.

"Maybe we have," she stammered.

"Where do you live?" His tone implied that it was in a castle on a hill surrounded by thorns that only he was fit to tackle.

Jana's mind, like a lost homing pigeon, groped for a location to give him. "I don't know. I mean, I only arrived this afternoon." Her I.Q. was dropping around her ankles.

"I know the perfect place for you."

Jana threw a desperate glance to Cassie's side of the weigh house. Cassie had vanished.

Chapter 2

Why was she speeding south down Highway 99 behind Andy's yellow Honda? Was it another heat-induced decision? Peter Milford was picking her up at the motel in exactly an hour, and she had to find a drugstore, buy a dress (if she could find one), check into her room, bathe and dress.

The sun filtered obliquely through the eucalyptus trees, the oleander clumped thickly along the median, offering a pleasant dividing line. Irrigation ditches next to the road and in the fields glistened black, gold or red, depending on the height of the shadows cast by the nearest crops of tomatoes, grapes, almonds, peaches or apricots.

For some reason, the mountains at sunset no longer appeared so far away—particularly the high Sierra Nevada range to the east.

Until she had met this blond Adonis, remaining in California long enough to visit Yosemite National Park, which was somewhere in those mountains, had been all the pleasure she had looked forward to from this trip.

Andy turned into a heavily-shaded residential street. Maybe she *would* keep this Mercedes. It was completely in tune with California, the state it had been built to be driven in.

Andy had pulled in and stopped in a circular driveway in front of an ivy-covered, wooden post fence.

Grinning, he jumped out of his car. "Before you say a word, I must tell you that before you is a compound of three houses. I live in one, a friend of mine is housesitting in another and the third is closed up for the summer. My friend has been looking for a roommate for the remainder of the summer—you two can work out the small fee.

If there was one thing Jana had outgrown after her first two years in college, it was female roommates.

With Andy leading, she ducked under the branches of a blossoming magnolia tree and hurried down a rock path lined with nasturtiums and maroon dahlias. The perfect flowers appeared to be growing out of a perfect green carpet. Baby tears. In Chicago, they grew in pots. She preferred it that way.

He led her to the shimmering oval pool in the middle of the complex. The pool's blue surface was marred by a bulky brown object that, if such things existed, could have been a floating Barcalounger.

"Gretchen," said Andy, "Gretchen, come out and meet your public."

A flipperlike hand paddled the chair into a slow-motion turn, and a girl with thick glasses, pigtails and huge feet, balancing a book on her chest, revolved into view.

"This is your new housemate. Her name is Jana."

"Yeah?" The girl squinted and pushed her glasses up with her nose muscles before shoving them into place with the back of her wrist.

"Jana's the new weighmaster at Mariposa. She needs a place to stay for the summer."

Gretchen closed her book. "My classes are in the morning; I study out here all afternoon; and I need quiet at night."

She sounded as if she had a summer cold, although Jana feared it was her usual sniffling tone.

"And I don't allow wild parties." Jana glanced down at herself. She had unrolled the blue skirt, slipped her suit jacket over the tube top. She didn't look like a party girl.

"Gretchen is referring to me," said Andy. "She's an anthropology major at Cal in Berkeley. She can't afford to make less than an 'A' in summer school, or she won't be allowed to return in the fall."

"I had a course in anthropology when I was a sophomore," said Jana. "Strange cultures, exotic locales—I loved it."

"Urban anthropology," said Gretchen, squinting again, "is my interest: the unseen among the seen; the institutional structures held up by people toiling out of habit to perpetuate and strengthen the boundaries of their unexamined lives." She waved across the pool at a pepper tree as if a city hung in its branches.

"Don't worry, Gretch," said Andy. "We work long hours at Mariposa and you won't be seeing much of Jana. You'll like the long days best, Jana, because you get paid by the hour."

Gretchen sprawled across the seat of her armchair island, propped the book up on her very flat chest, and maneuvered a paddled turn as she said disinterestedly, "Watch what you track in when you show her through."

Once inside the house, Jana was pleased to see that her room would be in a corner of the house quite apart from Gretchen's room—the room she was shown first. With clothes hanging from the sides of the dresser mirror, the corners of drawers and the edges of doors, it looked like a merchandise jungle. Heaps of clothes in the corner resembled an excavation site. The room might provide Gretchen enough material for her doctoral dissertation—if she could dig her way out of it long enough to enter graduate school.

Andy seemed to know the room that would be hers and she followed him to the other end of the hall. The room was neat and clean, but otherwise awful. The walls were painted black and it had a smoky-mirrored ceiling over the kingsized waterbed.

The stark contrast to her white, beige and cream-colored bedroom in Chicago could not have been sharper. In her apartment, so severely did the sun glint across Lake Michigan and hit its walls, that she could have worn sunglasses in the daytime without wondering why. The person who had designed this room was obviously sick of the sun and wanted his own private burrow.

In her own apartment, there were no overtones of darkness. Even the closets contained bright lights. And there were no ratholes like Gretchen's room. Not even in the back of a drawer. Her once-a-week maid had told her she was the neatest of all her "people." She also gave Jana frequent lectures that usually began, "Miss Robbins, you can't always be putting everything back where you got it. You're s'posed to be out having some fun. And if you're too perfect, you'll scare off the men. I cleaned a woman's apartment down on Fourteen. Everything was in little boxes. No crumbs on the floor. No spillovers on the stove."

"Was?" Had the woman died of neatness?

"She got a better job in New York. She was forty-five years old and that's all she wanted: a job in New York."

"How do you like it?" asked Andy.

Jana's pupils had dilated, so with the help of the discreet track-lighting she could see all she wanted to of the bedroom.

"I've always wanted to live in a projectionist's booth," she quipped, still feeling worried about the woman who had moved to New York.

Without so much as a smile, Andy continued, "The complex shares a maid and two gardeners and you needn't worry: you won't ever be asked to vacuum the pool. I would have asked you to move in with me right away," he said, "but I could see immediately that you were from the east and were probably not. . . ."

"Andy, I'm late. You tell Gretchen that I'd like to stay, and if she doesn't mind, I'll be here tomorrow after work."

Andy walked toward her, smiling with the most sensual lips she had ever seen: a full lower lip, an extra curve at both sides of the top one. Had she seen his mouth in a photograph, she might have considered it cruel. But when examined as part of his perfect, golden-brown body, it held interest far beyond the average mouth. His deep tan allowed his teeth to reveal themselves like the velvety white magnolias in the now-darkening trees.

He was so close that Jana looked down at her wrist with embarrassment. She would have studied it even if there hadn't been a watch there.

"I do have to hurry."

"Why, hon?"

"I've made arrangements to have dinner with someone—and my suitcases haven't arrived and. . . ."

"I understand."

And he did. First stop: a discount drugstore in a small shopping center.

But Jana saw a boutique next door to it that had a mannequin in the window wearing a melon-colored, strapless, silk-like dress. If only she could pick up one in another color, she would feel much better about her evening with Peter.

Seeing her interest, Andy steered her into the store. The only dress in her size that she liked was a one-strap silk in soft light blue. It swathed her midriff and breasts, causing her nipples to show just a little. Andy approved heartily, and she liked the way she felt in it. She also found a pair of cream-colored sandals, which she bought in the same store without trying them on. After that, she ran into the drugstore and scooped up a toothbrush, toothpaste, some makeup base, mascara and clear nail polish.

Andy drove in front of her on the way back to the motel and, to her chagrin, accompanied her to the room, insisting that he wanted to see how she looked in the dress.

As Jana bathed, she heard him turn on the television, and when she emerged from the bathroom she found him slumped on the bed. Grabbing the dress, she slipped it on in the bathroom, and when she reappeared his evaluation was, "Fabulous, super."

The time was 7:20, and someone was knocking on the door. When she opened it, she saw Peter's moderately pleasant expression twist into displeasure as soon as he saw Andy. "You work fast," he said to the lounger on the bed.

"I might remind you," said Andy, "that the lady is going out to eat with you, not me. I'd say you're in line for the fast work award, Milford."

"Are you ready, Jana?" Peter was ignoring Andy.

"Look, man," said Andy getting off the bed, "the lady lost her suitcase and had nothing to wear. Don't you think she looks great now? And she did it all for you-oo-oo."

With a motion of his head toward the door that reminded Jana of a gangster in a movie, Peter ordered Andy to exit.

Jana was furious at Peter's dictatorial manner, peeved at Andy's casualness, and angry with herself for being in this uncomfortable motel room situation. She disliked going from here to a meeting with Peter. It was a bad way to start a discussion on which so much was riding.

Peter had already been reluctant, to say the least, to have her at Mariposa. If there were any more snags, she was sure to lose the momentum she had gained at Havermeyer. Her plans leading to her next promotion would be sure to be slowed if she returned to Chicago without the Mariposa situation settled.

As she sat in Peter's flashy silver Jaguar, she wondered if all Californians lived in television situation comedies. Maybe that's why they film most of them in this state, Jana thought.

Peter turned onto the highway, and Jana's feelings were soothed by the smooth ride of the car. She felt safe enough to close her eyes and formulate a working plan for the evening. Whenever she opened them, the cozy lights of the dashboard —complicated enough to be an instrument panel—reassured her that everything was under control. And when one of her hands automatically turned palm-down to feel the bare softness of her new dress, one that had no place in her Chicago wardrobe, she was glad to be where she was and not on an airplane headed east.

Judging from her previous encounters with Peter Milford, Jana concluded that an understanding with him while he was driving was hopeless as long as he had such a good excuse for ignoring her.

Through her peripheral vision, however, she noted that his lips were hard and set, as though he were squelching a list of new recriminations.

Sooner than she expected, they had skirted the downtown area of Fresno and stopped outside a small stucco house—the gate house of a large estate.

The ornate wrought-iron gate rolled silently into the stucco wall, and the Jaguar glided through the opening and down a road lined with giant Christmas tree–sized firs. Peter was driving slowly now, and even though most of the view had been cast into leaden sundown silhouettes, Jana could see a large rectangular swimming pool. It looked like an aquamarine on black velvet, lighted by diamondlike underwater lights and held down by underwater stairs and white columns at one end.

"That is so beautiful," Jana whispered, forgetting their game of who would speak first.

Peter stopped the car, helped her out, and led her through an arched passageway sculpted in a high shrub.

It was like walking through a keyhole into another world. Beyond the pool was a Japanese garden, its pagoda-shapes barely discernible, its pools glimmering and punctuated by perfect rocks and boulders.

Jana had a sense that there might be something beyond the obvious flatness of this valley; something more than the uninteresting grid of criss-crossed streets, the tiny attempts at tall buildings, the endless middle-class sprawl of tidy yards she had glimpsed from the plane that morning.

As if warning her, Peter finally said, "The house we're going to isn't the original Milford home. That is located out at Mariposa."

"Where your aunt lives?"

"Who told you about her?" he snapped.

"Cassie only mentioned that she lives in the white house across the road from the weigh house."

Peter motioned toward the two-story, tile-roofed structure that stood at the center of the landscaped gardens. "This house belongs to my dad. He's recovering from his illness and a new marriage at his beach house in Santa Cruz."

To Jana, the Spanish-style house seemed to have grown like one of the trees in the garden. She couldn't imagine any other house being there. A modern house would have elbowed with the landscape; a colonial would have been pretentious. But this dusty, colored stucco with twisted narrow columns and arched windows was perfect.

She looked at Peter to see if his face had registered any changes since he began talking about the house. She thought he had warmed up. If she could only keep him talking, by the time she understood the house she might understand him.

"Nobody has resided here full time since I was a small boy. The house itself is not in the greatest condition but, fortunately, there has always been a dedicated gardening staff that has kept up the grounds. They live in various small houses scattered around the estate."

Peter's countenance grew softer and more human as he spoke. Jana could see him clearly now, because the lights from the pool were being reflected by his cream-colored trousers, icy green shirt and natural-colored linen jacket.

This Milford setup was more than she could ever have obtained in twenty or thirty years of hard work. You really had to inherit money—or marry it, she concluded.

The night air suddenly felt heavy and cool and the light stole that had come with her dress had been left behind in the car.

Peter noticed at once that she was cold. "Our dinner is being served where we have a view of these gardens, but we'll be indoors. We have some rough things to talk about and I want to make it as pleasant as possible."

"I think you already have," she said, taking his arm as they returned to the car over the dew-damp grass.

Inherit it. Or marry it. Jana couldn't believe such thoughts had occurred to her. She had always been of the school that believed that waiting for a man to choose her was not her style. How could it have been? There had been so many men who had swarmed around her. But she had had so little time, and the man she had chosen traveled almost as much as she did.

A maroon Rolls Royce was parked in the driveway at the back of the three- story house. Jana's heart dropped.

"Do you have company?"

"The car," he said, "goes with the house."

Jana noticed then that the paint, particularly around the upstairs windows, was peeling, that the curtains were closed in every room and the shades pulled. If it hadn't been for that maroon car, she would have thought that Peter was taking her to an uninhabited place. And if the grounds had been neglected as much as the house, they would be dry and yellowing, the swimming pool cracked and empty.

Jana pictured herself helping the house to bloom and flower so that it would be what the great house of a great family should be. A house needed care and attention—and love.

They walked in through the kitchen. Peter introduced her to a cook named Pilar whose gray uniform was straining at the buttons down its front.

As they continued through the house, Jana wished they had entered by the front door. Then her first sight would have been the curved stairway and the custom-made beige, turquoise, brown and cream-colored tile laid in the center of the foyer to form an enormous "M."

Jana looked up the stairs and along the burnished wood balcony. She imagined the rooms that stretched off the back into three wings.

"You live here alone?"

"Yeah. I squirrel up in the room I had as a kid with my T.V., books and tape deck. Except for meals, which Pilar usually prepares, it's a little like camping out with electricity.

"I haven't hired more staff because I won't want to run into somebody every time I walk out the door. And if Mariposa has to be sold, this house will go, too."

Peter led her down several stairs into a living room whose walls were heavy with life-sized portraits.

Jana stopped to examine a painting of one Harold Arthur Milford. She had only time to notice that his eyes were the same as Peter's when Peter said, "Let's go in to dinner. We have a lot to talk about."

"But who is he?" Peter was acting as if these pictures, hanging there for anyone to see, were private.

"He was my great, great grandfather. Legend has it that he entered a jumping frog in the same contest Mark Twain wrote about up in Calaveras County.

"Those other men on both sides of him are also grandparents."

"They look adventurous," said Jana, noting their one-foot-in-front-of-the-other stance. "And prosperous."

"It's a Milford trait to go around looking as if we had millions even when we don't—a condition that was true most of the time in those days. And for all I know, it's true now, too. I'm not privy to the Milford books—only to Mariposa's. And you know the trouble that place is in."

Jana walked on to three portraits of Milford women: the first was riding a horse; the second painting in a woods. The third stood looking out a window at orchards that could have been Mariposa's. This woman had purple eyes that were almost eerie.

Jana envisioned her own portrait. It would be the only modern one on the wall, different and distinctive. Her portrait would stand out uncamouflaged in this room. But she would fit into the room and the family several ways. With her skills and her drive, she could bring this place into the twentieth century. The mansion would be the seat of Milford greatness once more. Jana Robbins Milford. She tried the name on for size.

"Would you come on?" Peter said gruffly. She followed him to a small round table set in a glassed-in alcove a few feet away from a large dining table that looked as if it would seat at least two dozen.

Peter didn't know that he had everything. He had a little idea of upgrading Mariposa. But he had no idea about preserving the past. At least, judging from his pressured explanations in front of the portraits, he seemed not to appreciate the past that money could not buy—a past Jana would never have unless. . . .

At the table, Peter poured a Milford Chardonnay into monogrammed crystal glasses. Jana placed her heavy white napkin in her lap and could feel the rough monogrammed "M" on it with her fingertips. The silver napkin ring was edged with a cursive "M." When she reached the end of her avocado, lettuce and pignon nut salad, the plate was hand-painted with a large gold "M."

Half expecting an "M" to be neatly stamped or branded on his forehead, Jana looked up at Peter. Thank goodness, he had been spared, at least externally. However, judging from his earlier overreaction to having a woman at Mariposa, Jana felt sure the initial of tradition was engraved on his mind and heart. Even his stomach was probably filled with little *m*'s— reminders of the lifetime diet he had been fed.

After Jana was half through the main course—fish, with squash, mandarin oranges and olives—she realized that she had not been able to prompt Peter into conversation. Perhaps, as he picked at his food, he was allowing her to eat before the kill.

Surely, she wasn't important enough to him to upset him. In fact, when she tried to see herself as Peter must see her, as a stranger passing through this vast estate, she must seem very small and unimportant. Perhaps that's why he had brought her here: to put her into perspective.

Jana felt thwarted, but not enough to cause her to stop eating. Only that morning she had been an ambitious, hardworking woman who planned to free her mother and brother and Spenser from money worries for the rest of their lives. She wanted her brother to be free to specialize in the kind of medicine that interested him most, whether it was lucrative or not.

Spenser, of course, couldn't be counted on for money. To keep him in microscopes and chemical equipment for testing old works of art would cost her a fortune if he worked for himself—as he wanted to do.

Jana's resolve always strengthened when she thought of her mother wearing herself out in the credit department of Marshall Fields—a job she had been forced to take after Jana's father disappeared. Jana had sworn she would never be in that position. No man would ever walk out and leave her loaded with children and no way to feed them. She would show—whom? Herself. She could do it all. Nothing like that would ever happen to her or the ones she loved. Not ever.

Finally, Peter offered the information that as a child he had lived in Paris, Rome, Lausanne and London, as well as San Francisco and this mansion. He had studied law at Stanford and then, after some "unfortunate experiences" in California, moved to Washington.

Jana asked him about his mother. Only then did his voice rise out of a monotone to say sharply, "She lived her own life and my dad and I lived ours."

Recognizing that she had offended him, Jana braced herself. It was Peter's turn to say something offensive. Already, there was a pattern to whatever game they were playing.

Peter leaned back from the table. "If you remain at Mariposa, you will continue to pose as a college student who lucked into a damned good summer job." His voice now had the tone of a modern major-general.

"You'll be paid four dollars an hour—the same as Cassie's salary."

"I can't take money from Mariposa."

"If you weren't there, we would be paying somebody. If you feel so guilty about it, perhaps by the time you leave you could find some worthy cause to donate the money to."

"Like one of your aunt's projects?"

Peter was disapprovingly silent. "I don't care what you do with the money," he finally said. "But whatever it is, I don't want to hear about it."

"What do you plan to do with me after the harvesters arrive?"

"You mean, *if*?"

"They are supposed to be on their way."

"If they do come and you need to talk with me about them, we'll talk in the office."

"When?"

"When I say so. As you have already noted, being in the weigh house is better than driving a truck. You'll always be in the same place. You'll hear things, and people will know where to find you. Cassie runs an all-day open house there. She works hard, but when there's a lull, which is sometimes half the day, everybody goes there to talk. If Cassie or the women on the platform haven't heard the rumor of the day, it doesn't count.

"The drivers have a lot of influence on the pickers. They have also been resisting any mechanization. I don't know what you can say to them, but from what I've seen so far, you tend to get what you want by some means or another. I think you can have a big influence on their attitudes."

"Why not level with everybody and let me roam the ranch—at my own risk?"

"Right. With your pale complexion, big blue eyes, long blonde hair and your flashy-washy little Mercedes, you plan to walk around among guys who are a thousand or so miles from their wives and girlfriends."

"Do you know what you just said?"

Peter looked at her with surprise.

"You're saying I'm in danger because I'm a woman—not because I'm a representative of Havermeyer. Which is it, *Mister* Milford?"

Jana accepted more coffee from Pilar, refused then accepted a liqueur made from Milford oranges grown in the southern part of the state.

"You don't understand subtleties, do you, *Miss* Robbins? Perhaps you will have a clearer picture if you are told one of the complications. My dad is recovering from a heart attack. He and Moose have based Mariposa on men, not machines. They think it's most profitable, and both men are unable to cope with changes they have opposed all their lives. Haven't you heard the Milford advertising on T.V.?"

Of course she had. It was appalling: "We live from hand to mouth. We can help you live that way, too."

"My father has run Mariposa for the last twenty-five years—with Moose's help, of course. I'm not in a position to fire my dad, but I'd let Moose go if I could. However, as I make more and more changes, I'm hoping that he'll leave of his own accord.

"The two men have always been popular with most of the workers here, but they're out of touch with the way things have to be done now. There are laws regulating migrant workers and they want to ignore them as thoroughly as possible.

"There aren't many workers anymore who are willing to take on the sticky, messy, heavy labor of picking peaches. In fact, it has become one of the most unappealing of all the jobs in the valley. But, ignoring this, every year, my dad has sent out reassurances to the local people who work here in the summer that Mariposa will never have machines. And even people like the sorters, the drivers, the men in the machine shop who are the year-round farmhands are nervous and resentful of the changes I'm making here.

"They haven't seen anything. I'd like to see this place a model that could turn California's bad name with migrant workers into a blueprint for the country to follow."

Now Peter was sounding exactly like one of those idealists who had been infected with pilot-project fever while working in Washington.

"And I don't just mean experiments that would fade away after a couple of flattering newspaper articles, but ones that would form the groundwork for basic institutional changes in our migrant worker setup in this country. It would take four or five years just to set it all up, but once the foundation is laid, I'd like to spend at least half my time spreading it to other growers."

Peter's sincerity touched her. Beneath his scowls and rhetoric, Jana sensed another man. Her hands ached to stretch out to help him, to touch the person expounding these ideas. Instead, she blurted out, "Why do you call the ranch Mariposa?"

"The official name is the Mariposa Packing Company. Mariposa, you know, means 'butterfly' in Spanish. Miss Mari's name is taken from the word."

Sensing her interest in the woman, Peter said, "Miss Mari owns only the land her house is on, but she has hidden influences on the workers—ways to sway them to her point of view, and she always has one. You would think that Miss Mari had caused quite enough trouble in the Milford family without butting into Mariposa's business at this time in her life. She's a very stubborn woman. I don't know if you can win her over. Anyway, as I was saying, there's a town further north named Mariposa. Also a county. But we don't own them."

"I'm surprised," muttered Jana.

"I'm talking too much," said Peter. "But I want to emphasize the fact that there may be serious trouble when those harvesters arrive."

"I hear you." He reminded her of a child who was anxious about a new toy that had arrived unassembled and without directions. He wasn't the only one to face problems with mechanization. It happened all the time on farms, in vineyards and in orchards.

"What kind of trouble are you expecting?" she asked innocently.

"Sabotage, sit-downs—even assassinations. When men are afraid, they'll protect themselves at the expense of anything and anyone."

"I know," she said idly.

"You don't know anything. Did you learn it at some damned school? No. All you learned was how to ravage the world with money-making machines. I don't like the idea of harvesters at Mariposa any more than the men, but I know it's necessary.

"What I've got to do—and the way you can help me, I think—is to try and convince everybody that while their jobs may be in danger in the future, we'll pay them this summer, if not by the pound, at least by the hour. This should satisfy all but the best and most vocal workers."

Jana leaned forward. "It's because of shoddy, backward management practices that Mariposa has been dragged down. Don't you think you are presenting yet another harmful practice?"

"If I hadn't announced that policy, all the men and half the sorters would have taken jobs last week with the Calimyrna Corporation. I wouldn't have had anybody to pick peaches—peaches that were dropping off the trees while the Havermeyer Harvester people were sitting up in their Chicago highrise making big promises to me about how their machines were going to save me money. I had counted on the damn things."

Jana was learning that Peter was not always as angry with her as he sounded. He honestly thought he could turn Mariposa into a model ranch. He looked almost angelic as he described his profit-sharing plans. Jana was so charmed by his altruism that she hesitated and then decided against providing him with alternatives that she had on the tip of her tongue.

Peter was an enigma that was slowly unfolding to her. If she had met him at a party, she would have assumed that he was a man without problems because he was a man who had everything. But she knew he didn't have everything. He needed one more addition to his life—someone like her. Someone who could help him with his work and set things around the house moving in a forward direction.

Here was a man who had convinced her without saying a word that her future was no longer in her hands—the future she had been so sure of this morning. Jana almost looked in her palm to see what was there and why it had become so elusive.

"When I was in Washington," he said, "I attended committee hearings on farm and ranch problems. The lawyers, senators and representatives, as well as the bureaucrats, had no idea of the concrete nature of the problems.

"I saw men like my dad testify—men who thought that as long as their migrant workers had a cot in a bunk house and an occasional truck to take them into town and a rare day off, that was 'the American Way.'

"Mariposa has all the possibilities for being a fine model. If I can make it work here, I can take my plans to the Milford vineyards and down south to the orange groves."

"I think I could help you make this transition smoothly if I were freed from the weigh house," Jana said. "Can't you level with everyone? Don't you think I would have more authority if they thought I was something more than a college student?"

"Didn't Cassie already give you a bad time about being from Harvard? What do you think she would do if she thought you were from Harvard *and* MIT, and on the management conveyer belt at Havermeyer, working your way to the top with the impatience of people who run up the stairs of an escalator? People out here don't respect that kind of scramble for power," Peter told her hotly.

"Especially not you?"

"That's right."

"What else can I do besides chum around with the truck drivers?"

"You can chum around with the women on the platform. Most of them have been here for decades and the machines are going to wipe them out of their jobs and they know it. The machines will sort the peaches in the fields; if you could come up with something you think those women could do, I'd—I'd pay you a consultant's fee."

"A *third* salary!" Jana sniffed as though she were the Queen of England. "I actually thought you were going to say you'd be grateful. Or is that not a currency with which you're familiar?"

She was being obnoxious, and when Peter didn't reply she felt less justified than ever.

He shoved his chair back from the table and, without waiting for her, walked through the living room.

Jana followed him slowly. He was pacing at the feet of the Milford portraits, which showed the assurance and control he was now fighting to display.

"I think we're finished. If you change your mind, if you are threatened by anyone who discovers you work for Havermeyer, you'll return to Chicago on the next plane, is that clear? I'll take you to your motel now."

They had been in the car for about five minutes when Jana said, "I think. . . ."

"You may keep your opinions to yourself, Miss Robbins. If you can't, you can get out and walk."

The silence that followed was so heavy she thought she was going to be asphyxiated.

After stopping in front of her motel, he said, "And another thing. You are to be civil to Andy Goodwin."

"I am."

"I'll bet. But you are to be no *more* than that."

"What a bastard you are. Andy was kind to me today. *He* actually cared that I had no suitcase, no clothes."

Peter surveyed the front of her dress, the shoulder that was bare, ripped the key out of the ignition and touched her arm.

"Keep your hands off my private life and off me," she said, wrenching open the door and bounding out of the car.

As she struggled with the damned key, which was too loose in the keyhole, Peter leaned out of the window on the passenger side and said, "If I see you with him longer than five minutes, you'll find out whose hands are on your *professional* life. And that's all that really matters to you, anyway, isn't it—Miss Robbins?"

She was still struggling. He shouted, "And from now on, why don't you tie your hair back in a little wad again. It suits you better."

Later, when she was in bed, Jana thought that if she counted all the points she had lost that evening, she would never fall asleep. Instead, she considered Andy, inch by inch, rolled over and slept a more or less pleasant, if restless, sleep.

Chapter 3

"Who's there? What do you want?" yelled Jana as she ran naked to the door. The room was unnaturally dark, but her wristwatch said it was 7:00 A.M.

"It's Andy. Let me in. The phone in your room doesn't work."

"I'm not dressed."

"Open up anyway. I'm standing in a downpour."

"Go sit in your car."

"Come on, Jana. I've brought you more clothes."

Her second day in California and she was already involved in another television sitcom. Wrapping the bedspread around her, she threw open the door to Andy. He handed her a pile of clothes: a faded blue sweatshirt, a pair of jeans and large-sized sneakers, compliments of Gretchen.

"You and I are going to the mountains," he announced. "And you had to have something to wear."

"What do you mean?"

"Mariposa's closed for the weekend. I just got a call from Moose about a half-hour ago."

"Then this will be a good day for me to find an apartment of my own. I've decided I'd rather do that than stay with Gretchen."

Andy grabbed the top sheet off the bed and wrapped it

around himself like a cape belonging to the landlord in a melodrama. "But you must go to zee mountains wiz me," he said.

"But I can't!"

"You must!" He was playfully hugging her. Her toga was slipping. She yanked it around her more tightly.

"Zen *I'll* take you to zee mountains. . . ." They tumbled on the bed giggling, laughing, touching. Jana remembered Peter's angry appearance in this room the night before and his warning returned to her, along with the time they had spent together. She felt a dry pain in her chest and climbed off the bed.

But Peter was not the entire reason she stopped the horseplay. Nor was he the entire reason she refused Andy's invitation to the mountains. She simply did not do things on the spur of the moment. Here she was wrestling like a puppy on a bed with someone she hardly knew, while wrapped in a bedspread that was barely in place.

"But, Jana," persisted Andy, "we'll stay with my stepsister *and* her husband *and* their little girl and probably the child's nurse. Doesn't that sound proper? Come on, Jana, we can be there in time for breakfast, and if you don't want to, we don't have to spend the night. Even considering all this rain, it's only an hour away."

"But I need to find an apartment."

"Look at this weather. You would drown. And you don't even know Fresno. You'd get lost. And you certainly don't want to be cooped up all day here—or for that matter at Gretchen's. Now, do you?"

Nor did Jana relish the possibility of another confrontation with Peter—not while she was so confused about him. For the first time in her life, she was skeptical about the goals that had brought her here in the first place. A new set of personal, more ambitious goals had moved in and were taking an unbalancing toll on her. And she had always thought she knew exactly what she wanted.

If she did go to the mountains, Peter would probably never know. Obviously, he and Andy were not on the best of terms and there would be no discussion about it. And being with Andy would give her an opportunity to discover more of the background of Mariposa and the Milfords, more about Peter. The trip would be more than a pleasant excursion: it would be time profitably spent. In fact, she could probably fill in all the missing facts and feelings that Schultz had never bothered to discover or add to his report. Jana knew she was rationalizing, but pushed that knowledge aside.

"All right," she said. "You've convinced me."

When Andy hugged her, they did not kiss, although Jana wanted to more than she could believe. He did, too, she felt, but it was as if he didn't dare.

Jana attributed her own feelings to the surprise of being turned loose on an unexpected holiday and of being freed from any sort of possible entanglement that day with Peter.

After checking out of the motel, she followed Andy to his house. They parked his Honda behind Gretchen's Toyota and set out in Jana's Mercedes. Andy said the heavier car would hold the wet and winding roads better.

As they sped through the wet streets and out to the highway, Andy explained they were headed west toward the coastal ranges where his stepsister, Susan, and her husband, Ken Williams, had recently built a house.

Jana was conscious of Andy's physical presence to the exclusion of all thoughts about Peter or Havermeyer. Each time he stroked her arm or patted her leg, it was with the natural touch of a friendly, exuberant boy. She, however, imagined what might happen later between them. Again, she felt a little off-balance. Andy must be four or five years younger than she. He was probably conceived when she was in kindergarten.

How different he was from Spenser, who was twenty-eight, complex and moody. She had become accustomed to responding to the nuances of Spenser's every word and gesture. Andy's nonchalance and openness was making her giddy. He exuded a physicality that invited her to touch him.

Spenser said he loved her because she always took the trouble to listen to his feelings. But it had taken months. Here she was reading Andy almost immediately, and she sensed that he was, indeed, what he seemed to be: friendly, frisky, guileless. He was sunny California on a rainy day, and she wanted his warmth around her.

With all the effort she had put into Spenser over the past two years, he had never come near to arousing her like this. Since the day they had met in front of a Paul Revere tea service in the Boston Museum of Fine Arts—the day she picked him up—she had cherished and studied him as if he were the only work of art she would ever possess. And he was

worth studying, she had told herself, because he was devoting
his life to "Art." But if they hadn't been apart so often, she
would never have been able to keep up the energy a
relationship with him required.

And here she was sitting next to Andy who was spilling his
life all over her, openly showing how much he liked her, and
she hadn't done anything to cause him to open up.

He had grown up in La Jolla. He was ten when his father
married Susan's mother and they moved to a bigger house on
the beach. Susan was the oldest; she had a younger sister and
they shared a sister who was born after their parents married.
"Her name is Ginni and she's a pain," Andy told Jana.

She gathered that Andy was twenty-five, had been in the
Army, flunked out of law school, and was now enrolled in an
MBA program at San Francisco State. He was unhappy with
his major, but planned to make a lot of money after graduation.

Jana felt her thoughts drifting to her own rigid childhood,
caring for her brother every afternoon in a sparsely-furnished
apartment. Andy, however, continued talking about his
Kansas-born grandparents who had had the gumption to go
west during the Depression, of his father who had been
appointed a U.S. attorney in San Diego but had quit and
"made a killing" in corporate law.

When Andy described an Andrew Wyeth painting over
their dining room table, Jana thought of the TWA calendar
photograph she had, as a child, hung over their kitchen table.
When Andy described their maid, the slumber parties his
sisters had held in the "girls' wing" of his house and his room,
which opened out onto the beach, all Jana could see was the
dark hall that connected the apartment where she had grown
up—and where her mother still lived—with the sidewalks
where she had supervised her brother's play.

When Andy talked about cookouts on the beach, all she
could remember was preparing dinner for a mother who was
so tired when she arrived home that she often had to cry in
order to release the tension before she could eat.

What was Andy doing those days when she had hurried
home from school, slapped peanut butter and jelly on a slice
of bread for her brother and studied the refrigerator for
dinner ideas? Where was he when she scrubbed the kitchen
and bathroom floors, and polished the echoing hardwood
floors of the living room and bedrooms? Andy was probably

surfing and walking on the beach with girls who wanted to touch his beautiful body. No wonder he had flunked out of law school. He had probably expected to glide through it as he had glided over the waves on his surfboard.

Jana half-resented Andy for having such an easy life, which he was all too glib in describing. There was nothing she wanted to tell him about her growing up. The only way to go in her life had been straight ahead. At least, she had figured that out in time.

Andy was a child of the beach, and beaches had always symbolized a way of life that had been closed to her. Even when she had been in school in Boston, she had rarely taken advantage of them. Lolling around on a beach was out of character. She had spent her summers scooping ice cream, being a mail clerk at Marshall Fields and, finally, typing for a commodities brokerage firm. Jana had hated those jobs, and endured them because she knew they were only a means to an end, a way out of her life of never-enough.

When she heard Andy mention Peter's name, Jana was drawn back to the present. "Susan divorced Peter. He always wanted children and she didn't, but she finally agreed to have one."

"Peter Milford?" Jana asked.

"The one and only. Hell, I might as well tell you. Susan and Peter have a love-hate divorce. When Ken was out of the country on a case a while back, Susan and Peter, shall we say, renewed their sex life. Lisa is the result. Susan planned to have an abortion, but Ken discovered what she was going to do. . . ."

Jana's thoughts were racing. There had never been any indication from Peter that he had ever been married, and it hadn't crossed her mind. She resisted meeting Susan, yet she couldn't wait. Jana couldn't imagine any woman divorcing Peter Milford once she had managed to marry him. But the fact of Susan having Peter's baby, while married to someone else, was hard for her to deal with. It meant he had a permanent tie to another woman, which left her feeling unsettled. Jana's life had always taken a straight path, and now there were more curves in the road than she knew what to do with.

"Susan agreed to have the baby and remain married to Ken, but only after they signed a contract that gives Ken major responsibility for Lisa at all times when he's home. He is also the primary parent in charge if, when she goes to school and breaks a leg or something, a parent has to be called. And Ken made Peter sign an agreement that he would never claim Lisa as his own in any way."

"But why didn't Susan go back to Peter?"

"I don't know. Maybe because Ken has proven to her that he's better for her career. She's an artist, and I don't think she progressed very much the two years she was married to Peter. They were always fighting.

"I even think that Peter respects Ken over the way he has handled this Lisa thing. God knows, it could have been a mess if he had objected. Ken's a good lawyer—a practicing lawyer. He's not one of those idealists who goes to Washington to save the country and, when he finds that's impossible, returns home to save the world."

Jana found it hard to conceive of Peter having had a recent relationship with the woman she was about to meet.

"How old is Lisa?" she asked, hoping that the child was six or seven.

"She's a year old," said Andy.

Jana could think of nothing to say. Her stomach felt like lead. In order to prove that she was not overwhelmed by Andy's revelations about Peter, she took the sleeve of her sweatshirt and wiped off the windshield on Andy's side. Andy was paying closer attention to the road, and visibility was down to a few feet beyond the hood.

Jana wished she had never agreed to this silly trip. Hearing Andy talk about his sister reminded her of all the wild, weird stories she had heard about people in this state where anything went. Obviously, this was the case with this free-spirited artist-stepsister of his. But instead of sounding creative, daring, barrier-breaking, her behavior sounded downright trampy to Jana. Welcome to Kinkyfornia. And how could a husband tolerate such behavior from his wife? And Peter, how could the great he-man allow another male to raise his child?

"I don't know," said Andy, "if we'll be able to see the sign pointing to Susan's and Ken's private road. Ken said it's an oval of wood with 'Williams Walk' painted on it—probably by Susan."

Jana had a fleeting hope that they would never find the sign and be forced to return to Fresno. What if Peter wanted to talk to her? What if he had thought over his behavior last night and wanted to apologize? What if, after sleeping on the situation, he had decided she should return to Chicago?

Andy had pulled into a combination gas station-curio shop. "I'm going to phone Ken," he said.

Jana was furious at herself. She had no business being on her way to visit Peter Milford's ex-wife. How could she have thought that another member of Andy's family would be as sunny and uncomplicated as he had at first seemed? She had to remember that Andy and Susan were related only by marriage. She wondered if his stepsister planned to have any other children with Peter or anybody else other than her husband. Surrogate siblings for little Lisa. How convenient. In California, artificial insemination was probably an unnecessary technique. After all, why choose the sterility of the laboratory when you could experience the steaminess of. . . . ?

Andy returned dripping wet and announced that Ken would be down in a minute to guide them to the house. "The sign is down, and he said we'd never be able to find it by ourselves."

"Pity."

"What?"

"Haven't you been there before?"

"I've been busy. Work and school, you know."

Finally, Andy added, "We used to be good friends, Susan and I. In fact she was my best friend, the only good thing about the mess my father got us into by marrying into a family of girls. Then she married a Milford."

Jana didn't want to hear any more about this Susan; she just wanted to drive back down the mountain. After what seemed to her like an hour, a dark green Cadillac pulled up next to them and a man with a beard and eyeglasses rolled down the window and yelled for them to follow him.

After they had driven up and around a mountain for a few minutes, they reached a clearing where a modern, chalet-type redwood house hugged the mountain closely at one end and hung over a ravine at the other.

They parked next to Ken under a rocky ledge that jutted out and formed a natural carport for Jana's Mercedes and a red Jeep Renegade.

As they ran through the rain to the house, a slim, auburn-haired woman opened the front door and began to shout, "Hurry, hurry!"

With Andy's help, Jana leapt up three slippery, round boulders that served as the front steps.

Once inside, Ken introduced his wife. Susan's long, wavy hair, slender figure and slightly-freckled face fit the image of an artist—but not the one Jana had counted on meeting. Her smile was calm and her manner was sweet and warm but not exuberant. Jana was surprised to find that she liked Susan on first impression.

What Andy had said about her didn't seem to fit. Andy had seemed so disapproving in the car, but Jana noticed that the peck he was giving Susan's cheek had become a prolonged hug. When Susan caught Jana's eye, she wriggled free of him. "Andy hasn't seen us in a while," she explained uncomfortably.

"My wife and I have invited him often enough," said Ken, "but he's always too busy."

Ken was older than Susan by at least fifteen or twenty years. He had a beard flecked with gray and bushy, thick, salt-and-pepper hair that pointed in several directions, particularly on top of his head. He seemed to like calling Susan "my wife," and said it without possessiveness but with total affection.

The group drifted naturally into the two-story-high living room. Jana was overwhelmed by the woodsy smell, the rain pounding on the skylights in the arched, cathedral-like ceiling, the trees so close through the one wall of glass, the fire crackling in the fireplace in the center of the room. It was like being outdoors in perfect comfort.

The atmosphere here was as natural and warm as the textures and materials of the house. And it was as harmonious, too. This was not a house into which the memory of another man or his child could intrude.

The house was as original as Ken and Susan. They had designed it and built it for no one but themselves. Was it a testament to a marriage that had been through bad times and survived? Whatever it was, Jana had fallen in love with the love she felt here. Ken and Susan had worked hard on this house. She was glad to be here, glad not to be in Fresno.

Jana wandered into the kitchen that was on the other side

of the fireplace's brick wall. The countertop eating space ran along curved windows and overlooked the dripping green mountains.

A teenaged girl with short, curly, strawberry-blonde hair was standing at the sink, dreamily staring down at the wet landscape.

"Wake up, Ginni," said Ken. "I want you to meet a new friend."

Ginni turned around. She was a baby-faced duplicate of Susan.

"Ginni's my favorite sister-in-law," said Ken.

"He's only saying that because my other sister, Debbie, isn't here, and because he wants me to like him as much as I liked my other brother-in-law."

"I know you like Peter better than you like me, but there's nothing you can do about it right now." Ken put an arm around Ginni. "So why don't you stop sulking in the raspberries and come out and be friends? I'll wash the berries in a minute; you come on out in the living room and be pleasant."

"No," said Ginni, pulling away. "Andy's out there."

"I think he and Susan went downstairs to see about some dry clothes for Jana. And you might as well face it: Andy will always be your half-brother. Besides, you hardly ever have to put up with him anymore."

"Thank heavens."

"Ginni, I'll tell you what. If you're nice when you're around him today, I'll take you into town later and buy you something pretty to wear to the square dance tonight."

Ginni flung her arms and dripping wet hands around Ken. "Oh, thanks, bro-in-law. I'm beginning to like you better already. And I forgive you for not taking me to San Francisco this weekend.

"But let's hope Lisa wakes up soon so that I won't have to listen to Andy brag about tricks he did on only one ski last week or the mountain he climbed, or... ."

"Remember my present. . . ." warned Ken in a singsong voice.

As Ginni dried her hands, she said to Jana, "Your hair is beautiful. And so shiny. I'll bet it shines even more when it's completely dry. All my life, I've wanted long, straight hair, and I have this kinky stuff." She pretended to pull it out.

"What are you three talking about?" asked Susan, who was standing behind Ken, her arms around his waist.

"About how nice I'm going to behave for the remainder of the day," whispered Ginni, an eye toward the living room.

"You couldn't be anything else," said Susan, giving Ginni a light whack on the rear. "And thanks for cleaning those raspberries."

Ken hung an arm around Susan's shoulders and explained to Jana, "Susan picked the raspberries, but once she brought them into the house, her allegiance to them dropped. My wife is a nature girl: if it's outdoors, she loves to paint, plant, pick. But bring her inside and she spends all her time gazing out the windows, thinking of another reason to go out again. I thought this house would help by allowing the mountains and the trees to be seen so beautifully from indoors. . . ."

"It has, darling, it has. Don't you notice that, on rainy days, I'm able to spend almost the entire day in the house?"

"And I also remember that last week you thought up a way to paint with watercolors in the rain. You called it a new, wet-on-wet method."

"And now I call it terrible."

"I think I hear Lisa," said Ginni. She gave a playful grin to Ken and pecked him on the cheek. "I'll check on her."

"Have you two made up since your San Francisco spat this morning?" Susan asked her sister.

"Sort of," said Ginni. "You've married a man who has a way with words."

There was an awkward, split-second pause. Susan broke it by saying, "Don't I know that."

No matter what had happened between Susan and Peter, and no matter how recently, Susan and Ken were good together. Jana prayed that, for their sake, Susan wasn't still seeing Peter. She was so enamored of the two of them that she didn't think to hope it for her sake, too.

A screech came from the living room. "Andy, stop," Ginni said. "You're as awful as ever and you still hit too hard."

"Uh-oh," said Ken. "I'd better take over in there."

Susan leaned against the counter. "I was hoping that those two would get along. Neither Ken nor Ginni were thrilled to hear that Andy was coming—mainly because we were planning to go to San Francisco this weekend.

"Don't feel bad. When it started raining, we changed our minds, but we had brought Ginni up here to be our weekend babysitter. It was to have been her first trip to the city. Then Lisa developed a slight fever and she was up half the night, and when Andy called, I thought it might be fun—especially when he said he wanted to bring a friend. He's never done that before.

"Ken had the bright idea to call a boy Ginni's age who lives down the mountain. A few minutes later, he telephoned and asked Ginni to a square dance tonight. She's feeling very grown up. I'm sure she was thinking a date for a square dance would make a much better story to tell her friends than babysitting her niece in San Francisco."

As much as she liked Susan, Jana suddenly felt terribly uncomfortable, and offered to stem the raspberries. This friendly, confiding atmosphere should have put her at ease, but it was the opposite of the purposeful, directed air she usually breathed. Instead of relaxing her, the easy equilibrium in the house unsteadied her.

"I'll bet you're awfully domestic," said Susan.

"I hardly ever have the chance anymore, but I used to spend a lot of time in the kitchen." Jana didn't add, "when I was growing up."

"I can't get over how relaxed it is in California."

"Loose is the word," said Susan. "But a certain amount of it is good for a person. I sometimes think that if I lived on the east coast, I would be one of those New England sea-types who painted every cobblestone, every weathered shingle—in the Andrew Wyeth copycat-school style. But living out here, I've always wanted to fling my paint. Don't worry, I'm not a Jackson Pollock yet. But, recently, I have been able to paint hints of color or shadows rather than perfectly formed 'things.' Do you paint?"

Jana shook her head "no."

"Sing, play the piano, sculpt?"

"None of the above," she said, trying to remember what it was she did do. "I have a friend who's an art historian. He's in Florence now, working on the bronze doors of the Baptistry." She remembered that Spenser sometimes made a good conversation piece.

"I hope he's not carving extra characters in the door by the light of his flashlight."

"He's helping a professor with a book." Jana could have elaborated. She had entertained many dinner parties in Chicago with tales of Spenser's exploits for the good of "Art." But here, in the midst of real topics—like raspberries —the subject simply dried up in her throat, if not her heart.

Susan produced a colander for Jana to dump the berries into. "I hope you and Andy didn't stop on the way up here, because Ken and Ginni have made an enormous breakfast. Ginni 'created' the cinnamon rolls. They're gummy with sugar and pecans. She's a great little cook."

"I am, aren't I?" Ginni had returned. "Lisa's half-awake. Don't you think that I should remain in the nursery with her?" Ginni was nodding a prompter's "yes" to Susan.

"I think you probably should," said Susan. "After all, if she sleeps too long, you might have to miss the dance tonight!"

Ginni bowed in exaggerated gratitude and, taking huge steps, crept on tiptoe through the living room. Susan and Jana followed her as far as the three-sided couch in front of the fireplace, where they joined Ken and Andy. "When does school start, Andy?" Ken was straining to make conversation.

"The end of September. I'm looking forward to this being my last year."

"You'll be glad when it's over and you're working for some fancy company. Maybe they'll send you to Japan again."

"I doubt it," said Andy. "My dad says I won't have the kind of career I want if I spend all my time in Japan."

Jana had a feeling that a lot of hostility lay beneath the surface of this conversation. What were the key words? "My dad?" "Japan?"

"Andy loved Japan when he was there in the Army," said Susan.

Andy smiled with relief as if he had been praised to the hilt for an important accomplishment.

"You should show Jana some of the *sumi* paintings you did there. They were wonderful," Susan continued.

"They're somewhere in La Jolla—probably in the garbage. I wasn't too careful with them, because I always thought I would take it up again. But as my teacher—a Buddhist sage—told me, you have to lead a quiet and orderly life to be a proper *sumi* artist."

"I think I'll heat up Ginni's rolls now, and we can eat." Ken was obviously escaping.

"Jana, I'm going to take you downstairs and give you the dry clothes I laid out for you. Andy says you're a little short in that department." Susan motioned toward the stairs, which were cut in the floor of the living room. On the first floor, the dark hall was lined with large, low chests with hand-painted, carved tulips and landscapes on the sides and front.

"I was told by Ken's grandmother when she gave us the chests that they were from her home in Switzerland," Susan told Jana. "She instructed me on the original colors of the tulips and the tiny landscapes, and I practically painted them by number."

Susan motioned toward a door. "This is your room. I thought you'd probably want it to yourself. If not . . ."

"This is lovely," said Jana as she looked out one of the windows down into the valley. The other one backed onto the mountain, which was so near that all she could see were a few sprigs of wet grass and tons of pebbles and dirt. Of course, that's what mountains were made of.

The view in that direction was compensated for by two enormous oil paintings: one of a lake in autumn with tall trees and reddish-orange shrubs reflected hazily in the water; the other of the exact scene in early summer with green, yellow and lilac trees and bushes reflected in the light, blue-gray water. Both ponds were deep enough to dive into on the spot.

"Don't touch the summer picture. I completed it only yesterday. I would have left it upstairs, but with Lisa sticking her hands into everything, I knew it wouldn't last—at least it would no longer be *my* concept of the pond."

"It is beautiful," said Jana, suddenly remembering that she hadn't seen a sign of there being a child in this house. Not a toy or a highchair or anything.

"Andy was telling me about your little girl on the drive here. Is she asleep?"

"She might be. We have a small nursery wing at the other end of the corridor. It's joined to the house, but built apart with its own wall—like a condominium. Don't get me wrong: having a nursery doesn't mean there are going to be any more children. It's my own money, too, that pays for a full-time nurse. She's not really full time: she goes home to Coalinga on weekends when Ken is home."

Jana was uncomfortable again. She could live very well without hearing more. Although she didn't think she wanted children, she would have the good sense to stand by her decision without a lot of complicated architecture and an entourage of nurses and maids and a contracted husband.

Jana had sensed a flaw in Susan, and she now felt freer to blame her for fooling around with Peter Milford after she had been married for several years. But Jana also knew that Susan made her uncomfortable because, with her tidy plans, she reminded Jana of herself.

"I'm an artist first, a wife second and a mother third," Susan continued. "I merely put them in the order in which they came—which, for me, happens to be the order of their importance. I made the mistake once of getting all gummed up in an oppressive family situation. I told myself that if I ever married again, it would be on my terms."

Even if the terms included an ex-husband and his baby?

"Fortunately, Ken is mature enough and in love with me enough to put up with it. I don't say it's been easy for him, but since marrying Ken over six years ago, I've done my best work. I've had several shows in San Francisco and Fresno and I even have a small following of people who actually collect my paintings.

"Now that we have Lisa, Ken could have put me in debt to him or curtailed my activities. But he hasn't. You may have sensed that he is an unusual man. Nothing I do seems to drive his love away—and believe me, I've pulled some whoppers. Andy told you about Lisa, I suppose. It drives Andy crazy."

Jana nodded. She never expected Susan to bring this up, and was not prepared to discuss it. Susan perched on one of the Swiss chests, chin on bony knees, her beautiful, tapered hands clasped around her legs.

Jana sat down on the bed and faced her. This was the unselfconscious beauty that must have attracted Peter. She watched the sculptured gold ring on Susan's left hand glint messages to the emerald and gold studs in her ears. How this original, single-minded woman had managed to escape the graceless atmosphere of La Jolla with her individuality intact amazed Jana.

Susan dangled one leg off the chest.

"Now that you've met Peter Milford, Jana, what do you think about my ex-husband?"

The question surprised and in a way offended her. It was almost too personal, and the response to it had barely been thought and certainly never said aloud.

"He's complicated," she murmured.

"I mean physically," said Susan. "Isn't he the most sexually *compelling* man you've ever known? Don't you feel it? He pulls you toward him without acting as if he cares whether you're in the room or not. The touch of him is physically addictive. I think I've beaten it, but I'm not sure. Even now, mother and wife that I'm supposed to be, I try not to be around Peter too often."

"It is unusual, I suppose, that after having been married to Ken. . . ."

"Peter and I resumed our relationship—at least one side of it—when Ken spent a couple of months in Canada on a case."

"How did he find out?"

"I told him—even before I knew I was pregnant. Miss Mari—have you met her?—thought that I was having the baby only because Ken wanted one so much. He was married for ten years to his first wife and they never had children. I suppose he thinks it might be his possible inability to have children that would make this our only child—I don't know.

"I'm wildly attracted to Peter—when I'm in certain moods. And I had a lot of those moods while Ken was gone. But I've come to love Ken. I tell you that in case you're wondering why I stayed married to him—or why, for that matter, he didn't divorce me over Lisa."

Jana wanted to say, "Do change the subject." But Susan saw her spot the signature on a painting of a pond. It said, "Susan Milford."

"I did that when I was married to Peter. I use Ken's name now. I suppose I should let you change clothes. But as long as I'm rattling on, I should tell you that I really hate divorce. My mom thought life was escaping her and she divorced my father and married Andy's dad, who is much younger than she. He and Andy moved into the house my dad had built. I suppose you could say that the only good result of that marriage has been Ginni."

"You don't like your stepfather?"

"He's not even nice to his own son. For example, Andy's good at solo sports—like swimming and mountain-climbing. He paints better than I do and he loves classical music. Denver—my stepfather—acts as if none of these count. He wants his boy to be a "team player," both in sports and in his work. Andy, Ginni and my mom all deserve better."

"But what about you, Jana? Andy tells me you're studying business at Harvard. You can tell me the truth: are you there to find a rich husband?"

Jana wanted to tell her the truth, but she couldn't remember what it was. She had to continually remind herself that she was a student and not somebody who had been out of graduate school and in business for a year.

Jana glanced back at the signature—Susan Milford.

Without waiting for an answer to her question, Susan continued, "Peter and I eloped in the middle of one of those crazy Mariposa summers. I went out there to apply for a job—in the weigh house—and although I didn't get it, I met the Crown Prince. If I hadn't been so young and selfish, it might have turned out differently. But, we'll never know."

"What do you mean?"

"I was only twenty and thought of myself as an artist. If I had painted as much as I argued with Peter and balked at what he wanted to do . . . no, it wouldn't have worked out. I hated being married into a family where everything was stamped with an 'M'—including my husband.

"He wanted children right away. Can you imagine? I think he knew from some primordial instinct that that was the way men held onto their wives. I've always maintained that if you took him out of that family, there might be some hope for him. But he wanted me to be a campus wife during the school year, and on almost every weekend, I was supposed to run from one Milford party to another looking pretty, agreeable and preferably fertile.

"If Miss Mari had been at all those ordeals, I wouldn't have minded so much, but she wouldn't go near them.

"Old man Milford was all hands and no heart, and made rotten jokes about how many babies I was going to produce. I think he had just divorced one of his wives and was especially horny. Well, never mind, that's all over."

"Did you leave Peter?"

"I threw all my clothes out the front window of that mansion. A photographer from the *Sacramento Bee* happened to be snooping in the area and snapped a picture of the little episode. Peter paid to keep it out of the papers, but he was just as mad as if it had been relayed around the world by satellite. He said if I walked out of that door I could never return. Of course, I didn't want to. But he's been chasing me with that chemical pull of his ever since. I don't even think he can help it."

Jana removed one damp, oversized tennis shoe, then the other. She let her feet suffer on the cold slate floor.

Susan started for the door, then stopped. "I hear Peter's

managing Mariposa this summer. I suppose there'll be no
stopping him now. He'll be running all of Milford Enterprises
soon, I'll bet."

As soon as Susan had disappeared into the hall, Jana
unfolded the light blue corduroy pants and matching turtle-
neck sweater that Susan had found for her.

Upstairs, the men were laughing, and the sound of a
Mozart piano concerto permeated her corner bedroom.

In a way, Susan was a spoiled young woman. Jana could
easily imagine the merry tailspin she had kept Peter in during
their marriage. While Andy had surfed and Jana had worked
and studied, Susan had probably been sent to the best art
teachers, gone to the best parties. She must have made a
handsome divorce settlement with Peter. Otherwise, how
could she have the money to support a separate nursery and a
full-time nurse? Surely, she wasn't able to do it with the
money she made from her painting.

The stereo must have been turned up to full volume, Jana
thought. It was shaking the entire foundation of the house,
which seemed a feat considering the solid floor.

As Jana walked up the stairs, admiring their treetrunk
thickness, she heard another noise coming from her bedroom. She turned back and half-ran to the bedroom door.
Just as she did, a porridge of mud crashed through the
windows from the back of the mountain, and oozed like
mocha icing across the bed.

Jana attempted a scream, but could only gasp. The Mozart
was climaxing. No one upstairs seemed any more aware of
trouble than the musicians on the recording. The sunny,
intricate music was being counterpointed by thuds of mud.

Jana stood up. A new wave of mud slammed her into the
wall. She grabbed at the banister, but mud was mounting the
stairs faster than she could.

The Swiss chests were sliding around the hall, bumping into
each other like electric cars at a carnival. Jana climbed on top
of one of them and stretched both hands around the slippery
banister. The small light-fixture in the ceiling swayed and
flickered out. A new surge of mud gushed down the hall,
jamming her into the stairs. Before she could regain her
breath and balance, the slime was crushing in on her like cold,
heavy blankets. One of the chests slammed into her back,
knocking her flat again. She was relaxing, and the mud was
whirling heavily over her shoulders, neck, hair.

Lifting her arms toward the direction of the ceiling, Jana felt something pull on one arm. It was pinned and then wrenched. The crushing, cold thickness was sending her to a dark underground cavern filled with lovely music by Mozart. The floor was shaking, the windows rattling.

She heard someone say, "Run with her, run."

Jana heard the cracking of wood. Andy was carrying her, running with her, laying her down in the back seat of the Mercedes.

Without saying a word, he slammed the door and ran toward the house.

Jana looked out the car window. Did she imagine seeing the kitchen section of the house crash into the ravine? Did she dream that she saw Ken slap Susan and push her down on the ground? Susan *was* crawling, crying on the ground, screaming, "Lisa, Lisa." The nursery was still intact, but it was surrounded by the flow of debris that had crashed into her bedroom and poured through the halls.

"No. Oh, no!" screamed Susan. The house above Ken's and Susan's was slipping down the mountain. The only obstacle in its way, besides small trees that were splintering like toothpicks, was the nursery.

Chapter 4

I must help Susan, Jana thought.

No one can help her. The mountain wants it this way. It's Susan's punishment for intruding on nature.

She didn't believe that.

Punishment for not loving a child enough?

"No! No!"

Jana shook herself to full consciousness and reached for the car door handle. It did not budge. She had never touched it: the reach had been mental. Her arms were hours behind her intentions, and pulling herself upright had added to her dizziness.

All she could see outside were torrents of heavy, gray rain and a miniature figure—Susan, small and helpless before the mountain.

As the splintering, shapeless house above crumbled down the mountain, sliding, rolling, Susan was throwing herself into its path in her attempt to fling herself closer to Lisa, to Ken, to Ginni, who were somewhere inside the remains of her redwood dream house.

Jana staggered from the car and stumbled toward Susan. The roar of the mountain was overlaid with the hiss of the awful rain. Each square foot of atmosphere was like a squeezed sponge, drenching them with terrible sheets of water.

Susan was cold and unmovable as she stared in horror at the house poised above her child's nursery.

The bulk of the neighbor's house paused above the nursery in the timeless movement a basketball player or dancer uses to hang suspended in mid-air. During that split-second, Ken appeared at the front door with the screaming Lisa in his arms and ran toward the sheltered cars.

Susan, with Jana's help, picked herself up and, falling every few steps, staggered toward her child.

But where was Andy? And Ginni?

"Get into the car with them," ordered Ken. "I'm going back for Ginni."

As he spoke, the delayed crash came, and the mingling of beams and the inevitable final plunge as both houses tumbled spectacularly down the mountain.

"Oh, my God." Ken slumped down onto the back fender of his Cadillac, then to the ground. "Oh, my God."

Susan was crying along with Lisa and rocking her at the same time.

Ken rose and ran through the clearing toward what had been his perfect house. "Andy, Ginni!" he was screaming.

He headed for the back of the house, the part that had hugged the mountain, the part near the nursery. Seeing that passageway totally clogged, he ran in the other direction—the slow, more dangerous way, around the side of the mountain.

Wiping her eyes, Jana saw that a boulder bared by the deluge might provide a passageway to the area of the nursery.

Jana jumped out of the car and pulled herself up the mountain with the help of heavily-rooted plants. She willed her eyes to search out moving figures through the rain. "Andy! Ginni!"

She could barely hear herself.

Then she saw Andy tugging and heaving at a treetrunk-sized square log—part of the stairs. Beneath the log, she could see a bare, bleeding, distorted foot and a motionless, denim-clad leg. She would help Andy; together they could lift the massive hunk of wood off Ginni.

"Andy!" Jana yelled. "Stay there. I'm coming down to help you."

But, already, he was clawing his way toward her. Instead of helping, she was hurting the chances of rescuing Ginni.

Andy's lips were blue and quivering. A cut above his left eye drooled blood across half his face; his fingernails were bleeding, his hands were scratched, and his once-blue eyes looked dry and hot and were bleached gray, a horrible gray.

Jana wanted to push past him and run to Ginni. She looked again at Andy's eyes. They seemed to be evaporating into gray dust.

"She's dead," he said. "She couldn't get out. Her head's splattered like a ripe berry. I don't want you to see it, don't look down there. A beam hit her. A big beam. She's dead. Like a ripe berry, that's how her head looks."

Andy grasped Jana and held her so tightly she thought she could not take a breath. He was crying, moaning. The sounds were like a wild dog howling with excruciating pain.

She felt an old terror returning. When her little brother had been three years old, he had fallen off the banister in the lobby of their apartment house and had landed on a radiator, crushing the top of his head. It had been her fault. She had been in charge of him. Another time, he had hit a speeding car while on the skateboard she had given him for Christmas. What she had feared for her brother had now happened to Andy's little sister. She knew something of what he must be feeling.

She shook herself loose from him.

"Let's get out of here," said Andy.

"We can't leave Ginni there!"

"We have to. Only a crane can lift that stuff off her."

As they made their way back to the car, Andy said, "Ginni could have saved herself. She shoved Lisa in that closet. She didn't run away fast enough."

"Where is she—where's Ginni?" screamed Ken.

Andy pointed toward the debris of the nursery. He opened his mouth, but there were no words of explanation.

Ken started running.

"She's dead!" Andy screamed to Ken's back as he scrambled over the rubble.

Andy curled up in the back seat of Jana's car. At first she watched him from the front seat. He was not only grief-stricken: he was in shock. He must have hit his head harder than she had thought, although the cut on Ken's temple looked more serious.

Finally, she could see Ken return to his car. He was telling

Susan, who heaved herself against Ken's chest. Jana turned away. The view was too private, too tragic.

When the rain had become lighter, Jana saw Ken scramble toward the nursery. He reached out with a long stick until he pulled a pink baby blanket out of the rubble in the nursery. When she saw the blanket billow in the air and fall, she knew that it was covering Ginni's body.

After a while, Jana returned to the rubble around the kitchen until she found two undamaged jars of baby food. When she handed them to Susan, she was told that an empty picnic basket in the back of the jeep held spoons.

"People know we live up here," said Ken. "Somebody is sure to come."

Lisa was eating and crying at the same time. She was probably cold; Jana certainly was. She looked at Andy, whose head she was holding in her lap. He, too, occasionally broke into chills. Jana leaned over to hold him close, and found herself shaking.

Lisa, she noticed, was still crying. Jana left Andy to see about her. She cried most, they said, whenever her arm was moved. They thought it might be broken. Ken surmised that when Ginni had jammed Lisa in the closet, the child had resisted and the break or sprain had occurred then. She had no other bruises or injuries.

Andy jumped out of the car. "You live here," he said to Ken. "You know the way. We've got to get help."

"Anybody who walks down that road could be killed," said Ken. "Why don't you go right ahead?"

Andy returned to the car. "We'll be here all night," he cried. No rescuers would have time to hack through the debris to reach them in the remaining daylight.

After several more hours in the car, Andy was asleep, his head again in Jana's lap. Jana heard a noise that sounded like a giant machine gun. Without moving her arms, she looked up through the sunroof.

It was a helicopter.

She started to jump out of the car and wake up Andy, but the helicopter had disappeared. It was on its way to rescue someone else—someone who had called. They were parked in a half-hidden area. No one would suppose that anyone would be inside the rubble that had once been Susan's and Ken's house.

But the sound returned. This time it was closer. Jana slid out from under Andy, climbed into the front seat, turned on the ignition and honked the horn.

But it was unnecessary. The helicopter *had* come to rescue them.

Andy bolted out of the car and jumped around the clearing, waving wildly. He had either recovered or was hysterical.

There was a clear, solid open space for the craft in the center of the clearing. The rain was falling only lightly now.

As the craft hovered above its mark, Ken said he couldn't believe it.

"Why not?" Jana had been staring at a man who was looking down at them through the bubble of the 'copter.

"It's him, and this time I couldn't be gladder."

Jana stared upwards again. Instead of attempting to make out the identity of the pilot or the face that had been visible before, her eyes fixed on the emblem at the side of the helicopter. It was a round seal with the letter "M" on it.

And the face belonged to Peter Milford.

Did he know she would be there? Or did his heart still hover over Susan?

He was out of the helicopter, talking to Ken. She saw him put his hand over his forehead and shake his head with disbelief, then walk with Ken to the site of the pink blanket.

When they returned, Peter carried Lisa, and Ken guided Susan as he motioned for Jana to approach the craft.

Peter's mouth tightened when he saw Susan, and his eyes closed as he felt her pain and sorrow. Although he helped Jana up into the craft, his somber, pale face registered no emotion, nor did his black eyes actually focus on her.

Andy was the last in, and Jana thought how strange it was that no one spoke to him. It was, after all, his little sister who had been killed.

At first, the helicopter swayed and soared like a heavy balloon as it escaped from the clutches of the mountains. Soon they were flying over black fields and orchards, above the lights of towns and villages and past the right-angled grids of Fresno's street lights.

No one asked a question. No one spoke. Susan, who had been inarticulate since the accident, was now beyond tears, beyond hope of speech.

Where were they going? To the hospital? To the airport?

Not until she saw the rectangular jewel set in an even larger expanse of dark velvet did Jana know.

An ambulance was waiting at the helicopter pad, which was on the opposite side of the Japanese gardens and the pool on the Milford estate. The maroon Rolls Royce was there to transport the rest of them to the mansion, while Susan, Ken and Lisa disappeared into the back of the ambulance.

Jana followed Peter, who was racing in front of her. He went to a small study off the foyer, which she hadn't seen the night, the year, the life before. He dialed a number and ordered another helicopter from the airport. When he hung up, she stepped into his view. Ignoring her, he picked up the phone again and dialed another number, ordered a rescue crew to retrieve Ginni's body.

She opened her mouth when he hung up and he dialed again: a funeral home. Putting the phone between his ear and shoulder, he formed a wall so that the only way he could see Jana was to wrinkle his forehead and look out of the far corner of his eyes.

Jana could see that it would be an intrusion if she waited to speak with him—say she was sorry, say thank you, say something. Besides, Pilar was waiting to take her upstairs.

Jana was shown to a room. Andy, Pilar said, had been taken to one further down the hall.

The room had a balcony that faced the direction of the garden she had thought she would never see again. The pool, however, was hidden by the trees and the tall hedge.

Pilar dropped off an elegant, pale yellow satin nightgown, black velvet shoes and an old-fashioned, black silk robe with daffodils embroidered on it. Jana was sure they must have belonged to Peter's mother—the purple-eyed woman in the portrait.

Pilar surveyed the muddy figure she had just ushered into the room and walked toward the bathroom. Jana could hear water running.

"You'll come down for dinner," she said. "Mr. Peter is leaving and won't be back for hours, but he says his guests are to eat."

Was she supposed to eat in the black outfit?

"There are more clothes in the closet. You are to wear

anything you like. This was Miss Mari's room before she went to Europe. She hasn't used it since."

After bathing, Jana looked in the closet: silk pants, satin shoes and long silk tunics abounded.

She was too tired to choose. She would rather sleep. Jana slipped on the satin gown, which smoothed over her body. It was made for her and soothed her skin everywhere it touched.

She heard a knock and, thinking it was Pilar again, said, "Come in."

"Did you want me for something?" asked Peter. He had changed from a white turtleneck and Levi's to tan trousers and a navy shirt.

"I wanted to thank you," she said, holding an arm in front of her gown, which was cut almost to her waist. "How did you know we were in trouble?"

"When I heard the roads were out and that some houses were tumbling down in the area of Susan's house, I telephoned. The lines were down. I had seen the house. I knew those idiots in the house above hers had carved up the mountain in order to have a site for their sculpture garden. . . ." He grimaced and dropped his hands helplessly.

"I even went up there once and spoke to those people. They were fools."

Jana had been right. Peter had never gotten over Susan. He was still making an attempt to protect the woman who had rebelled at his protection.

"Susan's house had a sword of Damocles hanging above it." His voice choked. He tried to disguise it behind a clearing of his throat.

"Did you want anything else?" he said finally.

"I only wanted to thank you."

"We'll talk tomorrow." He closed the door with a terse pull, which thudded when it shut.

Jana lay back in the bed. She longed to love someone the way Peter loved Susan. To hold him to her—even when she was far away from him, as Peter was from Susan.

Why should she care that Peter had this kind of love and she did not? Perhaps it would never happen to her. A strong woman never needs the way others need her. And she knew she was strong. But she was also tired. She closed her eyes.

When she awakened, a hand was gently rubbing her satin stomach. Her head weighed three tons, and she could not raise it to see who belonged to the hand. There was also the smell of food. She felt a hand lift up her head. A spoon was nudging its way into her mouth with soup, warm soup that was trickling down her throat.

Chapter 5

Jana's head was weighted in the center with heavy metal. Whirling in slow motion, it drifted down her spine with a message that was unclear and unpleasant.

Crooning, "There's more, eat a little more," Andy shook her gently. Through the fuzzy bars of her blonde eyelashes, Jana saw an offering of homemade bread.

Andy plucked a piece of its buttery softness from the center and fed it to her. "Now a sip of wine?" Jana's lids closed as she contemplated the effort-filled answer.

However, swallowing the wine was easy. The cool-tasting, warm-temperature liquid freed her throat for more soup—but, please, that was all.

Andy kissed her eyes, her forehead. His soft arms were around her, his nose nuzzled her ear, her neck. She was at peace, not at war—as with the other one.

She was being lifted down onto the bed, covered with the sheet and a cotton-knit blanket. She was alseep and safe.

She awakened once and contemplated the closed glass doors leading to the balcony. They were covered with organdy curtains, which were perfectly still. Someone should open those doors. The valley weather was back to normal and the room smelled stuffy. But Andy was no longer there, and she could not walk all the way across the room.

How heavy she felt! And how she had loved those undemanding, totally giving, understanding arms of Andy around her. She had, for a time, misjudged him. He had untapped dimensions of generosity—dimensions that she looked forward to.

With closed eyes, Jana grasped for the spare pillow, pulled it down and leaned her stomach into it. Closer, closer, she inched the soft substance, until its mass was between her legs.

Stirring in the night, she found the pillow warmer and longer than she had remembered. Even her toes were touching it, at the same time as its softness covered her thighs. She rolled into its inviting bulk and lay her head on Andy's chest.

"Hello," he whispered. One of his legs, which on a surfboard had parted oceans, had replaced her pillow.

With her sleepy fingers, she explored the inside of his arms; with her lazy tongue, his face. His offering in the night had prompted her acceptance of the night.

But she had not the strength to guide him. He would have to find his own way. Even so, he waited for her lead.

The caressing—the urging of his full forces to gather themselves to answer her call—was really simple. Propelled solely by an intuition in her hands, she helped the throbbing insistence Andy shyly thrust toward her elevate itself into a hard horizon. With a shudder—her own, she believed—she lunged heavily until she was on his terrain, until she was rooted firmly, slowly, sinkingly, into the best California had to offer.

There were no earthquakes, no tossing storms. They were there and they were together, and slowly a tunnel of warmth was filling her. She acknowledged the gift, and with all of her holding all of him, she stretched to a tight, inward screaming until she could no longer bear the strength that was being called from her. Then she slipped away and slept, her head on Andy's chest.

When she stirred again, the continuation of an unconsummated dream led her to slip on her robe and wake Andy to get into his. Barefoot, she led him down the stairway's Oriental rug and over the foyer's cold tiles, the porch's cool cement and the garden path's smooth, dark pebbles.

At the head of the pool, she slid off the robe until it fell around her feet. Andy allowed his to fall on top of it. The two of them, along with the white columns and the poplars, were reflected in the dark mirror of the pool.

They walked hand in hand down the steps and, together, silently, slid into the water and swam toward the deep end. Jana turned on her side facing Andy. In unison, their sidestrokes allowed them never to break eye-contact. After two laps, they stood in the shallow water. Andy took her in his arms and, for the first time in the history of the world, his beautiful mouth drew hers into its depths. He murmured silent words down her neck, her breasts. Walking up one step, then another, she invited his message to travel.

Instead of sinking down onto the steps with him, Jana silently bade him recline in the water above the steps. She promised, with wordless praise, that all he could offer her she would return. Then, with a slow, muscular breaststroke, she propelled herself into deep water.

From the far end of the pool, she turned and saw Andy's readiness. Without taking her eyes from him, she swam, stroke by silent stroke, dipping her head in the water until she skimmed over his toes, feathered across his knees, grazed his gift.

With unthinking grace, she swerved and, with one stroke, turned and silently spurted her body toward the far end of the pool in a jetlike, luminous, underwater stream.

Emerging for air, she saw Andy, propped on his elbows, half-floating. His buttocks hovered above the white steps, supporting his body for the fiery underwater feast he had been promised. Jana slid silently through the elegant enormity of the space between them. The water caressed, held, surrounded, and floated her to him.

Once again, her tongue sought his as she cruised above him, but again, with a sudden splash, she flipped away with the twisting turn of a fish who was ready, but knowing there would be better bait, was wise enough to wait.

With purposeful, sensuous stroking, slowly, slowly, Jana turned and angled through the ultimate oneness of the night. Just as the fountain rose, she opened herself to him, diverting the direction of the shimmering male shower until they were a lazy summer storm, rained in and raining upon.

Imagining that their combined phosphorescence was filling the pool with shapes of glowing intensity, attendants of the night, Jana surrendered herself to aquatic arabesques, which exploded as fireworks rained beneath the garden sea.

They were gasping for air, rolling and rolling across the

steps in an easy slow motion until they were spun apart like angel hair.

Great waves lifted up Jana and held her. Terrycloth woven from white clouds enveloped her. Her robe was slid around her and, in unison, she walked back to the mansion with the unbelievable presence still beside her.

Only then did Andy speak to her and she to him and, as they stood on the side porch of the house from heaven, their two voices formed the same words.

"My darling."

"My darling."

It was only the daylight that brought limits: a past, a future, the impossible horror of the day that had passed, the wonder of the night that still lingered.

Jana could have remained in bed all day. When she was younger, she had often imagined that the four walls of her room held messages for her. As she grew older, the messages became longer and more specific, until each wall held the future that she planned for herself—and instructions on how to make sure she attained the future she wanted. The first wall to be filled in was school; the second included graduate school; the third listed a high-paying job, and the fourth a husband who would not block the achievements already gained from following the messages on the other walls in the room.

While her choice of jobs had grown longer, her selection of mates had become shorter, as she realized that she would never allow herself to be in a position where any man controlled her life—either professionally or personally.

Her need for someone like Spenser had been formulated during the summer between her two years at Harvard. She had taken some of her scholarship money and gone to Europe. Although such a trip wasn't included on her itinerary for success, Jana felt that it wouldn't hurt to have been to places like Paris, Cologne, Copenhagen, Helsinki, Athens or Amsterdam when she was with a group of businessmen who had been there also.

As she walked through antiquities older than anything she had ever seen—antiquities burnished with a beauty she had never been taught to appreciate—it had occurred to her that nothing truly desirable could ever be possessed.

Jana tried. She bought records of the operas she heard in Scotland at the Glyndebourne Festival. But she had been unable to listen to them when she returned home. She picked up a mosaic at the Baths of Caracalla outside of Rome. Ashamed, she had dropped it on the ground before leaving.

No one had ever told her there was more to life—intangible things, secrets of the universe—and she felt cheated because, if they had, she would have wanted them. She did want them. Whatever they were.

The week she had returned from Europe was the week she had met Spenser in the Museum of Fine Arts. She had picked *him* up. She had been the aggressive one all along. She had had to teach him everything. Last night with Andy had been instinctive. Could Spenser ever be enough for her again? Could she ever be less—or more—than she had been last night?

And there was Havermeyer: all tangible projections—game plans and lunch with "the boys." With Havermeyer and Spenser in her life, she was supposed to have it all.

But she had never known to want an Andy. He had turned the walls of her room into a solarium. He was the transparent ceiling, allowing the sun to shine and all that was natural to fill her. How lovely—how loving—it had been with him. She felt like a growing plant, stretching toward the sunlight.

Jana dressed in the clothes that Pilar had laid out for her: soft, pink silk blouse, soft, pink cotton pants—a little blousy, but blousy was back in style. The sandals were white and fit perfectly.

Her door flung open and Jana was hoisted up into the air and into Andy's arms like a big-little-girl. His kisses were in her hair, and hers were in his.

He set her down. "My darling, would you believe that we have to work today?—according to bossman, Peter."

"I'm ready," she said.

"We deserve a vacation."

"Andy, Peter's done so much for us."

"Peter's money, you mean. Helicopters. Big-time connections. He told me a few minutes ago that he had made arrangements to accompany Ginni's body back to Fresno after the men free it from those . . . think of the coyotes, even the birds. What must have happened to her during the night?"

"It's not Ginni, Andy. It's her body. If anything did happen to it, it's macabre and horrible, but it didn't hurt *her.*"

"Jana, Jana. We belong together. Now, tonight. Every night."

His steamy, warm body was ready for her.

"No, we can't," she said, wanting to. "We can't."

"There's a car downstairs waiting to take us to Mariposa. Terrific, huh?"

"What about Lisa?"

"Peter said that after the doctor set her arm, Susan and Ken took her to Miss Mari's for the night. You can see them this morning. But tonight," he continued, "just think what you'll gain by not living with Gretchen."

"Did she change her mind?"

"How could you think of living with anybody but me?"

The walls of her room were spinning around: east, west, north, south, the skylight had blurred the messages. If Peter ever discovered that she was living in the same complex—much less living with Andy!—he would interpret it as a major betrayal. She had four walls with her life written on them, and nobody had ever written a word for her. No matter what role Andy was going to play in her life, she would never allow him to be the cause of losing all or part of one of them.

"Andy, every night can't be like last night."

"Why not? I love you, and we can make it in this world as long as we're together. I haven't begun to show you what *I* can do to make you happy. Last night was full of *your* surprises."

"No, Andy. I can't."

The Rolls Royce only took one passenger to Mariposa. An unhappy young man arrived in a yellow Honda some time just before noon.

Chapter 6

Knowing that Jana had been in the mountains when Ginni was killed, the women at Mariposa hung around her scales at the weigh house.

Did you see it happen? We heard the girl's head was smashed. Why wasn't she rescued? We heard they grabbed the baby first and it was too late to save the girl. Is it true the house was completely destroyed? We heard they'll never live there again.

Jana fielded the questions as politely as she could. She was reluctant to talk about the tragedy, because she was having a difficult time shaking herself away from it.

There were the more private observations, too, which Jana only heard in snatches: *We heard that Pete's gone up with the men to bring back the body. He still thinks he's a member of that family.*

By mid-morning, Jana was ready to quit her weighmaster job. Mariposa needed her business expertise too much. The peach trucks had been arriving slowly, detained by road conditions in the southwest orchard. There had been trouble with the pickers, who had been stranded on the ranch over the weekend because Moose had not paid them on time. Cooped up all weekend, there had been plenty of fights among the men.

In addition, she needed to telephone her Chicago office. There was no phone in the weigh house, and even if there had been, she wouldn't have used it in Cassie's presence. But where were the harvesters? Halfway between California and Chicago? Or had they been stranded again by the same labor dispute with the truck drivers that had halted their arrival the first time?

Whatever Havermeyer thought she was doing here in "Peach Pit City"—as one member of the President's team had referred to Fresno—they would never guess that she had witnessed an untimely death, or the uprooting of a family from its home. Not to mention the sudden sexual awakening of the special representative. . . .

"It was a good thing," said Cassie, "that I introduced you to Andy Goodwin. I hear you're moving in with him."

Jana turned slowly to see if Cassie were teasing. She wasn't. Her pouting bottom lip was pursed tightly against her top lip, and her eyes were half-closed as she perched on her high stool, her legs crossed and swinging triumphantly.

"You heard wrong, Cassie. I was thinking of moving into one of the houses in the complex where he lives, but if those are the kind of rumors you are hearing, I can see it's a terrible idea."

"By all means, move in. Of course, you will never go around admitting whom you're living with: you'd stand no chance at all with Pete if you did. Don't think I haven't thought of that, kiddo.

"Interesting, isn't it, how Susan's family and Peter's continue to intertwine? It's like two vines growing around each other. One or the other of them is always causing them both to be twisted and distorted. And now the death of that little girl.

"I remember her running around here two years ago, when Susan spent a week with Miss Mari. That's where Susan goes when she's on the outs with Ken."

Cassie's voice had an air-infused, trancelike quality about it. If Jana could have seen Cassie's face, which was now turned toward her window, she was sure that her eyes would be fixed, unseeing, on one object.

"Yes, sometime after that, Susan found out she was pregnant. That's when they drew up that contract. She was practically on her way to an abortion clinic in Frisco. You know about the contract, don't you?"

"I know enough."

"I was dating old Pete that summer. Yes, he was here, spending his vacation—in case Susan needed him. I wasn't fooled. You know, Pete and I, we've gone our separate ways now and then, but we always swim toward each other after a storm. Don't be fooled, kiddo, into thinking you can dazzle him with your shiny blonde hair and your Harvard credentials."

The more Cassie explained the ground rules across the weigh house, the more revived Jana felt. Peter Milford: everything she had dreamed of, all in one package, came complete with a spicy little sidekick. The fade-out, desert island-type of romantic love had never appealed to her. Not in the least. Peter, as a trophy, might indeed be worth some trouble. And he *had* been fairly civil to her when he stopped by her room the night before. She looked forward to the "talk" he promised.

"Jana." Cassie's voice had risen in pitch.

"Yes?"

"I said, I imagine you're wondering, if Pete and I are such a pair, why aren't we married? Because, every time that Susan crops up, I lose a good six months. But, honey, I don't intend to lose a minute on account of *you*—is that clear? I may not be as smart as you, but I'm ten times more experienced. This is my territory."

"Your credentials are in order," said Jana, happy that the trucks had begun to rumble in with half-loads of peaches.

When Andy arrived, Jana asked him if he would take her to see Susan during her lunch hour.

"Why?"

"Because you already know Miss Mari and I think it would be nice if you introduced me to her."

Even though the truck behind him was honking, Andy hesitated, then said that he would do it. Jana held out her hand to him. He grasped it tightly before leaving with reluctance.

If only Andy had been endowed with Peter's family! How much easier it would have been to plan her goals around someone who so obviously cared for her.

What about Spenser? She hoped he would find someone with *her* drive and initiative in Italy this summer. Whenever she thought of Spenser, she saw him bent over a meticulous problem in a laboratory. Compared to Andy, who was the sun, Spenser was a fluorescent lamp. Common sense argued that she was overclassifying Andy. The back of her neck argued that she was not.

At noon, Jana picked up her handbag and walked with Andy across the dusty road toward the wild tangle of eccentric trees and clumps of flowers and bushes that belonged to the friend of plants, animals, wild rivers and fresh air whom Jana was so anxious to meet.

Inside the fence, they were overrun by an enormous collie, a tumble of blue-gray kittens, a three-legged tabby and a chicken with a limp.

Ken's face appeared at the oval glass on the front door, and Jana smiled. He banged out the door and slammed it so hard behind him that the glass rattled. As he tore open the screen door and slammed it, too, the porch shook. The side of his head was bandaged, but she was prevented from asking about it because underneath his beard he was swearing—at Andy.

"Don't let me see you near Susan or Lisa or anybody who is important to our lives. You get out of here and stay out!"

Jana opened her mouth to defend Andy against Ken's irrational ravings, but remained quiet. Andy was well-equipped to defend himself, and Ken was obviously overcome with grief and unaware of what he was saying.

But Andy was saying nothing. Instead, he backed down the steps and walked sideways toward the front gate. When he reached it, he did not wave or explain, but with fear in his eyes, he disappeared to the other side of the jumble of greenery.

"Sorry," said Ken. "Come on in. Susan's finally asleep and, fortunately, Lisa is too. But Miss Mari wants to meet you. She'll return in a moment."

"Ken, what's wrong between you and Andy? What did you mean that you didn't want him around his own sister again?"

"Jana," he said, putting his hand on her arm, "You ask Andy. No one knows better what I'm talking about."

Jana collected her thoughts by looking around the living room. The light filtering through the windows was elegant and lacy because of the varied hanging plants it passed around. The brightness caused the plants to look black—like wrought-iron creations of a skilled artist. Jana loved every shape, every color, every shadow in the room. Even the creaks in the floor sounded like soothing modern music. Everything in the room fascinated her. This house was so filled with variety that she would have been happy to sit in a chair for hours, listening and looking.

She glimpsed the breakfast room, where glass shelves had been constructed in the windows. They held dozens of antique fruit jars, their delicate colors ranging from the lightest pastel blue to purple, green, gray and pink.

The wallpaper was patterned with rows of tea roses, and had obviously been hung years ago. Several old photographs in round frames covered with convex glass hung on the wall. Some were so dark that nothing could be discerned clearly except their eyes—those black Milford eyes.

The odor that permeated the house reminded Jana that she hadn't eaten since Andy had fed her the night before. Or had that been a dream?

"Peter was up almost all night," interjected Ken. "He's made all the arrangements to recover Ginni's body. We'll be meeting him in Fresno for the flight to La Jolla. I think he and I can finally be friends." Ken's eyes were red and, even with his heavy beard, Jana discerned other signs of grief on the remainder of his face.

"It was through my friendship with Pete, you know, that I met Susan. I convinced Peter to study law, to get away from that father of his. Joe Milford never had the slightest understanding of the son he had, or of the way the constant Milford foot-on-the-neck pressure affected his son.

"Peter, has, unfortunately, always had the idea that Susan *planned* to marry me when she left him. And Peter has always thought that if he kept close enough watch, at some point I would fail Susan and he could step in and show her that she does, after all, need him."

"Is this tragedy proof to him—that she does?"

"No. I think he finally knows that if he had had my patience all along, he might have succeeded with Susan when they were married. But it's too late for him and Susan—just as it's too late for Ginni."

Ken sat down at the edge of a wooden rocker and put his head in his hands.

"I can't believe it," he murmured. "And yet I find it incredible that we didn't lose Lisa, too. What rules are operating? A life for a life? It didn't have to be. . . ."

"And you're the Jana I've heard about?" The woman who stood there with her hand outstretched was not the woman anyone had led Jana to expect.

This was not some dotty old maid with do-gooder tendencies—a woman who mended the needlepoint cushions at church or marched in front of city hall protesting. This was not a woman whose sidelines compensated for an empty life.

This was the woman with the purple eyes in the portrait at the Milford mansion. That had not been Peter's mother at all, but Marietta Milford as a young woman.

Now a woman in her late fifties, she was graying but not gray; her nose was thin but strong; and her eyes were a purply-blue color, like wine held up to a certain light.

Energy radiated from her as if it were her trademark. Her light blue cotton blouse was expensive enough to look like a custom-made St. Laurent. She wore it tucked into white pants of an equally perfect cut. Her calf pumps were black and shiny, and matched her thin black belt with a plain gold buckle.

Placing her hand on Ken's shoulder, she gave it a rub as she talked. "I suggest that you go upstairs and lie down until you and Susan must leave for La Jolla. After what I just heard out there on the porch, you'll be needing more restraint than you showed with your little brother-in-law."

"He's not really a brother-in-law, you know," said Ken as he turned and slowly weaved his way through the room.

As he clumped wearily up the stairs, Jana thought how odd and unfair it was that, in the face of tragedy, one still expected a suffering person to behave with a certain amount of decency. But you did. And she had. She was glad she had stopped herself from flying off the handle at Ken when he was screaming at Andy. Yet, she had trouble with the fact that she felt a dislike for Ken now. It wasn't fair, but she did.

And here she was under Miss Mari's penetrating gaze. Jana knew that the woman saw everything.

"Since Susan's asleep, I'll go on back to work," said Jana.

"First, come into the kitchen. I'm working out a different recipe for the peach preserves my Save Yosemite Committee is planning to sell for Christmas. I want to see how the women are progressing."

The pitch of Miss Mari's deep, contralto voice was as musical and as soothing as bamboo wind chimes. No wonder Susan spoke so fondly of her.

"You know our preserves are our biggest seller. It appeals to people that buying preserves helps to 'preserve' the park. The fruit we use is donated by farmers in the valley. I'm not

too impressed with their generosity, however, since the fruit
they give us is too ripe to go to the cannery, or too small to be
sold as fresh produce.

"Our dried fruit doesn't do as well. People—mainly in the
east—don't think they like dried fruit. Or they imagine there
are flies mixed up in it."

Miss Mari motioned to the figs in the drying shed outside
her gate. "A couple of days in the sun and flies come, flies go.
Some of them are stuck and die. You've heard the stories
about what ends up in canned foods. Of course, 'unidentified
furry objects' get heated up in the can, along with everything
else.

"I've never heard of a cannery or a food-processing plant
worker who didn't have some horror story to tell—have
you?"

Jana nodded blankly, all the while thinking that she had
some stories about the fake food produced at Engineered
Edibles that would curl Miss Mari's toes.

They passed two large gas stoves in the huge kitchen at the
back of the house. Miss Mari gave a few instructions to the
two women who were watching over the wonderful-smelling
vats of yellowish-orange brews.

She motioned Jana to a seat at the round oak table in front
of the fruit jar collection.

Miss Mari sat quietly for a moment. Her hands, Jana
noticed, were beautiful and tapered and offered a ballet
accompaniment to her words. Was she the one who had
taught Peter to synchronize his conversation with his hands?
Miss Mari's uncanny eyes were focused down on the smooth
grain of the wooden table. Finally, she said, "Jana, why are
you here?"

It was a pleading question—not an accusing one—and Jana
did not bristle. In fact, suddenly she felt like spilling out how
important it was that she earn money, help her family, give
them what she knew they had always missed. She wanted to
ask Miss Mari about Peter and say, "Here I am and here he is
and what do you think? Will you help me?"

Miss Mari waited comfortably through the long silence
during which Jana only managed to say, "Ahh. . . ." Because
her hundreds of thoughts could not fit into her mouth. In
addition, a censor was at work: how much had Peter told Miss
Mari about her?

"Everything," Miss Mari informed her. The burgundy of

her eyes drained to a lighter color as the flat light passed through the fruit jars.

Jana gave a start.

"Peter told me your pedigree and your business. And the next thing I know, you're ensconced in the weigh house in a job reserved for college kids—a job that people pass down to their little sisters."

"Miss Mari, it was Peter's idea. And if I had been the man he expected from Havermeyer, he planned to 'infiltrate' me into Mariposa as a truck driver. He seems to have some feeling that there is danger involved."

"He's right. You don't think that the local farm-equipment dealer has refused to sell Havermeyer products because it's good for his pocketbook, do you?"

"I hadn't been told. I didn't realize. Nobody told me that was the situation." When she returned to Chicago, she was going to blow the whistle on Schultz. Either he had done no homework at all, or he knew that if he revealed the problems at Mariposa, he would never be offered the China trip he'd wanted so badly.

"Nobody told you that the Calimyrna Corporation threatened that dealer? That's why the equipment had to come directly from the midwest." Miss Mari shook her head.

"I thought the safety problem had to do with the new group of men Peter was forced to hire because our machines did not arrive in time," Jana answered.

"Those men are innocents compared to the Calimyrna people. And, apparently, you are, too.

"I've seen my brother sell off the Mariposa cannery, which processed our fruit for the finest specialty stores in this country, and in Canada and England. Now, we're producing peaches that are so hard you can bounce them. That's what the Calimyrna canneries demand, and then they reject our fruit for size or, unjustly, for worms and insects. These can't really be hurt by machines, so let Havermeyer's harvesters shake hell out of them, I say.

"Of course, I shouldn't complain. Thousands of cases of the fruit that the Save Yosemite Committee dried for mail order last year have been rejected by the Calimyrna cannery. That corporation can't wait to pick up Mariposa at the same sweet price it stole our cannery.

"We used to have the most beautiful freestone peaches in the world here. I'm the only one raising them on this land,

and do you know why? Uneducated consumers. They have had their wits scared out of them by talk of cancer. They think that the sweet pink color oozing from the peach pits is an artificial red dye. And when freestone peaches are mass produced by labels they have no reason to trust—like Calimyrna—they won't buy the peaches.

"Mariposa's label was a sign of *quality*. The public knew we weren't going to squirt pink poison into *our* product. People trusted us. Whom can they trust now?"

Miss Mari took a deep breath. "I sound like a fanatic, don't I?"

"Not at all. I wish this had been explained to me before I arrived."

"What I'm saying to you, Jana, is that I don't like the idea of machines in our orchards—not for a moment. But I look at the quality of peaches we are planting these days, and I look down the valley to Bakersfield and up the valley toward Sacramento, and I see these damned machines stalking through the tomatoes and even the olive orchards, like creatures from outer space. And most of the places that use the machines wisely are making a profit, while Mariposa operates in the red.

"What it comes down to is that I'd rather for us to take on a few of these monsters than go to hell."

"Hell?"

"The hell of losing my home, my land—the first land my grandfather planted and irrigated. He was a friend of John Muir—you know, the man responsible for the national park system in the U.S.

"We preserve what we have: that's what makes real Californians. The rest are all Okies as far as I'm concerned, and my allegiance is not to them."

A beige wall phone behind Miss Mari rang. She answered it and handed it to Jana.

"It's your company: they've been trying to reach you for an hour."

"The harvesters are arriving tonight?" Jana couldn't believe that was what they were telling her.

"No. They have to stall. We're not. . . ."

"Mud," said Miss Mari. "We've had a big rain and they'll sink in the mud."

"We've had a mud problem here because of—of unseasonal rains. It would take a week to pull your trucks out, should they become stuck."

Jana hung up the phone with a sigh of relief.

Miss Mari winked at her.

"They said they'll phone again in two days. I have to talk to Peter about this."

"Don't worry. He'll find a place to hide them, if he doesn't think it's wise for them to be unveiled at this moment. Now, my assignment from Peter is to work on Moose. This is harder on him than on anyone else."

"Frankly, Miss Mari, I'm surprised that you're as receptive to the machines as you are. Peter said. . . ."

"Peter doesn't know anything about me. He thinks that just because Moose and I are . . . good friends . . . that we feel the same way. It's not so. But Peter's presence on this ranch has made it hard for Moose. He never expected it to turn out this way. He thought that once Peter had gone to Washington, he would stay there.

"But the real reason it is untimely for the machines to arrive today is that my brother's arriving tonight with his new wife."

"Peter's father?"

"Yes, and I'll have my hands full."

Chapter 7

"Don't worry," said Miss Mari, "Peter and I will size up Joe's physical condition, and if we think he's not up to it, we won't mention the harvesters."

"And if he is . . . ?"

"We'll lay all our cards on the table and, for the first time, I'll show Joe that Peter has my full support."

"Miss Mari, why haven't you taken a more active part in running Mariposa?"

"It wouldn't have been my style. I've always used my name and position to leap in—and out—of projects that interest me. But management is not one of them.

"Except for what you see inside the boundaries of my fence here, I've inherited no land. The cash and securities I received from my father more than made up for it, even though I would have preferred the land. But our father knew that Joe and I were so far apart in our philosophies that we would never have been able to run Milford Enterprises together. We would have ended up selling it, in order to maintain a life of some peace."

Miss Mari's eyes brimmed with huge blue tears, which miraculously never fell.

"Now," she said in a softer voice, "I want Peter to make

peace with his father and show him that he is worthy of running all of Milford Enterprises by turning around Mariposa's financial condition."

"Do you think Peter plans to live in the valley?"

"He is determined. And when that boy sets his mind. . . ."

"When he moved to Washington, I, along with Moose, thought he would never return. He worked for the labor department's legal division, specializing in laws covering migrant workers—the very laws Joe always thumbed his nose at as 'undue governmental intervention.' In fact, while Peter was there, I half-expected him to take Milford Enterprises to court over the conditions here."

"Do you think he returned because of his interest in 'cleaning up' Mariposa?" Jana dared not bring up Susan.

The Spanish-speaking women in the kitchen were laughing and talking so loudly that Miss Mari had to lean forward.

"I'd like to think that it's because of the land and because I've instilled some of my values in him. His father has always had money, money, money on his mind. You see, Joe is fighting mechanization, not out of any love of the land, but because he believes in doling out as little as possible to laborers. He also believes that Mariposa will lose its prestige if it gets around that we use machines. And to him, prestige means money. He is, as you can see, quite behind the times.

"Joe always said that Peter took after me—that he was too sentimental. I'm beginning to believe it. At first, I thought that the only reason Peter returned was because . . . because of his father's poor health.

"But last summer, Peter saw peaches dropping off the trees faster than our skimpy supply of laborers could pick them. There really is very little incentive these days for men to pick peaches: the pay is about a penny a pound, and the men average from six to ten dollars an hour. They have few fringe benefits, and no job security. No wonder laborers are hard to find. Peter has some pipe dreams about a year-round labor force. I'm afraid he got it out of a textbook."

"That's exactly what I told him."

Miss Mari eyed Jana. "You know, you look very much like Peter's mother. She was blonde, and in her way, delicate—like you. She had her steamy side, too, as I'm sure you do."

"What happened to her?"

"She thought she was an actress. When being a movie star

didn't work out, she claimed her talents were for the stage. She left Joe and Peter, and spent six months in New York at some acting school. That was the beginning of the end of that family. After she failed at that, she went to Europe and there, shall we say, fell out of the limelight and out of grace with the Milford family, that's for sure. Joe divorced her and she died six or seven years ago—in France.

"Lorene never felt she belonged in the family. Few do. She thought everyone looked down on the tasteless, ostentatious way she dressed. I did, of course."

"I slept in your room at the mansion last night," said Jana. "And these are your clothes."

"I thought they looked familiar. We're built alike, you and I, tall and narrow. But you have that lovely blonde hair.

"My mother had blue eyes—like yours. And when those Milford black eyes are blended with sky-blue eyes, you can see what you get."

"Your eyes are a wonderful color, Miss Mari."

"I often thought that I would be happy if Peter married someone with blue eyes . . . but," she straightened her back and held her shoulders up, "Susan has green eyes. It was after their divorce that he moved to Washington."

"He must have loved her very much."

"Too much. He wanted to possess her. But what examples did he have? Only me, an old maid, and his money-grubbing dad who wants to possess everything *and* everybody. Joe has diversified Milford Enterprises into areas we have no business in—like spices and chewing gum.

"The worst thing you can do is tell him about endangered species. He'll want to go out and grab them all up. He even owns several whale boats in Japan. He's blind to what selfishness has done to our beautiful state. And he has friends in Washington who always keep their hands off him and his exploits. His friends are rotten—and much more wicked at heart than he is."

The phone rang again. After a few seconds, Miss Mari hung up. "It's Moose. He says there's a line of trucks at Cassie's window that will take until day after tomorrow to weigh if you don't hurry back."

"Moose doesn't know about me, does he?"

"He has suspicions. Don't tell him. That's my job."

Reluctantly, Jana hurried to the weigh house and hopped

onto her perch, using the same method Roy Rogers employed to jump on Trigger.

Moose waved to the trucks and yelled, "You can split up the line, now. The lady from Harvard has decided to return from her two-hour lunch."

As Jana slid the weights into place and subtracted the weights of the trucks empty from the trucks full, Moose was screaming in her right ear.

"Unless you can act responsibly, you ain't gonna last long here. Cassie can do the job all by herself. I want you to know that I've got a ranch to run. Peter may have taken charge of the drivers and the pickers, but I've still got you and Cassie and the girls on the platform to worry about."

"Moose, I'm really sorry. I'll be on time from now on. It's just that. . . ."

"Don't tell me your problems. I've got enough on my hands. Who do you think you are? Dragging in here as late as you did?"

Jana was finding it more and more interesting that the sparks that caused the smoke on this ranch were never traceable to the real fire.

Still looking over Jana's shoulder, Moose added, "You forgot to carry your four. You know these are only tiny numbers, but they stand for thousands of pounds of peaches. I don't want the head office in San Francisco calling me and complaining."

"I would have caught it when I checked during a slack period."

"There won't be any slack periods today, honey. We're making up for lost time and, frankly, the rain has shaken down tons of peaches. Watch them turn them away at the cannery, saying they're bruised or some damn thing."

"Are they?"

"Wouldn't you be, if you fell out of a tree? And Peter has gone and bought machines that shake down the peaches on purpose. Hellfire. There's no hope around here!"

Jana laughed to herself as soon as he had gone. So that's what he had been saying all the time: *hellfire!* Ruby Ford came inside the weigh house and pulled up a peach box until she was literally sitting at Jana's knees. Ruby had been sorting peaches at Mariposa longer than anybody on the platform.

"It says here in this tourist brochure I just found that it takes tons of fresh grapes to make a batch of raisins."

"That's nice," said Jana, checking the accuracy of her last five truckweights.

Ruby was wearing red pedal-pushers salvaged from the 1950s, a sleeveless blouse dating back to the same time, and bifocal glasses with white frames and jewels embedded in their pointed edges.

"Imagine," she said.

"Imagine what?"

"How many flies can hide in a ton of raisins. I remember when all the peaches and grapes were iced down here before going to the canneries or markets. Now, most of them go in air-conditioned comfort.

"Remember when they brought in some of the clingstone peaches from the ranches up north for the first time, Cassie?"

"No," Cassie said from across the room. She was reading, or pretending to read, a paperback book.

"The first time I heard those clingstone names, I felt like I was on a glamorous tour . . . Halford . . . Gaume . . . Paoloro . . . Peak . . . Fortuna. . . .

"But they never did taste as delicious as our freestones, did they, Cassie? Remember Redhaven . . . Golden Jubilee . . . Triogem . . . Halehaven . . . Elberta?

"I also remember when Mariposa employed only wetbacks to do the picking. Ha! I'll bet Peter still does that—in spite of the line he spins about justice and liberty for all."

"I thought the contractor assured Mariposa that the laborers were in this country legally," said Jana.

"Don't kid yourself. There have always been hundreds of thousands sneaking across the Mexican border."

"Peter's gonna change all that around here," piped up Cassie.

"My little town can't accomodate any more of these foreigners," Ruby complained.

"Hispanics," said Cassie.

"They go to school with my grandkids."

"Half my class is filled with cute little Spanish faces. But most of the kids' families have been here so long that many of them speak only English."

Ruby turned to Jana. "I'll bet you've heard terrible stories about California because of the Cesar Chavez types. There are terrible things, but they're not *our* fault. We're being overrun by people from across the border—all our borders. It's like it was here during the Depression."

"Like you, Ruby?" asked Cassie.

"No. My dad came in Eighteen-ninety and survived the great San Francisco earthquake of Oh-six."

"*My* great, great, great or something grandfather arrived in *Eighteen-fifty*—the year California became the thirty-first state," noted Cassie smugly. "He just missed striking it rich in the gold rush of Forty-nine."

"I don't know what's to become of Mariposa now," said Ruby. "Pete is a city boy, really, and doesn't understand the orchards."

"Perhaps he intends to hire people who do know," suggested Jana. She might as well practice defending him. He seemed to be constantly cited for faults around here.

"If you ask me," said Ruby, "that fellow has been to school too much."

If anyone asked Jana, Ruby smoked too much. The woman was humped over, waving a cigarette, and the smoke was wafting directly under Jana's nose and out the window on the other side of her.

"Peter has spent too much time on the east coast," continued Ruby. "And what do they know?"

"They have peaches there, too."

"Those peaches don't count," she snapped. "Besides, you have to be born with the knowledge of how to run orchards. You have to know when the ground smells right for planting, and what it means when the dust blows and the air is dry.

"Peter has great intuition about tennis and airplanes, how to drink fancy liquor and drive fancy cars. He may even know lawyer lingo, but he knows nothing about growing peaches— or wives, don't you agree, Cassie?"

"I'll never be a peach, so I couldn't tell you. But ask me about the wife part in a couple of weeks."

Cassie ambled over to Jana. "How's Susan taking it all?"

"I didn't see her."

"You were certainly over at Miss Mari's for a long time."

"She and I had a talk."

"Oh."

"What Cassie means," said Ruby, "is that she and Miss Mari have never gotten along, and Lord knows, Cassie has tried to get in with the right people ever since she found herself stuck with kindergarten kids instead of a life of luxury."

"Ruby Ford, you know that's not true! Besides, I need to talk to Jana, and I think someone is calling you out on the platform."

Cassie moved in. Her head came to Jana's elbow as she stood at the tall desk.

"What happened to Andy over at Miss Mari's?"

"What do you mean?"

"Why didn't he stay there with you?"

What had Cassie seen? Heard?

"I suppose he had work to do."

"You know that's not true. We could hear the yelling all the way over here. Then we saw him shoot out of that gate and run to his truck."

"Why don't you ask Andy?" suggested Jana.

"I did! Ruby did, too. He wouldn't say a word."

It was now clear to Jana why Ruby had parked herself at Jana's feet—to dig out information, not to give it, particularly not about the history of California.

"Between the two of us," said Cassie, "I certainly hope you aren't having any trouble with Andy. I figure he's my life insurance."

"Oh?"

"As long as you keep your hands all over his irresistible body and off Peter's, then we'll have nothing to quarrel about."

"Cassie, what I do is not your concern."

"I only tell you now, Jana, because I don't want you to get hurt. Last spring, you know, Pete and I flew to Paris. I always thought it would be great to do it with Peter on a ship, but I figured he'd never have time. Instead, I covered us with a big blanket on the plane. It was nice, but of course we had to wait for the real thing until we were at the hotel."

"I hate to break into your reveries, but there's a truck at your window and one of your little friends is panting for you."

Had Cassie read her resolve regarding Peter? Or did she have the inferiority complex of most brunettes—fear of the mysterious power a blonde could hold over a man?

Jana didn't understand it herself, but it was true. During her freshman year at MIT, she finally got herself under control enough to gracefully turn down the five or six calls she

received each night for coffee, dinner, movies, plays, walks—
anything. The fact was that men liked to be seen with
blondes. It wasn't long before she had deduced it was no great
compliment to her ego, but to theirs. And that wasn't *her*
game.

"Okay," said Moose, his voice booming through the back
door of the weigh house. "Everybody go home. Right now.
There's been a little disturbance out in one of the orchards.
It's nothing big, but you ladies get out of here immediately.
Call in tomorrow morning, we'll probably have business as
usual."

As Jana had been driven to Mariposa that morning in the
Milford Rolls, she had no way to return to Fresno. Her car
was still in the mountains and Andy had disappeared after his
run-in with Ken. Besides, she had no idea where that complex
of houses she was supposed to be living in was located. She
had decided to go ahead and move in. She was too exhausted
to hunt for an apartment. And she sensed that if she buckled
now to Peter's wishes regarding Andy, he would never have
any respect for her.

"How are you getting home, Jana?" Cassie asked with
perfect timing.

"I—I don't know."

"Look behind you."

"No matter what they're saying about me at Miss Mari's,
I'm certainly not going to leave you stranded here," said
Andy.

Once they were on the highway, Jana said, "You'll have to
understand how upset Ken was. It had nothing to do with
you."

"What did Miss Mari say?"

"That Ken was upset. She even sent him upstairs to rest, so
he wouldn't fly off the handle again."

"He's a louse."

"Give him time, Andy. He'll apologize."

Andy's shoulders were relaxing. Jana moved her hand to
his leg, patted it and gave him a reassuring smile.

"Andy, I asked Ken why he was so angry at you."

"And?"

"He said to ask you. He seems to think it's pretty awful."

"That damned creep. He suspects me of everything. I
haven't done anything. He believes I'm the one who has told
everybody, including Peter, that Lisa isn't his child."

"Did you?"

"I didn't have to. Peter found out on his own. And you know how rumors fly."

"Isn't there more to Ken's anger than that?"

"I think he b-b-believes I spread a rumor about him being sterile. I don't know it for sure, but I'll bet you fifty dollars it's true. Why else would he have taken on the responsibility of Peter's child unless he thought he'd never have one of his own? Susan wanted to have an abortion. Ken said he doesn't believe in them. I don't know anybody who'd want someone else's baby—a constant reminder that his wife had been screwing around with that r-rotten Milford. I hate it! I hate everything about it! It doesn't seem to bother Ken at all. In fact, since they've had that kid, he and Susan have been getting along better than ever. It doesn't make sense."

"Andy!"

"My dad thinks they'll break up. He claims Peter is always lurking around Susan. He wants to file a case against Milford, get all the money he can get his hands on—for Lisa, of course."

"Your father would do that?"

Andy was taking the curves in the road with more confidence. "My dad's made most of his big money by striking out for what rightfully belongs to him and his—even though most people would let it go. Yup, he's a smart man: never goes after anybody unless he's sure they can pay off big."

They rode in silence for a couple of sun-hazed miles. Jana was surprised to find herself thinking that the valley looked fairly pleasant in the sunset—like a solemn space on the earth where all the excitement took place underground. Someone had even told her that Fresno had an underground garden where trees and plants thrived.

"Andy, thank you for answering my question about the problem with Ken. But could I ask you another?"

"Honey, you can ask anything."

"Did you spend much time with Susan and Peter when they were married?"

"Enough."

"Did they seem happy—at first, I mean?"

"I don't know. I think Susan found out right away that she wouldn't be able to paint as much as she wanted to. And the more Peter suspected that she hadn't married him just for his adorable self, the more insistent he became that she spend all her time with him. He tested her minute by minute, as though he couldn't believe that the obvious was true: the old boy had been taken for a ride. But, Jana, I don't want to talk about *him*. Let's talk about us. Last night was wonderful. Tonight, I've already planned what we'll do. A nice dinner at a French restaurant about a mile from the house, then we'll have wine and cheese at home—in bed."

He turned into the drive of the complex—and stopped behind Jana's white, rented Mercedes.

"Isn't that nice," she exclaimed. "Peter has had someone drive my car down from the mountains."

"Nice for him, you mean. Look who's sitting in it, waiting for your gratitude."

Peter unfolded out of the car. His face was ashen. "I tried to catch you before Mariposa closed," he said. "Cassie told me you'd left with him." Peter glared at Andy.

"Yeah?" said Andy. "Why didn't you try the telephone?"

Ignoring him, Peter said, "Miss Mari finally got Susan and Ken off a few minutes ago."

"That's nice, fella. Give the lady the keys to the car and we'll be going. Now, I suppose, you'll need a ride."

"Jana, I came to tell you that Miss Mari wants you at the dinner she is having for my father tonight. She thinks you might be able to say something to him that will back us up—if that's necessary."

"I don't believe this," said Andy.

"I'd love to be there," replied Jana, oblivious to his agitation.

"God almighty!" Andy turned and stomped toward the patio of the complex.

Jana rushed ahead to somehow explain why it was important that she be at the dinner. She heard Peter say, "I'll wait out here."

Chapter 8

Jana was in the shower before she remembered that her one dress was wadded up somewhere in the Mercedes, where it had been since she checked out of the motel.

She combed her hair and dried it with the dryer that was installed on an electric appliance shelf, along with a shaver and a curling iron. Spying Gretchen in the pool, she called to her out the window and asked if she would mind retrieving her dress from the car.

After what seemed like eons to Jana, Gretchen appeared with the dress, which Jana hung up immediately in the steamy bathroom.

Gretchen turned to leave as silently as she had come, but then came back into the room. "Your suitcases have arrived," she reported in her nasal monotone. "They're in the front hall."

"Thanks for telling me, Gretchen," Jana said drily. At least, she thought, I'll have clean underwear and my own makeup.

Jana opened the suitcase and rifled through it, looking for a pair of Pucci bikinis, the ones she liked to travel with because they looked halfway cheerful when they were hung up to dry. Nothing else in the suitcase looked at all cheerful, and Jana was disgusted with all the strange, dark clothes. She found the green and blue bikinis and slipped them on under the dress, which had turned out quite nicely, for all that it had been through.

She had forgotten to steam the matching stole but decided she looked better without it. Her one bare shoulder was quite lovely; she felt slightly risqué. But, after all, this was California. And, she told herself, you are going to a business dinner, don't forget. It could seal your whole future.

Jana hurried out the door feeling a rush of her old sense of control, mixed with the anticipation of just a little adventure.

She tackled Peter head-on. "What do the women at Mariposa know about me? Cassie, for example, and Ruby?"

She watched him closely to see how he reacted to Cassie's name. She need not have.

"Oh, them," he said. "They're always nosing around."

Jana was encouraged.

"Miss Mari is wonderful. Susan was right."

He drove on without commenting.

"I didn't know you had a background in labor law." Jana tried another tack.

"Somebody around here had to."

"Maybe you should have gone to my school and gotten a degree in mechanical engineering. But you didn't know you were going to be responsible for a mechanized farm when you went to school, did you?"

"None of it matters. You know where my dad is at this moment? Downtown at one of his lawyers', discussing the sale price of Mariposa."

"But why?"

"He'd rather sell it than change it. I'm thinking that Aline, his new wife, may have something to do with this. Or, he may have finally capitulated to his staff in San Francisco. That bunch is more interested in the vineyards, anyway. For the last four or five years, they've been attempting to persuade him to sell Mariposa and invest the money in land in the Napa Valley."

"I didn't know you were so fond of peaches."

"Milford Enterprises means nothing without Mariposa. Nothing."

"I know."

"You don't know anything."

If there was ever a time when she must endure Peter's shafts, it was now. Not just on his behalf—he was understandably keyed up—but on hers. If anything were to come of this Mariposa venture, she had to be very careful about what she said—or didn't say.

The heavy, slanted sunlight lying over the valley had settled the trees, plants—even the birds on the telephone wires—into a calm hush. It was really quite beautiful, and Jana was not in the least upset that Peter did not talk further with her. This meant that the explosion she had expected from him over her residence in Andy's housing complex would probably never take place.

Peter pulled up outside Miss Mari's and guided her through the green gate. All the animals seemed to know and like him—especially the collie, Honey, who whined with excitement and sounded as if she were carrying on a human conversation with him.

There was a scribbled note on the front door that said, "Be back in a minute."

"You can go inside if you wish; I'll wait for her out here." He sank down on the top step of the porch. Honey thought this gesture was on her behalf, and stuck her nose in his hand.

"I love this porch," Peter said softly. "I always have. When I was a little boy, I thought you could see the whole world from here."

Jana stood behind Peter and looked out at the Milford orchards. The evening was peaceful. Her dress was as soft as the evening light, and her feeling was one of blending perfectly with her surroundings.

For the first time, she was in the middle of something that made simple sense. Her feet were not flying along in their usual high-powered search for security. They were, if not firmly planted, at least close to real ground and real sounds: birds chirping, roosters crowing, cows mooing in the distance.

Jana preferred being on this porch, listening to these sounds in the hazy evening sunset, to an orchestra seat at a Chicago Symphony concert. *This* sunset and *these* sounds were not being played *for* her: they included her. They were part of her life.

With a contented smile, Jana looked at the jumble of a garden that surrounded the porch. Miss Mari was definitely not one of those gardeners who spent hours dividing a plot into neat squares. The bell peppers were planted around the steps, and the strawberries were mixed with billowing geraniums that had already reached the porch railing.

A white Volvo spun around in front of the gate, and Miss Mari, a whirl of pale purple cotton, raced up the path.

"Hello, Jana," she said, shaking her hand firmly. But when she reached Peter, she said, "And hello, my dear, my sweet, dear boy." She put her arms around him, inviting his head to lean on her shoulder.

"What you did for Susie and Ken today and yesterday—it couldn't have been easy for you."

Peter straightened. Honey leaned hard on his leg. He rubbed her ears, but said nothing.

"You mean your dad isn't here yet?" Miss Mari asked.

"He's down paying a visit to old beetface."

"Cy Leeman? That could only mean trouble."

"You're right. When dad heard that I let everybody go because of the heavy rain yesterday—and when Moose told him on the phone this morning that I was not planning to show up for the day—dad figured I wasn't running the place right—just as he had suspected. I think Moose is causing me more trouble than I guessed!"

"Peter, you're too hard on Moose," Miss Mari said as she ushered Jana and Peter into the house.

"And you're too easy."

"He's an artist. Jana, these stained-glass windows on both sides of the mantel, the blown-glass lamp by that chair, the wood sculptures of young ducklings stretching their necks to be fed, the modern carvings of crocuses sprouting up in the spring—Moose made them all. Someday, museums will want them."

"And all these," said Peter, "are precisely the reasons he shouldn't be running this ranch. He's always firing, blowing, soldering or whittling at something."

"Moose thinks you're his only problem," said Miss Mari.

"Well, he's not mine. I have bigger worries. Did you hear about the telegram that some of the pickers sent to the San Francisco office, claiming that I was going back on my dad's word that he would never mechanize?"

"Yes, I heard," said Miss Mari. "I may not run this ranch, but my place is still the hub. There's not much that escapes me. Let's have a drink. Moose should be here any minute, and I don't want you to be so uptight with him, Peter, that you fly off and say something you'll regret."

As Miss Mari poured the drinks, Jana caught a glimpse of her standing with her glass held in mid-air. The brown color of her scotch had a jewel-like glow, as did so many things in this house.

Miss Mari reached down and flipped on the table lamp. Lighted, it showed reddish-orange fruit clumped around its globe. "Persimmons," Miss Mari said, reading Jana's puzzlement. "If Tiffany ever had a successor, I believe it is—and here he is—the artist himself. Hello, darling. You're late."

Moose and Miss Mari? Moose, in a light blue seersucker suit, complete with a western tie and shined shoes?

Peter gulped down his drink and announced, "And here's dad and Aline."

A silver Lincoln Continental had appeared in front of the gate, and a white-suited chauffeur was helping out a man in a tan suit and a woman in a pink dress. As they approached the front door, the pink dress floated through the breeze. The woman twisted and turned, motioning to "the darling kitty," the "to-die-for roses," and the "precious, itty-bitty baby tears."

As though marching to battle, Peter bravely pushed open the screen door and carefully stepped onto the porch.

"It's been a long time, my boy," said Joe Milford, embracing him. "And you've met Aline, of course."

As if on a wave, the group barged into the living room. The man who was introduced to Jana did not shake hands with her. His right arm hung limply at his side and his speech, while backed by a vigor that surprised Jana, was painfully enunciated.

His dyed black hair and mustache made her think that somebody had probably told him, once-upon-a-time, that he looked like Clark Gable. But Clark Gable had never been so old.

He studied her closely for a minute, fixing his eyes for too long a moment on her breasts, barely sheltered behind the thin material of her dress.

Miss Mari shoved a drink under his eyes, but Aline snatched it away from him, sipping it first. "No alcohol; you can drink it," she announced.

Aline—her powder too white, her lipstick too purple, her dress too frilly, her heels too high, her straps too tight and her bracelets and rings too many—seemed oddly concerned that her husband might overindulge and overdo.

Suddenly, Jana had to retreat from the crowd, overwhelmed by so many Milfords at once. She skirted the photographs of Milford ancestors and took refuge near the mantel, directly under the solemn picture of a clean-cut World War II soldier. Jana wondered who he was, but knew from the eyes he was an outsider like herself.

Mr. Milford spoke slowly—an impediment that seemed to irritate him more than anyone else. "I've had a good talk with Cy. He said that Calimyrna had finally made him a decent offer for the place."

Peter, Moose and Miss Mari—all three—opened their mouths.

"But wait," he continued. "I've got better news. Some folks who want to use this place as a tax write-off have made an even larger offer, and I'm real tempted.

"I know all about your attitude this summer, Peter. But it's a passing thing. When the peaches are all in, you go on back to Washington or New York or wherever the heck you used to live, and get back into the center of things. I've raised you to be like that. You'll never be happy out here. I wasn't."

He sat down in the stuffed chair next to the persimmon lamp. "Don't worry, Miss Mari. You can stay on here. This is, after all, your land. We'll see that something nice is built outside your gate—a rice paddy or a retirement home. Heh, heh—that's a joke, Mari.

"It's a damned shame that, just when we got the land all watered with those wonderful dammed-up rivers, we should be driven out. But I'd rather see almost anything here than somebody come in with those new-fangled methods foreign to our soil, our trees and our people. What it all boils down to is that I'd rather sell than sell out."

He turned to Aline. "Wouldn't you say so, my dear?"

"Abso-loot-ly," she agreed, holding her glass of wine and toasting her nose with it.

"The young lady in the corner doesn't know that I'd still have been in that hospital if Aline here hadn't come along to marry me."

"Joe and me have known each other for years," said Aline. "He used to come into my bow-teek to buy presents for his other Mrs. Milfords, if you'll pardon the expression. When the wedding bells rang, I sold out. Made a good profit, too, didn't I?"

"Damned good," agreed Joe.

"Dad. . . ."

"Pete, if I could be sure I'd be feeling fit next summer, I'd say let's hold onto Mariposa for a while longer and see if we couldn't make it pay. . . ."

"I think Joe had better eat now, Miss Mari," said Aline. "He hasn't had a bite since we stopped on the road."

"Go on, baby, tell them what you call me at home."

"I couldn't." Aline blushed under her white powder.

"This is family—or almost—go on."

"Patoot," she said.

"Tell them all of it." Joe was smiling.

"Sweet Patoot—that's short for Patootie?" She ended her explanation in a question.

"Lovely," said Miss Mari, who looked up as if examining a leak in the ceiling before leading the party into the dining room.

Peter was the last in the room. Almost immediately, they were served small, thin steaks, and salads of fruits, lettuce, avocados and a touch of onion.

Aline extracted a set of scales from her purse and proceeded to weigh Joe's meat in a little plastic bowl.

"He's not supposed to eat but three ounces of meat a day, and he had a slice of bacon for breakfast that weighed a good half-ounce."

"Gracious," said Miss Mari.

Moose laughed uncomfortably.

Jana did nothing, trying to be as aloof as possible without being rude. Aline's ruffled wrists fanned away unwanted milligrams and sprinkles of sinful sugar. Miss Mari floated above it all like the hanging plants.

Finally, Joe pointed his fork at Jana. "Where'd you meet this young thing, Peter? She reminds me of my gal Susan."

"Susan has red hair, Dad. Jana is the new weighmaster who has replaced Sara. You remember Sara?"

"Sara? Sure." But his eyes said that he didn't, and his manner suggested that, since he didn't, it wasn't important.

"These ladies," he said to Jana, holding hands with Miss Mari and Aline, "and Peter, are all the family I've got these days. I hoped like everything that Susie would grow me a grandbaby, but, no, she waited until she married somebody else. The baby's a cute little thing, I'll bet."

"She certainly is," said Miss Mari, "and her name is Lisa."

Mr. Milford changed the subject abruptly, as if he hadn't heard. "Cy tells me that Calimyrna has bought the five hundred acres to the north, and that last spring they came in with machines and pruned hell out of the trees—pert'near mowed them down. Why didn't you tell me that?"

"Just a minute," said Miss Mari, "somebody's at the front door. It's probably one of my committee members."

Outside, Honey was barking ferociously. Jana looked out the window and saw the orange tops of two trucks towering over Miss Mari's hedge.

Without being able to read a single word on the side of the trucks, she knew that bright, blue letters proclaimed:

HAVERMEYER HARVESTER

"Everything from fruit to nuts"

Chapter 9

Peter pushed Jana's shoulder down with the gentle pressure of one shoving a beach ball beneath the water's surface, before dashing alone to the front door.

It took all Jana's effort to keep from bouncing up after him.

"Anybody I know out there?" Mr. Milford leaned forward and peered around Aline.

Miss Mari walked in the door as Peter walked out and, as she sat down in her place, she replied coolly, "Only some men who have lost their way. Peter's showing them where they can leave their trucks overnight."

Apparently, Miss Mari and Peter were convinced that this was not the night to discuss harvesters with Joe Milford, even though the subject had been forced upon them. What were those drivers thinking? How dare they arrive here when they had been told not to? Was it because the instructions *not* to appear had been delivered by a woman? It was hard to know why anybody did anything.

Jana sipped her wine and concentrated on looking pleasant, while wondering where Peter was directing the men in the two trucks. To the edge of the ocean, she hoped. If he allowed them to park anywhere on the ranch, the pickers would be sure to see them. The last thing Mariposa, Mr.

Milford, or she needed was for a commotion to start up tonight.

Moose stuck his napkin under his plate. "It's all right," said Miss Mari. "Peter has everything under control."

As if sensing the subject that was in the air—did he have Miss Mari's sixth sense, too?—Mr. Milford said, "I hear the Calimyrna people lost half their crop last year, or was it the year before, when they allowed some dang-fool machinery to come in and shake hell out of their trees. Most of the fruit that fell off was so badly bruised that their own cannery wouldn't take it."

"They're a bunch of fools," growled Moose.

To divert attention, Miss Mari helped her maid place a distracting dessert in front of Mr. Milford.

Aline's left hand reached out to inspect the dessert. To Jana's surprise, Miss Mari firmly grasped Aline's wrist and said, "*I* made this dessert, especially for Joe."

"That means he can eat this?"

"Say, Mari, this is the best ice cream I've ever eaten."

"Put that down! Ice cream's not on your list!"

"Aline, don't get hysterical. It's frozen peach juice."

"You don't say! We'll have to have this all the time at home. I'll bet they're freestones, huh?"

Miss Mari nodded.

"What the hell do you do with all the freestones you've got in this yard—and if I'm not mistaken, have planted on a few of my acres?"

"Tourists."

"You sell them to tourists?"

"We give them away."

"You never did have good sense, Mari."

"We're the only ranch in the valley with a peach center open to the public. We took the idea from the wineries. Children are interested in something *they* can eat. Everybody likes peaches, but even fewer people remember a good peach than can recall a good tomato. At least folks can grow tomatoes in their own back yards with relative ease—even if they live in Illinois."

"So you're giving away good peaches to these poor, fruit-deprived people." Joe shook his head in disbelief.

"We sell quite a number of products, too. Our Save Yosemite pack includes a jar of peach preserves, some dried peaches, a jar of peach butter and a recipe book for desserts made from peaches. We also show films that tell tourists how we grow peaches at Mariposa."

"How do you say the peaches are picked? Do you tell them how the competition gives their trees shock-treatment until the poor things drop their fruit like some poor sucker who can't. . . ."

Miss Mari hastened to break in. "I think I forgot to tell you that Peter has agreed that the 'picker of the week' is to be paid his highest summer salary the week he works off his prize—giving away peaches at the Tourist Center."

"You see what I told you, Joe," said Moose. "I don't mean to ruin your dinner, but things have gone haywire out here since that son of yours. . . ."

"Hush, Moose. We tell the tourists, Joe, when they eat a Mariposa peach, that the hands they receive the peach from is the hand that picks it."

"Sounds like a pretty good idea, Moose," he said.

Jana was again amazed that Schultz had never mentioned such a center.

"How many people you got filtering through your eleemosynary institution, Mari?"

"We had forty thousand last summer, and that was up from seventy-five hundred the year before."

Joe was definitely interested. "And the year before *that?*"

"That was the year we built the center," Miss Mari said gently.

Aline dropped her spoon heavily into the saucer holding her own bowl of peach ice. She didn't want anyone to remind Joe that his memory was so weak.

"Why don't we take a little walk?" she said brightly. "Every night, Patoot and I walk down to the ocean and back."

"Aline thinks the sun won't have enough sense to set without us."

"It's so *gorge*-us. I don't think I'll ever get used to living smack-dab on the ocean." She turned to Jana. "You know, I've lived in California all my life. . . ."

Miss Mari and Moose looked at each other.

"Except for the years I lived in Brooklyn, but even so, I've never had a view. Of course, for the past ten years, I lived above my bow-teek, and can you guess what I looked out on?"

Nobody wanted to guess, and the idea of a walk was becoming more appealing.

"The Trickie Dickie Topless Bar. Of course, I couldn't see inside, but let me tell you, those girls would sometimes be dragged off by those rednecks for a roll in a truck or a nearby motel—or even down on our beach. I've seen them. We've even had Giorgio, he's our man. . . ."

Peter sat down at the table, trying hard not to look upset. He had a streak of grease on one tan jacket sleeve.

"What was I saying?" asked Aline.

"That we've had Giorgio shoo off the fornicators from our beach."

"And you should hear the latest. They've opened Trickie Dickie Two out on the highway—you know where the road turns off at the Jack-in-the-box?"

"Why don't we walk over to the packing shed now, and you and Joe can pick out some figs to take home with you, Aline." Miss Mari moved to help her brother out of his seat.

"Figs. I don't know." Aline was shaking her tousled, hennaed hair. "Aren't figs full of sugar?"

"Then," said Miss Mari, "you can both find a nice figleaf to wear on your beach. One size fits all—and no sugar!"

"Now, girls," said Mr. Milford, "you two put your arms through mine and we'll take a shuffle around and I'll take whatever I want, be it figs or figleaves. Remember, Mariposa still belongs to me."

"Let's go, sweetie," he said, motioning to Jana. "You take Pete's arm. Don't be bashful. We'll have us an old-fashioned, after-dinner stroll."

Honey woofed a low, happy series of barks, and frolicked ahead as the procession, punctuated by Aline's chatter, moved through the gate in relative harmony.

Peter extracted himself from Jana's arm when they were safely behind the trio, and left her to walk with Moose.

After Aline had pinched and tasted the figs, Mr. Milford led her toward the back of Miss Mari's property.

"Hey, dad, Aline—let's walk this way." Peter and Honey were acting like sheepdogs keeping their charges out of a trap.

But Mr. Milford was not strolling at all. He was walking purposefully, and he only had to take a few steps before he could read the billboard side of one of the trucks.

"How did these Havermeyer trucks get here?"

"They wanted to be near the water spigot at the back of the property."

"Do you know that Moose and I have been fending off that bunch for years? Who have they sold their wrecking equipment to this time?"

Peter said nothing.

Mr. Milford disentangled himself from the arms of Miss Mari and Aline and whirled around to his son.

"Traitor! My own son a traitor to everything I've ever stood for!"

He sank down onto two upside-down peach boxes.

"Joe!" screamed Aline. "You're not supposed to be upset!"

"Shut up, wife."

Aline backed off, and Mr. Milford dropped both arms between his legs. Jana felt tears coming to her eyes.

"How much did the damned thing cost?"

"About a hundred thousand dollars each."

"*Each?*"

"We bought five, dad. The interest rates alone are averaging a hundred-fifty an acre per year, including this year, and we haven't even begun to use them. We also bought five hydraulic bin-fillers—at thirty-five thousand dollars each."

"Send them back."

"Impossible, dad."

"You should have known that you couldn't sneak around me and get away with it. You're trying to take advantage of me because I haven't been my old self lately. Well, let me tell you. . . ." He was growing short of breath.

Jana stepped in front of Peter.

"Sir," she said, "why don't you return to Mariposa when the harvesters are unloaded? Perhaps you'll be able to judge better what they can and cannot do. I'm sure that Peter gave a good deal of thought to buying them."

"They're not going to be unloaded. I'll blow the damned things up first. Where's Moose? Oh, there you are. Get this junk off my land."

"They're on *my* land, Joe," Miss Mari reminded him.

Jana pulled up a peach box and sat down at Mr. Milford's feet. Her dress was dragging in the dirt. She didn't care.

"It's not what you think, sir. Although these harvesters are shakers, they won't rattle the treetrunks and kill the trees."

"Those trees have been in the ground ten, fifteen and

twenty years. They're good producers. Disease-free, even rare," Joe said angrily.

"Sir, I've heard that these machines shake the peach trees so that they actually stimulate the root system and help the trees grow. And when the peaches fall, they don't hit the dirt or some hard conveyer belt. They fall ever so gently into a soft, upturned umbrella, where they are gently sorted and guided into fifty-pound bins right out in the orchard. From there they go into thousand-pound containers, and they're ready for the cannery."

"Yes, and that's only the beginning of our troubles. The cannery insists on peaches that are two and three-sixteenths inches in diameter, not two and one-fourth inches. How is some damned machine going to know that?"

"Mr. Milford, machines don't know very much, but that little bit of information has been drilled into their heads from the moment they were conceived."

"Conceived, eh? That's a good one." He smiled for the first time.

"There have been computer studies that have simulated what happens to peaches when they are harvested by various methods."

"Rubbish."

"And there have been actual on-site studies that have shown that with the right kind of equipment, there is less damage to the fruit than when it's hand-picked."

"Girl, don't tell me there is anything better than those Mexicans packing peaches in little green tissue paper and stacking them on the back of trucks for my drivers to take to the markets."

"Joe," protested Miss Mari, "we haven't done that in years. You're thinking of the days when Mariposa sold mostly freestones."

Aline frowned at Miss Mari for bringing up Joe's memory again.

"In fact," continued Miss Mari, "I've been hoping that you would plant freestones again in the southeast orchard. The trees there are about twenty-three years old, which is too old, and you and Moose know better.

"What the hell for? The canneries reject them: they taste too good, look too pretty. They float around in the cans like peaches are supposed to, and don't look and taste like softballs crammed in cans the way those clingstones do."

"Mr. Milford," said Jana, "I think I can promise you that Peter weighed all the options open to him when he purchased this machinery for Mariposa."

"I'll bet he didn't even know about the meta-orchards. And I'll bet you don't, either. What are you, anyway, a spy?" His eyes were twinkling.

"The meta-orchards are being tried a few places in this country, but there are some serious questions about them."

"Such as?" Joe challenged.

"When you plant your trees every six inches to a foot apart and allow them to grow in order to be harvested like wheat, you strip off the leaves as well as the fruit. Generally, from July to October, the leaves are photosynthesizing, putting nutrients back into the root system. Without their leaves, we don't know how long trees will last. The cost of establishing a meta-orchard is tremendous—some forty to fifty thousand an acre."

"Yeah?"

"I know for a fact that Peter considered it after his experience with labor last year, and decided that Mariposa should invest in the more dependable machines. Each one replaces forty persons."

"Men," insisted Mr. Milford.

"Peter felt that it just didn't make sense to put so much of Mariposa's resources into fertilizers, pesticides and taxes, and then to be so dependent on an undependable labor force. You know there's nothing worse than the sound of a peach dropping. It's like money falling out of trees.

"Peter is also considering alternate crops, to replace the dozen or so acres of figs that are grown here."

"Like what? Banty hens?"

"No." Now it was Jana's turn to smile. "Like almonds or walnuts. There is almost no labor problem with those crops, and the end-product is closer to being ready for the market than peaches—which have to go through a series of steps.

"But, as you know, Mr. Milford, harvesting is really a very small part of the growing cycle of a tree. It's not the most important part. There's nothing to harvest if you haven't taken care of the trees beforehand—if you've failed at irrigating, pruning, spraying. Peter is interested in developing a year-round labor force."

"Yes, and I suppose he wants to build houses for them, give

them a swimming pool, an ice-skating rink and a discount grocery store," Joe snorted.

"I don't know. I haven't talked to him about that. I think he's been hesitant because of your illness, but I think that now the two of you can talk, make some plans."

"But I'm selling Mariposa. There's nothing to talk about, remember?" Mr. Milford looked up at Peter, who was standing behind Jana.

"Mr. Milford, why don't you consider giving your son just a month? See how things go with the machines. It's possible that you may have an enormous harvest, even considering all the extra labor he has had to hire through no fault of his own, but because of Havermeyer. It makes very good equipment, but it's not the most thoughtful corporation. Money is the name of the game, you know."

"Hell, it's the name of *any* good game."

"Give me a month, dad. Arrange the sale, if you wish, but don't sign the papers."

"Go on, Joe, give the kid a month," echoed Aline with earnestness.

"What do you say, Mari?"

"I say, give him as long as he needs."

"You're a bleeding heart. I knew you'd say that. All right. You've got a month. But you make hellfire sure that everybody around here believes that these contraptions are *your* idea. Because I've already made it known I wouldn't have 'em."

"But, Joe," said Miss Mari. "It's important that everybody knows you are backing Pete. Don't you agree, Moose?"

He had stepped behind Aline and his forehead was wrinkled. "This place is becoming an experimental playground."

"Mari, I'll send a letter to Mariposa employees and I'll phone San Francisco. No, maybe I'd better not say anything to the main office."

"Why not?" asked Miss Mari.

"I'm afraid that word will get around and the grapepickers will think that the next thing we're going to do is pick grapes with a machine. That would be an impossible mess." He turned to Jana. "Don't you agree, darling?"

"I've heard there are some very efficient. . . ."

"My Lord, she talks like a spy. Smart little thing though, ain't she?" He winked at Peter.

Mr. Milford stood up, and as he walked toward the front of Miss Mari's, he said, "I thought today that Mariposa was a hundred percent gone. I never thought Peter would have the nerve to sink Mariposa's money in five harvesters. But I can understand the circumstances—and I can see that my illness put him in a spot."

He patted Peter on the back. "I don't blame you, my boy. And if you can manage it—which I don't think you can—I'll be proud. In any case, you've shown me that you can make decisions—wrong as they may be."

Peter opened the back door of the limousine, but Aline held back.

"Miss Mari, this visit has been perfect for Joe. I've never seen him as upset as he was when he thought he had finally decided to sell this place. And now look at him—talking and laughing. He's got a son he can be proud of. I tell you, until today, I had my doubts about that boy. And, Miss Mari, could you give me your recipe for that peach ice?"

The gray limousine had cruised past the office while Peter, Jana and Miss Mari, too stunned to return to the house immediately, stood there and waved, even though they couldn't see anyone to wave to through the smoked glass.

When the car was halfway to the main road, it stopped and backed up. When it had pulled up alongside the front gate again, the sun roof rolled back and Mr. Milford stood up and leaned his elbows on the car. "Any other peach ranch have forty thousand visitors?" he asked.

"No, Joe," said Miss Mari. "You know they don't want anybody eating their clingstones. People might discover what they taste like before they're disguised with syrup at the cannery."

Aline popped up beside Joe. "And don't forget to send me the recipe," she said as the car pulled away, the two of them waving to the group they had left behind like people being honored in a parade.

Not until the car had turned onto the highway and the dust from Mariposa's roads had settled down did Peter hug Miss Mari, then gallantly turn to Jana and say, "Hey, hey! We've got ourselves a little breathing spell."

"Thanks to Jana," said Miss Mari firmly.

"No thanks to Jana," said Moose. "It won't work."

"I don't know how those drivers dared stop here tonight. I told them—you heard me, Miss Mari. . . ."

"Never mind," said Peter. "If the trucks hadn't been here, we never would have faced the issue. And look how much better he felt."

"We're both grateful to you, Jana," said Miss Mari.

"Let's all go home," said Peter, "and get some sleep. May I borrow your Volvo, Miss Mari?"

"You may not. You may be my only charming nephew, but I'll feel much more charmed knowing you aren't chasing around in my only car."

"I'll take you home," said Jana.

"Thanks. You can drop me at the pool. I'll swim up and down until I'm half asleep. God, what a day."

"And I," said Miss Mari, "will have a long talk with Moose." She kissed him on the cheek. As they walked through the yard, Jana could hear her say, "You've been feeling neglected lately, and it's my fault. Let's finish that wine, what do you say?"

Peter was remarkably silent all the way back to Fresno. That was fine with Jana. She knew exactly what would happen next, and she was preparing herself for it. The night had been successful so far. But there would be more, much more.

Peter would ask her to join him at the pool. And how different it would be than with Andy. They would swim together, not passively, but ambitiously. He would beat her in a race; then, lifting her out of the water, he would lay her down on the monogrammed royal blue velour towels. She had seen them at the back of the cabana. He would kiss her, holding her so close that the kiss would penetrate her entire being and body. It would be the way he wanted it: she would make sure of that.

He might crush her at first, but she would gather strength and refuse to be crushed. She would hold herself open to him and, with his release of passion, there would be love. He would learn there was no other woman for him, because she had it all. She could help him at every step—in and out of the bedroom.

Jana watched Peter's hands on the steering wheel. Soon, they would be caressing her. Soon, she would know those hands.

As they were waiting for the gate to open at the estate,

Peter finally spoke. "I praised you in front of Miss Mari this evening, but I want you to know that not for a minute did I think you were doing anything but saving your own skin with Havermeyer."

The weakest, least violent emotions Jana felt were released, and she screamed: "Get out of this car, Peter! And *walk* to your damned pool."

Chapter 10

Jana drove unthinkingly through the streets. The car's engine could have run on her fury alone. She should, however, open the hood and see what *was* making it run. It sounded worse than ever.

Teenagers were hanging out in parking lots of grocery stores and businesses along the street. This must be a main drag for them. They were sitting on the parked cars, watching other cars drive up and down. She had no idea where she was, or how to get home.

Jana drove around the block and backtracked to a McDonald's she had passed. She would calm down, then ask somebody for directions.

She drove to the take-out window, ordered a vanilla milkshake, and parked in front of the establishment's one oleander bush.

Jana had thought that, tonight, Peter had not only begun to tolerate her, but had even started to like her. And, surely, he had seen how useful she could be to him, helping him to do what he wanted to do all along—save Mariposa, gain himself a little time to do so. Besides, who had been his ally until she arrived? Certainly not Moose. And Miss Mari had obviously been torn in her loyalties—whatever they were—between Moose and Peter.

Star light, star bright. Why couldn't I have been Susan, just for tonight?

That was it. If she had been Susan, she would be down there now, swimming with Peter, and he would be loving her. Had she *asked* that he love? No. They would make a terrific team. All she asked was that he recognize it.

Apparently, a show of skill and concern about Mariposa, while pleasing to Miss Mari and Mr. Milford, had aroused Peter's suspicions and caused him to dislike and mistrust her even more.

Dammit, as Mr. Milford would have said, Peter had had no right to ask her to that dinner if he had thought she was going to say something *against* Havermeyer.

In spite of the cold milkshake, Jana was inwardly burning. And never mind the smooth way Peter glided over Havermeyer's untimely delivery of the harvesters. Apparently, he blamed her for that, too.

Was any of this worth her effort? The worst businesses in the world were operated by families. Seventy percent of family businesses did not last into the second generation. And it was no wonder.

The lights flickered on the teenagers in front of her. They were playing in the mobile built for five year olds. Their beautiful bodies, practically naked in their skimpy shorts and halters, reminded her of Andy.

She had been humiliated by Peter. He had *used* her. And, yet, the evening hadn't been a loss. She had been touched at seeing how protective Miss Mari, Aline—even Peter—had been of Joe Milford. Miss Mari's home was a good influence on that family. Everything in it seemed to glow.

Even Miss Mari seemed to have an inward light that was the source of her energy. By contrast, Jana felt as though all her life her inner guide had been an awful, opaque stick—which she used to drive herself toward success.

But was she entirely heartless? She *had* quit her job with Engineered Edibles. She had been physically revolted to hear over and over that the corporation was riding on the wave—the gloppy, artificial wave—of the future. And she wanted no part in it.

That didn't make her any the less unhappy with herself. She backed up and pulled out into the street. A few seconds later, she heard the honk of the Jaguar behind her. It was Peter. Was he following or passing her?

She sped on.

He pulled the Jaguar in front of her and motioned her to a side street. Thinking there was something wrong with the damned car, she obeyed.

He leaned in her window and indicated that she should unlock the door and get out.

She did. Her car must be on fire. Peter looked like hell. Something terrible had happened: his father had been in a car wreck; Susan had committed suicide; Ken had a serious concussion, after all.

"What is it?" she gasped.

Peter pushed her against the side of the Mercedes and, with no pressure point less than any other, he crushed her in his arms, kissing her more deeply, more passionately, than anyone ever had.

There was no space in which she could respond. He had her pinned against the car, against himself.

"Come home with me. I need you. You were brilliant tonight. I couldn't admit it. I don't know why."

His hand was on her shoulder, just above her breast. On her breast. The thin layer of silk was too much. Tears were in his eyes and he was breathing heavily. His muscular chest was so large. Could she ever put her arms all the way around it?

Jana snatched the keys out of the Mercedes, rolled up the windows and walked straight to the Jaguar.

When Peter was not shifting, he was holding her hand, her shoulder. Five blocks. Four blocks. Three. Two. One.

"We can swim together. Cleanse this day from us."

"Ginni's death was as hard on you as anybody, wasn't it?"

"God," he said. "It was awful. And, today, when we went back up there . . . and then to see Susan so upset. It was her little sister. Ginni and I, we had always been special pals. But Susan. . . ."

Jana felt terrible for Peter. But she felt worse for herself. Was she going to be his Susan-substitute for the night? Was she really? Weren't there some things even worse than participating in the construction of a lousy lemon, a plastic pear?

"Peter, I've changed my mind. I can't go with you. I feel terribly saddened by what you are feeling. But I don't think I can help you through the night. It's something you'll have to face alone—or maybe eventually with Susan."

"What do you know about that?"

"Only what she told me: that you two had been married. And the rumor seems to be that you've never gotten over her."

"Is that all?"

"Yes."

"Is Andy waiting for you? Would you rather be with him than with me? It doesn't have to mean any more with me than it would with him."

"I'm not that indiscriminate, and, no, Andy is not waiting for me."

"Why the hell are you staying there, anyway, after what I said to you?"

"Peter, I'll see you in the morning."

"Do you know how to find your complex by yourself?"

She said she didn't.

"I'll lead you there."

Jana felt fortunate that he did, and that Andy did not loom out of the shadows as she slipped into Gretchen's house.

She lay in bed and was almost asleep when she heard a splash in the pool. Raising up, she saw Andy swimming back and forth from one end of the small pool to the other. When he emerged, he walked as if he felt as heavy as marble, and disappeared in the direction of his house.

Jana wanted him to be with her—she wanted his innocence, his ease, his touchable, edible body. But, if Andy was the sun, Peter was the moon, pulling, pulling her toward him, replacing the earth's relationships so that she couldn't remember where she had once been. Peter couldn't help it. He belonged to Susan. She had to understand.

Peter's force had pulled and directed her according to *his* emotions. And she had almost fallen for it, because she had been so driven by her own. . . .

"Get up!"

Jana turned. Gretchen was in the doorway. She closed her eyes. The sun flooded into the horrible room, glanced off the mirror and into her face. There was no getting away from it.

"Andy asked about you a few minutes ago," continued Gretchen. "He said that you should be at Mariposa especially early this morning. Since he's giving me a ride to my bone lecture, he has to leave a little early. Don't you want to ride with us?

"Damn this summer school, anyway," Gretchen moaned.
"I don't know if I can take any more early morning revelations. Yesterday he told us that in the story of David and
Goliath, any aborigine would have thought Goliath was a fool
for wearing all that armor, because anybody knew that the
best way to kill was with a lightweight slingshot and not spears
and hot, heavy, armor. Ever notice how anthropologists love
to deflate heroes?"

Jana didn't have the strength or the inclination to tell
Gretchen that Goliath was not the hero of that tale. She
wished Gretchen would leave, but as she dressed, Gretchen
sat down on the edge of the bed and watched as if she had just
discovered a new species.

Jana slipped into a pair of blue jeans—the pair she almost
had neglected to pack—and a pale orange T-shirt.

As she brushed her hair, Gretchen continued her running
commentary. "Where were you last night? Andy almost
drove me crazy, pacing up and down by the pool. He didn't
even have anybody over. This place is becoming so quiet that
I can't study."

"Gretchen, I didn't know the way home. After dinner at
Miss Mari's, Peter Milford had to guide me here. End of
story. Okay?"

"And what were you and Peter Milford doing? I think
that's really what was on Andy's mind."

"We were having a fight."

"Oh? A lover's quarrel already. That's interesting.
You know, fighting between lovers is a universal phenome-
non. I met this guy in my anthro lecture, and I've invited
him here today for a swim. What do you think I should
feed him?"

"Gretchen, I don't know. Whatever you have in the
refrigerator." Jana wasn't even sure where the refrigerator
was.

When she encountered Andy at his car, he kissed her stiffly
on the mouth.

"Thanks for waking me up."

"It would have been simpler if you had been in my bed."

"Andy, for heaven's sake, don't *you* get complicated."

"Where were you?"

"At Miss Mari's. You know that. I took Peter to his house
to get his car. And he led me home."

"I would have shown you the way. Why didn't you call?"

"Because I was tired and having him show me was the fastest."

With Gretchen all ears, Andy continued, "I missed you last night. It was supposed to be *my* night, remember?"

Jana was too tired to unravel the complications Andy was weaving. They drove in silence until they dropped Gretchen off.

"What did they say about me?" was the first thing he asked when they were alone.

"Oh, you were the main topic of conversation the whole evening," she said sarcastically.

"Peter made a lot of accusations, didn't he?"

"Andy, nobody mentioned you at all. Are you disappointed?"

He said nothing for a moment while he digested what she said. Finally, he added, "I talked to my mom. She says they'll have memorial services for Ginni next week. They're going to sprinkle her ashes over the ocean."

"Are you planning to be there?"

"Susan advised me against it—mainly because of Ken. The girls will be there. Mom can make it without me. They'll all sit around and talk about the black sheep of the family. Ken can remind everyone how Ginni—how she and I never got along, anyway.

"Dammit. If I could only get away from the entire bunch of them. They think they know me. They don't at all. I want to get as far from them as I can."

"Just finish up with grad school and you'll be entirely on your own," she encouraged him.

"I'll never be free of them. Denver has my life all planned. He says he's making it easy for me."

Jana debated about whether or not to comment further on Andy's dissatisfactions. She decided against it.

"Andy," she said, "have you ever been to Miss Mari's Tourist Center?"

"Sure."

"Where is it?"

"Across the road from the office and about two miles down. It's a well-kept secret—something Miss Mari sort of sprang on Mariposa."

"Could we visit there at noon?"

"Are you sure you wouldn't rather spend your lunch hour with the Milfords?"

Jana leaned back and pushed her feet to the floor. Perhaps she had done as much good in California as she ever would. From now on, the complications pressing on her from every direction might not be worth it. Only winning was worth it, and the chances for that seemed to grow slimmer with her every encounter.

Chapter 11

When she heard Cassie exclaim through her screened window, "Pete, honey, I loved our swim last night," Jana was glad she had not given in to her almost overwhelming urge to follow Peter to the end of his pool, the end of his world.

As for her daytime tasks: she still felt uneasy about remaining at Mariposa as long as she worked mainly in the weigh house. And when she heard from one of the drivers that Peter had called everyone to a meeting that evening, she was hurt, insulted and puzzled.

It probably concerned the harvesters. Jana could have helped him. She had the answers to questions he couldn't answer. Or if he answered too bluntly, she had ready examples of other orchards—besides Calimyrna—that had used the harvesters. She could have rattled off figures for Mariposa, or compared hand-picking to mechanical harvesting on the east, west and gulf coasts.

That was the trouble with this ranch: nothing was strictly business. Decisions were made on the basis of emotions Jana had never known.

Ruby poked her head in the door. When she saw Jana, she immediately retreated.

"What's up?" asked Jana, following her.

"You tell me," said the little woman coldly, as she turned

back to her job of pitching out undersized or damaged peaches.

Jana had no rapport with Ruby or any of the sorters. She had made no headway in persuading them to trust either her own or Peter's judgment. They saw him as the kid they had once known—a kid who was turning their lives around. Her, they didn't see at all.

Jana stared at the still-loaded Havermeyer trucks, conspicuously parked behind Miss Mari. They were mountainous objects between the house and the real mountains. How fitting, Jana thought.

What if she *had* gone with Peter the night before? Would it have advanced her position if she had poured it on: "What prowess, what heights, what ho—whatever. . . ." He would have melted. Men did. Women knew a line when they heard it. At least, *she* did. The timing had not been right. Jana was certain that if she had gone with him, she would not have been any more sincere.

But wanting to go home with Peter—with somebody— made her feel even more off-balance. What was happening to her?

Cassie laid down a *tatami* mat on the floor and plopped. "One, two, three, four." She kicked her legs up in the air, one after the other.

What if Jana said, Cassie, did you know you were Peter's third choice last night?

And what if Cassie said, And who was first?

Susan.

Second?

A Susan-substitute.

Oh, she would probably say, I've been his third choice for years. That's why I know I'll get him: you see, I'm the charm.

"One, two, three, four."

Jana came back to earth and noticed that Moose was standing in the doorway. He glared at her, removed his cap and scratched his head as he watched Cassie rolling and straining.

As soon as he had gone, Cassie gasped, "Have you ever . . ." puff, puff, "heard of anybody being rubbed with suntan oil by the light of the moon?"

Jana turned away.

"Well, you have now." Cassie was like a cat reaffirming claims to her territory.

Venturing out again onto the enemy bunker of the platform, Jana chose a peach for herself, sat down on a wooden bench. Should she eat it, or talk to the women?

"Jana," said Ruby, "did you know that Francine here has worked at Mariposa since she was sixteen years old? She has five children and, in all these years, Mariposa has paid her the only money she's made on her own. She wouldn't have missed her Mariposa summers for anything—not even a vacation. Do you think there will be a Mariposa at this time next summer, or will Peter have ruined it for everybody?"

"Sure," said Jana, smiling. "It may not appear like it, but he's just now laying the groundwork for a Mariposa that will be stronger than ever. Maybe he'll tell you about it at the meeting."

Jana wandered back into the weigh house, where she waited through the slow morning thinking that lunchtime would never come. When Andy finally honked for her, she ran with relief to his truck.

"I brought some cheese sandwiches for us," he said. "I thought that for dessert we could either sample Miss Mari's freestone freebies or a swirl or two of her peach ice. The Tourist Center is the only place in the valley that makes it. Restaurants and take-out joints serve peach ice cream and yogurt, but this is the real thing."

"It couldn't be totally peach ice," said Jana, "or the frozen liquid would stick to the machinery. It must have some kind of glutinous additive—that isn't necessarily bad."

"What?"

"A glutinous additive."

"Don't talk to me about that stuff. I heard the other day that people are working on imitation sliced peaches, which they're planning to hawk for frozen peach cobbler, pies, ice cream and puddings."

"Yes. They call it the Emperor's New Peaches."

Andy laughed.

"When I was at MIT, I worked on one of those imitation food projects funded by the government."

"You never told me you went there. In fact, I have a feeling there are lots of things you haven't confided to me."

"Andy, when have we had time?"

He stopped the truck outside a Quonset hut surrounded by trees and vines. Mariposa Tourist Center, the sign proclaimed. All profits from sales go to the Save Yosemite Committee (SYC).

"Hurry," said Andy as they rushed past the gift-shop counter. "The movie is about to begin."

They sat in the back of a small makeshift movie theater at one end of the Quonset hut, which was miraculously air-conditioned. Tourists, their mouths open, ready to be fed anything, were silencing their children, cooling off—or catching up on things they had not been able to do in their cars, like kissing and diapering babies.

"The peach," said a scratchy voice-over, "is known to most people as a fruit that tastes sweet without having as many calories as an apple." A giant peach was shown on the screen—doing nothing. "But to us here at Mariposa, a peach is known as *prunus persica,* a fruit of the cherry, plum and apricot family—a little gift of nature brought to the New World from China by the Spaniards, then carried into California by explorers, settlers and the Indians."

The voice, taped for classroom documentaries of the 1940s, continued: "The peach has five petals on its flower, which is usually—but not always—pink. The ovary—that's the reproductive center where the seed grows—becomes the fruit of the peach. And as the fruit ripens, there is an increase in sugar-content, and an emission of a volatile substance that gives the fruit its peachy smell."

"Let's go," said Andy, whose hand had moved up her leg.

She lifted it away and said, "No, I want to see how terrible this is."

"A nectarine is a smooth-skinned peach developed from the common peach through experimentation. We at Mariposa grow only real peaches."

The movie was showing men standing on ladders, dropping peaches into bags slung around their necks. The voice now sounded as if it had fallen down a well.

As the film switched into animation, the children in the audience clapped. Now, a furry white creature was standing at the base of a peach tree. It was the North Wind and he was shaking the peaches so hard that they fell to the ground, and every time one hit, it said, "ouch" and cried real peach juice.

"There is," said the all-knowing, well-articulated voice, "also the limb-shaker method, whereby the limbs of the peach tree and not the trunk are shaken. These peaches are allowed to land on a canvas conveyer belt, which supposedly cushions their fall, then jiggles and sorts the remaining peaches into boxes that are weighed by the machines out in the field.

"There is also the Big Bad Wolf machine, which blows the peaches off the tree." The film showed little, piggy-shaped peaches being hit by a hurricane.

"Needless to say," said the narrator, "Mariposa has never treated its peaches with such cruelty." Salesmen for the wicked machines were shown marching along a Mariposa road wearing handcuffs. They entered a building labeled The Society for the Prevention of Cruelty to Peaches.

"Now," said a new voice, which sounded like Snow White just after the Prince arrived, "Mariposa brings its peaches to you in a more heavenly, natural way." Muzak played, butterflies fluttered in, and out of the peach tree branches—every time a chubby animated hand picked a peach—a chorus of children's voices sang until the peach wafted into heaven. When all the peaches had gone, a chorus singing English words to the finale of Beethoven's Ninth Symphony rose in praise, and the orchard fell asleep to plan for next season's happy peaches.

The lights came on and the children screamed and clapped. People lined up on one side of the "peachateria" for bagged, chipped, frittered or iced peaches. Further purchases could be made in the snack bar or the gift shop.

"We have to be back at work in thirty minutes, Jana. We've hardly had any time to spend alone." Andy tugged at her arm.

"I want to look in the gift shop, first."

Against his will, Andy followed her. Jana was surprised to find peach brandy, and dozens of pieces of little brown jewelry.

"What are those things made of?"

"Carved peach pits. They're as hard as petrified wood. Moose makes them during the winter. These are not for sale, but people can place orders for them. As soon as Moose gets around to it, they'll get their orders. Moose carves the buyers' initials into every piece. Isn't that the dumbest thing you ever heard? Custom-made peach pits."

"I think it's rather sweet for Moose to do it at all."

"He'd do anything—anything at all—for Miss Mari. Now, let's go, Jana."

"Wait. We haven't been to the P.O. Maybe I'll send a package from the Peach Office to one of my peachy friends at home."

"It makes me sick. I need a big chew of licorice." Andy made a face.

"Jana! What are you doing here? And Andy? How are you?" A contralto voice rang out.

Miss Mari carried a basket filled with jars of peach preserves. "Have you seen the movie? What do you think of it? Be honest, now."

"We both thought it looked like something shown to second graders during World War Two."

"Andy!" Jana cried.

"I couldn't agree with you more. Appalling, isn't it? But, last summer, one of the women on the platform had a son home from college. He was interested in doing a project for his animation workshop. We thought of calling it 'Peachy Tunes.' It would feature Elmer Fuzz as the main character. So, you see, it could have been worse."

Jana was laughing with Miss Mari. Andy was not.

"Come on in the back room. I want to ask you what you think of a movie I've just commissioned. It hasn't been edited yet. It's about Yosemite and where all this money is going."

"Miss Mari, I'd love to see it, but our lunch hour is almost over, and you know Moose."

"Indeed I do."

"Jana's going to be holding down a big job someday, and the corporation will appreciate her sense of duty." Andy was being sarcastic.

"I'd like to see the movie," said Jana. "I've never been to Yosemite."

"Then I wouldn't dream of allowing you to view it. You should see Yosemite firsthand the first time around."

"And I thought we were about to see another terrible movie," said Andy as soon as they were in the car. He kissed her with relief. And then again. . . .

"Andy, we don't have time. Anyway, I'm sure the Yosemite movie is an improvement over the one they're showing now. Besides, I think the Tourist Center is a delight—considering that it's run almost completely by Miss Mari's volunteers."

"Did you really mean it, Jana, about wanting to see Yosemite?"

"I'll never have time."

"I heard that if there's trouble at the meeting Peter has called tonight, he'll close down the ranch for a day or two of talks with the pickers."

"Only the pickers?"

"Milford doesn't need to indoctrinate the drivers. They're college people, and won't form the steady work force he keeps promising everybody."

As Andy drove past the office, Peter leapt off the porch and hailed him down. He walked around to Jana's side of the car, looking disturbed but not angry. "I don't want to alarm you," he said, "but your scales and desk in the weigh house have been tampered with."

"What do you mean?"

"The scales are wrecked—at least for a couple of days—and your desk has got machine oil and mud all over it. Somebody's in there cleaning it up right now. I want you to get out of here for a few days until I can find out who did it. Go on to your house, and don't come back out here until I call you."

For a moment, Jana thought he was going to say, "Take the next plane out of here."

"But I thought you were having meetings with the pickers." Jana gave him a pointed look. She couldn't say too much with Andy in the car. "Won't you be showing them the harvesters?"

"No. The Havermeyer drivers have gone to San Francisco —I loaned them my dad's Rolls Royce. We can't unload the equipment until they return."

"You bribed them."

"Buying time, Jana, buying time. Now get out of here, before something else happens."

"I don't have my car."

Peter waved his arms in the air with exasperation. "Take Andy's car. Take Andy. Both of you, scram. But, Andy, watch out for anybody strange around that complex. And if either of you feel there is any danger, I want to know about it. Immediately."

Andy whistled, "Yosemite here we come," all the way back to Fresno.

Chapter 12

"But where would we stay in Yosemite? I've heard that everything is booked for years in the summer. And I'm not one to camp out," Jana warned.

"I'm sure of that," Andy said. "As soon as we arrive at the house, I'll telephone a friend of mine who is a national park ranger up there. We might be able to stay with him and his wife this weekend."

"That would be perfect." Jana did not want to hole up with Andy in a hotel room. Peter would be certain to hear about it.

"Of course," said Andy, "if you would rather camp out with the bears, the bugs and the burglars . . . ?"

"No thanks."

"There are as many as forty thousand people in Yosemite Valley on summer weekends, and they want to see all the sights that you probably have in mind—like Bridal Veil Falls, El Capitán, Half-Dome and the Cathedral Rocks."

"All that and more."

While Andy telephoned his friend, Jana tossed blue jeans, sneakers, a jacket and a raincoat into a suitcase. Impetuously, she also threw in a full-length, halter-style dress of thin material.

The last item she packed was a pair of heavy, cotton-flannel pajamas. She had heard it could be cold in the mountains, though after the San Joaquin Valley and the hot days at Mariposa, she couldn't imagine ever being cold again.

They drove out of Fresno at 4:00 A.M. the next morning. Andy followed Highway 41 northeast. He seemed jubilant, and talked even more than usual. Perhaps it was the early hour, but Jana was bothered by his talking. It seemed he should be as quiet as the world was.

"You know where the San Joaquin Valley got its name?"

"Of course I don't."

"From a bandit named Joaquin Marrieta. He was finally captured near Coalinga—a town west of Fresno."

"Fascinating," mumbled Jana, barely awake.

"Over ten million acres of almonds, peaches, plums, pears, cherries, apricots, prunes, raisins, olives, figs and—if you can believe it—many other fruits and vegetables, are grown here."

"I believe," said Jana, closing her eyes.

"You didn't know you were spending the summer in a famous desert, did you?"

"No, but I once considered living in the desert." Joining the Foreign Legion, to be exact, she thought. That was when her company in Davenport had assigned her to the artificial artichoke project.

"You've heard of the naturalist John Muir?"

"Yes, Miss Mari talked about him being a friend of her grandfather."

"Wouldn't you know that he would be a friend of the Milfords. They may know everybody—but they don't know everything. If Muir hadn't had such wide influence, Yosemite would have neon signs and hamburger stands everywhere. Thanks to him, the scenery is fairly well-preserved. The Sierra Club and the Wilderness Society still have to watchdog the park to keep the government from selling out. The Yosemite Park and Curry Company, which is owned by the Music Corporation of America—you know, the company that owns Universal Artists—runs all the concessions in the park, including the hotels and lodges. Shortly after that company bought into the park, environmentalists turned out in droves."

"You sound like a true Californian—the kind Miss Mari likes."

"I don't know about that. But the average native doesn't appreciate the beauty of this state, nor the necessity of preserving it. Old man Milford, I hear, is one of the worst. And if you ask me, once Peter gets enough power, he'll start doing a modern number of ravaging the land—just like his father has done."

"What do you mean?"

"I heard that Peter has already bought up huge supplies of DPCB."

"The chemical that gives cancer to rats? Where did you hear that?"

Andy ignored her question. "He's going to use it in spite of the fact that it's been outlawed. I'm glad I don't have to go to his stupid meeting with the pickers and the women. I couldn't bear to listen to any of his platitudes. I hope everybody gives him hell."

Jana glanced at Andy's profile. His nose was too pointed when viewed from the side. But she did want to see Yosemite.

They passed by the small towns of Coarsegold and Oakhurst. "Now, keep your eyes open," he said, "you're in for a surprise."

Suddenly, they were plunged into total darkness. Andy flipped on the headlights.

"It's the Wawona Tunnel. Are your eyes open?"

"No!" Tunnels always made her feel trapped. She had once had a children's book that told about a landslide that covered the end of a Swiss tunnel. She half-expected the same thing to happen here. Instead, as they emerged from the blackness, before her was Bridal Veil Falls splashing down from on high like streams of lace. At the same time, she could also see the soaring granite peaks of Cathedral Rock and El Capitán as well as Half-Dome.

"This scene is called Discovery View."

"Why did someone have to name it?"

"Don't you know? In parks, people name everything they can. It's their way of taming nature. You don't have to pay any attention to the names. Certainly, the rocks don't know what they're called. Nor the trees. Ponderosa, sugar pine, incense cedar . . . it doesn't matter to them."

"Andy. Stop." Jana had never seen a valley where the sheer drop from the top of the mountains was so great and the valley floor so flat and narrow.

"Frederick Law Olmstead—you know, the guy who designed New York's Central Park—was responsible for the original plan of the valley. It's gotten a little out of hand, however. There are over sixteen hundred structures down there, and the valley is only seven miles long and a mile wide.

"Before John Muir came along and proposed the glacier theory for Yosemite, it was thought the valley was formed because the bottom had dropped out of the mountains."

"Sometimes," said Jana, reaching over and kissing him on the cheek, "that's been my theory of the world."

"Me, too," he said, "until you came along."

"I never knew you were so interested in trees and mountains. You'd be a good park ranger."

"I think so, too. But there's no money in it."

"I didn't know you cared about money that much."

"My dad says. . . ."

"Look at the falls now. There are two rainbows in it. Could we stop?"

"Those falls are even higher than they seem. Muir, for example, thought they were sixty to seventy feet high, when actually they're six hundred and twenty feet."

Jana gasped appropriately.

"When Muir first visited the Sierra Nevada, men were cutting down these trees and using the wood for house shingles and stakes to hold up grapevines. He founded the Sierra Club, and even persuaded President Theodore Roosevelt to camp out here with him for two nights. It was after that that the President proclaimed Yosemite and a number of other sites in the United States as part of the National Parks system.

"One of Muir's big disappointments, however, was his inability to preserve the Hetch-hetchy Valley. During his lifetime, he saw it turned into a reservoir for San Francisco's water supply. It remains a reservoir today, and people are deprived of seeing the beautiful valley it must have been. But worse things than that have been done up here. They filmed a flop television series up here, and even painted some of the boulders the color called for in the script."

After parking the car, Andy guided Jana onto a shuttle bus designed to minimize traffic problems in the valley. She marveled at the giant ferns standing almost equidistant from one another, and at the awe she felt down in the enclosed spaciousness of these mountain walls.

It made her happy to see Andy in his element. His nose looked less pointed. But what was he doing studying business, anyway?

With delight, Andy continually pointed out animals and plants she never would have seen without him.

"That's an ouzel—that little bird wading over there in the stream. And look, up there—a Stellars jay. That little beggar loves tourists, because they give him a free lunch. And speaking of lunch. . . ."

He bought Jana a hot dog. The paths in the valley were becoming more and more crowded as the double-decker shuttle buses continued to bring in hundreds of tourists.

"They're adding more buses because visitors are now trampling through here at the rate of over two million a year, and the park is beginning to look a little shabby."

"I suppose the only real tourist problem is here, isn't it?"

"You'd be surprised." He pointed toward the vertical granite drop of Half-Dome. "That entire side of the granite is marred with rusty pitons—those little pegs that mountain climbers hammer in to hold themselves as they climb to the top. I removed dozens of them when I made my climb."

"You crawled up the side of that rock?"

"Sure. It took almost three days to maneuver two thousand feet."

"And you didn't sleep?"

"Of course, I did. I nestled on a ten-inch ledge and lassoed myself to étriers—little nylon, stirrup-type loops that I hammered into cracks in the granite. The second night, I rigged up a hammock and hung from the rocks. I slept—but the sleep wasn't exactly sound."

"You enjoy climbing around like that?"

"I'd have liked it better if you had been with me."

"Thanks, but that will never happen. How did you get down?"

"I jumped off."

"Andy!" It was fun to be with someone who wasn't juggling Mariposa problems in his head—someone who was having a good time showing off.

"Actually, I lowered myself down the backside of Half-Dome. First I had the help of cables, and after that I merely walked down on a well-worn hiking trail."

"I've never understood how mountain climbers keep from falling when there's no place to put their feet, or anything to grab hold of."

"You can't see the little toeholds from down below. Even a small crack is a fine place to hang a foot. Other times—when you feel as though you might be clinging by your fingernails, if only they were strong enough—you can use a substitute fingernail called a sky hook. They're made to grasp bare rock."

The scowl on his forehead completely disappeared, and his lips seemed to curl in a more gentle line. She forced herself not to reach over and touch his chin, his lips.

"There's the Awahnee Hotel."

"It looks like a nice place to stay," said Jana, observing the three-story, log-cabin structure.

"Sorry, I made other plans. But we are eating dinner there, do you mind? I thought we should have something nice to do tonight."

Jana was relieved that they would be in a small cabin with his friends. Andy's arm pulled tighter around her waist. He was ready for her at that moment, and it made her want him—almost more desperately than she had that night at the pool.

Jana looked up at the peaks soaring thousands of feet above them. Andy probably thought she was smiling because of the wonders of nature, when, actually, it was his own wonder that she was thinking of.

"Hey!" He snapped his fingers to break her gaze. "Let's hunt down the cabin."

They retrieved the car and made their way to the cabin. Except for the times Andy slowed down to point out a marmot, a chipmunk and a woodpecker, Jana watched the narrow road closely during the four-mile drive.

The cabin was just as she had expected: rustic, cozy and built of split logs. The owners, however, were not where she had expected them to be.

"They went to Bakersfield," reported Andy. "Now, if you'll just remember not to leave food outside because of the bears, you won't be attacked during your visit."

"But you said your friends were here."

"Never mind about them now. Yosemite is derived from an Indian word meaning grizzly bear. Don't worry: there aren't grizzlies up here anymore—but there are black bears—and they eat blondes from Chicago as appetizers." He lunged at her.

She couldn't help laughing. This was a new Andy she was seeing—an Andy who was enthusiastic about his surroundings. The first Andy had seemed so simple as he stood there in the weigh house. The second Andy was a strange, fearful person whom she had held and comforted in the mountains. And the third Andy was at odds with his own family, wasn't even attending his sister's memorial service. With each situation, Andy's complications compounded. If only she could encourage him to follow his own interests in the outdoors instead of chasing after his father's goals.

But how could she, when it seemed as if the search for money and security had driven her? But, she rationalized, money interested her as much as buzzards and bears interested Andy.

Jana walked around the cabin. It was cozier than a vacation place and packed with both summer and winter items: snow shoes, skis, photographs of hikers in shorts and snowsuits.

She loved seeing how people lived, right down to how they arranged the soap and scrub brushes in the kitchen. She felt comfortable here in this cabin—but intact.

The Milford mansion with its portraits, its cold mosaic tile, its unused silk and satin clothes, its pool and gardens, had assaulted her, and somehow changed her. After having been there, she had felt the need of history as well as wealth. The mansion called to her. It needed her. She would hire plasterers, painters. She would knock out a room here, repair tiles there. . . .

Jana stopped herself. She would never be a part of that house.

Of all the houses she had been in since she arrived, she loved Miss Mari's house best, where everything was scrubbed, translucent and loved.

It was homes like these that were foreign to her. She had always been determined to live in a house—not an apartment. And that took money.

After showering, Jana called to Andy. "Do you think I could wear a long dress to dinner?"

He walked through the door to see for himself. "I didn't mean for you to walk right in," she said. "I'm hardly dressed."

"That's quite all right." He touched her waist, her breasts, the towel slid down and she shivered.

"I'm starving," she whispered. "And we'll be late."

"Now's the time," said Andy. "The other night you were the one. Now it's my turn." He was stepping out of his trousers, molding his hands to her breasts, kissing her, leading her in front of the fire. He had already prepared a place for them on a blanket he had doubled and spread.

There was an innocence about being with Andy, and now she knew what it was. She had never fit Andy into any of her long-range plans. Andy was for pleasure. And the pleasure he could give her outweighed all other considerations, such as a heavy feeling that he was seeing her differently than she saw him.

A spark flew out of the fireplace. Andy jumped up.

"Burned?" asked Jana lazily, stretching up her arms for him.

"It was nothing," he said, spreading over her, taunting her, "nothing compared to the long slow burn I'm feeling from you."

The pine needles in the fireplace cracked and glowed; the aroma smelled like the bath oil that she used in Chicago.

Andy was copying her actions of the night at Peter's mansion. He was doing to her what she had done to him, only he did not have the buoyancy of the water to help him. When he hovered above her, he became tired or else leaned too heavily.

Jana wanted to rush him, take over. That would be wrong. But how long could she wait? Every time he touched her, she was ready. She touched him and wound her feet through his legs, rubbed them along his calves.

Their sentences were fewer and further apart. They were traveling along the periphery of a sensuous chasm into which they both knew they were about to plunge.

But instead of it being Andy's hour, it was becoming hers. She had to touch him. She could not wait any longer. The moments before his hardness was hers alone to do with as she pleased were unbearable. She could almost hear him growing. She wanted to open her eyes and look at him. Instead, she lay back and saw the peaks of the mountains outside the windows. As she looked up, one peak was the largest. She imagined she was seeing that peak through a speeded-up, fast-frame camera, and its seasons were changing from summer, winter, hot, cold, spring, autumn and winter, stop, stop. Like an icicle of frozen fire, the mountain was filling her.

She was making of it all she knew it to be.

"Wait for me, for me," said Andy. But she could not.

"It's all right," she said, but it really wasn't. Even so, his face was wrinkled, perspiring, earnest, as if his diligence with

her were paying off. His unusual upper lip had curled into an
ecstatic snarl as he congratulated himself on a long upward
climb that he was about to complete. He had finally reached
the top of the mountain. He was a downhill skier, racing,
sliding.

He wanted to make the climb again, do it right. All the
equipment was here in front of the fire. He wanted to more
than anything in the world. He was begging her.

She was tired. She wondered about Peter. Would he get
into a brawl with whoever had savaged her desk? It might
have been a prank that was unconnected to her.

That was a silly reason for her to leave Mariposa. She
should have argued with Peter. He seemed to be glad to get
rid of both her and Andy. Perhaps it had nothing to do with
her safety. He was showing his control of her. That's what
had been wrong just now. It had nothing to do with a failure
on Andy's part.

"Let me have you, Andy. I'll let you take me to that place
you've just been. Together we'll race, together."

With all her might, Jana released herself from time and
space and Peter, and flew just this once more to a new height.

As the fire died, Andy's pledges to her grew more heated:
"I'll never . . . We'll always . . . I promise . . . forever . . .
precious . . . love."

It took Andy longer to dress than it did Jana. She waited
for him in front of the picture window in the living room.
Darkness had already arrived under the heavy trees, although
it would be at least half an hour before their upper branches
knew about it.

Her dress was becoming, she knew. Starting with grada-
tions of light blue, it swirled around and around until at the
bottom its color was a deep purple—the color of the dark
spaces between the mountain firs.

Andy, wearing a tan gabardine suit, a tie flecked with green
and a green shirt so pale it was almost white, whistled at her.
She liked watching his eyes cover her bare shoulders and
follow her slender figure, which was closely outlined by the
dress.

"Funny, isn't it?" she said. "Here we are in this wild setting
and we're stepping out as though we're going to a fancy
restaurant."

"In spite of the location, the restaurant happens to be just
that," Andy told her.

Indeed, the leisurely dinner at the hotel was elegant. After several rounds of cocktails, it began with an appetizer of marinated mountain mushrooms, and continued with an *entrée* of filet mignon and a large vegetable dish of lightly-steamed squash, broccoli, and artichoke hearts.

Andy's conversation had slowed down a bit. He constantly hinted of better times together later that night. At the same time, Jana was wishing they could return to home ground. She had even thought about calling Mariposa to see how everything was going.

But she hadn't even dared suggest that they order a Milford wine. She was certainly afraid to suggest a phone call. Being with Andy when he was in such a good mood was too important. And it had been a trip she would never have taken without him.

As they waited for the dessert—a deep-dish rhubarb pie—Andy persuaded Jana to drink a Brandy Alexander instead of coffee.

Just as she had sipped the last strong drop of it, he grabbed her hand and said, "I love you."

Before she had time to reply, his jaw stiffened and he loosed his hold on her hand, sat straight up and stared toward the door.

"What's wrong?"

"Somebody I know is talking to somebody. . . ."

"That's not very explicit, Andy. Who is it?"

Since Andy said nothing, she turned around.

Standing in the doorway, his wild, questioning eyes surveying the room like a black beacon light, was Peter.

Chapter 13

Since Jana saw Peter first, she had the full benefit of watching the reverberations his face made when he saw her across the room.

His head was tilted up, his eyes were riveted on her the entire time it took him to stride across the dining room. He turned, swerved, even yanked a few chairs out of his way as he passed through the obstacle course of round tables, chairs and patrons full and drowsy from too much food and wine.

Jana completely forgot about Andy. All her energy was consumed by the anger, unwarranted, of course, with which Peter was charging toward her.

He looked like a lumberjack, dressed in hiking boots, khakis and a red flannel shirt. His hands were dirty, his hair was flying like a rooster's comb.

This was not a social call: it was an act of war. Even Andy, who often misinterpreted events, could not mistake this one. He automatically rose the moment Peter reached the table.

"Get up and get out of here," Peter said to Jana as if she were a slave.

"N-n-now just a m-m-minute."

The big bully was making Andy stutter. Jana had only heard him verge on it once before—and now she remem-

bered. It was when he had been upset about what Ken might
have said about him that day at Miss Mari's.

"Let's go," said Peter.

The patrons and waiters, as well as the maître d', who was
waving menus in one hand and a telephone in the other,
provided a vast audience. For them it was like a dinner
theater.

With one hand Peter was pulling Jana up by her elbow and
with his other he was hauling her chair back from the table.

"Stop! You can't do this to me," she hissed.

"I can and I will."

"You have no business h-h-here, b-buddy."

"She has no business with you, and I know it better than
anyone."

The odd thing about the embarrassing confrontation was
that Peter, who was the angriest, was speaking in tones that
could barely be heard, while every time Andy spoke a raspy
word, the dining room seemed to shake.

Jana was in the peculiar position of wanting to hush up
Andy more than she wanted to chase Peter away. What could
have driven him to barge in here like this? She was curious
beyond all bounds.

Andy's blond hair glistened under the lights and she
observed that all the cocktails and wine he had drunk were
having an extraordinary effect on him now. The flush of his
fury was coinciding with a heated rush of alcohol to his head.
He stumbled as he yelled, "You can't follow us around like
this."

"Peter," whispered Jana, "sit down if you must, and tell us
what you want."

Instead, he yanked her out of the chair and forcibly guided
her between the tables, hurting her arm with every step they
took.

Two National Park rangers charged in the front door.
"What's the trouble?"

"This girl is an employee of mine and she is in serious
danger over some trouble we have been having at Mariposa."

"Mr. Milford!" exclaimed the maître d'. "I didn't recognize
you."

What was Peter talking about?

"It's all right," the maître d' was explaining. "This is Peter
Milford."

Andy rushed to Jana's side and tried to tell the park rangers he was glad they had arrived, that a man was trying to kidnap his friend.

"Shut up," said the policeman, pushing him down into an easy chair. "You're drunk."

As long as Peter had an "M" on him, he had a free pass to do anything. No wonder Andy resented him so much.

"What is it?" she asked, unable to believe that she had walked to his car with him, that she was sitting obediently in the Jaguar and that he was roaring out of the valley with her. "And it had better be good."

The Jaguar screeched around hairpin turns. "It doesn't have to be anything. You had no right to leave the city. You have two jobs, remember, and because you were not there today, we could have had some serious trouble. In addition, I have every reason to believe that Andy himself was responsible for the damage done in the weigh house yesterday."

"Peter, you're talking like a madman. There was nothing wrong in the weigh house when I joined Andy for our visit to the Tourist Center. And you flagged us down when we returned. What's the matter with you? And why would Andy do such a thing? You have Ken's problem of wanting to blame Andy for everything. It's not rational."

"Are you finished? I know where Andy was at noon, but I have a good idea who did the actual damage. He paid one of the pickers to do it. I can't prove it, but I have a feeling."

"And I have a feeling you're out to get Andy for no professional reason. One of the first principles of management is to act on facts, not feelings. And whatever reasons you have for your feelings are not based in facts, so I suggest that you drop them."

Jana took a deep breath. "And besides, what's this about serious trouble at Mariposa?"

"I unloaded the harvesters."

"You told me you couldn't as long as the Havermeyer drivers were out of town. You deliberately told me to leave because you didn't want me there when you did it."

"Who's being irrational? The pickers demanded to see them. We unloaded them together. And it's a good thing, because Havermeyer has goofed again. The bin-fillers didn't arrive with the harvesters, and what good is all this damned equipment without them? That's when I needed you to call Havermeyer and complain."

"Did you?"

"No. I didn't want you to look incompetent—or indolent. Did you want me to say you were off sight-seeing?"

"My hero," said Jana as she sank down in the seat and, facing him, lay the side of her head against its back. "I'd elaborate, but I've had a lot to drink. I don't feel as angry as I should."

"I wondered why you hadn't thrown a bigger fit."

"You'd better be glad. If I were my usual self, I wouldn't have allowed you to bully me out of that restaurant—nor would I have stood meekly by while you insulted Andy and escaped through that dragnet in the lobby just because you threw your name around."

"Andy won't remember it. He was too drunk."

"Or it may linger as a worse incident than it was—if that's possible."

"I can handle Andy."

Jana reached over and looped her wrist around Peter's arm. "Let me see your hand."

Peter smiled. As soon as Jana had grasped it, she returned the smile . . . and was asleep.

They were at a service station and she had a golden cashmere blanket tucked around her. The bright lights were flashing; she closed her eyes.

When she felt the car slump down and the door puff closed, she looked up. Peter's face was near hers; his hand was pulling the blanket up around her chin. He was near enough to kiss her, but he did not. He'd better not try. She was peeved at him. Peeved. Put out. Potted.

Through her eyelashes she discerned a smile flicker across his face. His eyes were so nearly closed that she did not know what they were seeing. She was ashamed of herself. Of course she was. But everywhere these Californians went, they seemed to have hot and cold running wine. But Peter did not seem to mind that she could not argue with him properly. All in all, it had been a good thing to be whisked away so quickly.

But for what reason? And where was he taking her? And where was her poor, sweet outdoorsman, who had such big plans for the evening?

Peter was carrying her out of the car. She squinted as a porch light switched on. Her eyes flickered open and a contralto voice said, "What's happened to her? Is she hurt?"

"She's not a drinker."

"Take her upstairs."

"Be sure and wake her in time to get to the office by seven. That's nine in Chicago and she's got work to do."

"Did anything happen in the orchards today?"

"Too much, Miss Mari, that's the trouble."

Jana felt Peter touch her forehead, her lips. She closed her eyes before the light was out and never saw him leave.

Once again Miss Mari providing clothes for Jana. The shirt was violet and a St. Laurent. There were bermuda shorts to match, and the sandals she had worn with her dress the night before.

"I try to make one of St. Laurent's showings every other year," said Miss Mari as she buttered an English muffin for Jana. "Your shirt is from the forties."

"What did Peter say last night? Was he angry?"

"He seemed to enjoy carting you around in that blanket."

"I hate to think how Andy must feel. Peter was awful to him. I can't understand how I could have gone along with Peter's bullying . . ."

"He's very good at it, that's probably why."

Jana could have remained in Miss Mari's house the entire morning. The shapes illumined by the morning sun were different from the ones she had seen there at noon and in the evening. They required a new appraisal.

"I do love your home, Miss Mari. Everything from the fruit jars to that lovely painting in the dining room to the Oriental rugs to the squatty jars you pack the peach preserves in."

"I feel the same way about it. Yesterday, a man who owns a grocery store in New Rochelle, New York, stopped by. He was sent to me after he tried to buy every single jar of peach preserves at the Tourist Center. I only allowed him to have one for himself and one for his wife, but he praised the house so lavishly that I almost *gave* them all away."

"Miss Mari, have you ever thought about having more than your cook and a volunteer put up those preserves?"

"We're so short-handed at the Tourist Center that I wouldn't dream of depleting the staff further."

The grandfather clock in the dining room gonged 7:00 A.M. Jana rushed, hoping to reach Mariposa's office by the seventh chime.

One reason for her eagerness was that today, for the first time since her arrival, she would be participating in the real business of Mariposa. She would no longer be obligated to sit around weighing trucks while Moose and Peter fumbled as they introduced the equipment to the laborers.

So confident was she that she whizzed through the door looking the opposite of her lethargic last night's self. "Who is replacing me at the scales today?" she asked.

"Now what?" said Moose.

Peter stood up, appraising her as she scanned him: Levi's, a silver buckle with an "M" on it and a shirt worn Mariposa-style—with the sleeves ripped out. Jana brushed her hair back with her hand, fully aware that it was shining almost as much as her eyes.

"You're quitting?" asked Peter.

"Of course not. I'm ready, however, to do the job I was sent here to do."

"I'm the one who decides what you do and if, after your call to Chicago, you don't get to your post, I might sure enough have a riot on my hands."

"What do you mean?"

"That you are to weigh peach trucks for all you're worth today, and if anyone asks you about the harvesters, refer them to me."

Jana glanced warily at Moose. "It's all right," said Peter. "He knows—thanks to Miss Mari."

Two flies were crawling on one of the floorboards. Jana stepped on one with her left foot, the other with her right.

"Look, Peter. I feel that I'm wasting my time, your time, my company's time."

"Tell me, Jana, what little perk do you hope will be waiting for you if you return to your Chicago office with Mariposa successfully under your belt? Will you become president? Have a couple of thousand shares of the company's stock shoveled into your portfolio, get your picture on the cover of *Time?*"

"Oh, didn't I tell you? They're giving me China. I'll sell every tenth Chinaman a peach-harvester. There won't be one in the U.S. for two thousand years—by which time the U.S. will be part of China.

"And if you don't think that's funny, let me tell you something that is: you aren't as smart as you like to boast that you are, or you would use me to better advantage around here."

"All right, tell you what. I've just thought of something you can do right this minute. The ladies on the platform are making a scene. They're calling a press conference at noon. They've already sent three telegrams to Milford headquarters in San Francisco."

"And what does this have to do with me?"

"You can try to pacify them."

"What are their complaints?"

"Something to do with age discrimination, would you believe?" said Moose.

"Yes, I would. And I would add sex discrimination. After all, if women of a certain age had not been locked into one or two kinds of jobs, there wouldn't be this heavy concentration of women on the platform."

"My God," said Moose. "Sounds as if she plans to join them instead of reason with them. I thought you said she'd help us out, Pete?"

"How well do you know Ruby?" asked Peter.

"Better than the others. She and I have had more conversations."

"That's nothing. Ruby talks more'n anybody else," retorted Moose.

Peter added, "She's the gangleader of this little revolt."

"Why don't you ask her to come over here, Moose?" said Jana. While Moose was gone, Jana discovered that disgruntlement over the harvesters has caused Ruby and the women to search for every reason they could think of to be dissatisfied. There were no government regulations that might support them if the harvesters knocked them out of jobs, but if discrimination were the culprit—they might have a case.

"I don't have anything to offer them," said Peter. "And what's more, Moose is halfway on their side, which puts me in an awkward position."

"Peter, why don't you propose a week's stand-off? Let the women sort the fruit as they always have. This would mean that while the harvesters are shaking down the trees, the drivers and the sorters are still doing their regular jobs."

Maybe the fact that the bin-fillers hadn't arrived with the harvesters was, in its way, a good thing.

"That means," said Peter, "the only ones thrown off will be the pickers. You corporation people always like to pick on the poor and the minorities first, don't you?"

"Whose side are you on? If you're going to compromise, they must, too."

"What if Ruby agrees? What will we do with the women next week?"

"I'll tell you after she agrees."

The woman appeared at the door in her usual ironed and creased pedal-pushers and a bright yellow, sleeveless blouse.

"Call off this damned press conference, Ruby, my love," said Peter.

"Don't you sweet-talk me, Pete Milford. I've worked here longer than you have, and so has Moose."

"You should listen to me, Ruby, because I'm regrouping my thoughts."

"You're what?"

"Changing my mind."

"And?"

"And you and your cronies will carry on as usual for a week. We'll see what we can work out."

Without even looking at Peter or Moose, Ruby practically pirouetted to the telephone, dialed a number and said, "Put me through to the farm desk."

"Listen, Clay, honey, Ruby here. We've called off our press conference at Mariposa. No. No strong-arming. I might have something peachy to talk to you about next week, though, so ring me up on Monday, okay?"

"Honestly, Ruby, you think you can wrap every young reporter around your little finger, don't you?"

"Ain't it true, though, ain't it true." She whacked Peter on the thigh and marched out the door like a victorious warrior.

"Now what?" implored Moose.

"Yes, Jana. If this thing blows up. . . ."

Jana cut Peter's warning short. "We're going to put the women to work in other jobs."

"We ain't got no other jobs," said Moose, who could speak perfect English any time he wanted to.

"I have to talk it over with Miss Mari first."

"Then get over there and talk," said Peter.

"I can't do it until noon. Don't you see I have a long line of trucks that can't go down to the orchards until I weigh them in?"

"She's right," said Moose. "It would be a bad example if Cassie had to sit over there alone again and see Jana get special treatment from the front office."

"To hell with Cassie," said Peter. "All she's done this

summer is fan the flames of revolt those women are cooking up."

"Watch out, Peter," said Jana. "Cassie's probably the best friend you've got around here." She allowed the screen door to bang moderately hard as she tripped down the steps.

In the weigh house, Cassie, who was certainly not *her* best friend, said, "Peter said he was with you last night, is that right? You slept with him, didn't you?"

"That's your line, not mine." Slide. Balance. Record.

"Then where were you? I called Gretchen, and *she* said you had gone to Yosemite with Andy. But I think you were up there with Peter."

"Cassie, it's such a long story that I'm not even sure I understand it. But it's nothing for you to worry about. And if you must know, I spent the night in one of Miss Mari's upstairs bedrooms."

"Alone? I mean, I want to lay this thing out on the table so I'll know what I'm fighting."

"I was alone. No. I think there was a cat on the end of the bed—a blonde and white one."

"Is that the truth?"

"Ask her."

"Who?"

"You'd probably get on better with the cat, but for a definite confirmation, why don't you check with Miss Mari, too."

Chapter 14

Jana felt triumphant. When Andy's truck rattled in, she had no doubt about being able to conquer him, too. She put her fingers through the weigh house window and touched Andy's lips.

"Shhh. Don't ask. I stayed at Miss Mari's last night. We'll talk over dinner, okay? This one will be on me."

Andy was too shocked to deliver the speech he had obviously rehearsed.

"I believe you," he said. "And I have a feeling that we'll settle everything tonight."

"What's going on out in the orchards?" asked Jana.

"The wetbacks are out there trying to cope with those weird harvesters."

"Braceros." Cassie's voice projected across the room.

Andy continued. "And now we're being told to box up the peaches as usual—the bad along with the good—and unload them at the platform. And anybody knows that one of the reasons for buying the machines is that they weigh and sort. It doesn't make any sense. If you're going to automate, I say automate. If you ask me, Milford's pulling a sneaky trick to get around government regulations. You know what he did yesterday before he allowed those harvesters to be introduced to the pickers?

"I was told that he read a letter from Joe Milford about how this was a last resort, and that if the harvesters didn't work and work soon, the ranch would close. Everybody knows that with Milford money behind it, Mariposa could run another hundred years and grow only lollipops."

"And it would be a ranch with the same kind of reputation, wouldn't it, Andy?" said Jana.

"You think just because you go to school in the east that you know about business. But let's don't argue. I want to be with you tonight."

"That's a firm date," said Jana. "And nothing—I promise you—will cancel it. Yesterday was ruined through no fault of your own."

"Did I tell you how beautiful you look—in spite of the wild ride I presume you had last night?"

"I'm wearing Miss Mari's clothes again."

"She may have the taste, but you've got the bod."

"Shhh!" Jana glanced at Cassie, who had turned her back on the two of them.

Ruby marched through the door and Jana was forced to turn her attention to Ruby's complaints. "These peaches are bruised, pinched, nicked and mistreated. They'll never accept them at the cannery."

Jana went outside to inspect some of them for herself. "They don't look any worse than the ones picked by hand," she observed.

"Look here at this one." Ruby stuck a too-ripe peach in front of Jana's nose.

"That cut could have been made by a fingernail."

"Whose side are you on, anyway, honey?"

"Yours, Ruby. Remember, I was in the office early this morning sticking up for everybody here. Since the women at this ranch have traditionally held such stereotyped jobs, we may not be able to hang onto our specialties as the ranch mechanizes, but we can fight for the right to hang onto jobs—maybe even better jobs."

"Thatta girl." Ruby was smiling. "Say," she added, "this next batch is looking better. The boys must have gotten the hang of those harvesters. Hurry it up, girls, we're going to have more than ever to sort today."

At noon, Jana raced across to Miss Mari's. Honey wagged her tail and barked happily as though Jana were a member of the family. Miss Mari was on the phone ordering boxes for her dried fruit gift packages, and motioned her to sit down at the oak breakfast room table.

"I wouldn't put it quite that way if I were you," Jana told the frolicking dog who had brought her a red, mangled-looking ball. "That's not the reason I'm here."

"It's a pomegranate," said Miss Mari. "Honey used to eat persimmons and I thought it better for her to maul this tougher fruit than to actually ingest so much acid."

Miss Mari insisted that Jana eat a chicken salad sandwich, and Jana outlined her plan as she ate.

To her surprise, Miss Mari pounced on it.

"Why haven't *I* thought of that? Those women have all been at Mariposa since the days when we did things with care. They all have special recipes and can follow recipes for peach products to sell at the center, and I can't think of a one of them who wouldn't rather be over there in air-conditioned comfort than standing out on a hot platform fighting peach fuzz.

"Besides, so many of them would be glad to have a winter job. A lot of the women work at Christmas jobs in town, and I'm sure they would rather be out here at Mariposa."

"Miss Mari, if the harvesters are successful, I think we could afford to downplay the center's promotion of hand-picked peaches. After all, sometimes the fruit goes through less trauma when it's harvested by a machine."

"Yes, so you convinced Joe."

"It isn't exactly true, as represented in your movie, that the fruit goes from tree to hand to mouth. There's a lot of hauling and mauling that goes on."

"You want me to scrap that movie?"

"Only when you're ready to replace it with your Yosemite one."

Miss Mari opened her volunteer file box.

"When I begin to think about how much the women here at Mariposa know, I wonder how I could have put up with these amateurish volunteers."

Miss Mari closed the box and looked closely, lovingly at Jana. "You really are going out of your way to help us. Why?"

"It's important to me." Jana was unable to explain further. She rationalized that if she could, she would sound unprofessional—or even maudlin. When she thought of this house and

Mariposa, she got a lump in her throat, in spite of willing herself not to.

"I see so much here that needs to be done—and that can be done. And I like what you stand for so much."

"And Peter?"

"It's been a hard summer for him. I can't hold it against him for putting me through some of the hell he himself is going through."

"He's a complicated boy. Always has been. He's shown a ruthless side this summer and you've borne the brunt of much of it. He does know the violence some of these workers are capable of—and you are, after all, a symbolic target. I think that's why he flew off the handle when that accident happened to your desk and scale."

"Miss Mari, I hope that as long as I'm a target, I'm more than a symbolic one. It's *my* company that has caused so much of this turmoil, my company that delivered the harvesters late and on the worst possible day."

"Are you serious about Andy Goodwin?" Miss Mari asked bluntly.

Jana knew she could not wiggle out of Miss Mari's questions with an oblique answer.

"I don't know. So far, we've had some—what would you call them in California—spontaneous experiences?"

"Sex," said Miss Mari.

Jana blushed. "He's a couple of years younger than I am. In spite of his privileged background and all his sisters, I think he's had the life of an outcast—because of his father."

"I know Denver Goodwin," said Miss Mari. "He's always been a loud-mouthed opportunist. That's how he's made most of his money. He barely misses going to prison almost every other year. He's a terrible influence on Andy—on anybody.

"As for Andy, I've only heard Ken and Susan talk. I've never been around him much. Sometimes he acts strange."

Miss Mari did not look as if she wanted to know him better. It was unfair. The entire Milford clan and their cronies had ganged up on Andy. It made no sense.

Andy had given her an insight into her own potential for tenderness, her own passion. With Peter, Jana always had to bite her tongue and treat his heavy handedness with levity. Good humor and assurance seemed to be the only things that made Peter stand back a couple of feet and let her go on her way.

The sooner Mariposa was quiet and the deal drawn up for the grape-harvesters, the sooner she would be flying home to Chicago—and Spenser.

Jana left Miss Mari's and returned to the weigh house. As soon as she arrived, she was told that the first load of shaken peaches had been rejected at the Calimyrna cannery. The driver had driven a few miles and returned. The load was rejected again.

When Ruby heard that, she almost hit the top of the shed. "Worm infestation! Too small!" she stormed. "Neither of those reasons are any more true than the man in the moon."

"You can see," said Jana, "that Calimyrna is really our biggest enemy. It wants to put Mariposa out of business any way it can."

"They could have mentioned the nicks on the fruit if they wanted to aim somewhere near the truth," Ruby continued. "But their complaints make no sense. Well, girls, I'm glad we reconsidered our press conference. The enemy has shown its face."

Peter, who had heard Ruby's declaration from inside the weigh house, walked slowly out to the platform.

"You had a good idea, Pete," Ruby said, "when you suggested that we wait a week before any more rabble-rousing. But I think I know whose brains were behind the idea."

Peter placed his hand devoutly over his bare chest. "Why, Ruby, break the news to me gently."

"It was Jana's suggestion, wasn't it? She's got more brains than you and Moose put together."

"I don't know about that," he said. "But I understand that Miss Mari's got a few good ideas up *her* sleeve—maybe they're even from the same source. We're calling a little siesta here at the ranch, and she would like all of you to come over for a little refreshment—right now."

"Like this?" said one of the women, looking down at her faded jeans. "I couldn't possibly go into that lovely house looking like a washerwoman."

"I never knew Miss Mari to care how anybody but herself looked," claimed Ruby.

"I suggest you all take her up on the invitation. You'll find it extremely interesting—especially if you are interested in higher wages and winter jobs," said Peter.

"You can't grow peaches in the winter, Pete, anybody knows that," Ruby admonished.

"Darn," he said, snapping his fingers. "I guess you're right. Maybe she's going to suggest that all of you go into the swimming pool business. Aren't most of them dug in the winter?"

"Hush up, Pete," said Ruby. "Come on girls, we'll see what Miss Mari has on her mind."

Cassie went along, too, as a skeptical bystander, muttering something about Jana cooking up wild ideas and drawing attention to herself because her desk was sabotaged.

Jana could see that Cassie was clearly disappointed when Jana never said a word during the forty-five-minute meeting. Nor did Miss Mari refer to her presence.

The other women's voices hushed under Miss Mari's spell. She did not consciously make people feel that she was superior, because her natural excellence inspired enormous confidence in her words.

The ideas about the Tourist Center, the gift boxes, the food—even the carved peach pits—were presented. When the question of money came up, Miss Mari laid out the figures that she and Jana had discussed, showing that if the Tourist Center and an adjunct mail-order business were operated efficiently, they could afford to support the Save Yosemite Committee as well as a trained staff.

Miss Mari also said that she was ordering a micro-computer, and asked who was interested in learning how to program it for the mail-order business as well as for the Tourist Center inventory and records.

Enthusiasm was high all around, and Jana lingered after the others had returned to work.

Miss Mari hugged her, then turned her face so the emotion in her burgundy-colored eyes could not be seen.

Finally, she faced Jana. "It was perfect. Because of you."

"No. Because of the women and your respect for them. They could have been totally against any change at all. There's been very little change since any of them began working at Mariposa.

"But how will you break it to Moose? The women are his responsibility. And what about Mr. Milford?"

"As for Moose, I might be able to handle him. He's been terribly depressed about every other change that has been made, so I can't guarantee how he'll take this one. But I know how I can butter up Joe. I'll pack him up the first mail-order package. I'll even make him some peach preserves with artificial sweetener to keep Aline from flying out of her ruffles. A spoonful of chemicals a day won't hurt him."

Jana thought of the truckloads of rubbish that were dumped into cocoa mix, cake mix, frozen foods and artificial cheese, and agreed silently with Miss Mari.

"In fact, I'll do it right now and take the box out to the airport this afternoon," Miss Mari continued.

Jana walked down the familiar steps of Miss Mari's porch. The whiskery little kittens were hiding on each step, ready to pounce on her feet as she descended. Honey came up to her for a neck scratch. Jana turned and embraced the house with her eyes. It was the symbol of everything that could save Mariposa. There might still be labor problems to be solved, but Mariposa was on its way to health. She could feel it. And she had never been so proud.

The house, the animals, the tangled trees, the bougainvillea and wisteria that sprawled over the porch, would be part of her forever. She knew what Miss Mari and Peter and Joe had been fighting for. It was something that could not be touched or measured, only felt.

Jana passed the packing shed, waved to the women on the platform and reached for the handle on the back door of the weigh house.

"You never ask me for *my* ideas," Cassie was saying. "What makes you talk to a new girl from the east who doesn't know anything about the land or what to do with it? I've tried since it opened to get a job at that air-conditioned Tourist Center. Miss Mari would never even talk to me about it."

"Miss Mari could only afford a couple of paid workers." The voice was Peter's. "Most of them were volunteers."

"Never mind all that logic, Peter. Show me that you care about me. Don't always chase around after *her*. Even Miss Mari is totally snowed. Just because she's Harvard. Are you sure she's not from one of the companies around here?"

"Tell you what, Cassie. For old time's sake, I'll take you up on your offer tonight."

"And a swim?" Cassie was pushing.

"They drained the pool," he said. "A crack."

Jana noisily pulled the screen door open. A truck had been on her scales for a couple of minutes, and she couldn't wait outside any longer.

Chapter 15

"That's the dress you bought to wear to dinner with Peter."

"You helped me pick it out, Andy. Besides, when have I had time to shop?"

It was their first private time together after the abruptly ended Yosemite trip, and Jana and Andy were both testing each other.

The arrangement was that Andy would choose the restaurant, but Jana would pay the bill. Andy claimed to know a marvelous place, but when he drove up to a plain, square stucco building, without even a visible sign in front, Jana suspected a mediocre private club.

She walked reluctantly with Andy into the dreary-looking building, where they were met by a Japanese man in a tuxedo. He bowed to Andy and said, "Good evening, Mr. Goodwin."

They were ushered down four small stone steps, where they were stopped by a large, wooden double door.

Once they had walked through that door, they were in Japan. Lighted *shojii* screens lined the hallway with what appeared to be translucent paper windows. A young woman in a kimono pointed to a row of cotton slippers. "Please," she said, and knelt to remove their shoes.

They padded along after her to a private dining room with a single low table in the middle. At the end of the room, a long, low chest with a vase containing a single sprig of pine was silhouetted simply against another screen.

"Our own room for the evening," said Andy in his softest, huskiest voice. "You're so beautiful, I don't want to share you with anyone."

Jana knelt on one of the square blue and white cushions and Andy fell on his knees beside her. He seemed at a loss for words and stared at her so intently, Jana was forced to turn away.

The kimonoed woman brought two steaming-hot washcloths in a basket, and Andy insisted on rubbing Jana's hands with them.

"Andy, I've been thinking about your future."

"You have?" He kissed her impetuously.

"How do you feel about your business courses?"

"I hate them. Most of the people in my classes, even though they're younger than I am, know more than I do already. They're even eager."

"Does your father know how enthusiastic you are about other things?"

"Yes. He laughs at me. He cuts me short when I talk about forestry or Japan or painting. My father says he wants the Goodwin name to mean something in California. And, after all, it's the old man who is paying this time around. And speaking of paying, I've already paid for dinner. I know you, uh, students, are always strapped for money."

The woman who was serving them approached silently with a large container of soup, which she ladled into red lacquer bowls. It was flavored with chicken broth and had a few noodles floating in it. Andy had already filled Jana's tiny cup with saki several times. It was the saki that Jana found more interesting, but recalling the evening before, she resolved to go slowly.

Andy watched the delicate young woman admiringly. "In Japan," he said, "women spend years learning how to conduct tea ceremonies. No young girl's education is considered complete without such knowledge. Every movement, every container has a meaning. In Ikebana, flowering arranging, the position of each branch and flower, holds a meaning of significance, too."

"Now I know why you brought me here. You're still in love with Japan."

Andy removed his jacket. His soft, cream-colored cotton

shirt seemed the color of his fair hair. "And I'm in love with you and I figured that if I put the two together. . . ."

"How long were you in Japan?" she asked as she wondered what to do with his pledge of love, how to respond, where to put it, whether or not to allow herself to feel it, too.

"I was there for a couple of months a few years ago. It was after I was released from the Army. I'll probably never live in Japan, but I'd like to have a home someday that is Japanese— uncluttered and with every object useful and meaningful.

"Once I thought that a house was the most important thing in life. I wanted to live in a place like the Milford mansion. That was before I saw simpler houses in Japan. . . ." Andy's voice trailed off wistfully.

"Did you visit Peter and Susan at the mansion when they were married?"

"Not very much. Peter was always stingy when Susan was around. He would never allow any of Susan's family—except Ginni or my mom—to stay with them more than a night or two. He always said *I* was more trouble than I was worth."

"What I don't understand," said Jana, "is why you returned to Mariposa this summer—and since the bad feeling between you and Peter obviously still remains, how you ever got a job there."

"What has Peter said about me now?" Andy's voice rose.

"Nothing, really."

"I got the job because of Susan. She still has a lot of influence with Peter. And if he hadn't given me the job, I had some old cards I could have played."

"You mean you could have blackmailed him?"

"If it came down to that, yes. There are still things Peter doesn't know about Susan, and even though it might hurt her, I'm not beyond using the information. It would devastate him. But I'm saving my ammunition. It will come in useful one day soon, I have the feeling."

Before Jana could say anything else, Andy turned his attention to preparing their meal.

A wok of liquid in front of them had come to a boil. A tray of fish heads, shrimp, vegetables and tofu was set before them. Andy dived for the first fish head and plopped it into the brew. Jana stared at it compulsively. The fish stared back through its one unsubmerged eye. Andy added more heads, but the eye of the first head boiled to a white pearl, fell out and disappeared. He began dropping vegetables into the liquid.

"You know, when I was in Japan, the people loved me. They thought I was a blond wonder. All I had to do was walk down the street and I received smiles, even invitations. I could have had any girl I wanted. A producer offered to hire me to make commercials—they use a lot of blonds to sell products to the Japanese. They'd go berserk over you, darling. Simply berserk."

Andy dropped several squares of tofu into the wok. "I've heard it said that if you can nab beancurd with chopsticks, you are a true Japanese." He delicately pinched up a square and, just as it was outside the wok, it fell into slippery pieces on the table.

"So much for your career passing for Japanese."

Andy substituted one of the china soup spoons as a better method of retrieval and filled a plate for her. "You'll like it."

"Andy, I already do." Jana tasted the tofu and avoided the fish. "I don't want to argue with you but, you remember, you promised I could pay for the dinner."

"No. You were only doing it to make up for the blow my ego suffered last night. I don't want Peter Milford to have anything to do with what we do together."

"I know Peter can be rough to deal with."

"Yes. But he doesn't have to treat me as if I were a twerp—a nothing."

"I never heard him say anything like that."

"It's not something you say; it's what you *do*. It has to do with my dad, too. When Peter and Susan married, dad said to me, 'You've got all the connections now, boy, go for it. With my brains and the Milford connections behind you, we can get you elected to any office in the state a few years after you're out of law school.'

"That meant I had to be a lawyer. As an undergrad, I majored in political science. I can't remember a thing I learned."

"I thought your father wanted you to go into business?"

"That was after I flunked out of law school during my first semester. Unheard of."

"I could have told you that you'd hate it."

"Jana, how I wish I had known you then. Everything I wanted to do, I somehow ended up doing the opposite. I think if we had been together early, it would have been different.

"I think it was what dad made me do in connection with law school that helped turn Peter against both of us."

"But Susan wasn't married to Peter then, was she?"

"No, but my dad never drops ties that may be useful one day. That's something I'm learning from him. I didn't have the grades for Stanford law, but the Milford name goes a long way, and Peter agreed to push for my entrance. I made certain promises to him, you see. And this summer, I made them again. Yes, Peter and I have our little secrets. Someday, he won't be able to offer me anything in return for my requests. That will be an interesting day."

Jana wondered if Andy were bluffing in order to prove himself as important, as powerful, as Peter. She was glad when the bowls of bright green lumps arrived.

"Green tea ice cream—the perfect meeting of East and West," said Andy. "Taste it, but don't eat too much because I've ordered my favorite dessert—which has very little to do with Japan except that I first ate it there."

They were served trays of sliced bananas, whole strawberries, sliced pears, halved apricots and chunked pineapple along with a hot vat of liquid chocolate.

"Chocolate fondue," said Andy dunking a strawberry into the sweet, heavy goo and feeding it to Jana. "Perfect, isn't it?"

"It certainly is." She speared her own slice of banana and ate it while Andy instructed the smiling woman who had so silently served them that they wanted to be alone.

After filling himself with both desserts, he leaned back on one elbow and watched Jana, touching her occasionally on the arm, the leg, asking her several times if she were comfortable sitting Japanese-style.

"Who are your friends in Chicago?" he blurted out.

"You want to know about men friends, don't you?" Why had he said Chicago and not Cambridge, Mass.?

"There's only one man there and his name is Spenser. He's in Italy for the summer."

"Do you think he's pacing the floor every night wondering if you've found somebody else? I certainly would be if I were he."

"He's very involved with his work and I doubt it."

"I don't understand why you didn't marry the first rich man who asked you."

Jana laughed. "First of all, none asked me. No rich ones, anyway, and I never planned to marry early. For one thing, I couldn't afford it. I have my brother in pre-med and my mother's in an awful job. The money I make has to go to them for several years."

"You're admirable, fun, beautiful—what more is there?" asked Andy.

"Rich, I suppose." She laughed. But she wondered why she felt as light-hearted about it as she did.

Andy's right hand was playing with her hands. He couldn't seem to bear not to be touching her. She found it pleasant enough. But so many complications had intervened since Andy had stood there in front of her like the sun.

He pulled her to him. Leaning into his chest was always so comfortable.

"It's all right. No one will disturb us. The blond boss-man has left orders."

Jana was ready to be loved, and here was Andy loving her. So why was the agitated image of Peter always with her?

"What are you thinking?" he asked, as he stroked her hair.

"How my first impression of you hid some of your complications. And I was wondering how to help you be what you really want to be."

"I only want to be with you. And you know what I was thinking? I'm glad you're one of the smart women—because if you weren't, you would already have been swept off your feet by somebody who offered to take care of you in exchange for a few favors in the bedroom and appearing with him in public.

"I'd like to meet your mother, your brother. What would you think if I transferred to a school near you?"

"You mean near Harvard?"

"I mean near Chicago. Isn't that where Havermeyer Harvester is located?"

"So you *know!*" And who else had he told? And how many were accurately guessing?

"The harvesters were the reason Peter rushed up to Yosemite last night, Andy. He was furious because I had left town and wasn't at the 'unveiling ceremony' that was demanded by the men," Jana admitted.

"I figured it had something to do with those damned machines."

"I had no idea he would allow them to be shown without telling me. It was his own fault. He should have invited me to the meeting."

"Maybe he thought some of the anger might turn in your direction."

"Maybe." Jana didn't want to say anything further.

"Now that our confessions have been completed, let's promise each other that we won't talk about Mariposa or Milfords or machines for the remainder of the night."

"May I make another confession?" Jana asked, relieved that the subject had been tabled.

Andy kissed her nose lightly.

"I think if I had met your father at the beginning of the summer, I would have agreed with him about money."

"And you've changed?"

"I'm changing. Unlike you, Andy, I've always lived close to asphalt streets, and as an angry reaction to the job I had with a dreadful outfit called Engineered Edibles, I decided to study agribusiness. I thought that, as a woman, I would be highly visible, and with my credentials from Harvard and my degree in mechanical engineering from MIT, I would have a head start over most of the men. None of this has served as much of an advantage since being here in California. In fact, it has been one of the factors that has made the women on the platform suspicious of me. Cassie dislikes me quite heartily because of my background, among other things.

"If I've been able to do anything helpful in the short time I've been here—such as showing Miss Mari the increased potential of the Tourist Center—it has not been a result of my business background. Last year, for example, I never would have helped her with the Tourist Center."

"What's different?"

"My feelings. I understand the Milfords' feeling for their land. I even understand to a degree what Peter has been going through. And if you could have seen Joe Milford when he learned some of the ways Peter was managing Mariposa and how proud he was. . . . And I've learned to love Miss Mari's house. It's the cornerstone of everything the Milfords do, and without it. . . ."

"Yes, I've never thought of that," said Andy. "And all the time I was dazzled by that mansion."

"What I'm trying to say, Andy, is that for the first time in my life, I've made so-called business decisions because of love. I love Mariposa. And anything I've done since I've been here will earn me no brownie points at Havermeyer. And, yet, I feel good about what's happened.

"All Havermeyer cares about is selling the Milfords a fleet of grape-harvesters." Jana stared at the single sprig of pine on the long, low chest. If only life could be that uncomplicated, she thought.

"Now it all comes to light: that's what you're really here to do, isn't it, Jana?"

"Sure. However, the more I read in the agriculture journals, the more I think that Havermeyer's grape-picker is of inferior design to at least two. . . ."

"Leading brands?"

"Right." Jana snuggled closer to Andy. "And ours are more expensive, too."

"Vy iss you tellink me all dis?"

"Because I have come to think that this kind of love and care should be the basis for decisions—and not power or money or fear that somebody in my family won't have enough. And I think it could be how you decide what to do with yourself. It would prevent you from tagging along after your father's wishes."

"It's too late for that," said Andy, changing the subject quickly. "You know what I'd really like to do? Go around the world with you on one of those luxury liners. We could have a suite of rooms and leave them occasionally, but we would spend most of our time together, very close together."

He pulled Jana toward his wall of muscle. She wanted to wrap her arms around him, kiss his neck. She loosened his tie. A rich reservoir of warmth was flooding over her. She shut out the sounds she heard beyond the *shojii* screens.

"It's not too late, Andy," Jana protested as she pulled herself apart from him for a moment.

"I told you, Miss Robbins. If only I had known you earlier."

"You can change. I'm changing. I can feel it."

"But look at your qualifications: a degree in this, another one in that; a job with this one, that one. And what about that guy—Spenser?"

"He was part of my plan."

"Were you and he as good together as we are?"

Jana smiled and kissed him lightly. "Not at all." He crushed her to him as he lay down on the floor.

There was a loud commotion outside. "We'll just say hello," a voice said. A shrill "No, no, no!" and an outpouring of Japanese followed.

The screen shot open and there stood Cassie and Peter.

Jana was so stunned that she could not roll away from Andy and had to wait until he could move her.

"Well, well," said Cassie. "We saw your car outside, Andy, and thought we'd say hello. We thought this was a *restaurant*."

Jana smoothed down her dress. Peter's chiseled features were cutting into her soul. The black weapons of his eyes were hurting her. He was the one who slid the screen shut with a shuddering slam.

Jana was shaking uncontrollably.

"Damn the Milfords. Damn all of them," said Andy.

"It wasn't Peter, it was Cassie. You must have told her where you were taking me."

"I discussed it with her at length. Damn her, too."

"We shouldn't have been together like that. This *is* a restaurant."

"I was only cuddling you, Jana. A lot more than that has been done here. And what we do is our business."

Jana wanted to return home, climb into bed and cry. She was too full of soft, drowned lumps.

"I suppose it's not a good time to ask you what I was planning to ask you tonight?"

"No, Andy," she said, as she stood up, "it isn't."

"Damn the Milfords."

Chapter 16

"Have you heard the news?" Ruby said to Jana when she arrived at Mariposa the next morning.

"Five *braceros* had a fight with their contractor, Carlo Prima, and Moose—on orders from San Francisco—fired the five. An investigation has been demanded, and it looks as if there's going to be a long strike. Haven't you listened to the radio?"

"Does this have anything to do with the harvesters?"

"Well, they don't help any, do they?"

"What about Peter?"

"The radio said that he's 'deeply concerned.' Now, to tell you the truth, I sincerely believe that Peter has our best interests at heart. But the rumor is that his dad is using him as a stoolie for Milford Enterprises and that no matter what he says, it won't carry any weight in the long run.

"I don't want to say too much, you understand," continued Ruby, "because I need the job and, besides, I'm sworn to fight for Mariposa because I want Miss Mari's plans for the Tourist Center to work out. But by the time Joe Milford was Pete's age, he was managing several of the Milford vineyards as well as a cling peach ranch up by Modesto and a cannery near Merced. Pete hasn't got the knack. When you're as old as he is—thirty-four or thirty-five—you know what you want

153

and you're already doing it. As Moose says, 'This ain't no pilot project.'"

Jana protested. "But Peter has been anticipating trouble this summer. He's spent more time working to avert it than he has on the peaches."

"Sure. He would. Because he's a labor lawyer—disguised as a ranch manager. Pete's father has lost contact with the land to such an extent that he didn't know better than to put him in at Mariposa for a season or two. Moose could have done a better job."

"I don't agree with you there, Ruby."

"I walked past the office a little while ago. There's a group of men seated around a desk and two of them are wearing business suits. Whenever the San Francisco people move in on us, we're in trouble. They never show up when we're happy."

From her standpoint on the sorting platform, Jana could see that there was not a truck in sight on the ranch.

She peered down the dusty road between the north and south orchards. There were no trucks, not even ones filled with grapes that sometimes stopped off at Mariposa. The dust on the roads had not been stirred since the morning fog and mist lifted.

Across the road from the weigh house, rows and rows of figs were drying in trays. Flies and dust had matted them into the blackish-brown end product. That fruit should be removed today.

Cassie walked in and went right to her stool, saying nothing to Jana.

"You watch out for her," whispered Ruby. "She'll walk over anybody to get what she wants. That Peter Milford shouldn't be tormenting young people like you and Cassie. He should have settled down long ago. Who knows? He may have a wife and five children on the east coast."

Jana dismissed Ruby's wild speculation.

"I'm reading a terrific book," said Cassie out of the blue. Jana jumped at the announcement. Cassie must feel guilty.

"What's it called?" she asked. Cassie waved the paperback above her head and Jana read, *Will Love Defy the Haunted Castle?*

Jana smiled. "Let's hope love wins."

"True love always does," proclaimed Cassie.

Now that Cassie had at least spoken, Jana felt more at liberty to drop the personal tensions she was feeling. She stared blankly down the road, sure that the stillness at Mariposa was disguising the activity actually taking place. The silent turmoil seemed a fitting background for her own confusion.

Andy was holding himself out for her—like a ripe peach. Peter, invoking the name of Susan, had toyed with her. One approach was appealing, the other appalling. She could free Andy from so much; Peter would never allow her to do anything for him. He already had it all—except for Susan— and if he continued his relentless, gentlemanly pursuit of her, he would probably have that, too.

"Here they come!"

The women were all standing up, leaning out to see the road better. Dust was billowing on the horizon, and it was more dust than any one truck could stir up.

The yellowish cloud rose higher and higher as the commotion drew nearer. Within two or three minutes, the weigh house platform and office were engulfed in the fine dust kicked up by what seemed to be the entire pool of ranch trucks. But instead of being filled with peaches, the bed of each truck was jammed with men standing up, holding onto the rails.

Moose shut the doors and windows of the office. The men in the trucks were yelling, "Decency and dollars! Decency and dollars!" Others were chanting, "The five were framed! The five were framed!"

Jana rushed inside the weigh house and parked herself at Cassie's window for a better view. "Do you think Peter will give them what they're demanding?" Jana asked.

"They'll end up with more money all right, but it won't be because of what Peter says, but what the men from San Francisco decree."

"But I thought the main issue is the men who were fired?"

"That's the catalyst. And it's a good issue because Carlo is unpopular with the laborers. He's probably more at fault than anyone, and he very likely may have mistreated the men.

"You and your harvesters are, of course, one of the main reasons for the strike. I hope you're proud of yourself."

So Cassie knew about her Havermeyer connection, too. That must mean everybody did. What kind of corner had

Peter backed her into? The dangerous one he claimed, or one that put her in her place?

Peter was walking out to the circle of trucks. He looked exhausted. Sweat trickled down his face and onto his light blue T-shirt. He held up both hands in an attempt to stop the procession. But it did not come to a halt.

"Why don't they do what he asks? The drivers are Peter's friends."

"Who says?" was Cassie's off-handed reply. "They think Peter is against them. His name is Milford, you know."

The circle of trucks resembled a wagon train. Peter leapt into one of the trucks. After a few moments of circling with it and talking to the driver, he jumped out. The men in the back of the truck jeered at him, yet Jana observed that almost immediately the truck slowed down.

The driver hung his arm out the window, indicating a stop. Soon, all fifteen of the trucks were parked in a double circle around the weigh house and office. A man in a blue suit emerged from the office.

"That's McNair," whispered Cassie. "Albert McNair is president of Milford Enterprises, and has been since Joe Milford has been ill."

"McNair, are you interested in listening to us now, or should we call in the television stations?" asked one of the pickers, who identified himself as Moe Perez.

"He's bluffing," said Cassie. "Nobody wants outsiders here during the first hours of a strike."

"I'm ready to talk," said McNair, as he hesitantly walked down the stairs of the office and approached Moe, who was standing on the bed of a truck.

McNair fished out a pair of sunglasses from his breast pocket and slipped them on.

The rumble among the men became a roar.

"Take'm off. Take'm off."

McNair did so immediately.

Behind the circle of trucks, grapes were being tossed out of a truck that had arrived the day before. Another truck was being rocked back and forth. A pickup drove in, and a dozen men carried crates of rotting peaches and dumped them in front of the office.

McNair was pulled up on the truck bed. One of the pickers jumped up behind him with the intention of knocking him off, but Peter quickly swung himself onto the truck, and after a moment's rough conversation with the picker, all hands were removed from McNair—to the nervous man's relief.

At that moment, three patrol cars sped through the front gate, their sirens squealing.

"Oh, brother," said Cassie.

Peter, however, approached the officers, shaking hands with each one as though welcoming them to a party.

"I'll bet Miss Mari called them. She's all for law and order when it comes to protecting her patch of property," Cassie sniffed.

"Maybe it was a good idea. These guys might hurt somebody."

"The cops probably think that the men are illegal aliens. They don't know Peter well enough to realize he would never hire them, even though it's not against the law to *hire* one, just to *be* one.

"Pete's father operated this ranch in the dark ages. He didn't see why labor couldn't be as cheap as he could get it, and he thought the government was wrong to crack down on the aliens. But the men always adored him." Cassie shook her head.

Peter was leading the two officers over to the truck of grapes, which had almost been tipped over. All was silent as he reached up and pulled off several bunches. He passed them to one of the men. After a few tense moments, the others followed his lead and began passing around peaches, grapes, figs and raisins. Laughter and talk rose as though the gathering were a celebration.

McNair, the other Milford Enterprises executive and Moose had disappeared inside the office. Jana did not trust what Moose might be telling them behind Peter's back. She watched Peter wave goodbye to the officers, who were now laden down with gifts of fruit.

As soon as the patrol car was out of sight, Moe held up a megaphone and yelled, "I want all you men to listen to me. First, where's McNair? And you jump here, too, Milford."

Again the pickers booed as McNair hesitantly walked out of the office, his shiny black shoes now covered with dust, his eyes squinted closed from a combination of fear and sunlight.

Moe yelled, "What you just saw happen with the cops was an example of the way Milford can throw his weight around. If it means anything to you, he's had experience in labor law in Washington. We don't hear much about it, but he's handled several landmark cases that have gone to the Supreme Court. His old man has sent him here this summer to pull a few fast ones on us."

Somebody threw a peach that missed McNair by five feet, but he ducked anyway and was laughed at.

"Speak up, McNair," said Moe.

The man cleared his throat and shaded his eyes with his hands. "What I want to say to you men is that we in the home office are doing everything we can to work out the problems here."

"What are you doing about our jobs?—never mind the problems. What about the harvesters? And where will we work next?"

"This dispute is very complicated."

"Moose fired the five only because he's out to get rid of every man that he can—because Mariposa doesn't need any of us. It's too late for most of us to find other jobs. We're sticking here, and as an act of good faith, we want the five men to be rehired."

McNair looked at Moose, who looked down to a stick at his feet and shoved it with his toe.

"F-first," said McNair, "we must determine if the men are guilty."

"Go to hell, go to hell, go to hell," shouted the men.

"You can't take law and order in your own h-hands," said McNair in a weaker voice. The men were on their feet raising their hands in the air. Someone threw a couple of gritty figs. Peter managed to catch one of them, but the other hit McNair in the ear.

When he had recovered, he said, "Exactly what is it that you men want?"

"Higher pay, job security at least for the summer, decent treatment and proper training on the new machines."

"The harvesters are a local decision," said McNair as he fumbled for answers that he did not have.

"Then go back to San Francisco and sit on your can and leave us to work this thing out with Milford."

One of the men stuck a bucket used by the pickers behind McNair and pushed him and his pin-striped suit into it. McNair was stuck in more ways than one.

Peter helped McNair out, turned the bucket upside-down and sat him down on it properly. Then he held up his hand for quiet.

"You've already been offered the same price per pound for peaches that you pick up out of the catch surface. You will receive this pay until the carts arrive. This makes you men the highest paid laborers in the valley for the weeks that are involved.

"This is an unfortunate delay on the part of Havermeyer, but Mariposa and Milford Enterprises are paying for it—not you men.

"I'm sure that all of you have heard of the arrangement that has been satisfactorily worked out for the women who sort on the platform. The same kind of care is going into plans for year-round jobs either here or on our other property for any of you who want it.

"Moe mentioned my work in Washington. I am completely dedicated to decent working and living conditions for the migrant workers—but there have been too few of you to work when we needed you. That's why Mariposa has purchased the machines and why we need your cooperation.

"I understand that some of you men made as much as twenty-five dollars an hour the days you had help from the machines. That's at least fifteen dollars more than any of you have ever made before, isn't that right? How many are twenty-five-dollar men?"

Moe was one of the first to step forward. Twenty or more others joined him.

"But we haven't seen the money yet, Pete," Moe said. "The offer seems too good to be true."

"If we had to do it for the remainder of the summer, there wouldn't be money to pay you."

"We want our money now," said a short man in once-white baggy pants and a blue work shirt.

Peter leaned down and spoke to McNair, who was looking less and less dignified as he perched on the bucket.

"I think it's time we met with your leaders and negotiated a deal. Now, don't get excited, no work will take place on this ranch until we have come up with an acceptable package."

"And we won't negotiate unless we can be guaranteed a flat hourly pay of eight bucks for each of us during the first week of the negotiations," said Moe.

"Man, we'll lose the best part of the harvest if we don't settle sooner than that," protested Peter.

"Take it or leave it."

Peter jumped off the truck bed and helped McNair, who

would have jumped off and broken his ankles without aid. He motioned for Moe, Moose and McNair to follow him to the office.

After a few minutes, Moe yelled through the megaphone that he had a simple list that had been presented to the men by Milford, and that the men would meet inside the circle of trucks for as long as it took to make a deal.

"Fair enough, fair enough," chanted the men. There was a lot of hooting and shouting and Jana was sure that the men would agree with Peter's reasoning. If he had asked her, which he had not, she would have said that his offers to the men were too liberal. But, in his own way, Peter was a generous man—at least to some.

Ruby braced herself on the sorting table. "I'll say this for Pete. He may not know anything about growing peaches, but he sure knows how to handle men."

"I'm going to run over and see if I can bring Peter anything for lunch," said Cassie. "What are planning to do with your time, Jana, dear? Visit your good friend, Miss Mari?"

"That's a good idea. I think I will. And, Cassie, did you see Andy anywhere this morning? I need to talk to him for a second."

During the confrontation, she had forgotten all about Andy. In case he was looking for her, she wanted to tell him where she had gone.

"He's probably out there with that bunch, although I don't see his truck. But if I see him, I'll tell him that you've secluded yourself with the great Miss Mari."

Peter dashed in the door of the weigh house, but gave Jana only a startled passing glance. He handed Cassie one-hundred dollars and asked her to buy enough food to last the people in the office for a couple days.

Cassie leapt up and hugged him, told him how wonderful he had been out there in that dangerous situation, and promised to do anything she could for him through this difficult ordeal.

Although he walked right past Jana on his way back to the office, she might as well not have been there, so perfectly did his black eyes ignore her.

Chapter 17

Jana tapped on Miss Mari's screen door and peered into the dim interior.

Miss Mari appeared to have settled down for a long siege and had already turned on the blown glass lamp. It illumined her face as she sat buried in the easy chair next to it.

She wore a white, loose, long-sleeved dress, held a wine glass in one hand and with the other was scratching Honey's ears. She was already a little tipsy.

"Come on in if you're alone," she told Jana.

The living room was the stillest place in the world. The noise outside had not intruded on the space already filled with rare shapes and memories. Too bad Peter and the men couldn't have negotiated in this room and had the benefit of its hush to remove their angry shouts, and its shapes to smooth the awkward edges of their arguments.

"I knew I hadn't opened that bottle just for me. How's it going over there? Honey doesn't know whether to leap the fence or remain here and protect me. That army of angry voices must sound like amplified screams to her."

"Peter and Moose are waiting in the office in case the men present new demands."

"I should send them over some food. But I don't feel like it."

"Peter sent Cassie for a big order."

"A domestic little darling, isn't she? Reminds me of one of those mayflies—always in your way, never really contributing anything substantial. Well, mayflies come and mayflies go, but year after year, Cassie flutters on. Someday she's going to catch him. Oh, well, I suppose she and Aline would get along—although I think Aline is a genuine sort, don't you, Jana?"

"Miss Mari, why are you so down?"

"I don't know. I think this is the end. Moose was over and he sees little hope in the situation. Peter is out of his element, and he won't listen to anything Moose says. Pour me another glass, dear. You are having one, too, aren't you?"

Honey rested her head on the floor, but her ears were cupped straight ahead and refused to relax.

"Have you ever noticed that Peter never does anything the easy way? He never was like the Milford men. He always has his eyes focused on something that none of the rest of us see. He questions situations, people."

"To me, his eyes seem to be exactly like the ones belonging to the other Milford men," Jana said.

"Yes, he fooled his father for years with those eyes. They looked the same, but they were different. The other Milfords wanted to take home butterflies, tear them apart, own and possess them, pin them down with their stare. Peter only wanted to understand the butterflies. Question them. How was it to live in a cocoon all those days and find yourself so changed?

"My mother and grandmother learned how to adapt to a Milford marriage. My mother, for example, spent as little time as possible at the mansion in town. Lenore, Peter's mother, finally tried her hand at gardening. She ripped up the orange trees, hauled in dirt for the hills around the pool, then she excavated some of the hills in order to build a bigger pool and, finally, she dredged up additional ponds in the Japanese garden.

"I think that Joe felt if she could run around the world buying plants for the gardens, she would settle down. But, oh, no, she could only have the most original plants. She traveled to Japan, but wasn't content just to cart home what she could get through customs—boulders, goldfish, an original thirteenth-century bridge. No, she settled in and studied Japanese legends with a Japanese storyteller, Buddhism with a priest, and *sumi*—Japanese brush painting—with one of Japan's leading artists, claiming she desired to know the meaning of every blossom and boulder.

"The columns you have seen at the head of the swimming pool were, she said, taken from some island in the Mediterranean. I forget which one, because she was always changing the name of it. I've meant to have them checked out by someone to see if they are authentic. I rather doubt it."

"She sounds like a fascinating woman. Why won't Peter speak about her?"

"His memories—the few he has—are not pleasant. More wine, dear."

The dark purple glittered like a liquid crystal ball—one that was swirling backward in time. Jana poured herself a second glass.

"You know," said Miss Mari, "Lenore looked a great deal like you: straight, flyaway blonde bangs. She also wore her hair long, around her shoulders, only occasionally putting it up for special occasions."

"Our resemblance must have been how I was able to get your brother's attention away from the harvesters so readily."

"That was part of it."

"And all the time I thought. . . ."

"You were also very good, very convincing . . . even Peter. . . ."

Jana thought back to her first day at Mariposa. Maybe the resemblance had been the cause of Peter's initial, rather violent reaction to her presence.

"I heard that Lenore, with her blonde hair, was a sensation in Latin countries and the Far East. Have you ever . . . ?"

"No, I've only been to China. My company sent me there last winter on an agricultural inspection tour."

"What an awful time to go. You must have frozen."

"I took a hot water bottle."

"You must have worked very hard, too."

It was true. It had taken the typing pool at Havermeyer weeks to transcribe her voluminous taped accounts of the agricultural needs of China—which Havermeyer could so profitably supply.

"I was the newest employee in the group. The men were out drinking themselves to sleep every night and touring farms with a hangover by day. I had taken a camera and a tape recorder and many notes, and was able to give them an account when they returned. The men on the trip could then comprehend what they had seen."

"What a way to go to such a wonderful country! You poor thing. Maybe you can return someday and see the place properly."

Miss Mari's reaction was certainly different from most people she had talked with. They had said, "How lucky, how fortunate to have had the opportunity."

Jana glanced down at Honey to see whether the negotiations had grown more peaceful. Her head was now down on her paws, and one ear was independently alert to the sounds beyond the fence; but the other one was horizontal and at rest.

"You also move with the same grace as Lenore. Did you ever study dancing?"

"No, but often I watched television and would imitate the dancers all over our apartment. Of course, the grumpy couple downstairs would claim I knocked plaster onto their dining room table."

Jana stopped suddenly. How drab her life had been compared to Miss Mari's!

"Your voice resembles hers too," said Miss Mari, who would not drop the subject.

"Lenore was from somewhere in the Midwest—one of those no-accent places."

Jana interrupted. "Every geographical location imprints more of an accent than California, Miss Mari."

"I suppose. We're too much of a melting pot here. We're a casting director's dream. I think that's why I liked Rennie at first. I was familiar with the business, had friends and fathers of friends who were in Hollywood . . . they even wanted me to take a screen test . . . I never did . . . maybe I should have . . . but I went to France and my life was changed. My life was out of my control, for the first time."

Jana motioned toward the photograph of the soldier on the mantel. "Because of him?"

"God, no! That's Al—short for 'alibi,' I suppose. He was killed at Normandy. But he's been very useful to me." Miss Mari toasted the photograph by pointing her foot in a memorial kick.

"My mother and dad thought I was in France because that's

where poor Al died. *His* parents believed it, too. As far as they knew, their son was dead, but had been engaged to 'the Milford girl.' Although nobody knew who Al was, or even me, they knew the Milford name.

"In their minds, I became a living memorial to their son. They would whisper, 'Never married. Couldn't find another good as our Al. It was made in heaven.'

"Don't look so sympathetic. I collected a fine allowance from my dad for years. In those days, American money could buy anything—even Rennie Vardot. Would you believe his name—Renaud Vardot?

"We lived in Paris, yachted on the Mediterranean with people who liked our company because we were so carefree. Occasionally, he would direct a film—which was usually subsidized with my money."

"No one in your family knew about him?"

"Joe didn't care; my mother, if it had occurred to her, wouldn't have mentioned it; and my father thought that only men 'played around.'

"Would you see if you can open that other bottle over there? The opener—you see it?"

The living room had grown dark and only the little lamp illumined Miss Mari's face. She swallowed half the wine that Jana poured for her and held out her glass for more, saying, "Might as well save you from getting up again."

Shuddering, she added, "Don't taste this one yet. Let it breathe for ten or fifteen minutes."

Jana nodded in bleary obedience.

"Nope, the only Milford who ever met Rennie was Lenore," continued Miss Mari, her speech growing slower and slower, her tone dropping lower.

"Of all things, I ran into her at the sidewalk café in front of the Grand Hotel. We saw each other occasionally after that. For a week or two, I thought she had changed so much that I would like her for a friend. I never had any women friends—too busy with the boys, you understand. Lenore, without the Milford family looking down their snoots at her, was different.

"Finally, I took her to my apartment to meet Rennie. They hit it off right away, and we gave a party in Lenore's honor. Hell, we even took her with us on a spring cruise."

"And she never told anyone about Rennie?"

"Old Lenore never returned to America. She never dared. She knew that if she did, Joe might strangle her, and if he didn't, I would."

"Miss Mari, you don't mean that!" exclaimed Jana, knowing by the grating sound of her voice, and the purple squint under her heavy lids, that she certainly did.

"Instead of pear trees, rare shrubs or more acting lessons, Lenore invested in an expensive French project—Rennie. She moved him into her hotel suite, bought him new clothes. He finally told me one day by letter—the coward—that he wasn't returning to me but that he would prefer, if I had a lover, to move to another apartment, because he didn't like to think of someone else in the bed we had shared.

"At that moment, and that moment only, I saw the value of marriage. If we had been married, I would have knocked him out of commission for the rest of his life. He had no money, but I could have ruined his reputation. But I didn't have to: Lenore did it for me. She killed his talent—and herself—in the process. They drank and traveled, drank and gambled. She ate little, drank a lot, and finally died of malnutrition.

"I read a few years ago that Rennie died in a nursing home in Leeds, England. What he was doing either in England or in a nursing home, I can't imagine. Surely, he wasn't that old?"

"How awful for you! Were you the one who told Joe about his wife?"

"I merely confirmed what he had already guessed from seeing photographs of them in *Life* and *Look*. One in particular showed them dancing in Monaco . . . when you begin the beguine, da-da, da-da-da. More wine, darling? It's certainly breathed long enough. Sometimes I think I have, too."

"How did Mr. Milford and Peter take her—her escapades?"

"Joe had his eye on another, anyway. I suppose you could say that he sold one and bought t'other. Poor little Peter was only six years old. He never understood, but his mother had been away for so long, he never exactly knew when he began missing her.

"And all these years I've lived a respectable do-gooder's life in the valley; the name of my grief has been 'Al.' Have you noticed, it always helps people feel better if they can put a name on your trouble? And I'm a big shot around here on Veteran's Day. People have probably bought more poppies from me than anyone in California. But now you and I know the truth, don't we, Jana?"

Miss Mari pointed one of her toes, and from her sitting position traced a red octagon in the rug, as though she were trying to make sense of her life by following a Persian design.

"Have you ever had anything like that happen to you? Ever lost a great love, and what's worse, discovered that you had invented the love and only lost the person?"

"Miss Mari, you took a risk with Rennie. I've never allowed myself to fall that far out of control."

"I see. You mean you've run your romantic life the way you did your tour of China, skipping over the intricacies, the danger, with an eye to power in the company, a secure future, a toe on a higher rung of the corporate ladder?" Miss Mari was not at all approving of Jana's sensible, already well-rewarded behavior.

Jana felt inundated with wine. She wished she could lean her head on a big, strong shoulder. Since the only one she had leaned on lately was Andy's, Andy would be perfect. That long, sweet pillow of a body. What could she say to Miss Mari? That only since arriving in the valley had she found herself treading around the rim of desire almost hourly?

Someone had once told her he had never sweated until he had taken his first hour-long sauna. Since then, he had sweated over the slightest emotion.

Andy had been her sauna, she supposed. The constant presence of his perfect body had innocently aroused her to react in a way that was far off her beaten track. Her response to him had almost nothing to do with the careful plans she had always made involving work, future, family and Spenser—dreary little Spenser.

Or could her emotions, which were so frequently out of control, have something to do with Peter? Peter and his high-wire tension, which began with the taut gaze of his eyes and continued as he strung her to his wavelength almost every time she encountered him.

Miss Mari's voice broke the pattern of her thoughts.

"I suppose I went a little crazy after I lost Rennie. It's allowed. Nobody has to remain on her original hinge all her life. And I swung back—a little tougher, a lot more cynical and ten times more leery of any real relationships."

Jana felt embarrassed, and checked Honey's ears for signs of the commotion outside. That one ear was still alert, but her eyes were closed in a fluttery sleep. The collie knew she should remain awake because all was not normal, but it was becoming increasingly hard to do.

"I should have been raised like the Milford men. I could have manipulated Rennie right out from under—yes, under—Lenore. No, that doesn't make sense, does it? I should have been raised like her."

"Do you think the Milford men are manipulators, Miss Mari?"

"They have a certain ability. Peter's not very good at it, though, is he? He lost Susan. But I saw him watching you the night Joe was talking to you. He may have found a replacement for her—at least a temporary one."

Jana resented Miss Mari for saying that. But, then, the woman could afford to view her only nephew generously. He was her only hope for saving Mariposa.

"Let's have some more wine, Jana. We must comfort each other, you and I."

Jana refilled Miss Mari's glass, but did not pour herself any.

"There, I've made you angry, talking about Susan. See, I've hit a tender spot, I knew it. But Susan is married to Ken now. Her responsibilities are walling Peter out of her life—probably forever. And she has guilt about her sister. If Ginni had only been in the main house, she could have easily been rescued.

"But I think Ken and Susan will make it. Ken is older and more patient than Peter was—than Peter will ever be. I tell Peter that Susan is finally with the man she needs. He gets as angry with me as you did. That's okay. I know when to be quiet." Miss Mari smiled at Jana's discomfort.

"How do you like the watercolor in the dining room? My mother, who could never afford a Turner oil, made a special trip to England to buy it. I'm thinking of giving it to Susan for her new home."

"Are they rebuilding in the mountains?"

"I don't think they'll be able to emotionally, but they haven't ruled it out. I tried to urge them to build near here, and even suggested part of my own land. But the way this place is overgrown and with my house smack in the middle of the ranch, just the thought of another structure made them feel crowded. And if Joe sells, where would they be? Living in the middle of some damned rice paddy."

"Isn't Ken wealthy? Couldn't he afford to buy Mariposa if it is sold?"

"If he did, this place would be an unlivable dustbin in a couple of years. It's already been hard for Susan to accept the responsibility of caring for Lisa. Ken told me the strain on her has been tremendous. Neither of them is interested in manicuring an orchard, and it takes attention that is almost that detailed."

Miss Mari was searching her glass as if looking for something good in it to speak about. "Only in the last year has Peter been able to be in the same room with Ken without bursting out in a threat."

"Since Lisa was born?"

Miss Mari looked at Jana suspiciously. "I guess you could say that. The little girl has been a blessing in a lot of ways. If it hadn't been for her, Peter would still be standing with his foot on Ken's neck every time their paths crossed.

"What do you suppose Peter and Moose are having for dinner? What are we having? It's past dinnertime, though, isn't it? Good, that means we don't have to eat.

"I certainly hope that Cassie didn't go out and buy fried chicken. Moose hates the take-out kind. He claims he always discovers little hairs all over it."

"You and Moose have been friends for a long time, haven't you, Miss Mari?"

"Too long, I sometimes think. I've known him since I was a child and *his* father was superintendent of this ranch."

"He seems terribly fond of you."

"Oh, he is. We've had a fondness going for years. Don't look so surprised. It was second best for both of us, but we've made do. At first, when Moose and I took up with each other, I thought I must be a nymphomaniac because I often wanted men whether I liked them or not. I thought, 'This isn't normal.' My mother never noticed my father, much less other men . . . unless. You know, she did spend a lot of time in England and we've only got that one watercolor to show for it. Well, you never know.

"Moose is attractive. He's always been in the wrong place at the wrong time. He should have had Milford money and been allowed to study art wherever he wanted to. He's more talented than anyone I know, and he's never had time to fulfill himself. I'm the only one of the Milfords to ever give him credit for his real calling. And now, just when he thought he was in control, Peter roars in and pulls the ranch out from under him.

"I'll bet a lot of people will be surprised when I marry him after all these years."

"Miss Mari!"

"If the ranch isn't sold, Peter and Moose will never agree about their methods for running it. And if it is—what will Moose do? Sometimes, the most comfortable accommodation must be made. Besides, I think Moose would be fun to travel with and, as soon as the Tourist Center is on its feet, that's what I'd like to do."

Miss Mari stared sleepily at the door. Jana grabbed her glass from her hand before it fell, but just as she did, Honey barked and Miss Mari was wide-eyed and awake.

The men were outside cheering.

Jana and Miss Mari rushed out on the porch as Peter rushed through the gate, his fist clenched in victory. The strike was over.

Chapter 18

Peter drove Jana home, which is where she insisted on spending the night.

"Where's your room?" Peter's voice seemed to be at the end of the hall where her room was located.

California was full of blurry nights. It must be the weather. Or the grapes. Or the grapey weather.

"Be late tomorrow if you wish," he said, "I'll have to teach Miss Mari not to inebriate my employees before the big day when their company's machinery goes into full operation. Yes, the men have agreed to it, does that make you happy?"

"Happy," she said. "But I'm even happier that the strike is over."

"There's still a lot of emotion focused on the machines."

"There is a lot of emotion everywhere, isn't there?" she said softly, and closed her bedroom door to keep from inviting Peter in.

Jana lay down on her bed and stared up at herself in the smoky ceiling mirror. She stretched out her legs and her arms into a butterfly design and studied what Peter's mother must have looked like, and silently cursed the woman for not choosing somebody else to resemble.

Jana thought of Miss Mari and Rennie. She wanted to cry.

Miss Mari had never found another Rennie. All these years, she had lived with nobody but herself—except for Moose, who was a comfortable partner.

Or had there been others and were they stories for another night? If so, Jana would gladly relinquish herself to their tales—and tears. They represented life, and Miss Mari had lived her life fully. What about herself? Where was her life being lived?

Unable to face herself, Jana closed her eyes. The image on the ceiling receded, and she dreamed of drinking gallons of pure, cold water. Her sleep was thirsty. Dry. Hot.

Andy was shaking her.

"Wake up," he said with urgency in his voice.

"I can't. I'm fraught with exhaustion."

"You're what?"

"Fraught."

"Hurry, Jana."

"It's not even daylight. Lie down next to me, on me, in me—but, Andy, don't hurry me."

"Jana." He shook her again. "There's a fire at Mariposa."

"Oh," she groaned, "that old weigh house, it's nothing but a match box."

"It isn't the weigh house."

"That office. All the debris under it. And dry as a bone."

"Jana, it's Miss Mari's house."

"No!" Impossible: that house, covered with vines of cool green and pink flowers, had to be protected against flames forever. But Andy had said fire.

"No!" she cried again, this time jumping up, still wearing Miss Mari's clothes.

"I'm on my way out there. Don't you want to go with me?"

"Of course I do." She was opening drawers, dropping clothes out on the floor, grabbing a light blue cotton turtle-neck and yanking it over her head. She was completely awake, totally sober.

As the Honda sped toward Mariposa, Jana asked one question after another. "It's not a bad fire, is it, Andy? Miss Mari has Honey: the dog would have barked. Who discovered it? When did it begin? It's such a little fire, it will probably be out by the time we arrive."

"I don't think so."

"What do you mean? How did you learn about it? Why didn't you tell me sooner?"

"One of the drivers who lives down the road from Mariposa saw it and telephoned me."

"And what about Miss Mari?"

He didn't answer.

She screamed. "Miss Mari? Is she hurt?"

"I was told that she had been hurt."

"Was she burned? Or did she have to jump? What does 'hurt' mean?"

Jana could see a glow in the distance—a bunsen burner-sized glow. In the scheme of the world, it was as nothing. It couldn't hurt a fly.

"It seems," continued Andy, "that Miss Mari was out of the house safely and then went back in. That's when the fire really went out of control. She probably went in to retrieve one of those damned pictures of hers. Milfords always have clung to every damned thing they could get their hands on. When she reached the porch, the roof fell in on her."

"But how do you know?"

"That's just what I was told. It may be incorrect information."

"How badly—just tell me how badly she was hurt?"

"She was knocked down and burned. Because of the flames, nobody except that damned dog could get to her."

"Andy, just be quiet and *hurry.*"

"I don't want you getting all worked up about this now. There's nothing you can do about it now."

Jana hated him, and the fear and hatred together dried her mouth, her chest, her throat. It was as if the flames had passed through her, too, and left her inside and out like a field of stubble.

As they turned into the Mariposa Road, an ambulance squealed past them.

"Miss Mari's in there. I know it!"

"You don't know any such thing. It could be almost anybody who was in that house visiting her. And from what I hear. . . ."

"Will you shut up!" screamed Jana.

Andy swerved off the road, screeching the brakes as he pulled to a stop. "I can't drive any closer."

Jana was already out of the car, sprinting like a weightless stalk in the wind, disbelieving what she saw ahead of her. Fire trucks, water spraying in the air, police cars with electrical bouquets whirling danger, television crews, flash cameras and fire roasting the second story of Miss Mari's house as it flamed out of every window.

"Who was in that ambulance?" she demanded of the first person who turned to her—a television cameraman.

"Some lady."

"How badly was she hurt?"

"She was unconscious. They think her neck is broken. She had severe burns." The idiot was smiling. "We got some great shots for tomorrow morning's 'Rise and Shine Breakfast Show.' Channel Two, don't forget to watch."

"You shut up."

A reporter stuck a microphone under her nose. "Are you a member of the family?"

She knocked the black stick out of his hand. Where was Peter?

Andy caught up with her. "I saw what you did. You're making a fool of yourself. I think you had better wait at home."

"You go to hell!"

"My theory is that the house is burning so nicely because it's so full of junk."

Jana flung herself around as if she were the eye of a tornado and slapped his face. Her hand missed his cheek and hit Andy on the side of the nose.

"You make me sick," she said, just as the blood gushed out. And in spite of the damage she had done, she darted ahead of him.

Ruby headed her off. "Can you take me to the hospital? I want to be with Miss Mari." The two of them were drenched in a spray that the fireman had directed toward the roof of the office and weigh house.

Andy ran up behind them and said they were in the way and had to get out of there.

"Ruby and I must go to the hospital, but first I want to find Peter."

"There he is!" screamed Ruby.

Peter was running from behind one of Miss Mari's shrubs with something in his arms. Not until he thrust it forward could she tell that it was Honey, now a short-haired collie where she had any hair at all.

Jana held out her arms for the sooty bundle, but Peter delivered the dog to Andy—who hesitantly took it. Jana knew what he was thinking: that his white shirt and pants would get dirty.

"Take her to Dr. Hansen down the road," yelled Peter. His face was black and scratched, his arm bleeding. Jana loved him.

Honey's eyes were open. Jana touched the dog's head and Honey licked her hand. The dog whimpered as the crash came.

Jana looked up in time to see the roof falling in. Peter dashed in the direction of the house.

Andy, whom Jana forced to hold the dog all the way to the vet's, sat in the passenger seat and Jana drove, with Andy giving her directions.

They stood by the examining table while Dr. Hansen checked for broken bones. He said that while the dog might be one of the first hairless collies in the country, she was going to be fine, but that he preferred to treat her burns and keep her for several days.

"I'll pick her up," promised Jana. "I'll keep her with me."

"No, you won't," said Andy. "No animals allowed at the complex, and I think Gretchen is allergic to dog hair."

"Then I'll move," said Jana firmly.

Andy steered her toward the car. As soon as she was in it, he shook her until her teeth felt loose. "You're acting like an emotional child," he said. "No one has been killed in this fire. And you haven't been hurt at all. It's not *your* house that has burned down, but you are acting as if it were."

"That's how I feel, Andy. I can't help it. What's going to happen? Peter only had a month."

"They'll sell out, that's all. No big deal. The house was old. You've placed too much sentimental value on it. It's as though you're superstitious or something."

He didn't understand. How could he? Andy had thought that the *mansion* was not only the most important of the Milford homes but, originally, he had thought it the most beautiful home he had ever seen. Andy had no feeling for the Milfords' land—or anybody's. He only wanted to possess her. She could feel it and it sickened her—especially on such a night.

He backed out of Dr. Hansen's driveway, saying that he wished he had asked where the bathroom was, so he could have washed his hands.

Andy had driven for about ten minutes before Jana realized they were headed toward Fresno.

"Stop!" she screamed.

He drove faster, merely questioning her by raising an eyebrow, but doing nothing about her demand.

"What are you doing? You turn around!"

"I think you should get some sleep."

"Don't you tell me what I need. You turn around and. . . ." She grabbed the steering wheel. She was screaming anything she could think of—that she hated him, would never speak to him again if he did not return her to Mariposa. She topped it off by calling him a selfish, spoiled, cruel bastard at a pitch that reached through his eardrums and registered on some vulnerable spot in his brain.

This time, when he parked, Jana walked slowly toward the flames, through the noises of two-way radios and hushed groups of neighbors who had come to stare.

She had not seen Moose anywhere. Had he and Miss Mari had an argument after Peter had taken her home? Had Miss Mari presented her plan to Moose, and had he been so displeased that he was punishing Miss Mari by exercising the only power he had remaining—that of an arsonist?

Maybe I am overreacting, Jana thought, her brain whirling. Moose was gruff, but even Cassie could find a soft spot in his heart any time she wanted to. And he hadn't said anything during the strike, although Jana could tell that he had wanted to.

Jana pictured Moe, McNair, Peter and Moose sitting around one of those old desks in the office. Every time Moose tried to say something, he would be silenced by one of them. But still waters ran deep. Moose knew as well as anybody that Miss Mari's house was a symbol for the success or failure of Mariposa. Maybe, seeing that he was going to have no part in Mariposa's future, Moose reasoned that he would be the final cause of its downfall. With a great effort, Jana pushed her suspicions aside.

"Now," said Andy, "are you satisfied that there's no reason for you to be here?"

"I am not. Miss Mari had other animals. And, besides, she returned to that house for something. It must have been important."

Jana pushed her way to the edge of Miss Mari's high hedge.

"You'll be hurt. One of these fire trucks will run over you.

Those hoses spray water hard enough to injure you seriously. You've got to get back."

Jana squeezed into the hedge so that she was completely out of sight.

She heard Andy yelling. "If you won't listen to me, I'll find someone who can make you listen. I'll find Peter—or a highway patrolman."

Jana inched on. The main part of the fire had centered in the kitchen of the house. The front porch and the living room, where it had originated, were now smoldering beneath the tons of water that had been sprayed on them.

She wasn't looking at the smoldering part. She was reasoning that, if Miss Mari had actually retrieved something from the house and been injured on her way out, she would not have been able to hold onto it. Whatever it was might still be there.

She stood waiting for it to reveal itself. What would Miss Mari have thought precious enough to return for?

The picture of her "alibi"? The lamp Moose had made? The family portraits? Some of the oil paintings by Thomas Moran, from his series of paintings of Yosemite?

No. It would be the little Turner watercolor her mother had brought back from London, the one she planned to give to Susan.

Thinking that she saw a glimmer of glass at the edge of the front porch, Jana bent down and raced over to it. The glass was a broken window pane.

"Get her out of there!" she heard someone yell.

"Jana!" The voice belonged to Peter. She glanced past the gaping hole in the hedge made by the fire truck. He was being held by firemen, who were grasping both his arms.

Jana slid through the muck and ashes to check both sides of the porch steps. As she did, she saw a corner of a picture frame. It was upside-down, but she knew at once that it was the Turner, and that it would be trampled by firemen who were still dragging hoses through the house, if she did not remove it.

With one hand hanging onto the wisteria vine, Jana reached down and snatched the picture. The glass was broken and water was beginning to seep in. Instead of leaving Miss Mari's yard the way she had come in, she ran out the front of the gate, picture in hand.

Peter and Andy were running after her. She didn't stop

until she reached the platform of the weigh house and, immediately, carefully, she extracted the picture from the frame.

Andy was calling her crazy; Peter was telling Andy to shut up, and Ruby was rustling around for a clean peach box to put the picture in.

"I used most of them for the kittens. We took them over to the house for my husband to look after. At least, that's something he can do."

Jana saw Peter walk around to the office where he sat down on the steps. Carrying the peach box, she followed him. She wanted to explain, to reach out to him, touch him. But if she did, she might cause more pain to his cuts and seared flesh.

He looked down into the box for a long time. Then, he studied her face with the same exhausted gaze. Finally, he said, "Miss Mari will be grateful."

"Peter," she said, "what happened?"

"At first, it looked as if a spark hit the roof of the porch."

"From where?"

"Maybe from one of the trucks this afternoon. And maybe also somebody threw an oil-soaked rag on the roof."

"Nobody would do that—would they?"

"It's possible that it was an accidental fire, but more probably it was sabotage."

"But who?"

"Somebody who was disappointed that the strike was amicably settled by the end of the day. Someone who wanted Mariposa to be out of commission for a longer time than it was."

"Peter, where's Moose? I've been thinking that Moose has been a very unhappy person."

"Jana, you're getting wild ideas. Moose went to the hospital with Miss Mari. He'd never do anything like that."

"I'm going to the hospital, too—with Ruby."

Andy stepped up behind her, and braced his foot on the step in front of her, almost surrounding her with his body. "You're not staying there long," he said. "You've done quite enough for the Milfords today—including risking your life to save that painting."

"Andy, you, of all people, shouldn't begrudge the rescue of a Turner. And you know good and well that the fire had spread around to the other side of the house. I was perfectly safe."

"Unless more of the porch fell in."

"Let's go," said Ruby. "Jana and I are going to stay at the hospital all night if we are needed."

Jana followed Peter's eyes as they watched the house, which was still in flames toward the back.

"I wish they would let it burn to the ground," he said.

What would make him feel that way? Was it because, through enormous odds, he had fought to end the strike, had won a few weeks from his father in which to prove he could save Mariposa—and, now, the symbol of Mariposa had been destroyed?

"If we're going to the hospital, come on, Jana." Andy was impatient.

"Yes," chirped Ruby. "Miss Mari may need us."

Jana was reluctant to leave. Peter's eyes had no brightness of their own: they were yellow, then red, as they reflected the flames.

"Andy, why don't you and Ruby go ahead? I'll wait and go with Peter," Jana offered.

"No," Peter replied. "I've got to arrange to have several of the men stand watch tonight. If anybody has any funny ideas about running off with anything, we'll shoot hell out of them. Besides, I don't want you around here: you're too closely identified with the harvesters. You could have been the victim, and not the house."

In protest to Andy's behavior, Jana sat in the back seat of the car. Mainly, however, she wanted to be as far from the intrusion of anyone else's thoughts as possible.

Andy was saying he couldn't see why Peter needed guards —because there was nothing left to steal, except the harvesters, and who would want those?

Ruby was clearly even more excited than she had been the day she and the other women had called a press conference. She was warbling a history of tragedies that had happened in the vicinity, her voice pitched loud enough for Jana to hear.

"Happened up at the cannery last year . . . he inhaled chlorine steam. Bleached out his hair and eyebrows, too. The poor soul died an albino. . . . Coupla fellas slammed into the back of a mower on Route Ninety-nine. Severed one head, took off the top of the other."

Jana tuned out in order to be able to leap to Miss Mari's aid, as surely all who truly cared about her were doing.

Chapter 19

At the hospital, Moose's face was the color of moon dust. His words crumbled out in dry, barren chunks.

"Critical condition. First-degree burns. Bruises. Broken leg. Shock. Unconscious. In operating room."

Jana sank down on a mustard-colored Naugahyde couch in the waiting room, as Moose disappeared to be closer to the patient.

He never said broken neck. At least, that, Miss Mari didn't have—did she?

Andy was poised to crash down next to her on the couch.

"Not there," she said, holding her hand over the cushion next to her.

"Don't tell me you're still mad?"

"Someone has spilled something sticky—soda, I think." The glistening streaks on the cushion confirmed it. Andy sat opposite her on the edge of a square, backless bench with cushions matching the couch. Head on hand, elbow on knee, a leg sprawled toward her, hating the soot and blood on his T-shirt from carrying Honey, he looked as uncomfortable as she was sure he was.

"How's your nose?"

"Okay. How's your hand?"

With a smile now possible between them, Jana had more space in her thoughts to concern herself with Miss Mari.

Andy picked up a rumpled, wrinkled *Woman's Day,* which boasted a feature article on how to eat for thirty-seven cents a meal.

Ruby, her own nose barely reaching the desktop of the nurses' station, had positioned herself next to it like a little bird waiting to open her mouth and swallow the first crumb of information that might be tossed.

Tonight, Ruby wore polyester pink plaid pants and a pink sweater. She had tied a scarf over her head—a red and blue plaid one—which brought the image of a bird into unforgettable focus.

Jana closed her eyes, not in prayer as she probably should, but because her brain was whirling a litany of unbelief.

Only tonight, surrounded by the Tiffany-like glow of that little lamp, Miss Mari had attempted to trace a pattern of sense to her life with only bare toes, a Persian rug and one glass of wine after another.

Everything in that house had glowed with depth, sorrow, perfection and the round hopes of the future.

And now? What if Havermeyer called her back this week? She would refuse to return. Miss Mari would want her to be here. Peter might need her. Mariposa, the Tourist Center . . . and she, above all, needed to remain.

Jana had to face another worry. Had all that wine been the cause of Miss Mari's accident? Was her judgment not sharp enough to guide her out of the house once and for all? While Jana was struggling with little things like the buckle on her sandal and staring up at that damned smoky mirror in her ceiling, was Miss Mari, stubborn, bleary, fighting her way back into the house for the watercolor?

Andy jumped up and attacked the soft drink machine with quarters. He brought Jana a soda of her own to spill. She couldn't bear breaking into her thought to say thanks aloud and, instead, absently smiled at him. She took a sip of the riotously fizzing drink, and again closed her eyes.

Ruby returned to report that she had nothing to report, but that she suspected all was not well. "They won't tell us anything because we're not family."

"Don't say that in front of Jana," said Andy, "because she thinks that she is."

Jana felt hot lead squeeze between her eyelashes and begin to disfigure her face.

Seeing the tears, Andy retaliated for his nosebleed by showing a lack of concern. He stretched, rose from his bench and said, "I'm going outside for a walk around the hospital."

Jana stretched out her arm on the couch and leaned her forehead on it. There are some men, she had been told by her mother, who react peculiarly in the face of tragedy.

When her brother was born prematurely and was in an incubator for four months, her mother had said that her father had refused to see him: if the baby lived, he would never look that scrawny and birdlike again; and if he didn't, what was the point?

Shortly after Kyle was brought home from the hospital, her father had disappeared. The medical bills were enormous; he couldn't function under their weight. That was her mother's rationalization. She had heard it recited until she had memorized the exact syntax of her mother's moanings. "If only I had given *him* more attention; but there was the baby and you were starting kindergarten. . . ."

Andy expected attention from her, and that was usually easy to give, but not at a time like this.

In the mountains that day of Ginni's death, Andy had been sluggish, useless and almost unconscious until the helicopter had arrived. She remembered that when her three-year-old cousin had drowned in the backyard, her uncle went to bed for three days and slept soundly until he was awakened for the funeral.

"Women are stronger," was her mother's conclusion. "Perhaps because men, unless they are in war, never face death until they are old. They aren't primed for a cycle in which pain and the possibility of death occurs with each new life."

No, Jana wouldn't be irritated with Andy. At least, she resolved not to show it. It was no night to reform the pattern he had developed over a lifetime.

"Peter has just arrived," Ruby reported breathlessly.

Jana looked up expectantly.

"He's been taken to see Miss Mari. She's out of the operating room."

"Did they say anything?"

"Nothing. And that's bad. Where's gorgeous George?"

"Out for a walk."

"He's a big help. Just like my husband."

"What do you mean?"

"I don't know. This isn't a night to be criticizing anybody, is it? I mean, faults and all, we're all better off *with* each other than without. Besides, here he is."

"You didn't stay long." Jana held up her hand to him and he pulled her to him, slowly, gratefully. As Jana leaned into his arms, she knew. Although everyone has to face life and death alone—alone *together* is better. All Andy needed was love; and at this moment, Jana loved everyone. She was convinced it was this love of life, which, more than anything, would help fight the threat of Miss Mari's death.

"Let's go home," said Andy, "and be together."

Ruby gave Jana an I-told-you-so look.

"Not now, Andy."

"I just saw Ken and Susan, with Lisa in her pajamas, driving into the parking lot."

"Did you tell them where to go?"

"I haven't spoken to Ken, nor will I, until he apologizes to me for the way he treated me that day at Miss Mari's—and for all the lies he has spread about me."

"Andy, we need your natural, loving nature; we don't have room for the other tonight. No grudges, please. We have to stick together—and help Miss Mari live."

Susan, carrying Lisa asleep on her shoulder, swiftly approached. Her green eyes were tired and teary.

"What happened? We heard on the news. . . ."

Ever-ready Ruby gave her report.

"And where were you?" Ken asked Andy.

"In bed. By myself."

"Why didn't anybody help Miss Mari out?"

"Don't worry, Ken. I wasn't there."

"A lot of good it would have done if you had been."

"Ken," snapped Susan, "leave him alone."

Lisa stirred and whimpered.

"Let me hold her before she wakes up fully," said Jana. "You and Ken go on and see what you can find out. Moose and Peter are back in there somewhere."

"How is Moose holding up?" asked Susan.

"He looks terrible," said Jana.

"Yes, terrible," agreed Ruby.

Ken added, "Just when things were looking up for those two."

"Ken, don't talk like that!" said Susan. "Miss Mari is alive. She's going to live. She has to."

Jana rocked Lisa, slowly, slowly. The fluorescent light was so bright, nothing like the sunlight swirling through a fruit jar or a stained-glass pane or around the heavy lace of Miss Mari's hanging plants before earning its right to enter a room.

She hestitated to speak. If Lisa awakened, she would know for sure that it was not her mother holding, comforting, loving her. Whispering, Jana said, "Andy, since we're the only ones using this waiting room, don't you think we could turn off those awful overhead lights? The table lamp will be enough."

Jana sat down and rocked Lisa again. Where would she have been were she not in this room with the warm little girl in her arms? What had her life been like before she knew the family—the families—that had produced this moist little face, the fat pink hands, the little feet wearing the duck house-shoes?

"Little girl, little girl, where have you been?" she started improvising words to the folksong. Jana addressed her own once-Lisa-sized self. And where are you going? And will you have cuddly babies like this? I wish you weren't asleep. I'd like to see your eyes. The eyes of Peter's baby.

Holding Lisa made Jana feel that there was a wall of baby between her and the world. Was this the fourth wall of her room—the wall she had not yet written on?

"Peter makes pretty babies, doesn't he?" said Andy.

"I think all babies are pretty. There's no sense dwelling on whose baby she is. Talk like that can ignite and hurt a lot of people. I think you should forget it." She sensed her voice rising, and resolved to be quiet.

Lisa stirred and Jana held her on her shoulder and patted her.

You sensible engineer, you Harvard grad, where did you get the idea that the future was only a direction in which you looked, not a place where you belonged? Miss Mari's house had no blank walls saved for the future: every wall was a showcase where jewels, exuding the aroma of burgundy, lived in the present to tell about a day gone by, a day in the future.

Miss Mari, my walls are crumbling. I need you.

When would Lisa wake up? Baby, baby, what color are your eyes?

Jana lay the child down on the couch and rested the little

head on her lap. Little girl, you are loved for only being you, now, but it won't always be so. Someday, you will be grown up like Andy, and what you are will be the reason you are loved.

What are *you*, Jana Robbins? What do you really want? Success, money, a respectably chosen husband who will enter you in ways that only you teach him, or will you settle for what you pray will be granted to Miss Mari: life? Life alone.

But life is never alone.

She remembered words from a poem called "Love's Philosophy."

> *Nothing in the world is single;*
> *All things by a law divine*
> *In one another's being mingle;*
> *Why not I with thine?*

Shelley had had it easy: he probably knew who "thine" was. But for her? If she had to choose at this moment, would it be Andy—so easy to touch, or Peter—so difficult to reach?

She looked around for Andy. Moose had come in and was sitting in a darkened corner.

"Did you see Andy anywhere?" she asked softly.

"He said he was expecting a phone call and went home. You're supposed to call him when you're ready to leave."

Moose paced restlessly to the soft drink machine: Tab; orange; Dr. Pepper; Sprite. So many decisions, he seemed to be thinking.

"She's in an oxygen tent," he said without turning toward Jana. "They haven't even set the bones in her leg."

"But why not?"

Moose turned around. Tears were spilling from his eyes. "They're waiting to see if she lives."

"No!" protested Jana, bursting into tears—for Miss Mari, for herself, Peter, Moose . . . and for the little life asleep in her lap.

"Here," said Moose gently. "You lay Lisa's head down on my jacket and slip out from under her."

"It's okay. I won't do that again."

"I saw you with her earlier, hon. You'll feel better if you walk around a little."

Jana did as she was told. Standing by Moose, she turned and looked down at Lisa. "She's sweet, isn't she?"

"Miss Mari wanted Peter to have more than one."

Jana did not react. Moose was too spent to realize what he was saying. But what if she hadn't known that Peter was Lisa's natural father?

"Miss Mari told me that you knew."

"We didn't talk about it."

"Don't you know by now that half of one's conversation with Miss Mari goes on in silence?"

Jana smiled. It was true.

"I spent the evening with her after you left. She was in a fine mood."

"But not very sober."

"Hell, yes. She perked up right away after she heard about the strike being over. That woman can drink straight bourbon all night and be as sober as a stick whenever she chooses to be."

Moose broke the silence that followed. "She told you about us, too, didn't she? She's got some funny ideas, and it's hard for me to cotton to most of them. What she's trying to turn me into is a kept man—a gigolo."

"Moose! You're not the gigolo type."

"Ah, but I could be. No, seriously, I could never go along with Miss Mari's idea of marrying her and traveling here and there with her. I like to remain in one place. My hobbies. . . ."

"Miss Mari calls it art. . . ."

"Whatever it is I do when I'm not worrying about Mariposa gives me all the traveling to other places that I'll ever need. Do you see what I mean?"

"Moose, did you and Miss Mari quarrel?"

"We usually do. Let me see, I'd say that I'm almost sure we quarreled very little tonight. We talked, drank some more wine—at least I did—and went upstairs.

"I remember, the quarrel was about my staying the entire night. I usually do. But I kept having the notion I should check on the damned harvesters. We left them down at the machine shop. Have you seen it? About a mile and a half down the Orchard Road? In spite of the strike's seemingly-satisfactory settlement, I felt real uneasy. Hell, I walked out right under that porch roof, where something must have already been smoldering."

How could Jana have ever thought Moose might be connected to the awful events that had followed? He loved the house and Mariposa as much as anyone, and had contributed to it in hundreds of ways.

"Did you hear anybody, see anyone?"

"Nobody. And there the harvesters sat at the shop, ugly as ever."

"I mean, did you hear or see anything odd outside Miss Mari's?"

The silence that followed existed only between them. Lisa murmured, a doctor was paged and three nurses' aides giggled at the soft drink machine.

When they had gone, Moose said, "Did Miss Mari tell you that she felt Peter and I would never see eye to eye, even if Mariposa hangs together?"

"But that fits in with her plans to travel, doesn't it?"

"I know all about her traveling. She says she'll be gone two weeks and she's home in nine days. When she goes off for a weekend, she's driving through the gate on Saturday afternoon."

"Moose, she told me that you are too talented to spend all your time on peaches."

"It's not the peaches. . . ." His voice choked. "It's everything about the place."

"I know, Moose, I know." Jana leaned his head on her shoulder and held him as he sobbed.

"Moose, Miss Mari loves you very much. You must believe in that love. Hold onto it. It's the only kind of life that counts right now."

"She's a helluva lady. Our lives have always been caught in the crossfires of circumstance. She's gone out and sought hers, mine have settled on me from my father. It's hard to find a meeting ground."

"Moose, she's your biggest supporter."

"Not anymore," he said. "She's rooting for Peter."

"I meant that she believes in your art."

"That's not enough," he said. "And who knows? Peter may know more about the ranch than I do. But I've never had Joe's financial support; Peter can sign checks, which I never could. I'm going to stand up for what I think is right—especially after this accident—but who knows? I may have to eat my words and go on the road with Mari."

"You can see her now, if you want to." Peter was standing at the entrance to the waiting room.

"Is she conscious?" asked Moose.

"No. Go on, anyway. She might know you're there. You know how she is about these things."

"Peter," whispered Jana, "how is she?"

"Not good." His voice was scratchy. His eyes were like tiny pools of tar: dull and visionless.

He walked over to Lisa. Her hand was in front of her mouth. He touched it lightly. After a few moments, he asked, "She doesn't suck her thumb, does she?"

"I don't think so," said Jana. "She puts her hand over her mouth as a substitute gesture. My little brother used to do it. It's easier to outgrow than thumb-sucking. Don't worry."

Peter sat down on the space remaining on the couch where Lisa was sleeping. Jana had the impression he had never had this much time with Lisa since she was born. She and Moose remained in the shadows of the room, although Jana wanted to weep for Peter, if he was not going to do it himself.

Peter slowly pulled himself to his feet and, after rubbing his eyes, joined Jana and Moose.

"She's a right nice little girl, Pete," said Moose.

"Don't you ever let me hear you mention her again!" snapped Peter, his words hissing angrily like an aerosol spray, filling the room with a dangerous chemical that could ignite at any moment.

Jana flipped the bright ceiling lights back on. This smart move deflected the hostility between the two men, but caused Lisa to wake up and begin to cry. "Daddy, daddy," she whimpered.

Jana rushed to the child and picked her up, but Lisa only cried louder. Was her arm in pain, was she hungry, did she want a drink of water, milk, juice? Why hadn't Susan left her a bottle, a jar, a box of cookies?

"Daddy, daddy." The little girl was almost delirious and, between screams, she would cough a croupy, scraping cough, which seemed certain to tear her throat to pieces.

Jana paced, bounced, circled and tried entertaining Lisa with the brightly-colored offerings in the soft drink machine. Lisa would have none of it. For all Jana could tell, she was neither looking nor listening. She was completely in another world, where each one cried alone, for himself and to himself.

Peter seemed to be held between two reins: one pulled him out of sight, out of mind of the child; the other—and this was the one he responded to—dragged him to her.

He grabbed Lisa out of Jana's arms, hung her over his

shoulder and, with big strong pats on her back, her diapered bottom and then her back again, he made the little girl feel safe.

Riding on that strength, Jana thought, who wouldn't be?

Moose was either too angry with Peter to remain in the same room with him, or else too moved by Peter's actions to watch.

Jana started to say something, but was met by the feeling of being in the presence of one of the most private moments the world would ever know.

She kept her distance, watching closely as Lisa's screams died down to whimpering, to silence. Only then did Peter hold her out in front of him, bracing her in the crook of his arm, looking closely at her face.

He didn't smile; neither did Lisa. But she watched his eyes, and a connection was made.

A few seconds after that, Jana heard the same voices Peter could hear: those of Susan and Ken. Peter turned around and handed Lisa over to Jana.

When her parents entered, Peter never again looked toward the child.

"What did you find out?" asked Jana.

"Miss Mari is still unconscious—for reasons that they don't understand. We plan to stay here a couple more hours," said Ken. "I suggest that you get some sleep. You've got a lot to deal with during the day."

"Peter," said Jana, "did you call your dad?"

"It was a fight to keep him from flying in tonight. I promised I would call him again before daylight."

Ken looked out the window behind the mustard couch. "Then you'd better hurry, or he'll be out on the front lawn in a helicopter before you know it."

Jana considered asking Peter for a ride, but it seemed a time he would want to be alone. There comes a point when two people share so many intimacies in the course of a few hours that any more would be intolerable. Jana had been the only one to observe Peter with Lisa. And this was something that he could only cherish alone.

She wanted so much to give him something. It was all she could think of.

While he was on the phone to Santa Cruz, Jana called a taxi.

Chapter 20

That Mariposa and Miss Mari's fate were twinned instead of doomed was the fact Jana clung to. As soon as Miss Mari regained consciousness, she began to improve immediately, and although there were minor mishaps, Mariposa's peaches were moving to the cannery on schedule—mainly because Peter was having them carted to an independent cannery instead of to the one owned by Calimyrna.

Miss Mari was only allowed to have family visit her, but this included Moose, Susan, Ken and Jana. She was receiving hundreds of telegrams and letters from those who had been helped by, or who had worked with, her in various organizations.

The big excitement in Miss Mari's hospital room was preparing for the special dinner the Governor was giving for Miss Mari the last week in August.

"I've got to get well, and fast," she announced. "That man has been avoiding me for the last few years, and I have a list of proposals three feet long to talk over with him."

When Jana, Ken or Susan were not at the hospital, Peter or Moose were. Jana had been requested back at Havermeyer the week after the fire, but had applied for and received permission to take an early vacation. This gave her time to

work with the women at the Tourist Center, even though she
was still working in the weigh house most of the time.

Peter had no idea that she was there on her vacation time,
and had argued with her continually about moving to an
apartment with a security guard. Just because the harvesters
occasionally were out of commission with unexplained mechanical failures was not enough reason for her to move, she
had concluded. The Mariposa machine shop, with its four
good mechanics, had even conceded that the problems could
be related to the normal amount of bugs in new machinery,
rather than to any intentional interference with them.

With Jana's schedule, she had very little time to be with
Andy. In addition, he had spent a week on the coast with his
father setting up a business deal that he said would not only
pay for his remaining year in school, but even set him up
when he graduated.

Sometimes, he talked about moving to Chicago.

"But what if I decide to move to California? This valley, for
example?"

"You'd hate it: cold, seepy fog all winter, which rolls in for
no purpose at all. It's better to be in a cold place where you
know what season it is. At least, when you suffer, you
understand why."

"Ever been in a Chicago winter?"

"I'll stay indoors with you. Tell me about your apartment.
Tell me what you're like in Chicago."

She couldn't; she didn't know anymore.

Sometimes, she thought of Spenser. She would release him
from all the promises she had extracted from him—promises
that were now hazy. Children? No children? They had never
planned to live together. She would end up with all the work.
They had drawn up a contract. She wrote it, and he had
agreed. "A well-delineated relationship," he had called it. "It
will last for centuries." She could see a Spenser of a future
century reconstructing the crumbled document with tweezers
and a microscope.

When Jana did see Peter in passing, he was distant except
when he asked a question about Mariposa. He had no time to
mix with the workers and left that up to Moose, who, since
the night at the hospital, had occasionally listened to Jana as
she explained Peter's point of view to him.

It hadn't been an easy time for her. Jana knew that Peter

saw Susan almost every day at the hospital at times when Ken
was working. Perhaps this was why he rarely asked anything
of her: just seeing Susan, talking with her regularly, was all he
needed.

The names Miss Mari carried around for her mail-order
business were, by the time of the fire, in the process of being
fed into the new computer and had been saved from the fire
by being at the Tourist Center. Some of the women from the
platform were already hard at work on all aspects of the
center.

The pressure of being in the middle of so many changes
must have been more than Jana thought. One day, driving to
Mariposa, she begged, "Rain, rain." If she could only get
away for a few days. "Fantastic Fresno" was supposedly a
launching place for those who went to Lake Tahoe, Yosemite,
San Francisco. But she hadn't been anywhere since that
quickie trip to Yosemite.

It was a Monday when she drove through mildly cloudy
weather thinking, "Rain, rain." It was that Monday when
Peter approached her as she was leaning down to the floor of
her Mercedes.

"My dad wants to see you," he said. "I'll pick you up at
your complex in two hours."

Peter sounded grave. But that was always the case these
days. Was there to be news of Mariposa's sale? Was Mr.
Milford in town for the day to visit Miss Mari?

Jana changed to a new pair of pants, which would have
been faint pink if they hadn't had a touch of orange in them.
Her blouse was of wide, delicate stripes of gold, pink, blue
and white, her sandals were new and their light brown leather
was untouched by Mariposa's grime, which had been worse
than ever since the fire because there was soot in everything.

Checking herself in the mirror, she decided she loved
having a tan.

"You'd better look hard, because two weeks away from the
sun and you'll be a paleface again," she advised herself.

Peter actually seemed to notice that she had changed
clothes and took a moment to appreciate her appearance
before saying: "Dad has heard about the accidents at Mariposa. Yesterday, he received the insurance report on the
cause of the fire—arson—and also the minor damage to the
machinery."

"Peter!" Jana was exploding with impatience. "Did he ask you to bring me to see him, or do you want me to sweet-talk him again?"

"I suppose you'll do whatever you want to do. When did you ever do otherwise?"

"Plenty of times—like right now. If I had time for an afternoon off, I'm not sure I would spend it this way. And, anyway, I haven't time."

They were in the country, speeding through an area she hadn't seen before. Peter was quiet, as usual.

"Do you think you and Moose are getting along any better?" she asked. "I've had quite a number of talks with him."

"You certainly have Moose eating out of your hand."

"It would be better for Mariposa, if you'd be a little more considerate to him. After all, he's been the backbone of Mariposa for years."

"You still don't know anything, do you? I would think that being around Miss Mari as much as you are, you would have caught on to some of her remarkable intuition. What you see is what you get, isn't it? You never notice subtleties."

Jana felt like wrenching open the door of his fancy, perfectly-tuned Jag, jumping out and running along the highway screaming, "Enough, enough!"

Instead, she steamed until she realized that they were not headed toward the Milford estate, not even by a roundabout route.

"Where are you taking me?"

"You are accompanying me to visit my father. I thought I made that clear."

"Where?"

"Santa Cruz."

"But that's hours away!"

"Only about three. Don't worry, you'll have a rest in a minute, because we're making a stop."

Jana could smell the pine trees. There was a horrible memory connected with them. The car was bumping along a tiny gravel road, which wound around a mountain. She looked to him for an explanation.

"Ken asked me to stop on my way to the coast and see what I think about him and Susan building here again."

"Susan is here?"

"Yes. She and Ken have been considering a new site for the home they're going to build. They said they hadn't found any place they liked as much as their old location."

Jana almost flew at him. She wanted to say, "I know what you're up to and it's *sick, sick, sick*. Susan is happy with Ken; leave her and Lisa alone. Go out and have some babies of your own with Cassie, anybody."

But, she reasoned almost immediately, Peter's countenance always took on the sweetest aura when he saw Lisa. And the best of him was present when he spoke with Susan—a situation that had definitely not been present during their marriage.

Besides, why was *she* so concerned? The flurry of ideas in which she had once imagined herself in possession of one of the Milford "M's" had departed. When had she stopped fantasizing about winning Peter and whole-heartedly thrown herself into helping Peter win Mariposa?

Was it when Andy had said with such sincerity that he loved her and she had wanted to love him? When Havermeyer no longer held such a controlling interest in her future? Or when she learned that Peter wanted only Susan or Susan-substitutes and no one else?

The latter, of course, was the answer. She could have shuffled Cassie to the back burner in twenty minutes if it had only been the case of another woman. But Susan—whom she liked tremendously—had become Peter's unreachable ideal. It was easier to be disappointed by an ethereal, idealized person, because such people so rarely walked on earth, anyway.

"God, I hate to see this place again," Peter blurted out as he turned into the clearing and parked next to Ken's green Cadillac.

Ken pointed up the mountain. "Susan's up there painting. Hey-hey," he yelled, "come on down!"

Susan was crouched on a ledge with a large canvas propped on a table-top easel in front of her. She was gazing out from under her white visor cap to a view they couldn't see. Every few moments, her brush would touch the canvas in a series of fast strokes.

"Either she can't hear us because of the wind—or she's in a painting trance and can't hear us—or she doesn't want to be disturbed," reported Ken.

"I would hate to miss her," said Jana. "Peter, why don't you honk your horn?"

Three short beeps and a long one caused Susan to wave at them, anchor her canvas behind a rock, and disappear around to the other side of the mountain.

"It'll take her about five minutes," said Ken, who seemed relieved that she had responded to the honk. Life with Susan must be one long, unpredictable experience. It must have driven Peter crazy.

"Susan is painting some of her old scenes, and I've been walking around the property," he added. "We're facing up the place, deciding if we want to—if we could—build here again."

"I don't know how you could even think of it," said Peter.

"I don't want that kind of judgment from you," said Ken sharply. "What do you think about the work that's been done above us?"

"Risky."

"We can't only consider what's happened here. Susan still sees beauty here. Ginni did, too."

Peter's Adam's apple was choking him. He walked alone toward the ruins of the house.

"Where's Andy?" asked Ken. He didn't care.

"Working," she answered primly.

"The coward. If it hadn't been for him, there would be no question about our rebuilding here. And Ginni would still be alive."

Jana whirled around and shouted at him. "What are you saying?" When people wore beards, you could never tell whether or not they were serious. At least not to what degree. She suspected that Ken was only being vindictive, and that it was his natural attitude toward Andy.

"I told you to ask Andy," he said. "If you didn't care enough to ask, then don't pester me about it now. I don't want to talk about it."

"I *did* ask him."

"And?"

Jana closed her eyes. How should she put it?

"He said it had something to do with Susan."

"Yes, he's used that threat to weasel himself into several situations where he had no business being."

"But what are you talking about—that Ginni would still be

alive if it hadn't been for Andy? That's a cruel and awful thing to say."

Ken was shaking his head. "And all this time I thought—Peter and Susan thought—that you knew what happened out here that day, that you knew Ginni's life was lost needlessly.

"And you're right, it is cruel to put all the blame on Andy, because in the long run, it was my fault. I never should have depended on him. You see, I ran into the nursery first. Ginni's foot was caught in some rubble. She pointed to the closet and screamed, 'Lisa's in there!' I indicated to Andy that Ginni needed help. I told him to get Ginni, and I ran for Lisa. As I left the nursery, he was still there, but when I turned around to see if he and Ginni were behind me, I could see him running clear of the house.

"That's when I saw the house above us—you know how it hung there, as if waiting for us to free the girls. Andy had looked up at it and, instead of freeing Ginni, he ran away from her.

"By the time I could make a second trip into the nursery, there wasn't much of a nursery left."

"No," protested Jana. "No. Did you ask Andy what happened? He wouldn't do that. You saw how he helped me—how brave he was."

"I saw him pull you out of the mud on our stairwell without so much as soiling his sneakers."

Susan and Peter converged on the conversation at the same time.

"What's wrong?" Susan asked.

"I just told Jana about Andy's part in Ginni's death. She didn't know. She really didn't."

"The hell she didn't," snarled Peter.

It was a conspiracy. This smug little group, too wealthy for their own good—how easy to blame Andy instead of, say, Ken. Why couldn't *he* have managed to help Ginni out at the same time as Lisa? He *was* the first one to reach the nursery.

Jana was so shot through with disgust and disbelief that an accusation would have shattered what little equilibrium she had remaining. But there was no need.

Ken said softly, "Jana, I could have saved Susan's little sister. I had time. If only I had known that he would not."

Jana looked Ken straight in the eye and said, "If only you had known that your house was built in a dangerous spot, you would have built elsewhere, too, wouldn't you?"

"Let's go," said Peter, taking her arm and leading her to the car. "I've told you what *I* think, Ken. You let me know what you decide."

Before Peter turned on the ignition, Jana said, "Let's get this trip over quickly."

He gunned his expensive motor and shot down the gravel road to the highway. The white lines down its center were soothing: they were short and even and needed no unraveling. To think of the pressure Andy had lived with all summer! And the accusations—they were unjust—but even if they had been correct, Andy was the only one who really knew. Why had he lied to her? Jana had the idea that he didn't want her to know anyone could think so badly of him.

"But, Andy," she heard herself thinking how she would talk to him, "it's not a matter of thinking badly; it's a matter of life—or death."

After several silent hours driving through the mountains and small vineyards, Jana began to see glimpses of the ocean. Peter's car squealed through the gate to a large house north of Santa Cruz.

A maid greeted, "Mr. Peter," which made him sound like a hair stylist, and Jana walked into the gleaming white, modern stucco house. It was built to be sparsely furnished in the manner that would fit a beach lifestyle. Instead, the rooms she could see were crowded with gee-gaws and plastic statues and stiff, carved furniture made of dark wood. The walls were hung with dark oil paintings of grapes, apples, pears and probably peaches, but she couldn't tell.

"Howdja like it?" Aline, tanner than ever, wearing white silk pants and a flowing gold and white pleated tunic top, floated through the door and motioned Jana to follow her out on a terrace.

The protection of a well-pruned hedge of geraniums seemed to be all that kept them from tumbling down a cliff to the ocean.

"Howdja like the Eyetalian furniture?"

"Very . . . ornate."

"It's ghastly and you know it. I'd rather sit on the floor than on all that junk. You know how long it took me to learn it was junk? One day in San Francisco museums. Hell, I can soak up culture as fast as anybody—faster probably, because I've been exposed to so little."

"Maybe you can redecorate."

"That's one of the things Patoot is talking to his son about—not furniture, but the fact that in a couple of weeks we're taking off for a round-the-world cruise. Before we leave, we've hired an auctioneer to hold a sale on the premises. Shopping for new furniture will give me a little project while we're away. Doncha think that's a great idea?"

On top of the morning's revelation—true or untrue—the hypnotizing brilliance of the ocean down below, and the incessant barrage from Aline, Jana felt that her head was caving in.

"And let me tell you about my Patoot. He's been so much better since we visited Miss Mari's that day. It's been hard keeping him away while she's been in the hospital, but she said he'd be upset to see her the way she looked, and that soon she'd be good as new—is that true?"

Shouts could be heard coming from another room. "That's Patoot and his offshoot. I'll have to say that Peter makes his old man's blood pressure flip off the map sometimes. Hope he doesn't get him too wrought up. I buried one huzbin already. I married Joe thinking I'd put a little zip into him, but so far, it's been all strikes and accidents and fires. Hey, I do believe they're already breaking up their little meeting."

Peter and his father and McNair appeared on the balcony. Mr. Milford was slapping Peter on the back.

"Jana, this boy of mine is really something, don't you think? You know what we've just done? McNair here has brought down all the papers, and we've just turned Milford Enterprises over to Peter."

"You mean Mariposa? That's wonderful!"

"Dammit, I mean the whole shebang! Before you know it, the Milfords are gonna have more money than ever!"

"I wouldn't count on that for a long time, dad. We need to pour a lot of money into improving the company's entire program for migrant laborers, planning for shifts of some workers from Mariposa to the vineyards. . . ."

"Okay, okay, I don't want you to bother me with any of that. Aline and I are making too many plans of our own."

Mr. Milford's voice was strong and, in his white shirt and trousers, he looked almost as tan as his wife.

He grabbed Jana by the shoulder and shook her until she thought her head would shatter at the temples. "And it's just great news that you'll be staying on at Mariposa. Peter told me some of the things you've done. We expect an all-out effort from now on—none of this dividing your time between us and the damned Havermeyer bunch."

Mr. Milford sat down next to Aline. "Those two look pretty good together, don't they?"

"Dad," interrupted Peter, "about those grape-harvesters. . . ."

"That's your problem. Aline and I, we're taking ourselves a big cruise, aren't we, baby? You and McNair had better get back to work."

He looked over at Jana. "And you, too, young lady."

She could hardly contain herself until they reached the car. Peter was laughing. "All I hoped to attempt today was to get an extension on the Mariposa deadline. And that's what I thought he called us out here for.

"I also intended to report on how inept McNair was when it came to settling Mariposa's strike, and I found that McNair had already owned up to his inadequacies and that he, in fact, recommended that dad turn everything over to me. He's going to remain on at Milford Enterprises in what he called a 'transitional advisory capacity.'

"Now I can form my model corporation, now everyone employing migrant or foreign-born laborers will look to the Milfords. That's the only reason to have money and power, you know: to make changes for the better in an industry that is all too far behind the times."

"You talk a good line," she said. "It's too bad your father believed you."

"What do you mean? I thought you were behind me?"

"Just get me back to Fresno as soon as you can. I'm leaving in the morning. I'll have no part of your lies to your father about me staying on at Mariposa. You didn't have to say that. He would have given you the moon, anyway."

Peter screeched his car into a fast turn, parked it behind a restaurant.

"I can't drive on an empty stomach," he said. "Get out."

Chapter 21

Walking behind her, his hands clasped tightly on her arms as if she were about to make a run for it, Peter led Jana into a restaurant called the Angler's Dream.

To the average observer, they probably appeared to be lovers who were unable to walk a step without touching. If anybody knew that appearances were deceptive, it was Jana. Should she warn all of those dining so leisurely, enjoying the sunset through tinted glass, that they were on the verge of being wiped out by a volcano—the one due to erupt in her at any moment?

But here she was, sitting down at the table like a regular person. There was something wet, like hot drops of water, balanced precariously on both her bottom eyelashes. While Peter Milford went about the easy task of choosing a wine, she smiled at the waiter and took a menu out from under his arm.

That's where she hid out. Squid . . . sardines . . . sole . . . shrimp . . . the fishy smells of the names beginning with "S" were making her s-s-s-sick—at heart.

"Would you . . . Jana, would you like to inform me of your choice, or would you prefer to confide in the waiter?"

How far did he think he could push her? How many millimeters did he think he had to go?

"I can't order. I'm not hungry for anything here."

"Eat it anyway."

"I'll eat when—if—ever this trip is over, thank you."

Motioning for the waiter, Peter announced with authority: "We've decided to have two abalone steaks, broiled, please. And," he added, eyeing Jana, "the young lady is in a hurry."

Jana leaned back in her chair and crossed her arms in front of her cotton-candy-colored shirt. Peter held up his white wine. "I knew this wine when it was only a bunch of grapes. It's from the year I first worked in one of the smallest of dad's vineyards—which is not too far from here. A toast?"

Jana's hold on herself tightened. She tucked her chin in and glared at him through eyes shaded with lids that hung like stiff half-awnings.

He lifted his glass and clinked it against her own, which was standing unclaimed on the table. "To this, a very good year."

"Speak for yourself."

She had arrived in this overripe, erratic state knowing exactly what she wanted and exactly how she was to get it and now, she knew only that she had been wrong.

"What kind of year has it been for you?" he asked.

"Fine. Splendid."

"What's set you off?"

"This was supposed to be a business trip, and that's the only reason I came. I have not participated in so much as a minute of business since I was foolish enough to get in your 'flashy-washy' car. Now I discover that you had a reason for dragging me along—so that you could, for some reason, exhibit me as a Mariposa trophy to your father at an opportune moment.

"The only good thing about this trip is that it's made me realize how quickly I have to get out of this state.

"Now, if you would like to talk about the progress you think has been made at Mariposa, the complaints you have with Havermeyer, the project plans for Mariposa in the next two, three . . ." Her voice cracked.

"Four comes next," he said.

"If you would even like to ask me what I think about Havermeyer's grape-harvesters as opposed to those sold by two other leading companies, that, I'd be glad to discuss."

"Okay. Let's hear it for the grape-pickers. I am, for the first time, in a position to place that large order that is the only reason Havermeyer sent you out here in the first place."

"If I really wanted to pay you back—in part—for some of the awful, awkward positions you have put me in this summer . . ."

"Ones you have gone along with . . ."

"I would tell you to buy Havermeyer. But if you will simply go down to one of the Napa Valley dealers, you will see there are two companies that make less expensive harvesters. The competitors have a better over-all design, and therefore inherently offer more durability."

"You don't say?" He looked amused instead of grateful. She could have thrown her wine at him. Instead, she drank it in three gulps.

"In addition, we have never discussed the potential importance of the Tourist Center in the scheme of Milford Enterprises. As I understand it, your father has never believed in having a center in your vineyards. You might pattern one, to begin with, on Miss Mari's setup. It's not my business, but I also think you should be concerned with the poor image peaches have nationwide. Peach consumption is going down yearly. Have you ever considered that Mariposa's advertising program in all areas, including peaches, is behind the times?"

"You sound as if you have enough plans to take over the world."

"Since I'm leaving tomorrow, this is your last chance to hear them."

"Look, I've got to run a larger concern now. I'm not going to kill myself on grinding out sophisticated peach ads.

"That's not my business, or the business of any grower. Every time I see that Florida orange juice commercial on television, I think, California is grateful to you, little Florida. Know why? California grows forty percent of the country's oranges used in orange juice. Now, have you ever seen a California orange juice commercial? No. We let Florida do it all *for* us. Have you ever stopped in front of the freezer at the grocery store and said, 'Um, let me see, which is the juice from Florida and which the juice from California?'

"No, and you wouldn't do it with peaches, either. If we growers put on a giant campaign for peaches, you know who would benefit? Georgia. That's where everybody thinks all the peaches are from, anyway. Advertising is the job of Hunt and Libby's, Del Monte and A & P. What can a little outfit like Mariposa, or even Milford Enterprises, do in all this?"

Peter absentmindedly unbuttoned a second button on his

shirt as he delivered his speech. Jana's eyes followed his hands for a few seconds, before she remembered what she had been about to say. "What Mariposa can do and what you can do is to stop being so provincial, conservative and pig-headed. What's going to become of Milford Enterprises if you exchange one brand of narrow thinking—held by your father—for another? You may be an expert in labor law, but there are other areas that are important, too."

"But not," he said, "as important." He continued with his plans for turning Mariposa, and then the vineyards, into model places for year-round employees. Insurance, medical care, profit-sharing . . . As he spoke, she followed his hands, not his words. They were always perfectly in tune with what he was saying, and whether Jana agreed with him or not, his hands always did. She had never seen a person who was as singleminded as Peter.

A few weeks ago, a dinner with Peter alone in a restaurant would have meant that her plan was going according to schedule. Now, there was no schedule and, if there had been a plan, it wouldn't have included Peter.

"While we're waiting, let's take our wine and go out on the balcony." He was already helping her up, guiding her to the door. His presence was tremendous and she was forced to spend this time with him. It was painful to feel used, when all she desired was to feel wanted for herself.

She barely saw the harbor, the lazy bustle on the boardwalk down below. She shivered.

"Cold?" asked Peter, slipping an arm around her waist, his long fingers reaching up around her midriff.

Jana swallowed her second glass of wine and mentally pulled away. Then the curve of his arm and shoulder, his huge hand, pulled her closer in a thousand unspoken apologies, in the promise of answers that he would like to give.

She could smell his warm breath, which, mixed with the sweetness of the cool salt air, was perfect. She could feel his thumping chest through her shoulderblades, down her spine.

"Mr. Milford," said the waiter, standing between them and the balcony entrance to the dining room, "Your dinner is about to be served."

The abalone smelled—okay—and the shells were beautiful.

"I collected abalone shells when I was a boy. I must have had a couple of hundred. I heard that the Indians used them for money and I felt very rich. Go ahead, taste yours—

abalone has the texture of scallops and tastes like a cross
between oysters and clams."

It *was* good and she hadn't realized how hungry she had
been. He watched her intently, with pleasure. Did he expect
her to starve just to get even with him?

When he chewed, she was more daring about observing
him. His hair was a mop of uncombed, straight, shining dark
fringe. She wanted to lean over and push some of it back.
Wouldn't that be a surprise? Where did he get that haircut
anyway? It was as if he had, months ago, gone to a stylist in
San Francisco, and no barber in Fresno could equal the job.

"Miss Mari's very fond of you," he said.

Why did he have to bring that up? The quivering communi-
cation that they had had from the beginning was pinning her
down again. He had no right.

"Dessert?" No. "Coffee?" No. "Let's be on our way."

When they reached the front door, the waiter rushed out
with an abalone shell. "It's for you. The gentleman says you
would like one."

Jana was holding a pot of rainbow in her hands. Its colors of
pink, purple, silver and blue curved and nestled in her hands.
This would be her last reminder of California.

"If we hurry, we'll be able to see all those colors on a much
grander scale," said Peter.

They drove for half an hour, until the late afternoon ocean
breezes were stronger than ever. Peter parked behind a sandy
hill and led her up to the top of one of them. What Jana had
been expecting, she didn't know, but they were facing an
evening ocean panorama of endless green water that met a
horizon of dusky purple. The avalanche of waves swelled,
roared and rolled in from the depths of the ocean, over and
over again.

She took in the ocean with her eyes, the wind in her hair,
the unforgettable, clean, pure, salty smell. And as she did,
she could feel Peter by her side, watching her, sensing who
she really was.

"Let's walk down by the ocean," he said. They approached
the water's edge together, although they were not touching.
The waves were circling onto the flat beach, leaving rings of
frothy necklaces. A new wave looped up higher on the sand
than the ones before, and Jana jumped out of its way. Peter
allowed the water to slide over his shoes, but when it had
receded he removed them and tossed his shoes and socks up

on the beach. Jana threw her own near his, and smiled as she felt the custom-fit cool of the sand.

As they walked, she found little shells and pebbles and gathered them until her hands were full. Slowly, she dropped them one by one. These moments were not collectible.

The edge of the water served as a marker for the shining sun's colors, which shifted on it like bits of glass in a kaleidoscope. The clouds rolled and turned from gold to green, purple to pink.

Peter, in his own thoughts, was not as distracted. She lagged behind him on purpose, in order to see him in this perfect surrounding for as long as she lived.

He stood alone, his reflection driving a crisp, clear image deep into the wet sand. Then, rhythmically, it melted in the next wave.

The departure of his image was not violent. It fit in with the universe. Her leaving California could be the same way.

The all-consuming sky, the minute changes around her feet, were causing Jana to strain in order not to miss the transition from one color to the next. It was like standing in the middle of an orchestra because you were unwilling to miss a single sound. She backed away and saw herself, walking behind Peter. They were never together. They never had been. The pattern of their lives was as clear as the pattern of the sunset.

Jana looked out at the horizon, intending to cherish the long, lazy disappearance of the sun. She blinked only a couple of times and the ocean gulped it down. The sun was gone. Only the clouds, which could see far over the horizon, were reflecting their own multicolored version of the sunset.

Jana turned to Peter. He took her hand and urged her to run with him. They reached the top of the dune. He turned around and there was the sun again. But this time it was a bold orange, not a fiery yellow, and everywhere there was a glorious, motionless light as the ocean fluttered and glimmered and the clouds flew about in a string of tiny iridescent wings.

She smiled and breathed deeply. Peter's tousled hair rippled with the irregular gusts of the ocean breeze. His profile, from high forehead to strong jaw, settled into gentleness as he watched her enjoyment.

Jana gathered her hair at the nape of her neck and, sighing, released it slowly. He touched the hair as it fell to her shoulders. His dark eyes were softened by the sunset—or by her sigh. Taking both her hands, he started to speak, but did not.

Jana stared down to see what her hands looked like when held in his: the interlocking of their fingers seemed too casual a connection to explain the surge she felt within her.

Again, more slowly, Peter led her silently down to the water's edge. Her feet no longer made firm footprints when they walked in the wet sand. Instead, indistinguishable little gullies, which the tide quickly filled, indicated their fleeting presence.

After they had walked and walked, Peter stopped and again took both her hands. She was unable to watch his eyes, which had so often been alien to her. Again, it was his hands, which he was entwining with hers in a delicate tangle of tenderness. Her slim hands were being wound in with his strong but acquiescent fingers, which allowed only enough space for the air to spin intricate, invisible webs around their touching.

His hands had held wonder for her from the beginning. And she had been right. They curled, they caressed, they understood.

Now that Jana was free to touch them, she was impatient: she criss-crossed her fingers with his palms, he looped their little fingers together in feigned casualness, her hands raced to weave a cocoon around his.

As he touched her cheek, reluctantly she let his hands leave hers. This time, not their hands, but their arms, the curves of their bodies, were synchronized.

When their lips met, they were not hungry or searching but generous and giving as though having been royally fed, they were passing on the fullness, the sweetness, to each other.

There was no wanting in that moment, no begging or strain. It was as if they were forever destined to touch in exactly this way at this time.

Standing at the end of the darkening earth, a dusky chill swirling in upon them, reaching toward each other, brushing their lips together lightly, then with eagerness, their warmth radiated as though they were replacing the missing sun.

Peter held her away from him, his hands tightly locked on her arms, his face peaceful.

At the water's edge, by the sun's afterglow, not only were their figures silhouettes to anyone who might have been watching from afar, but silhouettes to each other.

Chapter 22

Peter's hands sculpted her as if she were a dream he was dreaming to completion for the first time. They were around her, over her, in her. Hurry, she need not remind him, hurry, he knew.

There a blouse, there trousers, pants—the tide, if it were daring enough, could have them all.

Here, the universe pounding over her, on her, her body being molded into the sand, being pushed into a crater of love.

Light and dark, smooth and rough, all belonging to one man, were forming her anew. Love burst inside her inner shores, slashing, breaking, blasting until she became part of the same roll of thunder that hit simultaneously, leaving her submerged in the sand, covered entirely by heavy, heavenly clouds of warmth.

The winds sizzled against the dunes; the grass applauded in a rustling standing ovation, while beneath them, around them, creatures hidden in the sand blew bubbles of celebration into the air—balloons of the beach, which announced the wonder of this night.

Jana rolled out of her sandy mold and, with her hands, urged her evening artist to return. The swirling of the tide was in his hair, receding, advancing, receding, as were her hands. Learning quickly from the ocean, she had found his smooth pebbles, his gleaming driftwood. She cherished their shining softness, and growing hardness. With a wildness and speed unknown to her, Jana's hands caressed his chest; her knees dug into the sand, her loins sought for the mound of life belonging to the beach creature capable of loving to its fullest only when inside her locked resolve.

As she tasted his neck, his chest, her hands lavished themselves along his ribs, across the sweet, heaving hairs of his chest. She touched the sweet, cold medallion around his neck. Shyly at first, then hungrily, she tasted the warm gold with which he had already shared his wealth.

His hands flamed across her back, down her legs, and traveled quickly to press her down onto him as she held him between her legs.

Their dark mingling was like night wine and, as they shared its fullness, sections of the heavens shifted, acres of the earth were rearranged.

They were side-by-side sea creatures, slipping away from their earthly apartness, flowing in the same ocean stream.

Inside her, purple shapes fluttered. Outside, the long, low call of a bird. What bird? What sound? It was her own riotous, heaving fulfillment. This it was that both of them had feared would happen; this that they would fear no more.

This ultimate inwardness was turning them inside out for each other. "Jana-Jana-Jana," the first beach words, were answered directly a dozen times by her silky shudders.

Her legs stretched around him. Locked on his golden gift, she was being arched to ecstasy. As the strength of his body elevated them into a series of bridges, tidal pools celebrating their rapt oneness rushed to fill the space burrowed by their love. The final bridge bolted them together in a single heaving of rapture that spanned the universe.

Still locked around him, Jana touched his eyes, his beautiful eyes. She laid heavy kisses on his neck. He turned her over into the wet warmth of the ocean space beneath him, and his tongue skittered across her stomach, her breasts, her neck, lips, eyes, ears, until the complete tasting of their tangled kiss brought them full circle to a single stillness, accompanied only by the pounding of their hearts and the rhythm of the waves.

Next, the slow-motion gathering of their clothes, the long,

mingled walk back to the dunes. Nestled in sandy closeness, they waited to see the flickering stars disappear one by one into the floating fog.

The sand cooled and Jana felt damp and salty from the mist dropping out of the gray around them. He brought a sleeping bag from the trunk of his car and they curled together with "Jana-Jana" the only words until Peter finally said, "I never meant for us to remain so long."

"Maybe we can watch the sun rise."

"That won't happen for hours yet."

Could they have a real swim, could they walk together again down to that beach? Yes, yes. Jana held up her arms and Peter lifted her to him. As they looked out into the dark, the black cloak of the universe sealed their privacy.

Peter walked into the water first. The night was so dark that Jana lost sight of him almost immediately. He soon yelled, "The water is warmer than the night air—doesn't that sound inviting?"

Plunging into the heaving water, Jana was not terrified of the strange, intimate swirls that touched her in places where only Peter had. She felt her feet on the sandy ocean bottom. Peter's hands were on her waist.

She wanted to sink down onto her knees so that the water would completely cover her, yet she stood, with Peter's arms on her shoulders, his kisses on her lashes, his hands smoothing down her throat and shoulders. But he fell to his knees as he lightly cupped her breasts in his hands. He kissed the underside of them gently, murmuring, "You are beautiful, so beautiful."

She wanted to wrap herself around him. She wanted more of him inside her. There was no limit to her craving for him—a craving that had burst into a reality after all these weeks.

During several attempts at swimming, trying to follow Peter, she was constantly rolled under by the black waves.

Sensing her fear, he swept her up in his arms and carried her to the car, where they were faced with their soggy clothes.

"We could stay here all night," he said, motioning to the sleeping bag.

"Let's take it down near the water, so we can hear the surf."

"And be smashed in our sleep by a dune buggy? You can

hear all you need to hear from between these dunes. Look, they make a hammock for us."

He helped her dry off with the one towel, and held open the sleeping bag for her. It provided a mattress on the sand and a shelter from the fog and salty mist. He did not zip it, and lay down beside her.

His eyes, always questioning, were now looking in wonderment at her. His hands were cherishing her slowly.

Peter's blown hair, his whiskery, rough chin, his smile, which was more evident around his eyes than his mouth—she loved them all. The extent to which she would be free after tonight to express this love had no place between them tonight.

She lay her head down just over his heart, which was beating faster than hearts do. She rubbed her smooth legs against his sandy, salty, hairy ones, and their tickling sensation called her back for more.

She was at first embarrassed to run her hands over him now that they were on dry land. The muscles that quivered just under his skin shocked her with their power, and each time her hands skimmed around his ribs, touched his tight stomach, lowered to the place of his now-solved mystery, she knew she was in the presence of great strength. And, yet, he was so tender. The chest that had heaved in and out so violently that first day in the Mariposa office, and so many times afterwards, was now a welcoming pillow.

When Peter touched her, it was with the care one would use to turn the fragile pages of a rare book. Obviously wanting to read every inch of her, his passion was wordless, lingering. As the night stole away, the fog hovered lower and lower, and they slept, each with a hand between the other's thighs.

Jana awakened once, but remained as still as possible as she brushed off the residue of the salty air that covered her face. She turned and burrowed into his shoulder. As the air whipped around them, she concentrated on the closeness of his pulse, the music of his rhythmical breathing, the wonder of being with him at all.

When she opened her eyes again, a striped, pastel-colored cloud was hanging so low over her that she had to dodge it. The cloud had a sleeve that was flapping in the steady, dry breeze. It was held up by dried, gray sticks, and definitely resembled her own blouse.

Jana rolled out from under the shelter and squinted. It must be almost noon. Peter had disappeared. The light was so bright. Could she face him? Did daylight mean they had to talk? If so, what was there to be said? She had no words. She understood nothing. Slipping on the shirt and nearby pants, she climbed on top of the sand dune. There he was, that little dot out in the surf. He dived under and emerged, swimming inside the wave pattern. His powerful arms propelled him faster than she had thought it possible to swim in the ocean.

She sat down on the dune and absorbed what might be her last peaceful, undisturbed moments with Peter Milford. If they started for the valley now, she calculated, they wouldn't arrive for at least three hours. She resolved to spend those hours living in the present. No questions about the future, because there were no answers; no regrets about the past, because the explanations were too complicated.

Already, there were three people sitting under umbrellas on the beach. Why hadn't she concerned herself with people the night before? Living for the moment had served her well then. She would not abandon it now.

She looked down into the dune grass next to her, wondering if the little bugs that had hopped around her face during the night had been sand fleas. The dune grass was blowing in her face, stinging her wrist with tick-tocking regularity.

She was being tapped and reminded of something: a duty? Something was nagging at her.

Andy. What he had feared between her and Peter had happened. But did it matter? She was leaving tomorrow.

The reason for that abrupt decision hovered around her shoulders: it was because of her anger over the lie Peter had told his father—the lie about her staying on at Mariposa.

The Peter of the daylight hours had nerve. The Peter of the night had unsurpassed concern and tenderness for her.

Something else was nagging her: Susan. But if she lived in the present, accepted the gift of last night, the loveliness of their next hours together, no Susan could intervene. She hadn't thought of her once the night before. Could she say with certainty that Peter hadn't either?

Jana lay back on the dune and watched the clouds. They

were blowing into a continual series of shapes and changing almost as fast as she had changed this summer.

She shaded her eyes with her arm. What if she and Peter had been as politely stricken with each other as she and Andy had been? What would have happened this summer?

Her plans to bag an "M" for herself would have been completed with ease. She would never have gone to the mountains, never have spent any time with Andy, or probably even with Susan and Ken.

She would have completed Havermeyer's job in a week or two; had a pleasant dinner with Miss Mari; and returned home to announce her engagement to the heir of Milford Enterprises. By the time she returned to the valley, Peter's father would have sold Mariposa. Miss Mari's Tourist Center, struggling along anyway, would have gone down with the ranch. Without the strong backing of the Save Yosemite Committee, which would fold when Mariposa did, Yosemite would be overrun by money-hungry corporations. California's honor would be tainted, and the entire state would fall into the Pacific.

She would have Peter, but the reasons she had wanted him would be gone: no money, power, prestige, business. Jana grinned at her imagination. At least there was one good thing about the summer: she had felt a surge of real concern for the boundaries within which people wished to live their lives. She would never again wish to willfully invade those boundaries in order to fit them in with her purposes.

And, in learning about boundaries, she had begun to discern that her own lay deeper than she had thought, instead of being in the shape of an ever-expanding lasso, which circled around whatever she set her mind to.

When she had arrived at Havermeyer, her desk had been on the lowest floor of the top ten stories in their forty-story skyscraper. Even men with only a bachelor's degree, who had never worked at a real job in their lives, were assigned to bigger offices on higher floors. Jana's consuming ambition had been to move up.

She had climbed out of that bottom floor through drawing up plans on different sheets of paper. She finally consolidated everything into one plan: the China trip. She knew her work in China could make her mark on the company. She would be assigned a better office, closer to power, and gain an unusual experience quickly.

It had worked. She had even been invited to speak at a board meeting, where, as always, she made the kind of blonde impression she played to the hilt.

It hadn't worked with Peter Milford. Was it because she represented all his problems when he saw her sitting there in that awful blue suit?

What must he think of her now? She must stop analyzing and accept the next few hours for what they would be. Always, the two of them had been in trouble because of troubles from the outside that had intruded on them: Havermeyer, Susan, Andy, strikes, Yosemite, sabotage, fear of injury.

If there had been anything at all to their initial attraction to each other, would they have allowed all these things to matter? Not unless they carried as much weight as they had—which was more weight than that initial attraction.

It was incredible to Jana that Peter, with his wealthy family, had stood for a way out for her. That she wasn't entirely evil, however, was proven by the fact that she really had thought she would help out in the Milford businesses.

Jana raised up and searched for Peter. She finally found him—or the speck she thought was him—further out than anybody else.

The beach now had a dozen or more people on it. The women were spreading suntan oil on their legs, stretching themselves to the sun. The men were rubbing, being rubbed, lying down next to the women. What a strange way to live! Rarely had Jana relaxed that much. The pool at the complex had provided her only leisurely recreation since she had arrived. And swimming there had been something she had forced herself to do in order to get a tan. There was always Gretchen to contend with. She presided over her territory like a tyrannical troll.

Peter was swimming in closer. He had been in the water for a long time. There was probably no one at all on the beach when he went in.

His problem dawned on her: he wasn't wearing swim trunks. This was a family beach. All he needed was to be arrested as he made his long trek out of the ocean up to the sand dunes. It excited her to think about it. Peter falling, diving in between the dunes. She would be there waiting for him. Too bad this was a family beach.

Laughing, Jana searched around his car and found his pants on the back fender, stiff and dry. That would look silly: trying to slide into his trousers underwater. She settled for the towel and leisurely walked down onto the beach swinging it. Peter, probably on his knees, had come as close to the sand as possible. His raised hand shaded his eyes. Jana waved the towel over her head and hurried her steps.

"Were you looking for something?" she yelled.

"Give me that!" He was laughing. Actually laughing out loud. She loved that laugh. She loved him.

And that had been the problem all summer. She had never faced it. At first, she thought she disliked him thoroughly; then she thought she wanted him because he fit into her plans. As the summer advanced, she almost hated him for the way he treated her. He angered her for following Susan with his eyes, his heart, his Jaguar.

And what about her? What must he have thought about her and Andy? Particularly if he thought she knew about Andy's part in Ginni's death.

"Jana! Throw me the towel!"

She laughed and, wadding it, threw it almost over his head so that he nearly had to jump for it.

She waited for him to emerge from the water, throwing the towel around him as he did. And, suddenly, the beach, transformed by sunlight, seemed to be an impossible place for them to have made love the night before. And in the sunlight, she was an impossible person to have done it with the man she had fought all summer.

As they scuffled through the sand, they passed children digging holes to China. One was building a castle with a salt-water moat that reminded her of the pool that had formed under Peter the night before. Jana felt as if she were a person born to a new world.

She waited by the car while Peter dressed, and both of them said a silent goodbye to the beach that had the potential to wrinkle up their lives as thoroughly as it had wrinkled up their clothes.

Before they drove away, Peter stood her against the Jaguar and kissed her. The urgency was no longer there. Instead, she felt a patient, tender exploring as he pressed against her, searching her mouth, holding her close.

He cherished her. That was all Jana could think of. At night and under the sun, he cherished her. He was holding her head softly against his chest. When he raised her head and tilted her chin so that he could look her squarely in the eyes, he said what she had never asked to hear—probably because it was too wonderful:

"I love you, too."

Chapter 23

"You can see now that I was telling my father the truth about you remaining at Mariposa," murmured Peter as he released her and opened the car door.

Jana flared somewhere inside her chest. She studied his face for a moment before lowering herself into the plush bucket seat. How could he know? They hardly knew each other at this time the day before.

Peter headed down Highway 1. The implications of the shining circle of rocky coast, the cypress trees warped in a forever breeze from the sea, the winding road flanked on one side by low mountains, on the other by the spectacular views of Monterey, Big Sur, were small indeed compared to the interior terrain Peter was exposing her to.

"Charley Parkhurst won fame along this road as one of the tough, daring stagecoach drivers. Charley was found to be named Charlotte when she died in the late eighteen hundreds. And before we turn around, look up there—the William Randolph Hearst mansion—*la cuesta encantada*—the enchanted hill.

"Would you like to go in?"

"No." Please, no. I want to go inside your mind. Behind those black eyes, what are you thinking, why are you dangling promises before me that we have never come near to discussing?

They had circled around and were backtracking north along the same highway. He pulled over to a look-out point that faced the ocean. Without turning off the engine, without touching her, Peter, his voice low, almost choked, said:

"I want you to marry me. I want to see you at breakfast, watch you work during the day. I want our kids to be female forest rangers and male seamstresses, or whatever they choose. Every day, all day, I want to see myself and everything through your eyes as well as mine." The stunning scene before her was like a miniature painting held in the palm of her hand compared to this.

"Don't say anything. Not just now. I'm an arrogant bastard, but I can read, and I've been reading you all summer." He was holding her hand as though he were receiving a transfusion.

Applying himself again to steering the car, he shot up the road again. "That vineyard I was describing last night is somewhere around here. It's probably turned into a kind of secret garden now, because no one has cultivated it for seven or eight years.

"And how about some lunch before we head home?"

Jana smiled. Lunch was for earth people. But, in any case, she was starved.

Peter swung the car off the highway, and the Jaguar sped up into the hills past vineyards, any one of which might have belonged to the Milfords.

He pulled into a small, deserted-looking restaurant, which seemed expensive but not very promising. Jana balked at the idea of eating there. But they had to eat somewhere.

Peter jumped out of the car and, without inviting her to follow him, said, "I'll be back in a minute."

She watched Peter, in his wrinkled clothes, stride toward the entranceway with all the confidence of one wearing custom-made sports clothes designed for a day in the country. He knew what was before him, he had no doubts about the woman in the car behind him. This was an easy arrogance, not an abrasive one. It was new to Peter and not entirely unpleasing to her.

The man who had disappeared into the restaurant had

compressed more loveliness into her life in the last twenty-four hours than she had ever known. Whenever her thoughts raced ahead to the next twenty-four, she physically had to press her feet on the floor board to keep from going out of control.

Peter swung back into the car carrying white paper bags.

Jana peeked inside the first sack. She could already smell the bread, but there were rounds of cheese at the bottom and a second and third bag held two bottles of wine.

"Milford Chardonnay Sixty-six."

"That's what Miss Mari likes."

"I know, it's her favorite."

The car was bumping along a dirt road. Peter swerved into an overgrown vineyard and stopped by a broken-down fence.

This vineyard would be in use if Milford property were being run properly.

Jana carried the bags and Peter pulled out a small, tan blanket, one with a monogrammed "M" on it. Spreading it across the lumpy sod, he motioned for her to spread out their lunch.

"We don't have a corkscrew, Peter."

He retrieved a Swiss Army knife from his pocket. "These knives can do anything."

"There are no glasses. Are there any paper cups in the car?"

Smiling, he was back in a moment with a bundle of paper towels. Unwrapping them, he held out one crystal wine glass, then another—both from the Milford mansion.

Jana was hit with a bolt of jealousy. He had done this often with other women. Is this how he and Susan met in secret? He certainly wouldn't carry such glasses in order to drink with the boys.

Jana could only think of how she wanted to claim every inch of Peter's body right then and there. She threw her arms around him and, with the glasses still in his hands, he knelt down to the blanket. She was with him. The kiss was long and deep and right enough for her to feel much better about the glasses.

"We don't have to hurry about lunch," he said matter-of-factly. "I should check in at Mariposa at least by seven, and that gives us enough time to—to talk. That's what you want to do, isn't it?" He was grinning. He knew what she really wanted.

"Your eyes always look as if they know a nice, bright secret about me," he said.

"And until today, yours looked as if they were always asking me what it is."

"That's because," he said, holding up his glass, "today, I know. To our secret."

She went along with the toast, but then protested. "That's the trouble. I want to be in on whatever it is that's happening to us."

"You don't like it?"

"I don't understand it, I've never been here before. I feel . . ."

"Out of control?"

"Yes."

"And I've never felt more in control."

"But why is this happening to us now?"

"Can't you just accept it?"

"I have an inquiring mind."

"And body."

"Peter, stop. We have to eat lunch and . . ."

He kissed the wine from her lips and sat back obediently with only his hand on her ankle, which, after she had sat down with her feet tucked under her, was near him.

"But why now?" she asked again.

"I wasn't in a position to offer you enough until yesterday."

"Enough? What did you think I wanted?"

"Power, money. . . ."

"Peter!"

"It was true from the first day you arrived until . . . I don't know when it changed."

"That's not the only reason."

"There was Andy. I thought there was something significant going on between the two of you, and believing that you knew about that day in the mountains when Ginni. . . ."

"Something was going on. But then some things happened."

"Was it what Ken told you about him that finally made the difference?"

"There have been other things. He has become possessive. And his jealousy of you is not because of me so much as because of you being a Milford. And all the things he has been taught he is entitled to if he obeys his father and follows his rules."

"Some rules. But I do understand about him being possessive. When it comes to you, we all are."

"You've become awfully understanding."

"That's how I feel. Love let loose makes me feel—loving. What would you say if I had a talk with Andy—after you do, of course."

"About what?"

"Our marriage."

"You sound certain."

"I am."

She loved him. All the sharpness was out of his voice, his eyes, his movements.

"I don't know about you and Andy. He's jealous of you for so many reasons."

"The kid is strange."

"Peter, he's twenty-five years old. He's talented. He would be so happy following in Susan's footsteps and being an artist—or a forest ranger—but he's no kid."

"And he's not tough enough stuff for his old man—who is a bastard. But, hell, I could say to him: hang in there long enough, Andy, and things may change. Look what happened to me."

"You should have said it long ago. But I don't think that would be the thing to say to him now. Andy doesn't need to be compared or held up to anybody, particularly you. I'll have to handle him very carefully."

"Do you love him?"

"I do, in a protective way. He needs me."

"More than I do?"

"More—obviously."

"Jana, if you're going to be a Milford, you must stop looking for the obvious. That's not how we operate."

"And you must stop thinking you have a monopoly on intuition," she said sharply.

"Will you find it hard to choose between me and Andy?"

"I never had a choice." She laid her empty wine glass down on the blanket and moved close to him. He gave her sips from his glass, bites of bread and cheese from his sandwiches. The hum of late summer was in the air. The world was rushing to pack in all the life it could before the chill of winter slowed it down.

"Peter, what do you think about Moose and Miss Mari?"

"That their names both begin with 'M,'" he snapped.

"I mean about their love for each other."

"I'm suspicious."

"Is that because of your unquestionable intuition, or do you have a reason for being that way?"

"I don't think their love is real. I think it's convenient. The moment I saw you, I knew."

"But there are different kinds of love, don't you agree?"

"I don't know. Sometimes, I think that Miss Mari has flattered Moose by making him think he's an artist. . . ."

"He *is*."

"And Moose has flattered Miss Mari by reminding her that she's an attractive woman."

"And *she* is."

"And Miss Mari, who needed him at night, began needing him during the day, too, or thinking she did. She's got these wild ideas about traveling. . . ."

"Peter, what you're saying isn't what you mean. You're jealous, or something. Maybe you wouldn't be Miss Mari's main family concern if she married Moose. Maybe you wouldn't like that."

"Don't get Freudian on me, Jana. I'm not as hung up as you think."

"You act it sometimes."

"Shhhh," he said, "shhh."

"You see, we only get along when we don't talk."

"I love you, Jana, my Jana. We'll work it out."

"Do you believe that?"

"What I was thinking about Moose really had not all that much to do with Miss Mari. When I return to Mariposa, I plan to fire him on the spot."

"You would do a petty thing like that just because of him and Miss Mari?"

"No. Moose is one of the problems with the ranch. He has never questioned the orders my dad sent down to him. With only a tenth of his mind, he has gone through the motions of being Mariposa's superintendent. He's given his real energy to his stained-glass work, and even those damned little peach pit carvings.

"He has taken the road of least resistance, when he should have been questioning my dad, improving what he could on his own, not just maintaining the status quo. That isn't good enough for Mariposa.

"And with the ideas I have, I simply cannot have Moose

fighting me every minute only because he thinks he knows best, because changes mean he has been wrong."

"I wish there was another way."

"You've been telling me from practically the first day, how Mariposa is operating in the dark ages. . . ."

"Did I say that?"

"No, but you thought it."

Jana moved away from Peter. Sitting on her knees in front of him, she said, "I want to talk about Susan. If you married me, what about Susan?"

"Jana, I thought I had found my life when I found Susan. She was looking to be no such thing to me—and she was right."

But did Peter still love her? Could she ask that? Would he tell if he did?

"I thought I could change her. Heard that before?"

"How?"

"By being so interesting, energetic and, finally, so demanding, that she would devote herself to me—not to her work. She began to hate me. And I also thought I could make her want *my* children."

"How do you know what *I* want?"

"That's right, I haven't asked. Let's lay it all out on the blanket, shall we? What *do* you want?"

"Peter, I don't want *your* children."

"No?" Finally, she had surprised him.

"I would consider, at some carefully planned point. . . ."

"Watch it."

". . . to have *our* child—or children. Two."

"You're planning too close to the line."

"I can't give up all my bad habits, can I?"

"I suppose not. But what about Susan, don't you want to know more? Aren't you waiting to hear me say that I don't love her anymore?"

She withheld an answer. He could read it all over her face, which was waiting, poised, to hear him say no.

"I do love Susan. And I always will. She was my first love, and nothing can change that. But you—I have found you now. If I had known you ten years ago, I would have loved you, maybe even married you."

"If I had agreed."

One corner of his mouth smiled. "Of course. But one of us would have ruined it, because we would have put too much pressure on each other to live up to our plans for each other.

"For example, I'll be re-opening the houses my dad owns in Rome, New York and Nice, as well as fully staffing the mansion. Susan would have hated moving around so much. How could she have left behind a wet, unfinished canvas?"

"How could you have asked it of her?"

"I don't know. But ten years ago, Susan and I never talked about what we expected from each other. We merely stomped along, blaming each other for what we thought was wrong. We both did terrible work those two years. I almost flunked out of college, and the paintings she did were not remarkable. There was one, however, and I think she sold it, of a small lake up in the mountains. It was a sad picture—one she painted just before she left me, but after she had made up her mind to leave. . . ."

"Peter, what about Lisa?"

"She belongs to Ken and Susan. We will love her from afar. It's worked out so far."

"Has it really?"

"Did Miss Mari tell you about her?"

"No."

"Damn that Andy. He latched onto that and has milked it ever since."

"Peter, it's only been a year since Lisa was born, twenty-one months since. . . ."

"Jana-Jana, don't . . . let me love you as much as I do this moment."

Peter's shoulders were hot from the sun, his back was burning. The clouds in the sky were reeling their shapes, flinging them toward the ocean, bumping them into the mountains.

He shrugged out of his clothes and slipped Jana out of hers. His hips were churning under the natural growing season of their love. Instead of grapes dropping off the vines, there would be babies. She and Peter would tend them carefully, watch them grow under the same sun that had helped create them. They were mingling with the overgrown vines in the field, the leftover bread, the tears of happiness she had saved to be cried alone, tears that spilled and rolled back into her hair as their mingling flung them into the clouds.

They were together, close, comforting, comforted, and covered by sloshes of wine that they were spilling freely.

The sun let their love bask in peace, as it would if tiny seedlings had been planted in the field. They remained until the burning brightness above them was dressed in a cloud, and their blanket had turned damp from them and the ground.

Before they packed up to leave, Peter removed the long gold chain from his neck and placed it around hers. Jana closed her eyes. With her fingers, she followed the line of the chain between her breasts to where it hung just above her waist.

Holding the medallion, she opened her eyes slowly. Her fear was confirmed. The medallion had a raised "M" sculpted on it.

Chapter 24

Too soon they were driving through the straight streets of Fresno. They had passed acre after acre of fields of tomatoes, where two-story-high Havermeyer harvesters were grabbing up hard, green, square tomatoes that would be sprayed with ethylene and, ten days later, blossom out in a beautiful red color that belied their spongy tastelessness.

The miracle of it was that anything at all grew in this desert, even with artificial spraying, water, harvesting. Was there something artificial about her own rapid development this summer?

The streets enclosed square, even blocks. It was like driving inside a crossword puzzle. Her own square was no longer a blank. She had an initial that had been printed into it. But she still couldn't spell anything.

"Peter, let me drive on out to Mariposa with you tonight."

"You want to tell everybody, eh?" He liked the idea.

"I just don't want to be apart from you—so abruptly. And I don't want to tell anybody, not today."

"Not even Miss Mari."

"I want to see us through our eyes at first—to feel . . ." She paused.

"Certain?"

"Comfortable about it. After all, when you see me next to Cassie, you might change your mind."

"The hell I will!"

"That was a joke. I never worried much about you and Cassie."

"She marked you as the enemy the minute she saw you. She thought you were a fortune hunter."

"I guess I was, in a way."

She had her wrist on his shoulder as if she found it necessary to keep checking that he was there, with her. The drive north took on a friendly aura. This was to be her home—at least most of the time. She would be part of a family that had turned this valley into the richest fruit-producing land in the United States.

She could hear Fred, her boss at Havermeyer: "I never wanted to hire a gal in the first place. This doesn't happen with the men. They don't go around marrying their customers."

And his secretary, Alma. "Can you think of a better reason to leave? All that money?"

It was a good thing Peter wasn't a farmhand: they would never understand. Certainly, none of her colleagues at Engineered Edibles could figure out why she had not been happy there. If they could have, or if they hadn't been too tied down to admit it, they would have walked out with her. The valley, even without Peter, was better than those nasty strawberry-flavored globs her lab had worked so hard on, their work subsidized by lucrative government grants siphoned through universities.

What about Spenser? His work meant more to him than anything or anybody. He wouldn't fold. She hadn't written him once since arriving in the valley. But she had taught him that he could accomodate a certain kind of woman in his life. Having known her would help him meet another.

Andy would be her problem. Since they had met, she had been the most important person in his life. She never would have thought so at the time. He was bold, brazen, a woman-collector if she had ever seen one. Yet it was she who had taught him how to be with her, how to feel sexually brilliant, as he put it, instead of merely appearing that way.

She had never been as important, as depended on, as Andy had made her. She would never have allowed it to happen if she had understood what was really going on with Andy, as well as with her and Peter. Maybe she *was* obtuse, and observed only surfaces. She had always thought intuition was a woman's God-given endowment. It offended her to run across someone who had grown up believing it belonged to his *family*.

The drive from the highway to the Mariposa offices was a traumatic one. As soon as Peter turned onto the dirt road, they could both see that all was not as it should be. Instead of an orderly lineup of trucks, there was a jumble of them in the place where the tidy circle had parked the day of the strike.

A line of men was waiting to go into the office.

Peter jumped out and demanded, "What do you men think you're doing? This isn't payday."

Moe Perez stepped forward. "Moose is holding an investigation. Yesterday, the bin-fillers arrived and were unloaded down by the machine shop. This morning, when we arrived at work, somebody had slashed the nylon catch surfaces of three of the harvesters."

"Not just slashed them, but cut out huge holes," one of the men added.

"That's right. And now that we have the fillers and don't need the truck drivers to the extent that we did, or the sorters, we've only got two out of five harvesters working. When Moose ordered everyone but two teams of men out in the field to pick peaches as usual, they sat down on their buckets and refused."

"What the hell is Moose investigating?"

"Who slashed the nylon."

"And he's been doing that all day?"

"He said that nobody would be paid a penny until he discovered who had done it. Pete, the peaches are dropping off like crazy out in the east orchard."

Peter announced to Jana through gritted teeth: "This is it. That man is a menace. Why the hell didn't he wait until I returned? We've lost an entire day for no reason at all except that he had to play Sherlock Holmes."

"Don't do anything while you're so angry, Peter." She was begging him, holding him back, her hands clinging to one of his.

"I have the authority. Meanwhile, you figure out how we can replace those nylon catchers. What are they, twenty-five or thirty feet in diameter? You know we won't get any until next season, don't you? That's why you're standing there.

Well, do something about it. I've got my hands full with these men—and Moose."

Jana, looking like a rumpled ragpicker, pushed through the crowd to the weigh house. Before she opened the screen door, she made sure that the chain around her neck was hidden.

"Well," said Cassie, "have they found out who done it?"

"I don't think so. Moose is. . . ."

"Moose doesn't know what he's doing. He was as rattled as everybody else around here when they found those harvesters. It's really a shame, because by taking advantage of Peter's offer to pay them by the bucket instead of by the hour as long as the carts weren't here, those men were racking up more money than some of them had ever seen."

"Who does everybody think is responsible?"

"It could be anybody, of course. But I believe that most of the men were so impressed with the fact that Peter had not gone back on his word, even though they knew he was losing money on the deal, that they supported him. They were even interested when the automatic bin-fillers arrived. It was almost as if they had received five presents that belonged to all of them collectively."

That was Peter's goal—to make each man who worked for Mariposa feel identified with the ranch so that they would care what happened.

Ruby marched in. "Whoever did it should be tied to one of those harvesters and have the stuffing shaken out of him."

Jana looked out the window that faced the office. She could see that, from Peter's point of view, the men were being uselessly wasted today by Moose's investigation. But perhaps Moose knew something they did not: that more sabotage was planned.

All she had wanted was for Peter to make an appearance at Mariposa, then take her home with him to a real shower, a real bed and maybe a long swim. She wanted to test their being together on his home ground.

The door was knocked open and Andy said, "Let's go," before he was inside the weigh house.

"If you're thinking you should wait for Peter, remember how concerned he was about you last time when they got your desk with that oil and junk. You could be in danger now, too, you know. Did you ever think of that?"

She had not. Nor, apparently, had Peter. Besides, it didn't

ring true. No one would hurt a *person*. Sabotage was a criminal act, but it wasn't murderous—unless one thought of it as a way to murder Mariposa.

But with Peter at the head of all the Milford businesses, Mariposa was secure. Would it have been possible for someone to have learned about Joe Milford passing the reins of the company down to his son?

Peter's father would most likely have telephoned his lawyer in Fresno. He would know. And McNair would have made the announcement in San Francisco. Mr. Milford would most likely have telephoned Miss Mari, too. The word about Peter's new power would have gotten around.

The only true secret at the moment was between her and Peter. She was glad. It needed a place to safely grow for a while—especially with all this commotion that was preventing her from being where she wanted to be with Peter.

"You look a mess," Andy was saying.

"Thanks. Are you saying that because you're mad that you don't know where I've been?"

"Probably. But you still look awful."

"All I want to do is clean up and slip on some clean clothes. Cassie, would you tell . . . anybody who asks where I am . . . that I've gone back to the complex with Andy? And Ruby—do any of the women on the platform sew well?"

"Sure," she said. "Some of them even make tailored shirts and suits for their men."

If Havermeyer could not deliver the polyurethane-coated nylon shaker surfaces, she probably could receive the material in a couple of days.

Andy's Honda seemed like a kiddy-cart after Peter's Jaguar.

"Am I to assume," he said coldly, "that you plan to tell me where you've been?"

This was not the night to tell him about Peter. For one thing, she felt too weary. And when she was tired, she was too blunt. She would be sure to hurt him more than necessary.

"Peter's father wanted to see me. We went there on business."

For her part, that was true enough.

"Why are you sunburned?"

"We went down to the beach. Mr. Milford lives on one, you know that."

"And that's where you held your business meeting? Didn't you consider the terrace? Or the living room? It looks over the ocean, too. Lovely view."

"Andy, don't turn ugly because of this. There's no need."

"Sorry. Tell you what, you change clothes and I'll take you to dinner."

"I couldn't. I had a late lunch."

"Where?"

"I don't know—at some roadside place."

"The news came in today about Peter's new job. I was glad."

"That's wonderful, Andy, that you can say that."

"Glad—because I figured that now he'll move himself off to the San Francisco office and get out of my sight—and yours."

"What if he brings the home office of Milford Enterprises here?"

"He'll probably do it this winter, and I'll never return to this valley so I'll never know, will I?"

Jana pressed her hands flat against her temples and closed her eyes. What could she say? How could she say it? She saw the glint of gold dangling between her breasts. She covered her throat with one hand, played with her collar.

Andy began stripping off his clothes as soon as he was out of the car. Shirt in the courtyard, trousers near the diving board, briefs on the diving board.

Jana said she did not want to join him.

"Take off your clothes," he demanded.

"No."

He walked toward her, gave a wild laugh and pushed her in.

His arms were around her, stripping her, her clothes were floating. She was being pushed against the side of the pool. His legs, but not hers, touched the bottom. He was threatening her, lunging at her, stabbing at her. Her bikini panties were floating in the filter current, passing in front of the huge underwater spotlights like a wicked sea animal escaping from violence.

"Open up," he said, through gritted teeth. "Open up." His upper lip was curling, snarling, threatening.

"No!" she screamed.

"Touch me, then." He wrapped her hand around his

growing weapon and, with the pressure of his own strength, his anger rose to shooting strength.

He was holding her up, his knees jamming her legs apart, forcing her to straddle him. Jana was crying, screaming, her feet kicked, looking for the bottom of the pool.

"I hate you for this!" she screamed. "I'll always hate you for this. Let me go!"

"Say you love me, Jana."

"No!"

"Say it! I'm bigger and better when I'm mad. And I'll screw you all night until you know what I want you to say, until you feel its truth. No Milford is going to take you away from me after only one night. Say it, Jana, say it."

His entire hand was crowding between her legs. Jana managed to loosen an arm. She jammed her elbow into his right eye. As he screamed, she kicked him cruelly and, after lifting herself out of the pool, she kicked him again in the jaw.

As she ran into the house, she saw Gretchen rising from a lawn chair like something that had been hiding under a rock.

Sobbing, Jana locked the door to her bedroom and dialed Mariposa. The line was busy. Andy was knocking on her door, kicking it. She heard Gretchen call to him.

After hearing their voices out by the pool, Jana darted to the windowless bathroom, threw all the towels in the tub and curled up to drown in terrycloth.

The most perfect day of her life had become the worst; the innocent, beautiful body of Andy, the most vile. He would never touch her again. Never. She listened for sounds of Andy and Gretchen. She heard nothing at all.

After waiting half an hour, she opened the door slowly and checked for a glimpse of either of them.

She looked for the keys to the Mercedes. They were gone.

Jana ran to the phone by the bed and called a taxi, grabbed some blue jeans, a shirt and sneakers and, teeth chattering, hid behind a bush in the front yard until it pulled up.

"Take me to the best hotel downtown—one with good security."

She had frightened him. "The Hilton? That's fine. And please hurry."

The only way she prevented herself from crying all the way downtown was by straightening her clothes, combing her hair and putting on makeup. When she walked up to the reservations desk, she said with absolute authority that she worked with a Chicago firm, was in the valley as a consultant for Mariposa, and had met with an accident.

She was prepared to suggest that they telephone Mariposa to confirm her story, but the authority with which she delivered her speech to the desk clerk was so convincing that he merely bowed as he handed over the key.

Jana bleakly walked upstairs to one more lonely hotel room. If only Miss Mari and her home had been all right, she would have run to her. Miss Mari would have understood. Miss Mari would have advised her on whether or not to tell Peter about Andy.

Silently, Jana begged Peter to help her, comfort her, tell her she was safe. She was afraid he could never comfort her, because she could never tell him. What he might do to Andy was beyond her imagination.

Jana showered and scrubbed, then fell onto the bed. The words, "Peter, Peter" formed over her like skywriting.

She slept in those clouds where she was safe with Peter. But the sky turned dark. Instead of dropping hailstones, sour-skinned grapes began to fall. They turned into rough, black rocks, which were being thrown from a higher, more menacing cloud. A formation that looked like the beautiful, blond Andy was hurling the rocks at her and Peter. So close were they that if he threw at one, he would hit the other.

Crying, Jana awakened. It was 7:00 A.M. She phoned Mariposa. No answer. At the mansion, Pilar said that Peter had not returned that night. She called information for Moose's home number, reasoning that if he had been fired, he would be there.

"Pete's meeting with old beetface this morning," said Moose with disapproval. "Miss Mari told me."

Jana called that number. Peter had not arrived, but the secretary would give him the message to call her at the Hilton when he did.

Jana filled the bathtub, scooted down in it until her ears were in the water and her hair floating on the surface. California: the violence runs deep. Had it always been so? And what was she to do with it?

Chapter 25

The sun had set, and Peter had neither arrived nor telephoned. Had Beetface's secretary failed to give him her number?

Jana phoned Mariposa once in the morning and again in the afternoon. Both times Cassie answered, and Jana hung up without saying a word.

Throughout the day, she remained in a kind of enforced unconsciousness except for her phone calls.

They weren't all searching for Peter. Ruby told her that one of the women on the platform had a sewing machine that she used to make sails for her husband's boat. The woman was confident that, with help, she could custom-make the heavy nylon material to fit a harvester. That would at least work for the remainder of the season.

Jana phoned Illinois and ordered enough material for ten harvesters. There might be more vandalism.

She finally phoned Miss Mari. Peter had not been there. "Tell him I'm at the Hilton. I'll explain when I see you."

As she slept, the residue of one nightmare lingered long enough to refuel another. Finally, she snapped the chain when she realized that her head couldn't hold any more phantoms.

Room service would give her something sure and tangible

to wait for. She had thought she would be eating with Peter, a continuation of the last meal she had eaten with him in that vineyard, the last time she had looked up at the clouds lazily and felt safe at last.

She ordered something—anything. By the time it arrived, surely Peter would be there. Should she phone him again? Dammit, no. Even if he didn't care about her, however, he would be curious about her plans to put the harvesters in working order. But, knowing Ruby, she had probably already told him.

At the sound of someone knocking on her door, Jana made a sari out of the top sheet and, without asking who it was, flung open the door to a sun-tanned blond waiter, one of Andy's surfing brothers, no doubt. He wheeled the covered dishes into the room and his eyes shifted between her unmade bed, her unmade mind, and the two glasses, the two coffee cups.

"Young man," she considered saying, "go to New York or Boston. Don't take a car. Lock yourself up in classes and libraries all day, go to plays and sit in coffee houses on the weekends. Grow pale. Don't cover your soul with the crust of the sun and think you've accomplished something."

The waiter started to open the wine for her. "No, don't. My friend can do it when he arrives. His knife has a corkscrew on it—one of those Swiss Army knives. . . ."

He probably had no idea that he was the first person she had seen all day. He looked at her curiously as she babbled.

When he had gone, Jana climbed back on the bed and leaned over the food, removing the silver-plated dish covers. No wonder the food was covered: gray roast beef, faded, slimy brussels sprouts, accompanied by a dried-out hard roll, clammy peach pie and cold coffee. The only decent offering was the bottle of Milford burgundy. And that was for her and Peter.

At 11:00 P.M., she phoned the Milford mansion. Pilar said that she had not seen him. She phoned Mariposa on a chance. No one answered. Should she call Moose at his home? She refused to scavenge the city any more. Peter knew where she was. He could damn well get himself up here.

She had already decided: there was no way she would sob on his shoulder about the events of the night before with Andy. She couldn't be responsible for what Peter's already long-standing anger toward Andy would make him do.

She would simply sob on about life in general—about her sadness, unnamed; her happiness, unformed.

At 11:30, Jana dialed Andy's number, planning to hang up if he answered. She only wanted to know where he was.

He wasn't home. She was afraid. What if he were looking for her? Or, even worse, what if Peter had found out what had happened and had found *him?* They might be chasing each other down one of those dark lanes in the orchard. Andy was bigger, but Peter was smarter—too smart to engage in back-lot boxing.

Peter must have gone to the hospital to see Miss Mari. That was it. And she couldn't phone there. Would he tell Miss Mari about them, or would he wait? She hoped he'd hold off, so that the two of them could say together, "Miss Mari, we want you to smile with your lovely eyes on our union," and Miss Mari would say, "I will," and in a few weeks (months?), she and Peter would say, "I do." And, in the name of the Father and the Son and the Holy Spirit, she would be pronounced a Milford.

Jana touched the chain around her neck. It had almost happened already. And so far, there hadn't been a single tangible benefit.

She checked to see if the phone were on the hook. It was. She listened for the dial tone. It worked. She looked once again at the door. No message had been pushed under it.

Lying back on the bed, Jana lay her hand over that place that longed for Peter. Would he never call? Had they both been intoxicated, first by the grand announcement made by Peter's father, then by the beauty of the ocean and the sunny, fruity wine that had steamed through them; by their bodies aching to be one, and the abandon they had experienced on that patch of blanket that lay so rumpled in the overgrown vineyard? Was there nothing more substantial?

She, who was a lightning analyst of people, had looked at Andy that first day and read him wrong. Could she have done the same with Peter?

Raising herself up from the bed, slicking back her bangs, her long straight hair, she addressed the mirror. "You," she said, "know nothing about anybody, not even yourself."

It was midnight. Jana crawled down to the end of the bed and reached for the wine. Damn the waiter. Why hadn't he left her a corkscrew? Damn *her.* Why hadn't she allowed him to open it?

She stuck a fork tong into the cork and half-heartedly picked. She was remembering the day in the mountains when Ginni was killed. Everybody was jumpy, but Andy had been jumping the wrong way. While Susan and Ken huddled together, Andy had withdrawn, even as she held his head on her lap. That head. Heavy, unthinking, innocent—like lead.

It was his innocence that had appealed to her. That and his perfect body—the body of one meant to live on an island, unclothed, bathed by brown-skinned women with peonies behind their ears, orchids around their necks. Stroked, oiled, kissed, approved of forever. That's what Andy needed. And anybody who needed all that needed help—because that wasn't what the world was about.

Why hadn't she simply ordered a wine bottle with a top that screwed off? For obvious reasons—the Milford bottles were all sealed with corks.

Jana observed her progress on the cork: she had managed to remove several chunks from the soft, speckled structure, but had made no headway into the bottle.

She picked up a table knife. Its blade was too wide to attack the cork further than the bottle's rim. She felt nervous, angry: how could she wait another minute to hold up the glass to the light, swallow its jewels, bask in its warm, inner embrace?

Next, she placed the handle of the knife on the cork and her eyes scavenged the room for a brick, a rock, a hammer-like object. A shoe, that was it—that all-purpose tool of women down through the ages. A shoe maybe, but a sneaker? It would never do.

One hand still on the knife, Jana stretched and opened the drawer of the bed table. *The Book of Mormon* lay, maroon in color and positioned next to a dark green copy of the Bible, courtesy of the Gideon people.

Both groups may have anticipated her anguish, but neither had foreseen her predicament.

She felt foolish. If she, an engineer, could not work out a structural solution for extracting a cork from a bottle, she would be reduced to chiseling it away a little at a time. That was as aesthetically unpleasing as the thought of masses of spongy tree between her teeth and under her tongue. The other choice was to cause the cork to become impacted so that, without spraying wine all over the room, it would shoot down into the liquid. And that was the only method.

What should it be: *The Book of Mormon* or the *Bible?* The *Bible* was heavier: one little thump from it on the knife handle might accomplish the job. However, *The Book of Mormon* was an unknown to her. She had never heard it read as a child. It was, for her, an impersonal tool for the task at hand.

Balancing the bottle, knife and book on the table with wheels was an impossible arrangement. She grasped the bottle between her legs and scanned the setup. She was ready to smash it on the side of the bathtub, "I christen you. . . ." in order to sip the runoff.

She slid to the floor and positioned it between her legs, pounding gently on the apparatus. Wasn't there a toy that trained children to do this at a very young age?

It was working. And with each dull whack of the book on the knife, she awaited the perfect sound. At last she heard it, as the cork shot down into the bottle. But the blackish burgundy shot to the ceiling, and from there rained down on her in macabre drips. It was an overripe nightmare that had caught her at last, but proof of its reality was on the sheet around her and on the bed, the carpet and—worst of all—it was bleeding down the mirror like a sloppy transfusion.

"Oh, my God," she cried aloud, hurriedly drying off *The Book of Mormon* with the bedspread.

With a towel, she groped around the room like a caterpillar unraveling before her time.

Stripping out of the stained sheet she had so genteelly donned for the arrival of the waiter (and so expectantly tightened every few minutes in anticipation of Peter), naked, she leaned back on the bed.

From her position on the pungent pillows, she could see herself in the mirror. First, she toasted herself with every imbecilic name she could think of. With the second glass, she saluted herself with promises of doing better in the future. By the third glass, her only toast was, "to me, as is"—a peaceful plateau, which was enough to put anyone to sleep.

Instead of rushing to Mariposa looking like the Grapola Queen, Jana made plans to see Miss Mari at the hospital. In order to do that, she had to buy some clothes.

She stopped in a small boutique, quickly purchased blue knickers, a yellow skirt, a white linen jacket and three silk shirts—cream, blue and burnt orange. Jana also bought a glimmeringly perfect cream-colored pantsuit with a satin waistband to wear to the Governor's dinner honoring Miss Mari.

Her efficiency at such a time surprised her. She would look cheerful, whether she was or not. Wearing the blue shirt and the knickers, and new tan espadrilles, she caught a taxi to the hospital.

Before she reached Miss Mari's door, she heard the woman calling her name as she turned around in her wheelchair. "I just knew it was you," she said. "Look at this. I've been watching the news on television. There's been more trouble at Mariposa."

Thank goodness, that's why Peter had not phoned her. Now she knew.

"Carlo Prima was injured while making a minor adjustment to one of those harvesters. A bin crashed on him and it was carrying fifty pounds of peaches. They say he's down in the emergency room of this hospital."

Jana stood behind Miss Mari's wheelchair, her hands gripping its handles. The camera was panning from the rubble that was once Miss Mari's home to the idle men to the worried women and to Ruby, who obviously wanted to be the one whose opinion was asked.

Peter now filled the screen, his eyes darting from the workers to the television camera and down the road to the highway.

A reporter snared him. What did he think was the trouble?

Peter's brow wrinkled, his hand reached for the medallion that had always been around his neck and he said angrily, "I can tell you one thing: this is no accident. And if anyone who is connected to people who work at Mariposa has a clue, tell me, tell the police, write an anonymous letter."

"Whom do you suspect?"

"Officially, no one. If you ask me, what do I suspect, I'll say greed. For years, Mariposa has been approached by two groups of people: those who want to buy us out because they need a tax shelter and those who are seeking to develop our land as real estate—or a cheap imitation of Disneyland, as one landgrabber put it last week."

"He looks furious, almost vindictive," said Miss Mari.

"It was only two days ago that I became president of Mariposa's parent company—Milford Enterprises. I now have the power to put a stop to this kind of sabotage, this blackmail. And I intend to do it."

"Mr. Milford, I'm from the Los Angeles *Times,* and I don't have the background on this story."

"You'd better get it, lady, before you print the usual distortions that you Southern Californians have about valley people."

"I don't know what you mean."

"Just because you have the population down there doesn't mean you can write quaint stories about the colorful landowners grappling with the age-old plight of powerful corporations versus the little people. Milford Enterprises is a sophisticated company, and we have no intention of being intimidated by criminals."

Miss Mari was disgusted, and reached down to the remote-control button in her lap to turn off the set.

"Wait a minute," said Jana, her eyes unable to leave the face of this man she knew but couldn't fathom, "Peter's still talking."

"The facts are," he said, "this land will never be sold as long as I'm alive. And that gives you a pretty good idea of who the next target around here will be."

"That little fool," said Miss Mari, this time switching off the set with finality.

Jana slumped down in one of the mustard-colored chairs identical to the ones in the waiting room. Its pseudo–Danish Modern arms cut into her elbows. Her head was swimming. She should have eaten breakfast. She was absolutely not going to faint—not in a hospital.

"Put your head between your knees, Jana. Right now," barked Miss Mari. "I see what's happening to you."

As Jana let her head drop, she felt the welcome rush of blood. Miss Mari's still-bandaged hands held her while she said, "Stay there. No reason to hurry."

"I'm reaching for a pillow to put over my hard, old cast. That's it. Stay there. Jana, Peter was only being dramatic. It's very likely that when Carlo becomes conscious—as he may be this very moment—he can tell what really happened. It may have been that the person operating the buttons on the decelerator punched the wrong one."

Jana raised up. "No," said Miss Mari, "I don't want to hear your protests. I know Peter has just scared you half to death."

"He was here about midnight last night. Apparently, the two of you argued yesterday. He was upset about something concerning you. I was certain that with the two of you locked up in the same car all the way to the coast and back, you had more than enough time for a rip-roaring argument.

"Keep your eyes closed," she crooned. "Honey, there isn't a thing to worry about. I'll be released from the hospital in about a month. I'll find me a new place to live—maybe I'll even move into Moose's little house. We'd marry first, of course. Moose is a deacon in the Baptist church.

"And calling you 'honey' makes me think. I talked to Honey on the phone this morning. Moose put the phone in front of her, and we carried on a howlingly successful conversation."

Miss Mari rubbed a hand over Jana's neck, stroked her hair. "There, now, you *are* more relaxed."

She was a lump of lead and sinking by the second. How could Peter possibly have hinted that he had argued with her on their Santa Cruz trip? It was something else. He was angry at her for some unspeakable wrong she had done, something that probably had to do with Andy, but she didn't know what he knew, so how could she refute it?

In addition, Peter's *life* was in danger. She knew it, particularly now that he was acting president of Milford Enterprises.

What had happened to them while they were on the coast?

Her head still down, Jana told Miss Mari about the sewing team Ruby had organized, and Miss Mari related plans for photographing the Christmas mail-order catalogue.

"Did Joe say anything about the Save Yosemite pack I sent him?"

"Not a word. He was too happy about turning the company over to Peter."

"Genuinely happy?"

"I think so. He and Aline are planning a cruise around the world."

"Is he well enough?"

"He'll be here to see you before they leave. You can check him out. I thought he looked wonderful."

"What was the business he wanted to talk to you about?"

"I don't know. I think he might have wanted Peter to have company while he drove. If there was any argument on the trip, it concerned something Peter told him I would do."

"Well, you're not too sick to tell me, are you?"

Jana smiled into the pillow. "No. Peter told his father that I had made up my mind to remain at Mariposa—even help him out with the vineyards."

"And had you?"

"I have now."

Miss Mari held Jana's head up and kissed her on the cheek. "Jana, I'm so glad! That must mean that you and Peter are finally getting along."

Jana lay her head back down in the pillow. "I thought it did, too," she murmured.

"I just knew something might work out between the two of you, and it looks as if. . . ."

"Don't, Miss Mari, don't talk about that."

"Listen." Miss Mari sat up straight. "I think I hear Peter. He must have been down to check on Carlo."

The first words Jana heard from Peter since the day before yesterday were a harsh "What's wrong with her?"

"She came as near to passing out as anyone I've ever seen."

Jana raised up; she could feel her hair tangling awkwardly around her shoulders.

She looked up slowly at Peter. Something had happened. Once again, question marks of bold blue-black glared at her like baffled beads.

"I want to talk to Miss Mari—alone."

"Peter, there's nothing you can't say in front of Jana. Why she's practically. . . ."

"Miss Mari, I'd be glad to leave."

Was this the man who'd said he loved her, *too*? He must have misunderstood what "too" was echoing. If he had known, he would have realized that "too" meant "total"—without room for either accusing eyes or withheld words.

"Peter, tell me what's wrong. I've been waiting for you. I've needed you. Why haven't you come to me?"

"I've been busy."

"Tell her, tell us both what's in your craw," said Miss Mari.

"Jana, I looked for you last night."

"I left you three messages."

"I didn't have time to answer phone messages. My God, we're in the middle of a dangerous situation out there. And you took it upon yourself to disappear—as did your friend, your good friend, Andy Goodwin. That's why I went over to the complex looking for you last night. Nobody answered the phone, and I thought you might be out by the pool.

"That's where you'd been, all right. There were your goddam clothes floating in the pool, and Andy's, I presume, scattered all around.

"I was thinking of running a bed check, but that wasn't necessary. Gretchen came out looking pretty beat. She said that you and Andy were occupied, in your usual manner."

"I'm sorry you have to hear this, Miss Mari," Jana whispered.

"Peter, you have to listen to Jana. She has a story, I'm sure."

"Both of you, listen to me. You're two of a kind. Miss Mari, you threw yourself away on a good-for-nothing in Paris, and if that wasn't enough, when you were tired of him you introduced him to my mother, who wasn't as sensible, or as strong as you. She couldn't handle that kind of life, and it killed our family, killed her. Therefore, when you side with Jana, it means nothing to me."

"Peter, I meant what I said at the beach, in the vineyard, didn't you?" pleaded Jana.

He didn't answer. How could he? His face was made of petrified wood.

"You're acting like a fool, Peter," said Miss Mari, "worse than you acted before those T.V. cameras. If you won't listen to Jana, I suggest that you clear it up with Andy."

"No need," he said.

"What do you mean, Peter?" Jana choked out the words.

"I mean," he said, "that Jana had plans to leave the valley yesterday. I can't imagine what she's still doing here."

Like a frozen statue, Jana moved out of the chair, to the door. Without turning around, she heard Miss Mari say, "Jana Robbins, don't you dare leave until after my dinner in Sacramento next week!"

It was all she could do to find her way out of the hospital.

Chapter 26

As Jana climbed into one of the taxis in front of the hospital, she had a vague remembrance of having promised Ruby she would talk to her about the material that would be arriving from Illinois within the next few days.

Needing a purpose, she grabbed onto this one, and gave the driver directions for the expensive jaunt up Highway 99.

During the entire ride, Jana held tightly to the medallion around her neck as though it were her breaking heart. If she'd had her wits about her, she would have returned it to Peter at the hospital. She was glad she hadn't. The scene would have been too sophomoric. When she saw Miss Mari, she would give it to her—concealed in a little box. Obviously, Miss Mari was no more aware of what had gone on during the trip to the coast than Peter, who counted it as nothing.

Every time something awful happened in Jana's family, it had been their pattern to "oh-well" it, and immediately bounce back with some Pollyanna statement whose second sentence began with, "At least." In this case, Jana, if she had the energy, could say, "At least, I found out before it was too late. At least, I know what kind of a man he is now. At least . . . she wished she could believe a word she was thinking.

Peter's rage when it came to Andy equalled Andy's for

Peter. And *he* had less reason than Andy. He was fighting from strength. Andy was the underdog in every case.

It certainly confirmed her original belief that Peter must never know what really happened at the complex.

Operations were slow at Mariposa. Scattered trucks were driving up and down the road, and two were at Cassie's window.

Jana had the taxi let her out at the weigh house. She would clear out the few things she had squirreled away in the shallow drawer of her desk: velcro curlers, a *Guide to Yosemite* and a paring knife for peeling her unlimited supply of peach snacks.

Cassie whirled around on her stool and said most cheerfully, "When are you leaving?"

Her round, green eyes were so delighted that Jana felt a sudden desire to jam all the contents of her drawer into their old place. And how did Cassie know she *was* leaving? Peter couldn't have reached Mariposa any sooner than she did, unless he flew.

"Where were you last night? At least, you could tell me that. It's you I have to thank for Peter coming to me at two A.M. He's the one who said you'd be leaving soon. Too bad, we might have been friends if it hadn't been for Pete."

"Cassie, have you seen Ruby?"

"She's outside on the platform. This will be her last day out there. She's making plans to have a sew-in over at the Tourist Center. Some little cottage industry that you thought up to keep the old girls busy, I believe.

"But I have seen Andy. And, apparently, you haven't said a word to him about flying back to Chicago. He was really upset when I told him. Apparently, you two had some kind of lover's quarrel. Anyway, Andy wants to apologize."

"I can't see him. I haven't time."

"Nobody wants to see anybody around here, anymore. Peter doesn't care if he ever sees you again; you don't care if you ever see Andy. And me? I like seeing everybody."

On her way to the platform, Jana paused. Cassie was obnoxious but she knew everything that was going on, and her voice wasn't nearly as loud as Ruby's.

"Do you know why anybody would hurt Carlo?"

"Lots of reasons. Why don't you ask Andy when you see him? He and Carlo are old friends."

"What happened, do you know?"

"After dinner last night, the pickers were lying around in their bunk house playing cards, drinking beer. Carlo, who had been made one of the harvester operators, went down to the machine shop to check out his machine, which is one of the two still in commission.

"The rumor is that Carlo caught somebody giving the business to his harvester—or else caught someone tinkering with it so that it wouldn't work today and Mariposa would be left with only one machine out in the orchards.

"We hear there was a fight; Carlo had the wind knocked out of him, was shoved under that bin and . . . you know the rest: squash, down on his head, chest, stomach, hips. He looked like a bloody rag when they took him out of here this morning. The awful thing was that he managed to shove the bin off him, but had to lay under the machinery all night until somebody found him this morning."

"I thought somebody had been assigned to watch the harvesters?"

"Moose's job was to make the assignment. But I suppose you know that Peter sent him packing—even though he still lives on the ranch. Anyway, nobody assigned a watch, and the harvesters were there for anybody to mess with."

"I think I'll go down there."

"Don't touch anything. The police are returning in a little while."

Jana stopped again. "Cassie, do you think that Peter's life is in danger?"

"I don't know." Cassie was concerned, but also rather thrilled at the thought at the same time. "If he keeps poking around, issuing ultimatums on television, he may be asking for whoever is sabotaging Mariposa's men and machinery to pick on the big guy next time. Yes, that's it: he's asking for it. And nobody is more powerful than Peter, don't you know? I'm just sure the criminal will be caught soon."

Jana caught a ride with one of the drivers. As she hopped into the open truck, she saw Ruby bouncing down the road, her two little arms chugging like a train. "Wait up, Jana."

The driver stopped. His mufflerless truck idled at an eardrum-bursting level.

"Now, Jana, I want you to know I'm sorry for what happened to Carlo. But do you think that his accident will interfere with the Governor's dinner for Miss Mari? She has been looking forward to it so much."

"I don't think so, Ruby. Why should it?"

"You know what people are saying: that Mariposa is jinxed. I thought the Governor might be afraid to have a bunch of Milfords sitting around him."

"Ruby, I have to go. I'll talk to you later about the material."

"It's here."

"The material I ordered from Illinois yesterday morning?"

"Yes. Some of the girls have taken a pickup—one of their own, with sides—out to the airport to pick it up. They'll start to work on it this afternoon. I was over at the Tourist Center this morning, and they already had a pattern cut out from the old catch surface. They're raring to go."

"Ruby, you don't know how glad I am to hear the news." Ruby didn't know there was no competition at all in the good news department. Once in a while, Havermeyer did something right. Maybe it wouldn't be so bad returning there.

Jana asked to be let out about four hundred yards from the machine shop. This would be her last chance to walk through these orchards, her last chance to be alone here where she had been so happy—so unhappy—where she had belonged, where she had been thrown out.

At first, as she walked, she felt that the trees were cousins of the ones that had scared Snow White with their bony fingers as she ran through the forest. She squinted and looked down the row of trees, conscious of the patterns of light and dark rather than colors or small shapes.

She stood, listening to the sound of peaches falling. She no longer thought of it as money dropping to the ground, but as an indication of the bountiful potential of this ranch that had given—and taken away—so much from her.

Remembering that she was hungry, Jana reached up and touched the pinky-yellow fuzz of a peach hanging just above her head. The sunlight sparkled bright approval as the peach chose not to be picked, but to hatch in her hand.

She rubbed its fuzz down to smoothness and, leaning over to spare her new blue knickers from the juice, bit into the warm peach. The light sweetness of its flesh slid down easily. She could eat a second. Holding up her hand for another, it, too, belonged to her immediately.

Peter would find a way to make everything here continue for years and years. He would make mistakes. But it was his land, his money. And he would learn. The sabotage would stop. Perhaps if she had left earlier, it wouldn't have gone on as long as it had.

What would she tell Havermeyer about the readiness of Peter Milford to invest heavily in their grape-harvesters? She would tell them nothing. They could send somebody else out to give him the pitch. She couldn't have cared less if Havermeyer made the sale, but was worried about Mariposa buying the wrong harvesters. Before she left Fresno, perhaps she should wrap a scarf around her head, slip on sunglasses and make an inspection tour of the local dealers. She could leave her recommendations with Miss Mari, who could hint and hint until Peter understood the reasons for buying one or the other.

She walked toward the machine shop—a metal shed attached to a Quonset hut—a battered, greasy version of the Tourist Center.

Outside, the three sabotaged harvesters were lined up like odd insects that had fluttered down from their swarm after their wings had been ripped and slashed.

Their shaker head, like pincers belonging to an earwig, were in different states of openness. The rubber head-covers that clamped onto the tree were still clean.

The marvelous thing about these machines was that they could hug a tree in only seconds, shake off the fruit, catch it in the upturned umbrella and send the fruit to the bin-filler, where it would be sized and blown free of debris.

She hoped she never had to see another one. If she went to China—but after her failure at Mariposa, Havermeyer would never send her—she could concentrate on grain crops.

Suddenly, from three directions, the orchards began to eject men—pickers who had been hiding in the trees.

"What are you doing here?" she asked.

"We're standing watch. We know that the police are hoping to find one of us guilty of hurting Carlo. They'll say, 'Those wetbacks, they're always fighting among themselves.'"

"What do you think happened?"

"Somebody beat him up bad and couldn't face taking the blame, so they stuck him under one of those jinxed machines where he would be properly injured.

"We would never do that. But the police will try to blame Carlo's accident on one of us, anyway. That's why we're holding our own investigation, and why we're watching to see that nothing else happens to these harvesters you brought from Chicago."

So they knew who she was. As much as Peter had attempted to keep her separated from the pickers, they knew. And Jana felt certain that the pickers were right: none of them had taken part in the sabotage, or in Carlo's accident. She would bet on it.

But since when was she a judge of anybody's character these days?

The men, a group of about fifteen, dressed in khakis, ragged Levi's, straw workhats, baseball hats and a few in cowboy hats, all looked down the road. Jana joined them. A truck was racing toward them, honking. For a moment, Jana thought they all might be hit, but at the last moment, it swerved and, brakes screeching, spun around in the dirt.

Andy yelled from the truck. "Jana! You're not supposed to be down here by yourself." He was wearing the white tennis shorts and light-blue shirt with cut-off sleeves he had worn the day she met him, making it hard for her to connect him with the frightening man of the night before last.

"Get in," he said. "You're not safe out here."

Jana refused. She was more frightened of him, driving like a kid, reminding her of an evening that had turned her life—her love—around.

"I said, get in. I have to talk to you, explain, apologize."

The men were closing in on the truck. "She doesn't have to go with you. She's safe with us. What are you talking about? Hey, man!"

They began to rock his truck. He was terrified and Jana saw that his hands, although tight on the steering wheel, weren't able to keep his arms, his elbows, from shaking.

"Hey, *señorita*, you afraid of this man? We'll take care of him for you. He's been riding our backs all summer. Who does he think he is?"

"J-j-jana, please."

"*Callate la boca*," said one of the men, who reached into the truck and had Andy by the arm. "She stays with us, you stay with us. Let's see how you like that, Mr. Andy Goodwin, Mr. Lazyboy."

"Wait," said Jana. She felt sorry for Andy. She knew that the apology he was aching to make was sincere. She couldn't bring herself to side with the men in this group against Andy's weaknesses, which even they had perceived.

"Andy, these men have gathered here because they do not believe Carlo was injured accidentally. They are standing watch to see that nothing else happens. I have a right to be here. I'm still connected with Havermeyer. But I also appreciate your concern.

"Men," she turned to them, hoping they had sensed a respect in her voice for Andy, "you know that it was Havermeyer's fault, not Mariposa's, that the harvesters were late, that the bin-fillers did not arrive on time. But that was not a crime. What's been going on around here ever since is."

"But we didn't do it."

"Has anybody accused you? I certainly haven't."

"Yes. Mr. Lazyboy, sitting in the truck. He accused us when he raced down here like a cowboy saving you from the Indians. Right? Ain't that right?"

Andy turned the key in the ignition, and several of the men jumped into the doorless truck from the passenger side and grabbed them away from him, hacking his arm with painful chops as they did.

After Andy had grimaced for a few seconds, he said, "There are lots of people who could have done this. What if Peter Milford himself sabotaged this machinery, so he wouldn't have to pay up on the deal he made with the pickers?"

"That's outrageous, and you know it," snapped Jana. "Milford's been fair to us. We have no more gripes against him."

"Has he paid up for the weeks you have made more money than any pickers on the other ranches around here because the machines are doing your hardest work for you?"

"He will. He has to make the cash flow. . . ."

"Don't be stupid," yelled Andy, as though he were fighting for his life. "It's costing Milford more to pay you and the drivers than he would lose if the peaches rotted in the orchards."

"Is that right?" One of the men stepped forward. "Is that what Milford's doing? Is that what you're telling him? You've been leading him around by the nose ever since you arrived. You know what he's pulling. What is it?"

Jana glanced at Andy. He was resting his chin on his arm,

which was on the steering wheel. His eyes were half-open, his mouth posed in a comfortable smirk.

"I know, and you know," began Jana, "that Peter Milford's plans are based on the long run. He wants to develop good year-round workers. He is willing to put his reputation on the line to help any one of you establish a home for your families. He knows the ropes for getting you admitted to this country legally—if that's what you want. Do you know any landowner who has offered you such help?

"He believes that you want to work. Peter Milford believes in you. How could you not return this trust?"

She stood while the men talked, in Spanish, among themselves. At least . . . they had moved away from Andy's truck. At least . . . Andy had dropped that smirk from his face.

Jana thought she had become accustomed to the sun. But standing here in this clearing by the machine shop, she was burning under it. Yet, in the center, she felt cold, empty, out of her element. Maybe she did need a man to protect her. But where was he?

The men were surrounding her. Andy, still in the car, was watching with alarm. They had approached her to shake her hand, to tell her she was right about Milford.

"Now," she said, "I'm going back to the Mariposa offices with Andy, who has been so kind to offer me a ride. How about giving him back the keys to his jalopy?"

Instead, one of the men gave them to her. He had a solemn look on his face. "If you need us," he said, "we're here. . . ."

She thanked him, thanked them all. When she handed Andy the keys, she said, "Don't you dare peel out of here and throw up dirt in their faces. You drive like a grown-up and you take me straight to the Mariposa offices. I have to make a phone call to Chicago."

A phone call wouldn't hurt. She could thank them for expediting the material, and discuss when she would return to the office. She was also sure that a few questions had been raised about why she was still in California working, even though she was on vacation.

"Thanks," said Andy, "for helping me out. Those boys can be meaner than a turkey with his tail on fire."

"I don't know what you're talking about. It seems to me that, compared to what I've seen in the last few days, they are very gentle."

"Jana." He stopped the truck.

"Andy, you keep going."

The truck was idling. "I'd never hurt you—never."

"You would have if I hadn't broken away from you. I should never have moved into that complex. Peter warned me."

"To hell with Peter. I'm the one who loves you. He certainly doesn't. Cassie's been talking about nothing for the last two days except that louse."

"Andy, I don't want to discuss Peter, either."

"I heard about how he manipulated you to go with him to Santa Cruz and, when he returned, he had even manipulated his father into turning over the entire works. God, if I only had a little piece of it!"

Outside the office, Andy took her hand. "Jana, think about us. We never had to plot or plan: we came together naturally. We go together so well. I can do big things as long as I have you with me. I've got a part-time job—my dad arranged it for me. It's going to work into something big. I'll have lots of money. You won't have to work. We can have babies, beautiful babies."

"Andy, no. I have to return to Chicago. I have to arrange my life again. And while I wish the best for you, I know that you can't be part of it."

She spotted Peter and a patrolman through the window of the office. They were talking to Moose. He looked angry, and his head was continually bobbing downward before he spoke.

"Let's not talk here," said Andy nervously. "I'll take you to a nice place."

"I can't. I have that phone call. What do you suppose they're doing in there with Moose?"

"Probably accusing him of Carlo's accident. You know, Peter fired him the other night. Moose got drunk, and I heard he roared around this ranch all night and, finally, when his truck ran into a peach tree, he walked home.

"He hasn't got much use for Peter, and he's been around longer than anybody. You should learn something about Milford's character from him."

Andy's hand was reaching under her collar. "Hey, haven't I seen that before?" He touched the gold chain.

"It's nothing," said Jana, taking it out of his hands and slipping it under her blouse, feeling it slide between her breasts, wanting to sob because Peter's hands never would again.

"N-n-nothing?" Andy screamed.

"That's right. I was playing around and slipped it on—while we were driving. I was bored. I forgot to give it back. I'll do that right now. That's another reason I need to stop at the office."

"Jana, get your things out of that hotel. What do you say? Come on back home."

"We'll see." She had no intention of leaving the hotel until the day she was to fly to Chicago.

Peter had walked out on the porch and was gesturing to Andy and Jana. The patrolman nodded and approached them.

"I'm sorry," he said. "We'd like both of you to come into the office for questioning."

Chapter 27

As Jana and Andy climbed up the stairs to the office porch, Moose, his head down, his eyes not registering, walked out.

With Peter leaning in the doorway between the two rooms of the old, converted house, and Jana seated uncomfortably next to Andy, the policeman began the questioning.

"Where were you last night between nine o'clock and midnight?"

"At the Hilton."

"Don't you have a place to live?"

"Yes."

"Why were you in a hotel?"

"For personal reasons."

"Why were you planning to move to California?"

Jana looked up at Peter, and unconsciously found herself touching the chain inside her shirt.

"That was also personal."

"You realize you can't get away with answers like this in court."

"These questions have nothing to do with anything. My private life is not Mariposa's business."

"What is *your* business?"

"I'm a special representative of Havermeyer Harvester."

"Are you happy in your work?"

"Yes, in my work."

"Why have you applied for a job with the Calimyrna Corporation, and why have they offered you a job in their corporate office in San Francisco?"

"What are you talking about?"

"This letter arrived today for you at the house you moved out of so abruptly the other night. It says it's in response to your serious interest in moving to California.

"In addition, Mr. Milford over there telephoned Havermeyer in Chicago to report that the situation at Mariposa was way over your head and they said you weren't even working for them now—that you were on vacation. Following his call, we telephoned and asked what business you had here now and they said none."

"I was on the phone with Havermeyer only yesterday, and Peter himself asked me to arrange for the repair of the catch surfaces for those three harvesters. What are you people trying to pull?"

"Just checking your story," said the officer, who then turned to Andy.

"Mr. Goodwin, have you ever been employed by the Calimyrna Corporation?"

"I'm a student."

"*Have* you?"

"No."

"Did you know that Carlo Prima was once on their payroll?"

"He's not anymore."

"Do you have any grudges against Carlo Prima?"

"Of course not."

"Were you friends?"

"I knew him."

"Did you agree with his position on the harvesters?"

"He became very sold on them. I have no position."

"Did you know Carlo when his men had a contract with the Calimyrna Corporation?"

"I think so."

"It was only a year ago."

"Yes. But what are you driving at?"

"This morning, a lawyer, Cy Leeman, responded to a plea made by Mr. Milford on television, asking for information that might explain who was responsible for the trouble at Mariposa.

"He reported that, earlier in the week, a representative of Calimyrna had again approached him and predicted that Mariposa would be up for sale within the month—that they had inside information that confirmed this.

"Mr. Leeman related that he had asked the Calimyrna people not to approach him again because he had a feeling that they were behind 'undue pressure' that was being placed on Mariposa.

"What part in this pressure do you think Carlo was playing?"

"He was a victim, obviously—*if* what you say is true. I know nothing about it."

"Do you, Miss Robbins?"

"I wouldn't be surprised if Mr. Leeman's suspicions were true, but I, too, know nothing."

"Okay, Mr. Goodwin. . . ."

"I think these questions have gone on long enough."

"Look, fella," the officer loomed over him, "while we've been having our little discussion, I've noticed that you have a bruised eye, a cut lip and scratches on your hand. How'd all that happen to a dandy like you?" The officer looked disapprovingly at Andy's white shorts and blue shirt, and then down at his miraculously unsmudged white sneakers.

"I-I-I. . . ." Andy turned his head down in order to hide his face from Peter.

Jana said, "I stuck my elbow in his eye when we were swimming the other day."

"On purpose?"

"Yes. I was angry."

The officer waited.

"The reason is no one's business. It's personal. It has nothing to do with Mariposa or. . . ." She started to say, "or Peter Milford." But that was not true.

"Thank you," said the officer, "that will be all."

Andy was on his feet immediately. Jana thought of handing the medallion back to Peter, but could think of no way to do it without saying, by her actions, something she didn't mean.

What was clear was that Peter had the ability to juggle two problems at once and, in spite of the trouble at Mariposa, he had found easy answers in his search for ways to rid himself of her. He had cast guilt on her by using Andy, and now by using the Calimyrna Corporation.

It would probably be the smartest thing she had ever done to leave for Chicago immediately.

To Andy's dismay, Jana caught a ride to Fresno with Ruby, who was on her way to visit Miss Mari. Jana stopped off with her to say goodbye.

"I won't hear of it," declared Miss Mari. "If you're not at my dinner, it won't be complete. I've already made arrangements for you to ride with me and Moose in the limousine the Governor is sending.

"Besides, since you were here this morning, I've had a brainstorm concerning the Save Yosemite Committee, and I need to discuss it with you."

"Peter wants me out of town."

"What does this have to do with him? After all, this is my roast."

"Toast."

"If they didn't feel sorry for me because of the fire and all my aches and pains, it would be a spicy roast. Now, it'll probably be a somber, pompous affair, with people standing up and saying nice things about me that they don't mean. You've got to be there to cheer me up. If it gets too dreary, we can all go out afterwards to a nice bar. Ken and Susan will be there."

"And Peter?"

"If he goes. You know how he hates big flings where a Milford is on the menu."

"Miss Mari," said Ruby, "we women are moving into the Tourist Center next week, and I need to know if you're still planning to have our product sales meeting and, if so, where will it be?"

"Right here in the hospital. The doctors are only letting me out for my dinner in Sacramento—they're impressed. But I've arranged to have a double room—which is empty, of course—and we'll get down to business. If Jana is still here. . . ."

"No, Miss Mari. I won't be. I'll leave the morning after your dinner."

"That's all I had to check on," said Ruby. "I'll return to our little project." She winked at Jana.

"What's she talking about?"

"The women have volunteered above and beyond the call

of duty to tackle the sewing of new catch surfaces for the three harvesters."

Miss Mari was standing. "I'm walking into my dinner by myself. Would you like to have a sneak preview?"

"I think they're bringing in your lunch now."

"We had lunch for breakfast. This will be supper. At this hospital, we practically have breakfast as a midnight snack. But I want to talk to you about my brainstorm.

"You've heard of the Miss Strawberry character that originated, alas, not out of the strawberry patches of Santa Cruz, but in a greeting card company. It has expanded to dolls, sheets, towels, curtains—practically everything but toilet seats, which they seem to feel is beneath them.

"I was sitting here staring at that blank television screen, thinking, What could I do for peaches?—you know national consumption goes down every year. There's already a Miss Peach comic strip, which had nothing to do with peaches. I decided to have a character—in the form of a doll—with a name like 'Peachy Pie,' or something similar. Peaches are much more voluptuous than strawberries. This would not be a doll in a quaint little sunhat, but a real woman—do you understand what I mean?"

Jana grabbed a sheet of paper from a tablet by the phone and sketched a peach doll.

"Here." She passed it to Miss Mari. The doll wore earrings, bracelets, a sleek skirt, fashionably-cut pants and shoes with mid-heels.

"Yes," said Miss Mari. "I like her very much. But she doesn't look like a 'Peachy Pie,' to me—she's much too sophisticated."

Jana took the sketch back and wrote under the doll: "Miss Mari."

"I wouldn't like to be named after a character," said Miss Mari slowly, "but to have a character named after me—I think I'd like it. Hand me the phone, I'll call my lawyer about a patent.

"If this goes over even half as well as Miss Strawberry, Yosemite can say goodbye to the money-makers who are trying to invade the park and get down to the business of being a true wilderness."

"Miss Mari?"

"Are you referring to me or to my namesake?"

"You! Before you take on supporting a national park, I

wonder if you've thought about funneling some of the Tourist Center's money back into Mariposa. It needs it desperately right now."

"We won't make money that soon."

"You will next year if all goes well."

Miss Mari waved for a nurse's aide who was pouring ice water in one of the pitchers to leave the room.

She said in a whisper, "I thought of that after you arrived and showed me the potential of the Tourist Center. But without Moose at Mariposa, I decided to concentrate on the Save Yosemite Committee. I'm so disappointed at the way Peter dismissed him. The timing was bad, too. We have never been so close as this summer, and it's been one blow after another for both of us. Moose never believed that after all these years he would be turned out by Peter."

"If it had been the other way around, wouldn't Moose have fired Peter?"

"In a minute," she admitted ruefully.

Miss Mari turned to the phone to talk to her lawyer, and Jana sensed that the answer she had received concerning Mariposa was not a definite "no"—that a possibility did exist for Mariposa to receive some of the Tourist Center's funds. Jana could see the time when Mariposa was entirely free from the tyranny of the nearby Calimyrna cannery and of the inconvenience of the one they were hauling their peaches to now. If the Tourist Center—and the Miss Mari emblem—caught on, everything grown at Mariposa could be sold through the Tourist Center and the mail-order catalogue.

Jana allowed herself to feel just the least bit optimistic.

"Miss Robbins, your car has arrived."

Jana felt elegant as she walked through the front entrance of the hotel and stepped into the limousine.

Moose and Miss Mari, with her cast, took up the forward-facing seat. Jana sat down on the smaller seat sandwiched in next to the television and bar.

"You look terrific," said Miss Mari. "Doesn't she, Moose?"

"Thanks, so do you. That silver dress is lovely and hardly anyone would know about your. . . ."

"Aches and pains." Miss Mari completed the sentence and stretched out her arms to show that the long sleeves covered.

her burns and fluffed out the long skirt of her dress to show that her cast was hardly noticeable.

"It's good to see you, Moose," said Jana.

"I've been staying pretty close to home, lately."

"Too close," said Miss Mari. "All he wants to do is work on some project—but he won't tell me what."

"I've been hoping this past week that you might come over and help us at the Tourist Center. After all, yours are the most expensive items we sell," Jana said.

"That's a wonderful idea!" exclaimed Miss Mari. "I was planning to badger him into helping me when I returned, but the sooner the better, if you ask me." Miss Mari looked concerned.

The limousine had stopped at the familiar gate house. The limousine was circling past the pool. The limousine door was being opened and Peter ducked his head in.

"What the hell is *she* doing here?"

"Dear, I thought if I told you that, I'd have a harder time than ever persuading you to join us. Now, get in."

There was no room next to Miss Mari and Moose, even though they had the larger seat. Peter was forced to squeeze onto the seat—which was adequate for two children or two Vogue models. He draped his arm over the back of the seat in order to fit in next to Jana.

As she fought the tears in her eyes, there seemed to be a serious cave-in behind her heart. It was only an engineering problem, which could be set right in a few hundred years.

Peter reached around her, heavily brushing against her back, as he flipped on the television. No picture. Jana almost sobbed with relief. She couldn't have stood it.

"What's the matter with this T.V.?" asked Peter, yelling through the open partition to the front seat.

"A kid," said the driver. "He broke it yesterday while he was watching cartoons during the family's drive through Yosemite. His mother said they might as well have remained in New York all summer—the cartoons were the same. I wish they had."

"Peter," said Miss Mari bossily, "get your head out of that window." She punched a button that rolled up the glass between the back and front seat.

"Now, open that wine," she said.

"Which bottle?" Again, Peter had to lean around Jana, because the bar was on top of the television.

"Ours, of course."

"It's a bad year."

"I don't care."

"Miss Mari," said Peter, "I hope it's not going to be one of those nights."

"Only if it's necessary, my dear."

"I'll watch her," said Moose.

"I'll bet you will," retorted Peter.

His light gray suit served as an artillery range from which his eyes could shoot.

"I thought you left town," he fired at Jana.

"I wouldn't let her," said Miss Mari. "And before you cause too much trouble, I want to remind you, young man, that this is my night and I'm the one who'll choose the subject matter for conversation."

"What's in that package?" asked Peter, nodding to a large white box wedged between the television and the back seat.

"A surprise."

"For whom?"

"The Governor of the state of California."

Peter poured himself more wine. Jana wasn't drinking; neither was Moose. She was developing claustrophobia, she was sure that's what it would be called. There was no movement Peter could make without touching her. It was not merely intolerable: it was unbearable.

If everything had not blown up, she was unable to keep from thinking, she and Peter would have been together in the back seat of a succession of limousines. She would never have had to leave his arms during the trips—the nicest thing about limousines.

But this one was crowded with enough emotion to start World War III. Moose was on his best behavior—on behalf of Miss Mari. Peter, although he was not so admirable, was also under the strain of balancing his emotions.

The drive, which took four hours, was a strenuous one for Miss Mari, who had not set foot outside the hospital in over a month. But she seemed not to know it. While Jana and Peter sat stiff and dull, she and Moose talked. She seemed to know that the less cross-conversation there was, the pleasanter the trip would be.

Miss Mari found a selection of tapes and played one after another. The varied selection included songs by Sondheim,

Beethoven piano and violin sonatas featuring Yehudi and Hepzibah Menuhin, and country blues by Tammy Wynette. All kinds of people rented limousines.

When they arrived, Miss Mari and Moose were whisked away for photographs, and Susan appeared with Ken not far behind her.

"I didn't know this was going to be such a large affair," said Jana. Peter had dropped behind her to talk with Ken. "There were a thousand tickets sold by invitation only—proceeds to go to the Save Yosemite Committee," said Susan.

A photographer jumped in front of Jana and began snapping pictures. Others joined him.

"They think you're a movie star," whispered Susan, who in sequined green dress, gold belt and shoes, looked like a celebrity herself.

"I wish they would stop." Peter was carefully avoiding her. "Peter doesn't like it," Jana told Susan.

"He's angry," said Susan, "because the reporters aren't asking him about the trouble *at* Mariposa, but about the trouble *with* Mariposa."

Susan took Jana aside. "Have you seen Andy this week?"

"No, not for the last few days." She had been relieved, had thought he had decided to leave her alone. "I've been staying at the Hilton—I'm leaving for home tomorrow, you know. But are you worried about Andy?"

"Not really. But my mom said he had been down for the second time to see Denver. That's very unusual. He was quite close-mouthed around her, although he seemed very excited. She said he spoke quite a lot about you, Jana. I think you've done more to help him straighten up than you know."

"I'm glad, Susan. But you can tell your mother what I've told Andy."

"I know," said Susan. "But it's good to see him sticking in there trying."

It was Ken who escorted Jana and Susan to dinner. Peter was already at the table on the dais sitting next to Miss Mari, who was next to the Governor.

After the meal of steak, avocado salad, peach soufflé and peach liqueur from the Milford stock, the Governor stood:

"Ladies and gentlemen, we are here tonight to honor the most lovely woman in California—Marietta Milford, known as Miss Mari to us all."

During the applause, Miss Mari did not rise, but acknowledged the introduction and its reception with the grace and presence of royalty.

"Those who accuse farmers and ranchers of being anti-environment," continued the Governor, "don't know Miss Mari: she's a combination of Paris fashion and California heart, and that heart has gone out to preserving the best of her state. Yosemite National Park is a national treasure, and so is Miss Mari.

"The Save Yosemite Committee has its initials, 'SYC,' as its motto. It first gained fame when a television series glorifying cops and robbers was filmed in Yosemite. Its producers insisted on slapping paint on boulders, and flying helicopters low over the heads of bears, tamaracks and tourists. The series flopped and there has never been another.

"Let a developer attempt to sneak through a proposal for a high-rise convention center in the park—and yes, it's been done—all Miss Mari has to say is 'SYC' 'em. And that's the last of it."

The Governor presented Miss Mari with a plaque, moved a bouquet of hydrangeas and placed the microphone in front of her.

"Thank you, my friend—and my friends. I had no idea when this dinner was planned, that I, too, would have a gift—to present.

"In just one short week, with the help of a friend of mine from Chicago, I have designed a new worker for the Save Yosemite Committee. I have already been told by a Madison Avenue ad agency that this worker will make enough money to save Yosemite.

"Finally, we can drive out the hawkers selling bed, board and trinkets, and the selfish entrepreneurs who are carving up the land with their plumbing and covering it with their garbage, which, tidy as it may be, is never as tidy as they claim, and is a blight to our park."

The Governor looked uncomfortable. Susan whispered to Jana, "Miss Mari is getting in her licks and the Governor—who has supported the commercial side of Yosemite—can't do anything about it."

Miss Mari reached down and lifted up a sophisticated, all-cloth doll, with a stitched face the shape of a peach.

"Her name, Governor, is Miss Mari. From now on, she'll

be on every peach product sold at the Save Yosemite Tourist Center and through our mail-order catalogue. The doll, itself, will be sold in stores all over the country. Not only will Miss Mari help Mariposa, but we hope it helps the peach industry and the state."

Miss Mari grinned and pushed the microphone away.

The Governor, doll cradled in his arm, quieted the audience. He bent over Miss Mari, kissed her cheek and said, "Miss Mari, you're a doll."

To everyone's surprise, Miss Mari insisted on stopping for an after-dinner drink in a "nice, dark dive."

Jana saw Ken and Susan nod to each other, and when their Cadillac and the limousine pulled up at Hattie's Hideout, Ken was carrying a long roll of paper.

When they sat down, he said, "You know, Miss Mari, how you begged us to build near your house after we lost ours."

Miss Mari looked up over her Irish coffee, her eyes mocking innocence. "Yes?"

"We'd like you to take a look and see what you think of this." He spread out a large blueprint.

"A friend of mine—an architect—worked out what might be a good way for our two families to live close to each other. See? There in the middle is a swimming pool."

"I've got a swimming pool," said Peter. "Miss Mari can swim there any time she wants."

"Both houses are built in a moon shape," Ken was saying, "not a single room is square."

"That's always been my main complaint," said Miss Mari. "I could never understand why architects couldn't design rooms that had a nice shape."

"The rooms at the estate are shaped fine," said Peter.

"Listen here. I own the land in question, even though it's surrounded by *your* orchards. And I'll make the decisions about that land."

She was studying the blueprint. "But where is there a place for you to paint, Susan?"

"Here on the second story. The windows are on three sides, and the view would be over mountain ranges. And look, in your house, Moose's studio would be in the same place."

For the first time all evening, the grin on Moose's face was wide.

"That looks real nice. My glass will show up pretty in the windows, too."

Peter excused himself. "You stay right here," said Miss Mari. "I want you to be as happy about this as Moose and I are. Except for the Tourist Center, I haven't known what to do about the future, But, it seems," she said, laying her hand across Peter's, "that the future is looking especially bright for both of us."

"Yes. Only the present is like hell. I'll wait for you outside."

Chapter 28

The view overlooking Lake Michigan was one Jana had already seen when her airplane landed at O'Hare.

She had walked in the door of her apartment, and without stopping, had gone out on the balcony. She stood there in the awful blue suit she had originally worn to California. The suit was a way of mourning what might have been, as well as a way of recognizing herself when she arrived at the airport.

The clouds hung in heavy, billowing, summertime shapes. She had not traveled any distance at all: they were the same clouds that had reflected the sunset on the beach; the same clouds that had sheltered her and Peter in the vineyard.

There had once been a person who lived in this apartment who had never given a second thought to the white parade. What was she to do with her old self? Who did that other person know in Chicago? Nobody. Then what was she doing here?

Spenser, who had not returned from Italy, was already far from her. When they saw each other, the distance would only increase.

Jana dashed in from the wind, so strong she dared not keep plants on the balcony for fear they would blow off and land on a pedestrian.

She could hear herself explaining. "It was an accident,

officer. At the beginning of the summer, my *Dracena Margi-nata* was perfectly happy: no indications of depression; no root rot, fungus or need for extra moisture or food. Officer, I can assure you that the plant did not jump—nor did it fall: it was whirled out of the balcony where it lives each summer and, pot and all, was pitched into the skies. Totally free of its usual container, it was, at first, *terrified* it would lose its identity.

"But, please, put this in your report: it was exposed to the boundless life outside a square box and it soared with the strong gales. The fact that it eventually landed upside-down, not injuring, but making a certain impression on a group of people, was entirely accidental. Thank you, sir. I'll keep it indoors and it will never happen again."

This apartment offered no comfort. Honeycombed in a highrise, how would she ever walk on solid earth, hear the rain on the roof, smell the fruit-flavored breezes blowing in from the orchards, from the drying sheds, from bubbling pots on the stove?

She wouldn't. Before this summer, this apartment had been more than she had ever had before. Now it was like a thimble that held her former life, a spacious hotel room for her present one.

The northern afternoon light was cruel and chilly, and it squared off the rooms of her apartment into sharp, hurtful shapes that bruised her eyes every time they tried to gain perspective. Beige and cream, a little tan. Colors of sophistication. Colors of dried-out sticks. Throw-away colors.

Hot tears began to flow—tears she had carried across the Sierra Nevada, tears so large they could never have been cried in a crowded airplane—or even last night in her hotel room.

Jana's hand went to her neck. The chain was gone. She had slipped the heavy gold into a satin coin purse that had come with her evening bag. When Moose and Miss Mari's eyes were closed on the long trip home, she had slipped it to Peter through the Plexiglas partition. He had chosen to ride in the front seat with the chauffeur on the way home. He said he wanted to listen to an Oakland A's game.

He had rolled up the window again immediately after she gave him the little purse, and looked around at her a final time. Despite the bullet-proof partition, his eyes were not separated from hers. They were eyes which no longer asked questions, because they thought they had all the answers. She sought no protection from them. In that last glance, she was totally vulnerable. But until now, she had not allowed herself to receive the full impact of them.

How could she ever become a new person? Or return to the one she had been? The hurt in her heart was all at once. The convulsions racked her through and through. The force of her hurt was moving the clouds: that was no sonic boom.

"Can't imagine why you stayed out there so long," Fred said on her first morning back at Havermeyer. "It's a good thing you got out when you did. I hear they had more trouble yesterday. Somebody stole all the new bins.

"If Schultz had told us what was going on in the first place, we never would have sent you."

"Who, then?"

"A man."

"It wouldn't have made much difference," said Jana blandly.

"What about the grape-harvesters?"

"They're—sleeping on it."

"After all the time you spent out there? If you ask me, it's not your fault. Milford's more trouble than his old man. He talks a good progressive line, but—what does he know?"

Jana's only response was to settle back in her chair, her shoulders limp, her face set to endure whatever she had to.

"He called this morning. At eight o'clock. You know what time it is in California at eight A.M.? It's six A.M.

"He wanted to speak to you. He needed to order more bins—he said.

"I suggested that he discuss it with the Havermeyer rep who would be handling Mariposa from now on, that you were no longer on assignment in California because you had been transferred to the International Division."

"I have?" She was mildly interested.

"It's a big promotion. You're the only one Havermeyer is sending to the Canton Trade Fair this fall. The board was impressed with your verbal and written reports from your trip last winter, and J.B. realized what he had always known: most of the men consider Far Eastern trips just an opportunity for an Oriental bash. He says you're different, and that in spite of your good looks, you have a determination of steel and can work circles around the men. He's overlooking your California experience—blames all the little snafus on company foul-ups."

Jana was silent.

"Well?"

All that Jana could hear was Miss Mari saying: "Poor Jana."

"I guess I'll go."

"You should feel complimented. Last year, Havermeyer sent three men. I, harumph, was one of them."

"Now, let me see." He was shuffling papers on his desk. "After that, we have you scheduled for an agribusiness seminar in Cairo between the Egyptian government and U.S. businesses. You might be too busy, but if you're not, you can catch some of the Nile trips. I've been to all those places. Interesting.

"And from there, you go to Italy, where there's been trouble with our tomato-harvester in that southern project. Italians, especially in the south, are resistant to the concept of square tomatoes—and hon, if they won't plant 'em, our machines can't very well pick 'em, now can they? And if there's nothing to pick, there's no reason to buy our product. And that, as you have always been the first to realize around here, is what makes the world go round. Right?"

What could she do but concentrate with all her might in order not to say, "Wrong, Fred, wrong."

"I figure you'll be home just in time for Christmas."

"Thanks a lot."

"And, one more thing: before you officially leave the country, J.B. asked me if you could leave on a shortie assignment at the end of the week. I said that after you had received so many plums, it would be ungrateful if you refused a peach."

Jana started.

"There's a similar situation to Mariposa down in Georgia. It's one of those father-son, resistance-to-change affairs. Routine. You may have picked up a few pointers in California. Pass them along."

Jana, returning to her office, felt like a piece of chalk that was being used to draw a line around the world. The only thing good about seeing Fred was that he made her feel slightly angry, slightly alive. They would never pull this on her if she had a husband with even an extraordinary tolerance for the rigors of this job. Or children. Never mind discrimination against women: what about *single* women?

She could hear J.B. and Fred in their all-male meetings: "Why not? What else would she be doing?"

Corporate nuns. No business should be without them. Total dedication was all they asked. Somebody should tell these people, "Don't ask. Don't ever ask."

Each day that week, Jana made an appearance in the office. She attended fall sales meetings, where she was asked her opinion of the marketing possibilities in the San Joaquin Valley, and she heard herself say something that amounted to very good. She listened to three universities give reports on their research projects—government-funded—that would benefit the harvester industry. They weren't even subtle about doing the industry's research—courtesy of the U.S. taxpayer.

Perhaps it was the fog, or the acid-permeated humidity, but by Friday night, Jana realized she had walked through the week feeling as if she had been dipped in astringent. The pores of her mind were closed too tightly to absorb very much.

She talked to Miss Mari once in order to hear the report on her Save Yosemite meeting with the women. "Wonderful," was her opinion. "They are all so enthusiastic and, as for their sideline—sewing—the first harvester is almost ready to be fitted with its new catch surface. The women have worked night and day all week."

"What about the bins?"

"They were 'mislaid,' but turned up some time in the middle of the week."

The phone connection was surrounded with Peter, because each of them was so careful not to mention his name. Jana was saddened to think that because of his presence, she and Miss Mari might be too uncomfortable to talk very often.

"And what about *you?*" Miss Mari had asked. Jana explained the itinerary, and Miss Mari sounded distant and preoccupied when she said, "How nice."

Jana debated with herself about giving her mother part of the salary she had earned from Havermeyer that summer, or her entire Mariposa earnings. To rid herself of the experience, at least symbolically, she gave her mother the Mariposa money and deposited several thousand Havermeyer dollars in her brother's account.

On Friday after work, she was standing in front of her picture window without seeing the lake. And there were no clouds to hold onto: they had blown away in the flat, dry wind.

Why wait until Sunday or Monday to go to Georgia? She would leave tomorrow. Rent a car, drive around the countryside. Be close to the earth. She rushed toward the phone, thinking herself half-witted that she had persuaded herself she would be closer to Peter in Georgia than in Chicago, because Georgia had peaches.

The buzzing of the doorman diverted her dialing. "Your friend is on his way up," he said.

Spenser was home. The doorman wouldn't let just anybody in. He was early. *Why* hadn't he called first? Why hadn't she flown to Georgia that morning?

Jana brushed back her hair and looked in the mirror. She refused the message: you need lipstick. The doorbell was ringing in a jazzy Morse code. Cute. Spenser always thought he was so original.

"Just a minute."

A minute for what? For *me*. For who I've become—so that I can protect myself from being seen as who I was.

Never mind that she had on her old, quilted, light-green satin robe, or that she had nothing on underneath. Spenser wouldn't be there long.

Jana unloosed the chain lock, then the lock she had installed when she moved in and, finally, the lock that came with the door.

Before she could twist the door knob, the door was opening and the universe rushed in.

Peter was holding her, kissing her, answering all the questions she had before she could ask them.

He loved her. He had come to take her home. She knew it before he said so.

"How could you have gone away?"

"You told me to."

"Since when did you ever do what I told you?"

He looked approving—disapproving, relieved—tired,

happy—anguished, and she had all of him in her arms to make it all right.

"Mariposa needs you. Miss Mari's computer has hit a snag—it needs you. But I need you most of all, because I love you—only you."

They were standing before the picture window, they were dropping down on the white fur rug together—the rug bought before she had known it was a cloud. The sun was setting, the corners of the balcony framed the sky where seagulls flew in Matisse collages.

His arms were forever around her, his lips crushed and searched her mouth. The balcony was spinning, curving, turning. It was no longer a square, but a circle.

His hands were over her, loving her. Finally, his words rushed out, claiming praise, strength, tenderness. And his eyes were no longer a weapon, but a wand, transforming her forever into his beloved.

It was urgent, it was yes. Welded to his wildness, she was wrenching with wonder until they were grounded in the clouds and were one. Her body cupped his glorious fullness perfectly and, as the late evening sun slanted into the room, their cloud gleamed incandescently with the same glorious light they had made inside each other.

When it was time for dinner, Peter went to the refrigerator and discovered one item: a bottle of soy sauce. Their choice of food was settled, and Jana ordered four or five containers from a menu she kept tucked in a drawer next to the silverware. Peter pointed to the items: Won Ton soup, sweet-and-sour-pork, rice, vegetables.

"And we like it hot," he added.

After the lazy, lukewarm dinner, Peter wandered through her apartment touching its treasures: clay pots and figurines from Mexico, baskets from China, lithographs by Chicago artists.

"No wonder you and Miss Mari get along so well: you love designs and shapes as much as she does."

"But I have no jewel-like pieces."

"An apartment only needs one jewel, and this one has you."

"Not anymore."

Jana had already called her mother and broken the news, saying, "You may have lost a daughter, but you have gained an apartment." She had thought her mother would be happier than she was, but the surprise of Jana marrying and moving so far away had canceled out the pleasure of moving into a light-filled, roach-free apartment.

"What about China, Egypt, Italy?" asked Peter.

"Miss Mari told you?"

"Immediately."

Jana held his hand while she said, "Peter, although I was trying not to be, I'm still the same person I was in California. If you thought I was guilty of something then, why don't you now?"

"I don't believe I ever really thought that. But I realized there could never be love between two people where the possibility of betrayal would not be present. I know myself fairly well. I didn't think I could tolerate the uncertainty again. I was afraid of what I might do. I know what I almost did to Andy.

"I finally had to confess this to Miss Mari, who never let me alone for a minute all week.

"Her question was devastating: 'You want to live the rest of your life with a sad possibility—or with Jana?'"

Holding him to her, Jana said, "Losing you would have been a sadness I would have lived with forever. If you want to know what happened. . . ."

"No. The week I have spent without you has been enough time for me to realize I had jumped to conclusions. And if that had not been enough, there was Andy's black eye to confirm it."

They were on her bed, shoving off a suitcase, a pile of lingerie, a hair dryer, two sets of hot curlers.

"Now," he said, "and now."

He was turning to steel inside her. Soldered together by molten fire, they were building something big. Jana closed her eyes as he hurled her to depths.

Before they flew out of O'Hare the next morning, Peter phoned Mariposa. He was bringing Jana home. They would be married. He turned to her. "When?"

"This week."

For most of the flight, she lay with her head on his shoulder. Having rushed over so many rough spots, there was an easiness between them.

"And what about Havermeyer?"

"They'll receive a short phone call from me on Monday, to

be followed by an it-gives-me-great-pleasure letter of resignation."

Peter's Jaguar was parked at the airport. She would take him to Mariposa; then, if everything was all right there, they would drive to the hospital to see Miss Mari.

Before they were out of the car, Ruby drove up in her Toyota pickup—with Moose sitting next to her.

She had heard the news and it was about time, she said, that Peter settled down with somebody who wasn't flighty.

"I'm dropping Moose off at the machine shop," she said. "He's going to fit one of the harvesters with the new catch surface the girls have sewn."

"Moose is going down there by himself?"

"Why not?" asked Ruby.

"He doesn't work here anymore, remember," said Peter, acting as if Moose were deaf.

"It's absolutely necessary," said Ruby. "And that's that." She sped off before Peter could say another word. Jana saw his jaw muscles tighten. She put her hand on his arm. "It will be all right."

Inside the office, Jana put her arms around him, hoping to silently soothe his anger. As Peter's passion grew, he did indeed seem to forget Moose.

When the phone rang, Peter reluctantly picked it up. Jana heard him say that he'd be right down.

"Some of the men at the bunkhouse want to see me. If you don't mind, you can answer the office phone while I'm gone." He kissed her again. "And then," he said, "let's get out of here as fast as possible, go for a swim and. . . ."

"And what?"

"See Miss Mari tomorrow."

Jana waited at the office for a long time with nothing to do. When the phone finally rang, she heard a dull voice ask if she wanted to buy an air conditioner.

Flies buzzed on the screen. The temperature was over 105 degrees. She recalled her first day in this office, and how much the heat had bothered her. Today she even liked it. The office reminded her of that sauna that had changed her friend so that he never was the same again.

She decided she might as well see how the harvester looked with its homemade garment.

Jana could have caught a ride with somebody, but she preferred to walk down to the machine shop.

Feeling sadness as she passed the ashes of Miss Mari's home, she thought how lovely it would have been if she and Peter could have been married there.

A frog jumping into an irrigation canal diverted her attention. Peaches occasionally plopping to the ground marked time with her steps. The birds were singing so loudly that they seemed to form a thick layer of song around the treetops. And the dry heat continued to please her. In a light blue and white sleeveless dress, she was friends with the weather. She was a lover.

The sweet, pulpy smell in the orchards was wonderful. She couldn't wait to be here in the spring and walk with Peter through the blossoming trees. They would take a blanket. And some wine . . . and, of course, cheese and bread.

Odd, there were no trucks around the machine shop next to the three disabled harvesters. The bright green, rubbery material was only half in place on one of them.

"Moose!" she called. He had probably gone home already.

She walked closer to the green disc of material. It looked as if it hadn't been measured correctly. There were slashes in it. At first, she believed—wanted to believe—they were part of the pattern. But when she saw a jagged strip of material flapping against the tire of one of the harvesters, and saw the ugly hole where it had been cut out of the middle of the material, she knew they were not.

"Moose, Moose, it's Jana!"

Opening the door of the machine shop, Jana stepped inside. There was a loaded silence. It was as if the building were holding its breath. Greasy particles hanging in the sun, tossing like tiny brown snowflakes, provided the only movement.

The sun illuminated every speck of dust on the shiny paint of the small red tractor in for repairs.

Jana heard a noise behind her. It was the gasp of one who had held his breath beyond endurance.

She turned around and, beneath the hanging wrenches and hammers, saw Andy, flattened against the wall, staring at a place underneath the tractor.

"Andy, what's wrong?"

Never unlocking his eyes from the stare, he said, "I didn't m-m-mean to hurt him."

Jana ran around the tractor. Her heart lurched to her throat in horror. Moose was lying on his back, slumped against one of the tires. His legs were stretched out in front of him.

Jana knelt and touched his hand. "Moose, wake up." His eyes fluttered open.

"What's wrong? What happened?"

He put a hand to the back of his head, closed his eyes, and his head slumped forward again.

"He f-f-fell," said Andy. "He tried to interfere with my job. M-m-moose is a troublemaker."

From outside came the sound of screeching brakes, a slamming door, and Peter's voice calling, "Jana!"

Andy ran to the end of the shop and crouched in a corner. "Don't you tell him I'm here," said Andy. "He'll kill me."

Jana rose, but for a moment was undecided about whether to meet Peter at the door or stay where she was.

He was inside before she could move. Jana pointed down. Peter bent over Moose, checked his pulse. Moose's eyes again fluttered open.

"Are you okay?" asked Peter. Moose nodded.

"You stay there for a few minutes, and I'll help you up." Moose nodded again.

Still kneeling, Peter turned toward Jana and said, "Who did this?"

Jana opened her mouth but made no sound. Andy darted out of the corner and ran past Peter. But by the time he had thrown open the door, Peter's hands were on his shoulders and he was pushing Andy outside and throwing him against the corrugated metal side of the building.

"Moose caught you at it, didn't he? You're working for Calimyrna, aren't you?"

"None of your business."

Peter hit Andy in the stomach. "Don't!" screamed Jana.

"Answer me," yelled Peter, slapping Andy. "You destroy my property, injure an old man, sabotage something the women have worked night and day on. You're nothing but a criminal."

"Y-y-you take Susan away from me, and now you're after Jana. You did Susan no good, and the same thing will happen to Jana. You can't have it *all*, Milford. I won't let you have it all." Andy's eyes were shifting to one side, then the other. Was he looking for a way to escape, or something that could be used as a weapon against Peter?

He continued. "You think that because you have money,

you can have everything. Calimyrna's gonna make me rich. They're bigger than you are. They're going to ruin you.

"Susan never thought I had enough money to take care of her. That's the only reason she went to Ken instead of me after she ran out on you—yeah, Peter the Great. Susan ran out on you."

Peter's tanned face had turned burnt orange. "You're a sniveling little criminal."

"You're the criminal. You finally found a man weak enough to bully: you sleep with Susan every time Ken is out of town. You can't bully me. And now that Jana knows about you, she'll never marry you."

He turned to Jana. "Think how many Lisas there will be."

Peter raised a clenched fist.

"Peter, no!" screamed Jana.

"I'd be faithful to you," said Andy. "I'd take care of you."

"You can't take care of yourself," said Peter.

"I never meant to burn down a house or hurt anybody. I only wanted Peter to sell Mariposa to Calimyrna. That was my real job. I wasn't only a truck driver. I had an important job. Peter was supposed to sell first thing this summer. Then, Jana, you and I could have gone away together."

"You're always making excuses for yourself," said Peter.

Andy seemed not to hear Peter, or recognize his presence. He was talking only to Jana.

"Nobody except you ever listened to me, Jana. You're the only one who ever understood what made me happy."

A silent stream of tears was rushing down Jana's cheeks.

"I lost Susan, but I'm not going to lose you. I've been fighting for you all summer. It's been more important than making money. Peter doesn't deserve you. Together we could make it." Andy reached out for her hand. Jana let him take it.

"Peter won't make you happy. I can make you forget him. Jana, Jana," Andy pleaded, "I know that Peter went to Chicago to force you to say you'd marry him. You don't have to do that. I'm going to be a wealthy man, too."

Jana dropped Andy's hand. "That has nothing to do with it. I love Peter. I *want* to marry him."

"If you're saying that because you blame me for what's happened at Mariposa, you must believe me: I didn't mean for anyone to be hurt, or for Miss Mari's house to burn down. Jana, don't you know, if it hadn't been for you, I would have given up at Mariposa long ago? If it hadn't been for you, I would never have needed so much money."

"You can't blame *her*." Peter tightened his hold on Andy's arm.

"I don't. I blame *you*. You, who never needed anything; you, who never give and always take."

Andy turned to Jana. "You belong to *me*. I loved you first. He doesn't want anything but what Susan won't give him anymore."

Peter shoved both Andy's wrists above his head and against the burning hot metal of the machine shop. Andy grimaced but did not cry out. "Go away with me, Jana." He spoke in gasps of air.

"Where you're going, you won't be needing company," said Peter roughly.

"What do you m-m-mean?"

"Prison. You're a criminal, and you've been caught."

"Peter," said Jana, "let him go."

Peter looked down at her, and then over at Andy, whose blue eyes were wide open and their color fading fast, not from the hot, direct sunlight, but from fear. He wasn't even squinting.

Looking into those eyes, Jana saw shallow, icy-blue pools. She was frightened, too—for Andy. "Peter, let him go."

"Where's your car?" snapped Peter as he loosened one of Andy's wrists, then the other.

"The other side of the south orchard." Andy wildly looked around the clearing to the thicket of trees on all four sides, the soft, newly-plowed, damp ground under them.

"You drive out of here," ordered Peter, "and if I ever see you or your father in this valley, I'll open a criminal investigation that will keep you both coming and going through courts and prisons for the rest of your lives."

"It's not because of what I've done that you're threatening me: it's because of Jana. You're afraid because you know she loves me." Andy stepped forward and grabbed Jana. He was clinging to her. Jana felt her arms around him. She begged with her frown for Peter not to touch him. Through tears she was remembering how Andy had grasped Susan in his arms that day they arrived in the mountains, and how understanding Susan had been. She knew why now. There were so many *lovable* things about Andy. He did need her.

"Please, Jana. I can't lose you, too. I am so sorry for everything. I can start over if I have you with me."

Fighting for any voice at all, Jana whispered, "Andy, do what you know you must do."

"But where will I go? Jana, tell me, where?"

"Andy, my dear Andy." Jana was loosening herself from him, stepping away from him. "Paint, go to Japan, Yosemite. Climb the mountains you love so much, and don't climb a single one you don't love."

They both looked toward the Sierras at the same time. Andy stumbled backward a couple of steps, stopped and looked again toward the high mountains. Their peaks were barely visible over the orchard. Andy stumbled faster and, when he was halfway across the clearing, turned and ran.

Jana watched until she could no longer see him, then she felt herself being enfolded in Peter's arms. Burying her head against his chest, she shook with sobs.

When she heard Andy's car motor start, she remained close to Peter, safe in his strong, gentle arms. She never saw the yellow Honda speed past.

"Thank you for understanding," she murmured.

"I know," said Peter, "what lengths his father would go to get what he wanted. Andy was only trying to please him—as he has done all his life."

"Peter, I do love you. In every situation, you are always more than I expect."

"And you," he said, "are kinder and stronger—and more lovely—than anyone I ever hoped existed."

Their kiss was ended by the sound of a pickup bumping down the road toward them. Peter flagged it down.

"Let's get Moose over to the hospital for a checkup. If he's in as good shape as I think he is, we'll leave him with Miss Mari and continue this exchange elsewhere."

"My place or yours?" teased Jana.

"Ours, my darling. And the sooner, the better."

Dear Reader:

Would you take a few moments to fill out this questionnaire and mail it to:

Richard Gallen Books/Questionnaire
8-10 West 36th St., New York, N.Y. 10018

1. What rating would you give *Harvest of Dreams?*
   ☐ excellent ☐ very good ☐ fair ☐ poor

2. What prompted you to buy this book? ☐ title
   ☐ front cover ☐ back cover ☐ friend's recommendation ☐ other (please specify) _____

3. Check off the elements you liked best:
   ☐ hero ☐ heroine ☐ other characters ☐ story
   ☐ setting ☐ ending ☐ love scenes

4. Were the love scenes ☐ too explicit
   ☐ not explicit enough ☐ just right

5. Any additional comments about the book?

   _____

6. Would you recommend this book to friends?
   ☐ yes ☐ no

7. Have you read other Richard Gallen
   romances? ☐ yes ☐ no

8. Do you plan to buy other Richard Gallen
   romances? ☐ yes ☐ no

9. What kind of romances do you enjoy reading?
   ☐ historical romance ☐ contemporary romance
   ☐ Regency romance ☐ light modern romance
   ☐ Gothic romance

10. Please check your general age group:
    ☐ under 25 ☐ 25-35 ☐ 35-45 ☐ 45-55 ☐ over 55

11. If you would like to receive a romance
    newsletter please fill in your name and
    address:

    _____

    _____

    _____

VV G + ½